"Certainly a book about big questions. . . Perhaps Keren David's biggest achievement, however, is that these issues play second fiddle to the psychological authenticity of her troubled hero, and the longing she rouses in the reader for Ty's ultimate redemption."
Books for Keeps

"A thrilling adventure . . . an emotional roller coaster."
Julia Eccleshare *Lovereading.co.uk*

"Not a single page is wasted. A truly excellent sequel from this talented author. Highly recommended."
Write Away

"Another powerful, utterly compelling novel. For me, it is really a novel of our time and of our culture. Keren David is a master of suspenseful, contemporary writing."
The Bookette

Praise for
when i was JOe

"So good that you never actually notice just how good because you are far too busy turning the pages."
Sunday Telegraph

"An ice-cold thriller about identity, pain and veracity."
Daily Telegraph

Keren David

FRANCES LINCOLN
CHILDREN'S BOOKS

First published in Great Britain in 2010 and in the USA in 2011 by
Frances Lincoln Children's Books, 4 Torriano Mews,
Torriano Avenue, London NW5 2RZ
www.franceslincoln.com

A catalogue record for this book is available from the British Library.

ISBN 978-1-84780-101-2

Set in Palatino

Printed in Croydon, Surrey, UK by CPI Bookmarque Ltd. in July 2010

3 5 7 9 8 6 4 2

For my parents, Shirley and Joseph David

CHAPTER 1
Blood

They come to kill me early in the morning. At 6 am when the sky is pink and misty grey, the seagulls are crying overhead and the beach is empty.

I'm not at home when they arrive. I'm the only person on the beach, loving my early morning run – the sound of the waves and the smell of seaweed. It all reminds me that my new name is Jake and Jake lives by the seaside.

Jake's normally a bit of a sad person – no friends, poor sod – but here, right now, working on my speed and strength, I'm happy that wherever we are and whatever my name is, I can always run, my body is my own.

For a bit I even forget that I'm supposed to be Jake and I run myself back into my last identity, which was Joe, cool popular Joe. I miss Joe. It's good that I can be him when I run. I never want to be Ty again,

1

my real name, the basic me, but I still dream of being Joe.

Joe never feels lonely, running on his own. It's Jake who's miserable at school, where no one talks to him.

Jake never thinks about Claire – *my* Claire, my lovely Claire – because her name throws him into a dark pit of despair, but when I'm Joe I pretend I'm running to see her and I let myself feel just a little bit of joy . . . excitement . . . hope.

So it's a good morning, and even when I get near home and have to readjust to being Jake again, there's still a kind of afterglow that clings to me. A Joe glow for Jake the fake. I'm hot and sweaty and that's as good as Jake's life ever gets, but then, when I turn our corner, there are police cars everywhere, and ambulances, and a small crowd of people staring, and they're putting up tape to stop anyone getting through.

'Get back! Get back!' a policeman is shouting, but I push on forward through the crowd to the edge of the tape.

And then I see it. A dark pool of blood at our front door. For a moment the world stops, and my heart isn't even beating. I'm swaying, and everything is going whiter and smaller and I'm like one of the seagulls flying overhead, looking down on the crowd and screaming to the sky.

I don't know what to do. I think about just running away, so I never need to find out what happened. Then arms hug me tight and it's Gran, oh God, it's Gran, and she's pulling me over to a police car. My mum's hunched up in the back. She's making a weird noise – a kind of gasping, howling, hooting noise. It reminds me of when Jamie Robins had an asthma attack in Year Three – it was scary then and it's hideous now.

Nicki's whole face is white, even her lips, and she's staring right through me – and then Gran slaps her face hard and Mum stops the terrible noise and falls into her arms. They're both still in their dressing gowns. There's blood on Gran's fluffy pink slippers.

Gran sits with her arms around my mum, rocking her back and forth and saying, 'You'll be OK, my darling, stay strong, Nicki, you'll be OK.'

'What . . . who?' I ask, but I know. I'm already beginning to piece together what must have happened.

They must have rung our doorbell. Most days, it would have been my mum stumbling down the stairs to the front door. If she had, then I think they would have grabbed her, dragged her upstairs and searched the place for me. When they found no one, what then? Kept her gagged and silent until I came back, then shot us both, I should think.

But Mum didn't open the door. She's sitting here

in the car, retching and sobbing, doubled over like she's in pain. It must have been Alistair who went downstairs. Alistair, the guy she had just started seeing before we had to move here.

Alistair, who spent the night in her bed.

Alistair, who turned up last night, out of the blue. No one bothered to tell me why or how.

Alistair, with his gelled hair and muscled arms. He looks like a prat from a boy band, but he's OK really. He's a good cook. My mum really likes him.

Alistair, who works in a gym and trained Ellie so well that she's going to the Paralympics next year. She was the first person to realise that I'd got potential as a runner. Ellie's sister is Claire. I'm probably never going to see either of them again.

Anyway. Alistair would have opened the door. Mum must've told him I'd gone out running and he probably thought I'd forgotten my key.

He's half-asleep, hair all over the place. And they shout at him, 'Ty? Ty Lewis?' He stares, yawning and bewildered – he doesn't even know I have a real name, let alone what it is – and they must take that as a yes because then they shoot him. His hands are trying to keep his brains from spilling out. Then he drops to his knees on the doorstep and blood leaks from his broken body and he dies right there on the path. And they don't

4

hang around because they think they've done their job. They've killed me.

This isn't the first time that someone's tried to silence me forever. It's just the first time that someone else has died instead.

My mum's woken up by the noise of the shots. She's standing at the top of the stairs, screaming and screaming, and then my gran, who's lived downstairs for the last few weeks, wakes up too. Gran spots Alistair's body, the blood – she screams and rushes to my mum. And then she calls the police.

Then the cars arrive, sirens shouting and the tape goes up and I get home from my run.

* * *

At the police station, they put us into a room on our own and say they'll send someone to take our statements. Gran pulls her mobile out of her pocket and starts ringing: first my aunties then Doug. Our witness protection officer. The policeman who's meant to keep us safe from the people who want to stop me testifying in court.

It seems like hours, but then they all start to arrive. Gran's trying to explain to the local cops that we're in witness protection, and my auntie Louise just says, 'Take us to whoever's in charge.'

Then Gran and Louise disappear into a room with the police guys and when Doug arrives, he goes in there too. Doug looks incredibly rough. He doesn't even say hello to us. Mum and my auntie Emma and I sit side by side in the corridor outside and I'm straining to hear what's going on. All I can hear is Lou's raised voice. She's good at shouting. She has to be – she's a teacher.

Mum is still shaking and crying and no one is doing anything to help her except Emma, who's hugging her and saying, 'It'll be OK, it'll be OK,' in a really unconvinced voice. Deep, deep inside me there's a tiny muffled scream – *he's dead . . . he was shot . . . that should have been me* – but shock has sucked all the feeling out of me and I'm getting that distant feeling again. It's like I've been laminated.

'I'm fed up with this,' I say. 'I'm going in there.'

Emma says, 'Ty, you can't just interrupt,' but I say, 'Watch me,' and I push the door open. They all go quiet as I barge into the room. It's almost funny to see Gran sitting there in her pink dressing gown in a room full of cops.

'Look,' I say, 'we've been sitting here for hours. My mum's just seen her boyfriend shot. We all know they wanted to shoot me. What's going on?' I top it up with a lot of words that I don't usually say in front of my gran.

Louise shakes her head and says, 'Just because there's been a murder, there is no need for you to be foul-mouthed.'

'Oh for Christ's sake, Lou, you're not in the classroom now,' I say, and I can see the police officers smiling. I sit down at the table with them. She frowns at me, but I'm going nowhere.

'Right,' she says, 'I think we've finished here anyway. Ty, you're coming with me. We've lost confidence in witness protection for you. We'll co-ordinate with the police when it's time for you to give evidence. But only if we're satisfied with their security arrangements.

'Your gran's going to stay here with Nicki so that they can make their statements, and maybe someone'll be thoughtful enough to get them some clothes and then they'll have a discussion with Doug about where to go next.'

What does she mean? How is she going to look after me? What's going to happen to my mum? And Gran? Will the police even let me go?

Doug says, 'We'll give Ty twenty-four-hour protection now this has happened. I don't think you should be too hasty.'

Louise is very near completely losing her temper. I can tell by the way the end of her nose has gone pink.

'As far as I can see, Ty is pretty safe right now.

The bastards who are out to get him think they've succeeded. Until you release the victim's name, that'll be the case. I'm assuming you won't do that right away. So I've got time to get Ty to a place where no one will know where he is. And that includes the Metropolitan Police, and every other bloody police force in the country.'

'Are you suggesting *we* had something to do with this?' says Doug, who sounds pretty upset himself.

'I'm suggesting you launch an inquiry right away to find out how they got Nicki and Ty's address. I'll bet you'll find there was a leak somewhere close to home. And just in case you don't do that, I'm going to get on the phone to the Police Complaints Commission just as soon as I've sorted my nephew out.'

She's not finished with Doug. 'I want you to go to the flat and pack all Ty's things, so I can leave here with him in half an hour. And then you can concentrate on making sure that Nicki and my mum and Emma – oh, and me as well – have somewhere reasonably safe to go. You can keep your twenty-four-hour protection for us.'

She leads Gran and me out of the room. Doug follows, and when he sees my mum, he says, 'Nicki, I don't know what to say,'

Louise snaps, 'An apology would be nice, but

that's not allowed, is it Doug? That would be admitting liability.'

Then she asks for some privacy to make phone calls and a policeman takes her away down the corridor.

Emma's rocking Mum back and forth, and Gran holds me tight.

'Ty, my love,' she says, 'this isn't going to be easy, but Louise knows what's she's about. She's rock-solid that girl, always made the right choices. She'll know what's best for you.'

'I want to stay with you,' I say. 'I only just got you back.'

Gran's always been more like a mother to me than my own mum. I nearly fell apart without her these last few months. I can't believe I'm going to be taken away from her again. I cling on to her like I'm a baby monkey, not someone who's going to be fifteen in just over a month.

She kisses my forehead and says, 'I'm always with you darling, I always love you. But Nicki needs me more than you do right now.'

And that's it. Doug comes back with my bag, and puts it into Lou's car. I have a final hug with Gran and Emma. My mum is throwing up in the Ladies, so we wait for her, and I give her a hug too, even though she smells of vomit. She can't stop crying and I'm not even sure she understands that I might not see her for . . . for weeks? For months? For ever?

'Take care,' she says, 'Take care. Lou, take care of him.'

Louise says, 'Don't worry, Nicki, I'll do what's best.'

My mum stops crying, mid-sob. She does an enormous sniff, which doesn't even begin to retrieve the snot on her face, looks Louise straight in the eye and says, 'He's *my* son, Louise, don't you forget that.'

And my auntie says, 'No one's ever in danger of forgetting that, Nicki. I'll be seeing you soon. Take care of yourselves.'

Then she puts her arm on my back and leads me away underground, where her car is waiting.

CHAPTER 2
Buckingham Palace

I'm lying on the back seat of Louise's car wondering where on earth she's going to take me. Louise is driving like a maniac and I'm incredibly sick and drowsy. I'm going to fall asleep or throw up, it's just a question of which one first.

I asked her where we were going and she said, 'Shut up, Ty, I'm thinking,' so fiercely that I didn't bother asking again. I've been running through all her friends in my mind and deciding which one I'd least hate to stay with. Most of them are teachers and they're all a bit serious – the boring brigade, my mum calls them. But they all live in London. She can't be taking me there.

We stopped for about ten minutes, and I thought she'd buy me some food as I haven't even had breakfast, but she just whizzed me into a Snappy Snaps and got my photo taken, then chucked a Mars Bar at me and said, 'That'll have to be lunch. I want to get on with it.' Louise is a health freak. I didn't think she even knew about Mars Bars. I ate it lying down in the car, bumping along some country roads, which wasn't a great experience.

'Why did you get my picture taken? Am I getting a passport?' I ask her, and she says, 'Shhh, I'm still thinking,' so I start imagining flying off to somewhere like Spain and maybe she'd have to let me stay in a hotel by myself, and maybe I could get Claire to somehow meet me there. . .

'Can I get changed?' I ask, because I'm still in my sweaty running gear and even though I've thrown a hoodie on top, I'm smelly and damp and uncomfortable. But she says, 'Ty, there are more important things right now than how you look.' Louise is generally a bit snappy, but this is an excessively bad mood.

Eventually she starts talking to me. I'm straining to hear her voice, but the engine's noisy and her voice is soft and I'm too sleepy to follow what she's saying. I just try and make appropriate replies so she doesn't get cross with me again.

'Teacher-training . . . parents . . . you understand?' she says, and I say, 'Yeah. . .'

And then, '. . . strange . . . very nice . . . long time . . . little. . .'

'Mmmm,' I say, and then I must have dropped off completely because I only wake up when she stops the car and says, 'We're here.'

'Urgh. Where's here?'

'We've arrived. At their house.'

I'm hot and sweaty all over again, and my teeth are furry with Mars Bar. I didn't quite finish it and it's melted all over my hands and my hoodie.

'Oh, um, right.' I expect she'd be annoyed if I ask for a recap. She was droning on for ages in the car.

We're parked in a gravel driveway which leads up to a huge red-brick house. It's got a big front garden, with lavender bushes and tubs of flowers, and a leafy red vine covering the front wall. The massive dark green front door is probably the biggest I've ever seen. Louise must know some seriously rich people.

'Come on,' she says, getting my bag out of the boot, 'I don't want the car to be here for long, just in case.'

'But Louise . . . wait. . .' I say, trailing after her as she marches to the front door and rings the bell. She looks like she always does – clean and smart and tidy. I smell of stale sweat and I'm covered with chocolate. I spit on my hands and transfer some melted Mars Bar onto my trackie trousers. Lou puts her arm around me and says, 'Don't worry, they are very nice.'

The door opens. Two old people. They must be the

13

parents of one of her friends. The grey-haired woman is wearing a pale blue jumper and dark blue skirt and she's smiling – a really weird smile, kind of twisted. There's something a bit familiar about her, and I try and think which one of Lou's teacher mates she reminds me of. The old man is hugely tall and has dark bushy eyebrows and there's a frown on his face. He's got a tweed jacket on.

Louise can't possibly expect me to stay here – can she?

'Come in, come in,' says the woman, in a super-posh voice, and she gives Lou a big hug. I'm wondering when Louise will explain who they are. But she obviously thinks she's done that already. I'll just have to work it out as I go along.

She releases Lou, and they all turn to look at me, and I stare at my trainers which are still sandy from the beach.

'Tyler, welcome,' says the lady in her Radio Four voice. 'We're so very happy to have you here.'

I mumble something and Lou says, 'Ty's had a terribly traumatic day, Helen, I don't think he's up to much at the moment.'

'Of course,' she says. 'Come and sit down. I'll make tea.'

She shows us into a living room which is – I swear –

bigger than our entire flat in London. There's a huge piano in the corner, and the floor is made of wood and there are soft patterned rugs and a blue velvety sofa and armchairs and blue curtains that look like they are made of silk. It's so tidy that it feels like a museum, not someone's home. And I can't see a television anywhere.

There's a big mirror over the mantelpiece and I catch sight of myself in it. My face is pale and grubby, and there's a huge shit-brown smear on my chin. My hair, heavy with dried sweat, hangs in strings over my eyes. Oh, and my mouth is wide open.

'I'm Patrick,' says the old guy, frowning at me like he's really regretting allowing Lou to bring me within fifty miles of his house. 'Do you want a drink? Louise?' I shake my head and manage to close the gaping mouth and she says no, she'd better not, because she's driving. That means she's really going to be leaving me here. He pours himself a whisky.

'So . . . this is Tyler, eh?' he says to me in his deep gruff voice. 'Let's get a look at you, boy.'

He sounds like a sergeant major in the army. I duck my head, but Louise tugs my hood down.

He looks me up and down like he's deciding whether to buy me. I don't like it. I don't like him either. I pull the hood up again and slouch back against my chair, arms crossed. I stretch out my legs in front of

15

me so my trainers are on the cream-coloured rug. Louise frowns at me, then starts talking to Patrick about the house. Do they get many visitors? Will it be possible for me to stay there without anyone realising?

Helen brings the tea in on a tray. There's a flowery teapot and little teacups and a milk jug and a sugar bowl and a plate of biscuits that I think come from Marks and Spencer. It's like having tea at Buckingham Palace. In our flat you'd have got mugs, tea bags and Lidl economy custard creams. But it reminds me of Gran's best china which she only used on special occasions. I wonder if it's still in her old flat in London.

I drink my tea in about a minute and eat two biscuits – I'm starving. I was right, they *are* from Marks and Spencer, Gran used to get them every six months or so as a very special treat, but I bet these people shop there every day. I lick my finger to pick up the last crumbs from my plate. Then I realise that everyone is watching me, and I start nibbling my fingernail instead.

Louise is updating them on the last few months in my life. How I witnessed a boy being stabbed, and how one of the people standing trial for the killing is my best friend Arron. How another one of the accused – Jukes White – comes from a family of gangsters who want me silenced. How I'd been given a new identity and sent to a new school but had to be moved on – 'Ty can tell you the details another time,' she says. Yeah, right, that's really going to happen. And then she starts to tell them about how Alistair got shot.

My attention wanders. On top of the piano are hundreds of photographs, all in silver frames. I can see weddings and christenings, children in school uniform and happy family portraits. I count one, two, three weddings. There are loads of children; they must have a big family, but I stare at one – a little boy with dark, tangled hair and three older sisters. He must have a hard life, that boy. The girls look pretty bossy.

I've lost the thread of Lou's story. I'm trying to tune out the recent stuff, Alistair . . . shooting . . . police. The words float in the air around me. But then I hear her say, 'So that's when I rang you. I don't trust the police to keep him safe any more, and Mum needs to concentrate on Nicki, now that she's expecting.'

I jump forward. My teacup clatters to the floor and rolls on to the rug. She couldn't really have said . . . have meant. . .

'Nicki's what? What are you talking about?' My voice is hoarse and croaky.

Louise's hand is over her mouth. Helen is biting her lower lip. Lou shakes her head and says, 'Ty, I'm sorry. Ty, darling – I thought you knew. Didn't she tell you?'

'No one told me anything. What's going on?'

'That's why she contacted Alistair again. To tell him she was having his baby.'

'But . . . they hardly even knew each other . . . it was only the one night. . .' I'm so shocked, that I've forgotten that these friends of hers are listening. I'm just trying to work it out.

Patrick snorts, 'Typical,' he says. I'd know that tone anywhere.

Helen tuts at him, and Lou says, 'Steady, Ty,' but I leap to my feet. Teacups fly in all directions. The days are over when I let people disrespect my mum. My hands turn to fists and my arms tense up.

I step towards him, breathing hard. He's frowning at me. I yell, 'Shut up! Or I'll make you!'

CHAPTER 3
The Wolf

I don't *think* I would actually have hit him, but no one ever finds out because an enormous wolf-like creature flies at me, snarling and howling. It jumps at my chest, sending me crashing backwards onto the floor, and its huge jaw is right in my face, with a deafening noise and toxic smell. Flying gobs of saliva blind me, as its razor-sharp yellow teeth tear at my throat.

The next thing I know the wolf-monster is gone. I'm sitting on the floor with my back against the sofa and Helen's handing me a cup. I take a big gulp and almost choke. I was expecting water, but it's burning my throat and judging by the smell it's the stuff that the old tramps drink in the park . . . meths, that's it.

'Urgh . . . what the hell?' I say, tears streaming down my face, and she says, 'It's brandy, for shock.'

I'm touching my neck and face to check everything's still there. Miraculously there's no gushing blood or tattered flesh. 'Has the wolf gone?' I ask, looking nervously around the room.

Louise is on the sofa next to me, hand on my shoulder, and I think she's trying not to laugh.

'It was a dog, Ty darling. Wolves live in the zoo, not people's houses.'

My face is hot. I knew that it was a dog, obviously. It's just that the wrong word came out. Where I come from, a dog is a weapon, just like a knife. I've been a bit wary of dogs since a bad experience with a runaway Rottweiler when I was seven. Helen must think I'm a retard because she says, 'Anyone could make the same mistake.'

Then I glance out of the window and see Patrick with the galloping wolf-monster on a lead, and it turns out to be a collie-sheepdog-Lassie-lookalike. I gulp down some more of the brandy.

Louise says, 'Helen, can I just have a minute to talk to Ty, please?' and Helen says, 'Of course,' and stops picking up bits of china from the floor, and leaves the room. I bet she's standing just outside, listening.

I lean against my auntie hoping she's going to say that she's changed her mind and this is obviously never going to work and she's thought of some dog-free place to take me.

But she starts telling me off. 'Jesus, Ty, what are you like? Helen and Patrick offer you a refuge and the first thing you do is threaten to attack them.'

'They set their dog on me.'

'No they didn't. Don't be ridiculous. She reacted to your aggression.'

'He was disrespecting my mum.'

'He's seventy-five years old. You can't shout at him like he's one of your gangster friends.'

'I don't have gangsta friends.' I don't have any friends right now.

'While you're staying here, for Christ's sake, try and behave and give a good impression,' she says. 'Otherwise you're letting Nicki down.'

I don't care, because I'm so angry with my mum for not telling me that she was pregnant that I never ever want to see her again, anyway.

I take another big gulp of brandy, pull my knees to my chest and bury my head in my arms.

'Lou, don't tell me off. I can't take any more today.'

She takes the brandy glass away from me and says, 'I think you've had quite enough of that.'

Then she goes out of the room and I fall asleep. I only wake up when Louise taps me gently on the shoulder. She's got her coat on.

'I'm going now, Ty, but I promise I'll be back in a few weeks. You must stay inside all the time, ideally away from the windows, and do what Helen and Patrick tell you. And behave yourself. No phone calls, no letters, no contact with anyone. And dye the hair black again. It'll be useful if I need to move you again, and we could dress you as a Goth. Understand?'

'Don't go . . . Lou, please, don't leave me here. . .'

She leans down and kisses me. 'It'll be fine. It'll be good. You take care.'

She's gone. I hear the front door slam. She's left me. And I have no idea who she's left me with.

Helen comes into the room and sits down and says, 'Patrick isn't very tactful, I'm afraid. You'll get used to him.'

'Yeah. Umm. Sorry.'

She's staring at me. I know I look dirty and sweaty; she doesn't have to rub it in. I shift my eyes away from her and start looking at the photos on the piano again. Maybe I can work out which one of Louise's friends they are related to. Maybe it's Sally, the Geography teacher at her school. She's a bit posh. . . Hang on. What's that?

There's a picture on the piano that I recognise. It's me aged eight in a shirt and tie, when my gran insisted I did First Communion at church. What the hell is it doing here?

She follows my gaze. 'Louise gave it to us,' she says, 'I've always loved it. Were you surprised to see it there?'

'Um. Yes.'

She picks out another. It's a picture of a weird little kid. He's looking all sad, he's got enormous blue eyes and he's holding a fluffy white toy horse. He looks a bit like an alien. I think maybe it's the boy from the other photo – the one outnumbered by his sisters.

'Do you remember the horse?' she says. 'You loved it.'

What *is* she going on about? I never had a toy horse, I have green eyes, and I certainly never looked as strange as this kid. She must be getting mixed up. Old people get a bit confused, don't they?

'Um. No,' I say as politely as possible.

'So how is your mum?' asks Helen and it sounds like she's also on her best behaviour. 'This must be a terribly difficult situation for her. Thank goodness Julie's able to be with her.'

Julie is my gran. I suppose Louise must have told Helen her name.

'Err. I don't know how she is,' I say. 'She was in hysterics in the police car. Gran had to slap her face.'

'I'm not surprised. Poor Nicki.'

I'm scanning my memory trying to think if Gran or Nicki ever mentioned knowing rich people called

23

Helen and Patrick. But I'm certain they didn't.

'Well, Julie's wonderful in a crisis,' says Helen. 'At least you know your mum is being well looked after.'

To my horror my eyes fill up. My lamination must be peeling off. I don't want my gran to look after my mum. I want her to look after me. I quickly turn my head away from Helen, and catch sight of a photo which is definitely me. It's the school photo taken in the last year at St Luke's. It's in a little frame, lined up with a row of pictures of other kids in school uniform. I suppose they must be Helen and Patrick's grandchildren. So what's my picture doing there?

Jesus.

Oh my *God*.

Jesus *Christ*.

They can't be. Louise can't have. But what other explanation can there be?

'Would you like a sandwich, darling?' asks Helen, as I'm wildly searching for alternative theories. That one word 'darling' settles it. You don't use that for a random teenager who's just been dumped on your doorstep as a favour to a friend. Not unless you're bonkers or American, you don't. *Jesus.* How could my auntie do this to me?

I nod, struck completely dumb, and she goes into the kitchen. Left alone, I search frantically for something that will tell me if I'm right. I spot some letters on the mantelpiece and I pick one up and turn it over, looking for the name that's going to tell me that I'm right. There's nothing on the envelope so I pull out the letter and scan it for names.

God. Mr Patrick Tyler. *God.*

They're not the parents of Sally the posh Geography teacher. They're the parents of Danny Tyler, my waste-of-space, completely absent father, who's never bothered to contact us since he pissed off when I was two.

Right on cue, Patrick enters the room. Mr Patrick Tyler, who must be my grandad. Patrick, who I very nearly punched in the teeth. What a brilliant start to our relationship.

'Tyler, I'd prefer it if you didn't touch our personal papers,' he says, and the devil dog snarls at me. I drop the letter right away, but I'm not sure if I'll ever be able to speak again.

Helen's made me a cheese sandwich, but I'm too choked to eat it. She looks worried, and says, 'You must be exhausted. Shall I show you your room, and you can have a shower and a rest?'

'Yeah, thanks,' I mumble. I need to escape. She leads me up two flights of stairs and says, 'I'm going to put you in the attic because you'll have more space and privacy up there.'

I imagine a dusty, dark, bare, spidery room. 'Yeah, fine, whatever.'

But when we get up there, it's not like that at all. It's big, with a wooden floor and pale blue slanty walls and a window looking out over a huge garden. There's a whole bathroom just for me. If you look up, you can see the beams criss-crossing up into the roof.

There's a set of bunk-beds at one end, and where the wall gets slopey there's a big iron double bed with a patchwork quilt. There's a toy box, and a table with pens and paper and paints. There's a bookshelf with children's books. I can see a toy garage with loads of cars. A massive doll's house. A painted rocking horse sits in the middle of the room, and there's a row of old-fashioned dolls with china faces. I'd have loved this stuff when I was about six.

Right now, though, I could do with a TV and a laptop.

She puts my bag on the big bed and says, 'Will this be all right for you? I'm afraid it's kitted out for younger children than you, but if you tell me what you'd like, I can get things in for you. And we have lots of books downstairs; you'll have to have a look tomorrow. Do you like reading?'

'Um, no. . .' I say, mainly to kill the conversation stone dead. She's still smiling, but there's a little crease between her eyes. I feel like I've let her down, but I don't care. Anyway I generally prefer to see the film if there is one.

'Have a look anyway, you might find something you like,' she says. 'The others are all younger than you, that's why it's like this.'

I wonder vaguely about her other grandchildren. They probably read Dickens and Shakespeare all day long. And then it strikes me. These are my cousins. I might even have brothers and sisters. I can't believe this is happening to me. My head is aching just trying to take in all the possibilities.

'Have you got everything you need?' she asks, opening a cupboard and bringing out some big fluffy white towels.

'Yup.' Actually I have absolutely zero idea what Doug's packed in my bag. For all I know, it contains three socks and my mum's nightie.

'Sleep well,' she says, and I can see her thinking about kissing me and deciding not to. Then she leaves me alone. Thank God for that.

I'm desperate to go and have a shower, but I don't seem to be able to move. I think I'll just lie down on the bed to get my strength together. The patchwork quilt is kind of scratchy to lie on, so I push it off and find fantastic smooth white sheets and a soft blanket underneath.

I lie there and take deep breaths and think about what I've worked out.

I have grandparents on my dad's side. I'd never thought about them before, and if I had, I'd have assumed they were dead because they never bothered to see me.

They're really rich, but we never had any money to spare. So they never helped us, and nor did my dad.

My auntie Louise has been secretly in touch with them for years. Why? They know Mum and Gran but I don't think they're in contact. Why? Patrick seems to have a really low opinion of my mum. Presumably he thinks she's a slapper for getting pregnant when she was sixteen and my dad was seventeen.

This adds to the scraps I know about my dad: he's a good-looking, arrogant bastard who never did anything for us, and I'm better off without him. Lots of girls liked him. He studied law at Manchester University. He went to St Saviour's, a Catholic boys' school which is why my mum sent me there. Oh, and the only thing he ever gave me was a Manchester United scarf. He and Mum had a go at living together but it didn't work out. And I once thought my mum was hinting that he might have hit her.

They must know everything about him, including where he is. I could ask them anything about him. He might even be about to turn up here . . . why wouldn't he? But why would he, if he never bothered to see me before?

My head is full and the brandy is churning around inside me, mixing with the Mars Bar and the M&S biscuits but not in a good way, and I'm incredibly dizzy. And this bed is really comfortable. It's a blessed relief to fall asleep.

When I wake up, everything is dark and Alistair is sitting on the end of the bed.

CHAPTER 4
Dirty Laundry

Alistair is dressed in black denims and a white T-shirt and his hair is gelled into its usual ridiculous style and he looks nothing like someone who was shot in the head less than twenty-four hours ago. I'm definitely awake, so he must be a ghost. But I don't believe in ghosts. What's going on?

All I can hear is my breath, which is getting faster and sounds a lot like someone who's about to start whimpering or something. My heart is bashing against the sides of my chest, like it's a cat trying to escape from the cage that's taking it to the vet.

'What . . . what do you want?' I whisper.

He leans towards me. I edge backwards until I'm crushed up against the iron bed. There's cold metal on my back. I can hear him when he speaks. I'm awake, I swear.

'You killed me, didn't you, mate?'

'No . . . no I didn't, I didn't – it wasn't me. . . ' I bleat. I must be awake. I'm digging my nails into my arm and it hurts. But how can I be awake? He's dead. Could I be dead?

He's staring at me. 'Don't deny it. I died because of you. So you have to do what I say.'

Alistair always looked like a nice guy before, but now his smile is really twisted.

'You . . . you what?'

'What's so special about you, eh? Why do people have to die for you? These old people, they're risking their necks to look after you. You've been useless so far. Ungrateful little whinger,' he says.

'I don't . . . I didn't. . .' What does he want from me?

'I want to see you work hard for them,' he says.

'What . . . what do you mean?'

'You show them why they should keep you alive. Because, right now, I'm wondering,' he says.

Then his head explodes and I'm covered with blood and brains and splinters of skull – soft, wet, hot crap all over my face and hands and body.

'Aaaaaaarghh. . . ' It would be a scream, but luckily I have no sound in me. He's gone, but the mess is still there, I'm choking and coughing and I don't know where the light is and I'm too scared to move because of what I might see.

And then I sniff an unmistakable smell and I realise that I'm covered in my own vomit.

A light goes on downstairs and I hear Helen's voice call, 'Ty . . . Ty . . . was that you?' I don't answer, I can't speak, and after a bit the light goes off. I can see a bit more now and I move to the door and feel around for a light switch. I can hear snatches of the conversation downstairs.

'. . . just a thug,' Patrick is saying. 'Well, what did we expect? Louise has obviously been dressing up the truth about him for a long time.'

'Oh, come on, we can't judge that yet,' says Helen. 'Give him a chance, the poor boy.'

Then the voices turn into a mumble and I switch on the light. There's no one here. There can't have been anyone here. It must have been a dream – but I'm certain I was awake.

I creep into the bathroom and finally have the shower I've been longing for all day. Wrapped in a huge towel – actually the nicest towel I've ever felt – I investigate my bag. Doug has made a crappy job of packing. He's managed to ignore my pyjamas and – typical – has packed nothing from my underwear drawer at all. So, nothing to sleep in or put on tomorrow. I have four pairs of jeans, some T-shirts, three hoodies, some running gear and no socks. No toothbrush even, although the hair dye from when I was Joe is still there, because I never unpacked it in the first place. I hunt around the bathroom and find a child-size toothbrush and some disgusting bubblegum flavoured toothpaste. As I scrub with pink foam, I wonder which child left them there.

Luckily I had my iPod in my pocket, and Doug did pack the Manchester United scarf that my dad gave me when I was a baby. I pull it out and twiddle the fringe a little bit, which is how I used to go to sleep when I was little. Even though I don't have a very high opinion of my dad, I'm still glad to have that scarf.

I pull on some shorts and decide to do without a top to conserve my clean clothes. Then I strip the bed, piling the vomit-covered sheets and blanket together with my dirty clothes from today. I don't really recommend Mars Bar puke, it's pretty disgusting.

I'd rather not bother Helen, and I could easily just sleep in the bunk bed, but it occurs to me that if I could find a washing machine and put this on to wash now, then I'd save her any trouble and also I'd have clean underwear for tomorrow.

And I want to get out of this room, in case Alistair's ghost comes back.

So I tiptoe down the stairs. The wolf-monster-Lassie-dog is snoring in a basket, and I'm thankful that it doesn't stir as I try door handles and find my way to the kitchen. It's massive, but there doesn't seem to be a washing machine. That's odd – surely rich people don't go to the launderette – but then I see there's a little side room and it's just for laundry. There's a washing machine and a dryer, and an ironing board and a clothes rack.

The washing machine is full, so I pull out the damp clothes, then carefully hang them all up on the clothes rail. I put the sick-stained sheets and sweaty clothes on to wash. Then I notice the big pile of ironing. There are shirts and handkerchiefs and all sorts of things. I don't mind ironing, and when I was at St Saviour's I did a lot at home alone in the evenings. It helped me forget what a rubbish time I was having.

They have a really nice ironing board and a top quality steam iron too. John Lewis. I'm sure no one will mind me doing this. I'm a pretty good ironer, if I say so myself. But, as the pile gets smaller, I wonder if Alistair's ghost will think I've worked hard enough?

I finish ironing just as my washing is ready. I empty the dryer and pile my sheets and clothes in. Then I fold up all the dried stuff. I wonder if Helen actually wants me sorting out her underwear, but it seems a bit strange not to do the whole job. I've been doing my mum's laundry for years.

I'm sleepy now, but I want to wait until everything is dry so I can make up the bed again and no one need know what happened. I turn off the light and sit down on the cool, tiled floor and I listen to the soothing sound of the dryer, and everything's just about safe for the moment. I like this room. It's warm and small and all about getting things clean and sorted.

I sleep a bit, wake up for a while, go back to sleep again. I think about going back upstairs but before I can decide it's getting light and a soft wet nose nudges my toes. I lie as still as I can. The wolf-dog has found me. It sniffs and snuffles, then starts barking its head off, paws skidding and clattering on the tiles as it rushes out of the room. I don't move, although I'm icy cold. I'm shaking, wondering how I can escape before it comes back and attacks me.

But when it comes back it doesn't rip my face off. It brings Patrick back with it. I'm not sure I wouldn't have preferred being bitten. He's wearing his dressing gown and yawning and looking completely puzzled.

'What on earth are you doing in here, boy?' he says. 'You'll freeze to death.'

I wish I could just go on pretending to be asleep, but I can't with the dog yapping away, so I stretch and say, 'Sorry, I must have just dropped off. Oh, and, um, sorry I shouted at you yesterday.'

'We'll forget about it,' he says, in a growly sort of voice. 'Get up, lad; you'll need to warm up a bit.'

I notice he doesn't say sorry for disrespecting my mum. I can't get up because the vicious dog is still sniffing my feet, and nudging its nose against me.

'Are you scared of her?' roars Patrick, as though it's totally bizarre to be nervous of something with razor-sharp teeth. 'She's trying to make friends.'

I try to look brave and unfriendly, but he doesn't get the hint and remove his savage beast. 'Have you never had anything to do with dogs before? Give her your hand to smell . . . that's it . . . now stroke her head and back. That's right, you see, she likes you now. Come for a few walks with us, and she'll be your best friend in no time.' The stupid dog is slobbering germs all over my hand, and it could easily bite off a finger with one snap of its jaw.

'I can't go for walks. Louise says I can't go out of the house.'

'Hmmm,' says Patrick. 'Seems tough, all day, every day in the house. Enough to drive anyone round the bend. Go and get dressed now, we don't want to look at your body all day long, do we, Meg?'

Meg woofs in my face, which makes me jump. I get my washing out of the dryer and fold it all up neatly, trying to put off going upstairs. I'd like to iron the sheets, but it's maybe more important to get the bed made up straight away. Patrick is looking around the laundry room.

'Bless me, lad, have you been up all night doing the ironing?' he asks, as if it's a crime to iron a few shirts. I panic and lie.

'No. I didn't do any.'

'Who did it then, the ironing fairy?'

'I dunno. I just did my washing.' I feel like I'm in the headmaster's study and I haven't had a good record there recently. He knows I'm lying, anyway.

'Julie always was a champion ironer,' he says, 'No doubt she's trained you up in her footsteps, eh?'

What is he talking about? Why would my gran be doing his ironing?

I must have looked baffled, because he says, 'You did know that Julie used to be our cleaner, nanny and bottlewasher-in-chief?'

He's lying. 'My gran wasn't your servant!' I say, furious. My gran's been a school dinner lady for as long as I've been at school. But before that she worked in a bookie's and before that she had a really good job which she loved as . . . as . . . I'm not quite sure what that job was.

'Long time ago now,' he says, ignoring me. 'She was a great help when the girls were small. Danny was born just before she had Louise, so she stopped working for us then, but she always came to visit. We were in Highgate then, before we moved out here. Danny and Louise were friends before Nicki dropped her bombshell. . . Well, anyway, your grandmother was a great ironer, and your grandfather was the best odd-job man I've ever met.'

My grandad Mick *wasn't* an odd-job man. He was a master carpenter. He worked at the Houses of Parliament. And 'Nicki's bombshell' must mean me. Bloody hell.

'I'm going to get dressed,' I say with as much dignity as I can, considering that I'm virtually naked, I've just told a stupidly obvious lie about ironing, my legs are being licked by the daft dog, and I'm descended from sluts and slaves.

Going up the stairs, I'm grateful not to meet Helen, and there's no ghost in my room as I have another shower to warm myself up, get dressed and re-make the bed. In my jeans pocket I find my two notes from Claire. I re-read them, and wonder if there's a computer here, and feel bad because so much happened yesterday that I hardly thought about her at all.

I'm starving hungry. I wander down the stairs and back into the kitchen where Helen and Patrick are eating toast and drinking coffee. It smells fantastic.

Helen jumps up and makes me some toast and pours me a coffee. They're both looking at me a bit strangely and I immediately lose my appetite. No one says anything, and I nibble the toast and start imagining how upset they must have been when I was born. No one wants their son to be a father before he's done his A levels, do they? I bet they wish I'd never happened. I'm desperate to get out of this house, to go for a run, but that's not allowed.

Helen breaks the silence.

'Ty,' she says, hesitantly, 'Patrick tells me he found you down here, asleep this morning. Was there a problem?'

'Erm . . . I just needed to do some washing. I didn't mean to sleep down here; I must've just fallen asleep. It's a nice room, that laundry room.'

'Is it?' She obviously thinks I'm crazy. Maybe I am.

'If you prefer to do your own laundry, then just help yourself anytime,' she says. 'You really don't have to worry about helping out though, you're our guest.'

'Um . . . yeah, right . . . sometimes I like to just do it myself.'

They exchange glances. Patrick says, 'I'll just take Meg for a walk,' and the dog's ears prick up and she rushes up to him, barking her head off, which makes me wince. She's a pretty clever animal, though, I have to admit, to understand English. I bet she'd like running with me better than walking with an old guy.

Once they've gone, Helen pours me another cup of coffee and makes me some more toast. She's still going on about the washing.

'Look, Ty, I can show you where there are sheets and things if you need to change the bed . . . I mean, if you have problems again. . . You don't have to start doing washing in the middle of the night. I've even got a mattress-protector somewhere.'

She thinks I'm a bed-wetter. Brilliant.

'It wasn't that sort of problem. I threw up. And the stupid policeman who packed my bag didn't put in any underwear or socks or anything, so I was a bit short of clothes for today.'

She looks worried and relieved at the same time. 'I'm here for you if you are ill, or you need anything – you can wake me up at any time. I hate to think of you falling asleep on the cold floor. And of course we can buy you anything you need. Just make me a list.'

Of course she can, there's no shortage of money here. If I'd suddenly lost half my clothes in London, my mum and I would've had a major financial crisis. And that's because we never got one penny from her stupid son.

'Thanks a lot,' I say, but not like I mean it, and she gives me a notepad and I write down what I need.

We've finished eating, so I clear up the plates and look around for washing-up gloves, but she says, 'Everything goes in the dishwasher,' so I stack them in there instead. Then I remember the clothes that I put to dry on the rack and I wander over to the nice laundry room and ask,

'Shall I . . . would you like me to just finish off the ironing for you?'

'Do you really want to?' she says, and I nod. And when Patrick and Meg come back and he sees what I'm doing, he looks at Helen and she shakes her head and shrugs, and I concentrate all the harder on the job in hand.

CHAPTER 5
Claire

No one talks about my dad. The only time anyone even mentions him is the day I dye my hair back to black, like Louise told me to, and Helen kind of splutters into her tea and then says, 'Well, you certainly look like Danny.' I think she's hoping I'll be thrilled and excited and ask her lots of questions, but I don't say anything.

I've been doing more and more cleaning. It keeps me out of their way. They sometimes seem a bit surprised at how I like to work – taking all the saucepans out of the cupboards for example, so I can scrub everything spotless – but no one complains. Helen even says how useful it is that I'm so helpful because she's had to ask her cleaner not to come in while I'm staying with them. I think they could do with getting a better cleaner anyway, because there's a lot of dirt hidden away under furniture and at the back of shelves if you look carefully enough.

Patrick went to Marks and Spencer and bought me boxers, socks and pyjamas and then he bought loads of clothes from Gap, which wouldn't have been my first choice, but most of them look OK. I can't quite imagine actually wearing them.

At mealtimes there's a lot of awkward silence. I eat as quickly as possible, and move over to the sink to clear up as soon as I can. Helen tries to talk to me about school and stuff, but I don't seem to have many words right now, so I nod and mumble and shrug, and eventually she gives up.

Patrick spends most of his time in his study, which is where the computer is. I haven't asked him yet if I can check my emails. I keep out of his way. I haven't quite got over our bad start, and he's always hanging around with the dog. I don't like the way it watches me, like it's planning when to attack.

Alistair only appears some nights. He stands at the bottom of my bed, staring at me in silence, and I can't sleep while he's doing that. And I can't sleep while I'm waiting to see if he'll turn up or not. So most days I feel weary and I seem to ache all over. I'm always looking for him out of the corner of my eye and sometimes I feel myself twitching with nerves.

It takes me three days to get to the computer without them noticing. Patrick's taken Meg for a walk.

Helen's on the phone to someone and I sneak into the study to see if he's left the computer on. He has. Fantastic. And I'm logging on to my email account and there are three messages waiting, which must all be from Claire.

A few weeks ago I sent a stupid, stupid email to Claire. I don't know what I was thinking. I told her that I had hurt Arron in the park, but I didn't tell her any of the details. It was a kind of truth or dare moment – a test of what she would do. How much did she love me? I spent the next week in agony, wishing I could call it back, and then she wrote and just ignored what I'd said. And then I wondered if I'd sent it to the right address, or whether this email with its dangerous words – *I'm a liar, I'm lying to the police* – is bouncing around in cyberspace.

Anyway. The first message is just chat, about school and her family and stuff. Apparently my friend Brian is going out with Emily, who he's fancied for ages and is way out of his league, so that's quite big news.

Her second message was written two days ago:

We heard about Alistair. I don't know where to start. First, are you all right? Where are you? What happened to you? I am so scared that you were hurt when they shot him . . . he was with you, wasn't he? The police told Ellie it was mistaken identity and that he'd been staying with his girlfriend and I know he was seeing your mum, wasn't he? But how come he knew where you were? I don't understand any of it, but I am so scared that you are hurt. Please write to me.

Alistair was a nice guy, you know. He was a really good coach to Ellie and she is devastated, crying all the time. And she and her friends are just sitting together the whole time and talking about Alistair. No one can believe it.

Of course – no one else says this, but I can to you – she's also worrying about what it means for her prospects for the Paralympics, and how she will find another coach like him. It's not so easy to find someone who really understands disabled athletes, she says. Ellie's quite bitter about it and she's been moaning about how the Paralympics don't get the same status as the real Olympics.

Anyway I just want to hear from you. Are you OK? Are you safe? Let me know.

And then the third message, written yesterday:

Joe, I am so worried about you it's unbearable. I am trying really hard to keep to our pledge and not hurt myself, but I feel all this panic building up. I am trying to be strong but it is hard and I need to talk to you because since you sent that email I don't even know who you are any more.

Oh Christ. My heart is pounding and I am so angry at myself for writing the email in the first place and for whatever it was I did that allowed Alistair to get shot and for screwing things up so badly that I couldn't stay where I was and be Joe and look after Claire. I hit *Reply* and

I start writing:

Claire I am OK and you mustn't worry about me and I can explain everything all I want is to see you—

'I think you'll find that that's my chair and my computer,' says a dry voice from the doorway. Bugger. It's Patrick, back again, and Meg growling at his heels.

'I'll just be a minute,' I say, and type as fast as I can, *don't hurt yrslf talk to smone, pls Claire maybe i can ring—*

'Enough!' thunders Patrick, and I press *Send* and then log out, while he marches right up to the chair and stands over me. He's frowning so much that his eyebrows look like two hamsters huddling together in a storm.

'It's not that I mind you using the computer *per se*,' he says, 'but I think you should ask, not just wait until I am out and help yourself.'

What is his problem? It's only a computer for Christ's sake. You'd have thought he'd be pleased that I waited until he was out. Why does he have to be so angry and fierce and tall?

'I didn't think you'd mind.'

'No boundaries,' he says. 'We need to set down some rules while you're staying here.'

I can hardly concentrate while he goes on and on at me because I'm so worried about Claire. He's talking about making an effort . . . asking permission . . . respecting privacy . . . my own safety . . . and all I can think about is how I can find out Claire's number because I had to give up Joe's mobile when I stopped being Joe, and how can I call her?

There are these numbers you can ring which tell you phone numbers, I've heard them advertised on the radio. But I've not got a mobile.

'So this won't happen again?' says Patrick, and I shake my head and say, 'No . . . I'll ask. . . ' and he nods and says, 'Good. Well, I need to use the computer now, so can you find something to do?'

I wander into the kitchen and check the laundry room to see if any ironing has magically appeared, but no, I've done everything. I load a sponge with bleach and swab the kitchen top, and then wonder if it's too soon to clean the floor again. I only did it an hour ago, but the dog's probably been in here and it must be swarming with bacteria.

And then I notice Helen's handbag sitting open on the kitchen table.

I sidle over. I can see her mobile glowing up at me, shiny blue. I want it. I need it. I stick my hand in and pull it out. She's my grandmother, after all. Gran never minded me borrowing her stuff and I've always felt free to help myself to money from my mum's handbag – I'd have starved otherwise. I'm sure it'll be fine, and she'll never know anyway because I'll just quickly call

Claire and then put it straight back. She'll never notice. Anyway it's a basic human right to have access to a phone, isn't it?

I scoot upstairs to my attic room, lock myself into the bathroom and hide behind the shower curtain. No one can find me here. I call the 118 number and give them Claire's address and surname. And then I'm breathless with excitement when they say they're putting me through and I hear the phone ringing and I imagine Claire hearing it in her dark attic – except that I know that her mum made her move bedrooms to the floor below when they found out about her cutting herself.

'Hello?' It's Ellie who answers the phone, and just for a minute I consider telling her that it's me and getting one of her bracing pep talks. Then I think how badly she's missing Alistair, and I say, 'Can I speak to Claire, please?'

'Who is it?'

'Umm . . . it's Brian. About our English homework.'

'Oh hi, Brian, I'll get her,' says Ellie and there's a silence while I think how strange it is that a few months ago Claire had no friends at all and now it seems it's totally normal for her to get calls from boys.

In fact, Ellie took it completely for granted that Brian would be calling Claire. What if this story about Emily is all nonsense – and, let's face it, it sounds pretty unlikely – and he and Claire are actually seeing each other but she doesn't want to tell me? What if. . . But she's here.

'Hi? Brian?' she says, and I open my mouth, but I'm choked with jealousy and love.

'Brian?' she says again and I manage to croak, 'It's me. Joe.'

'Oh!' she squeaks, and I wonder if she's shocked that I've found out that she's cheating on me.

'I just thought . . . your email. . . '

'We need to talk.' she says. 'I need to see you.'

We need to talk. Wasn't that what Ashley said when she chucked me?

'I can't . . . I'm not allowed to go anywhere.'

'Oh Joe . . . I'm just totally shocked to hear your voice. Are you OK? I've been so worried about you.'

There's a lump in my throat like I've swallowed Sonic the Hedgehog.

'I'm OK. You don't have to worry about me.'

'I'm going to send you a list of all Ellie's races. I can easily come along to any of them. Maybe one of them will be near where you are and you can meet me somewhere.'

I don't think that's very likely as I have no idea where I am and I'm not allowed out.

'OK. I'll try.'

'Oh, I miss you so much,' she says, and I'm just

starting to relax and feel happy and remember how it feels to look in her blue eyes and feel completely loved, when I become aware of noise. Feet thundering up my attic stairs. Shouting. And then someone . . . or something . . . rattling my bathroom door. Damn. Who the hell is it? It doesn't sound like Patrick. Or Alistair.

'I've got to go,' I whisper and she says, 'Try and do this again.'

'OK.' Then the rattling turns into banging and I end the call before we can say goodbye properly. I shove the phone in my back pocket and nervously slide the lock open.

The door bursts open. It's not Patrick. It's not Alistair. It's a boy. He must be about thirteen.

And he looks so much like me that we could be twins.

CHAPTER 6
Goldilocks and Baby Bear

'You've been sleeping in my bed,' he says accusingly, like I'm Goldilocks and he's Baby Bear. A very posh Baby Bear, who probably goes to the bears' version of Eton and is planning to serve Goldilocks with an ASBO.

'Umm . . . err. . . ' I reply. This must be a cousin. Unless – bloody hell – my dad had another baby really soon after me and this is my half-brother. Surely not. Christ. He must have learned how to avoid getting girls pregnant after I was born. I certainly would've made sure I was a world expert on the subject. Although my mum's thirty-one and she obviously hasn't mastered the basics.

'Who are you?' he demands.

'Umm . . . no one,' I say, feebly. 'I'm . . . ummm . . . here to help out with the cleaning.'

'Oh.' He loses interest in me, just like that. You can see his eyes kind of switch off. He's filed me under Domestic Help and decided that I'm not worth knowing. Fine by me.

'Well I'm going to sleep in here. I always do. You'll have to move your stuff. Grandma will change the bed for me.'

No spoilt brat is telling me what to do, even if he might be my brother. He doesn't even look that much like me, now I've had time to get used to him. His eyes are blue, not green – *he* must be the alien with the toy horse in Helen's picture – and his hair is dark brown, somewhere between Joe's black hair and Ty's dirty blond.

'I don't think so,' I say, flat and uninterested. And I sit down on my bed and plug in my iPod.

He looks completely outraged and then charges down the stairs again. I wait until he's nearly downstairs and then I follow him as far as the landing, so I can hear what's going on.

'Grandma!' he's shouting, 'There's a cleaner in my room and he's been sleeping in my bed.'

I peek down the stairs and I can see into the living room where Helen and Patrick are standing, talking to a lady who's tall and lanky with bushy brown hair and glasses. She must be Mummy Bear, I think, although there's no sign of Daddy Bear anywhere. Patrick's face is great – his eyebrows shoot upwards like two hamsters on a trampoline, and his mouth twists like he's eating pickled lemons. I start shaking with laughter, and have to slap my hands over my mouth.

Helen looks incredibly flustered and says, 'Archie darling, we're just talking to your mother. I'm glad you've met Tyler, but there's a lot to explain. . .'

Archie's mum's head jerks up and she says, 'Tyler? Tyler's here? How on earth? Does Danny know?'

'Not yet,' says Patrick, which is pretty interesting news to me.

'But surely. . .' she says, and Patrick says, 'Look, Penelope, it's a sensitive situation. The last thing we need is Danny pitching up here and making a scene.'

'What on earth is going on?' she asks and Patrick glances towards Archie – who's now making a huge fuss of Meg in the corner, and getting dog slobber all over his face – and says, 'You'd better come into the study and I'll tell you the whole story.'

They disappear, and I can hear Helen talking to Archie and explaining to him that I'm not a cleaner but his long-lost cousin – phew – and won't it be nice when we all get to know each other. She comes to the stairs and calls me down, and so I have no choice but to be introduced properly.

'Archie's possibly come to stay for a while,' says Helen. 'Won't that be nice?'

'Oh. Umm. Is that OK?' I ask. Louise isn't going to like this at all.

'And you've got to move beds,' says Archie, 'because that's where I sleep.'

I give him an evil, menacing look that's meant to crush any hope that he's going to be allowed to boss me around. It doesn't work at all.

'Grandma, tell him he's got to do what I say,' he says, and Helen says, 'Oh dear, would you mind, Ty? The bunk bed's very comfortable and Archie does always sleep in that iron bed.'

Unbelievable. She's going to let him get away with chucking me out of my bed, without even saying please or thank you.

'Whatever,' I shrug, and I swear that I'm going to teach young Archie about respect. And then I realise what this means. She's expecting us to share a room.

'How long is Archie staying?' I ask. He's obviously at some posh private school. Maybe he'll just be here for a bit of half term and then he'll be off.

'Well. . .' says Helen, and Archie sticks his chin in the air and says, 'I got expelled, actually, and Ma has to find me a new boarding school.'

'You got expelled? Why?' This is worrying – he could

be here for ages – but also quite funny. Although not for Helen, who's looking a bit upset.

'Oh, this and that,' says Archie, making me think it's something completely pathetic which only a stupid boarding school would worry about. He probably organised a midnight feast, or refused to make the Head Boy's toast, or skipped 5 pm curfew to go and buy wine gums at the village shop.

He can see that I'm unimpressed. 'Actually I arranged a strippergram for the housemaster's birthday,' he says, full of pride, and Helen says, 'That's quite enough. You're in disgrace and you shouldn't be boasting about it. Now go upstairs and sort yourselves out. Are you sure you don't mind about the bed, Ty?'

The conversation in the study is getting noisy. We both pause on the stairs going past, and then we both stop at the top of the stairs and lean on the banister and listen. We're trying to ignore each other. Luckily, Helen knocks on the study door with a tray of tea, and she doesn't quite close the door when she goes in.

'So it's not really safe for Archie to be here,' Patrick is saying, 'let alone the work involved in having two of them here. And I'm not sure we can trust either of them to behave.'

'Oh, nonsense, they'll keep each other company,' says Helen. 'It'll be good for Ty to have another boy here. He's absolutely no trouble, anyway. Spends all his time cleaning and ironing.'

Archie looks at me when she says this and I'm sure he's silently laughing.

'I'm certain you're exaggerating any danger,' says Archie's mum. 'There's no proof, is there, that the shooting incident had anything to do with poor Tyler? If the man was Nicki's boyfriend – well, we know from Louise that she's hooked up with some bad boys in her time, don't we?'

My mouth is wide open. Bloody hell. What is she on about? What's Louise been saying? It takes massive self control, but I manage to stop myself running down the stairs to shout at her.

'Anyway,' she goes on, 'I have no choice. I've got a meeting in Chicago next week, then I'm off to Brazil and David's tied up with a major acquisition in Dubai until mid-December. Marina's au pair says she's got her hands full with the twins, so I can't leave him there, and Elizabeth's not got room. I'm getting my secretary to ring round schools, and I'm sure we'll find somewhere that'll take him.'

'Somewhere with a bit more discipline,' says Patrick, and she answers, 'The thing is, Daddy, he's so bright that he runs rings round most school teachers.'

I glance at Archie. He's looking incredibly smug.

And then his mum says, 'But what about *Danny*? Surely he ought to know what's going on. He'll go crazy when he finds out—' and the door is slammed shut again.

Archie rushes up the stairs to my room and I follow him slowly. I can't believe my privacy is going to be invaded. I'm never going to be able to sleep . . . what if he snores . . . or farts. . . And what about Alistair? I'll have to tell Helen that I can't do this.

I open the door to the attic and see Archie dragging the sheets off my bed and tossing the pillows up to the bunk bed. Under the pillows are the pyjamas that Patrick bought for me, and folded underneath them is my Manchester United scarf. I've kept it there for the last few nights because I kind of need it when I'm waiting to see if Alistair's there, or when he's staring at me, or after he disappears. It's just something to touch which calms me down. It's none of anyone else's business.

Archie spots the scarf and picks it up, hooting with laughter. 'You wear this in bed? You must be really keen . . . have you got Wayne Rooney slippers?'

He stops laughing when I shove him down onto the bed – my bed – stick my knees on his chest, one arm on his windpipe, and wrap the other hand in his glossy hair, pulling it tight until one eye slants upwards. 'Get your filthy hands off my stuff,' I growl, as he struggles and chokes underneath me. He's strong, but I'm stronger.

'Understand?' I say, and he tries to nod, so I climb off him. He coughs and gulps while I wrap the scarf up carefully and put it safe in my bag – then the little brat jumps onto my back and tries to throttle me.

For Christ's sake. I stand up, carrying him with me like we're running a piggyback race, and turn and slam him against the wall. His grip weakens and he slides off me – then grabs my ankle, bringing me crashing down next to him. And he's on top of me and we're rolling around, banging into the doll's house and the rocking horse, which are pretty painful things to bash into.

'What's going on?' says Helen, and we jump away from each other and scramble to our feet. I'm all prepared to say it was nothing really, but Archie starts, 'He attacked me Grandma, he tried to choke me and he pulled my hair and he really hurt me. . .'

I open my mouth to tell her what I think of her precious grandson.

And then her phone rings in my back pocket.

CHAPTER 7
Sorry

I try and ignore the noise – it could be coming from anywhere – while Helen says, puzzled, 'What's my phone doing up here? I could have sworn it was in my bag . . . have you seen it, boys?' Luckily, the ring tone cuts out, but then after a minute there's a ping to tell her that someone's left a voicemail, and Archie opens his mouth wide and says, 'That came from you . . . oooooh . . . you've hidden her phone.'

So there's nothing to do but pull it out of my pocket and say, 'I don't know how it got there. . .' and then it rings again, so she can't say anything to me, because she's too busy answering it.

'Oh. . .' she says, 'I think . . . I think I'd better call you back later.'

I'm immediately convinced it must be my dad on the phone. It's the way she looks at me – like she's not sure what to do. It's a look I recognise because that's how I feel quite often. Helen's face is quite like mine . . . which is a really weird thought considering that she's about seventy and a woman.

I wonder why they're not telling my dad that I'm here. What are they scared of? Is it because he's violent? I wonder what would have happened if he'd called and no one was in the room and I'd seen his name flash up.

She turns the phone off. Archie is grinning his head off and mouthing, 'You're in big trouble,' to me, and Helen's looking pained and upset. I think I'd prefer to deal with Patrick, rather than face her. 'I'm going downstairs,' I say, and I turn my back on them and walk down the stairs.

Patrick's only going to shout at me. I don't think he'll actually hit me or set the dog on me if I own up right away and say I'm sorry, and there's not much he can do to punish me – I'm permanently grounded and I haven't even got a phone to take away. I've had worse things happen to me than being shouted at by an old man.

It's just that I'm not feeling at my best right now.

He's still talking to Archie's mum in the study. I knock

at the door and push it open, trying to look really hard and like nothing bothers me.

'Yes?' he barks, 'What is it?'

'I . . . ummm . . . wanted to tell you something.'

'Yes? Spit it out.'

'Umm . . . in private. . .'

Archie's mum says, 'I'll leave you to it. I'd better make some phone calls, anyway. Tyler, it is wonderful to meet you at last. We'll have a chance to talk later, I hope.' She hovers around like she's deciding whether to kiss me, but luckily I repel her by wiping my nose on my sleeve.

Once we're alone, Patrick sits down and points at a chair for me. It's a big room – like every room in this enormous house – and we're sitting by a fireplace which has a real fire burning in it. I've never seen a fire inside before, and it's kind of hypnotic watching it. I want to stick my hand into the flames to see if they're real. Meg sits on my feet, which is uncomfortably hot and heavy, but I'm so nervy that actually it's quite nice to feel her soft, warm fur.

'So, what did you want to tell me?' asks Patrick. His voice is less growly now and I wish I had something else to say to him. Patrick kind of reminds me of Sir Alex Ferguson, except Patrick's posh and English instead of rough and Scottish. Sir Alex shouts at the Manchester United players all the time – they call it getting the hairdryer – but it really seems to work.

It's just that when Wayne Rooney gets the hairdryer he's obviously had days when Sir Alex said loads of good things to him like, 'Well done, Wayne, you played a blinder in the Champions League final,' but Patrick's never said anything like that to me.

'I . . . ummm . . . want to . . . errrr . . . confess.'

His eyebrows leap around a bit.

'Should I call Father Delaney?' he asks.

'No. . .' I'm feeling really stupid. Of course I don't mean that kind of confession. I forgot they must be Catholics as well. 'I wanted to tell you. I borrowed Helen's mobile, and I used it without asking. And I pulled Archie's hair.'

He pulls out his handkerchief and coughs a bit. Maybe he's got a cold.

'When did you take the mobile, and why?' he asks.

'Just now . . . I was going to put it back right away, I promise, but it rang in my pocket and she realised.'

'So, immediately after we had our conversation about asking permission before you use the computer, you went and helped yourself to the phone?'

'Umm . . . you see I needed to make a phone call very urgently. . .'

He points his finger at me, 'What about asking? What about your safety?'

'I thought you'd say no . . . actually I didn't really think, but if I had, that's what I would've thought.'

'Next time, think. And ask. Who were you phoning?'

'Just a friend,' I say. He lifts one eyebrow but I keep my mouth shut, and he doesn't ask any more.

'Don't do it again,' he says, 'Think of the safety of the rest of us, even if you're careless of your own.'

I sigh. I'm nearly fifteen. I've had my own mobile for four years. I'm actually wondering if I'm going backwards in life instead of forwards.

'We'll come back to that,' he says. 'Now, I want to know why my grandsons are pulling each other's hair. In my day, that would be a girl's way of fighting.'

No one calls me a girl. 'I could've hit him, but the last time I hit someone I broke his nose,' I say, raising the volume just a bit. 'I'm very happy to hit him next time though.' Meg nudges my hand with her nose, so I have to scratch between her ears.

'No need to shout. I'm not deaf,' says Patrick. 'Sadly, I'm sure there will be a next time. Try and minimise the violence, though. It'll upset Helen and I'm sure you wouldn't want that. Whose nose did you break and what were the consequences?'

'Umm . . . Carl . . . he was a boy at my last school. I got suspended and then we had to sort out the lost property cupboard together. Restorative justice.'

Patrick is enormously interested in restorative justice and asks me loads of questions about it. Then he asks, 'And why did you hit him?'

'He tried to drown me in the swimming pool. . .' and I have to explain all about the contact lenses I wore as part of my disguise when I was Joe, and why it was so dangerous when Carl ducked me in the water, and about how he'd broken my ribs as well by kicking me.

'And Archie? What heinous crime did he commit that you needed to punish him by pulling his hair?' he asks, once I've ground to a halt.

Meg's lying on the ground now, and she rolls over so I can tickle her tummy. Her fur is really silky and soft and I'm not thinking about germs at all.

'He was moving my stuff from my bed to the bunk bed. He was touching my stuff, stuff that's not his to touch.'

'I'll talk to him,' says Patrick.

'Does he have to stay?'

'Apparently so,' he says. 'I think it might be quite interesting for you and Archie to get to know each other. You've both grown up without brothers or sisters.'

'I don't want to get to know him.'

'You seem to have no choice,' he says. 'But you may have more in common than you realise.'

I don't think I've got anything in common with

that spoilt baby.

'Ty,' he says. 'I know you think I'm being dictatorial about the computer and the phone, and I'm sorry if you don't feel fully at home. But Louise did say no contact with anyone, and that means no email and no phone calls, and from what I know about teenagers and the internet, I'd prefer you to avoid dubious chatrooms and illegal downloads.'

'Yeah . . . but. . .'

'I suspect that so many huge changes have happened in your life recently that it would be understandable if you started to act . . . how should I put it . . . without discipline. If you start punching people, taking things that don't belong to you, and so on . . . because, compared to the things you've seen and the things you've experienced, nothing seems to matter very much. Understand?'

I'm not sure. I concentrate on stroking Meg's soft ears. He's right that things did get a bit out of control when I was Joe, but I don't know where he's going with this.

'I think you need me to set clear boundaries,' he says. 'From what Louise has told me, neither Nicki nor Julie have ever been really tough with you. Has anyone ever given you any discipline at all?'

I'm not really sure what he means. Is he going to hit me? Gran never ever told me off, but there was nothing to tell me off about. I used to go round to her flat and have my supper and do my homework and watch TV, and what's the problem with that? Nicki would explode at me pretty randomly, not all that often, and I learned to keep my head down and say what she wanted to hear. That policy worked well at school too. Arron used to laugh at me because I was such a good boy.

There was one boyfriend of my mum's, Chris the plumber, who said I needed a firm hand and more discipline. He used to boss me around and shout at me, and I was a bit scared of him. Once, I remember, we went out for the day with him and in the car going home he got angry – 'Crumbs all over the bleeding upholstery' – and he went on and on and in the end I felt something warm on my leg and I'd wet myself. I was only about five.

Nicki looked over her shoulder and saw my face and said, 'Tell you what, Chris, let's drop him off with my mum and then we can have some fun by ourselves.' When we got to Gran's, she shoved Chris's A-Z over the wet patch on the seat, and ran with me to the door and said, 'Mum, can you have him for the weekend? Thanks,' and ran back to the car. Gran had to take me to her salsa class because she hadn't got a babysitter. And I never saw Chris again.

After that, my mum didn't introduce me much to her

boyfriends. When she was seeing someone I mostly got packed off to Gran's. Sometimes they didn't even know about me and sometimes she would tell them I was her little brother. They didn't last long, anyway.

Patrick unfolds himself from the chair and towers above me. It's like looking up at a giant. 'I'm going to have a word with Helen and Archie, and then I'd like you to apologise to them,' he says. 'Think you can do that?'

Apologise to Archie? To *Archie?* He must be joking. But he leaves me alone before I can say anything.

I'm just looking at the computer and wondering if Claire's written back – probably not so clever to check – when Archie's mum comes in. She's got a big smile on her face and I can see there's no escaping her.

'So . . . Tyler. . .' she says. 'We've all missed you so much all these years.'

Oh yeah? No one came to look for me.

'Your dad in particular – he'll be so happy to see you again. Poor Danny, it's been very hard for him.'

Hard for him? What about me? I have to bite my tongue not to say anything.

'My parents aren't really in touch with him, but wouldn't you like to meet him again?' she asks. 'You must have thought about him a lot over the years.'

For Christ's sake. I'm not going to discuss with her what I might feel about someone who never even bothered to send me a birthday card. Her smile is wobbling a bit. She's probably wondering if I know how to talk.

'Perhaps you'd like me to call him?' she asks.

'No,' I say. 'I'm not interested. I'm just staying here while I have to and then I'll go back to my gran and my mum, and you can all forget about me again.'

'No one ever forgot about you,' she says, but I've had enough. I push past her and stomp up the stairs.

Patrick is talking to Helen and Archie. I pause outside and I hear him say, 'Tyler's come here with almost nothing, Archie, and you're not to interfere with his possessions,' and then I push open the door. Everyone's looking at me, and I can see Archie's annoyed that I heard him being told off.

'Sorry Helen,' I mumble. 'Sorry Archie.' I drag his name out and sound as un-sorry as I can.

'I think you can do better than that,' says Patrick. 'Try again.'

Jesus. It's like being back in reception class.

'Ummm . . . I'm really sorry, Helen, I shouldn't have taken your mobile without asking. I only did it because I needed to make an urgent phone call and it won't happen again. Maybe I can repay you for the cost of the call. I promise never to take your stuff without asking again.'

She looks a bit stunned and says, 'Thank you for

the apology. Of course you can use the phone whenever you want, darling.'

'No he can't,' says Patrick, 'Don't you remember what Louise said? No calls.'

I'm hoping that he'll have forgotten that I haven't apologised properly to Archie, but oh no, that would be too much to hope for.

'And next, your cousin,' he says. I think he's really enjoying this. Sadist.

'I'm very, very sorry Archie that I pulled your hair and I do hope you are not seriously hurt and I'll try never to pull your hair again,' I say through gritted teeth.

'Much better,' says Patrick. 'Notice, Archie, that Tyler has left himself a large escape clause. You'd better be careful how you approach him in the future. Now, what have you got to say to him?'

'Sorry for touching your scarf and laughing at you,' says Archie. 'I hope I didn't hurt your feelings too much. I was only joking.' He might as well have called me a pathetic over-sensitive crybaby. Patrick lets him get away with it, though.

'Excellent,' he says. 'I can see we're going to have great fun together. Now I'm going to take Meg for a walk. Archie, maybe you'd better come with me.'

I'm pleased when they all leave me alone. I need some breathing space, some time to get used to the ideas that I've got to share a room, that I have a cousin, and an aunt, that Patrick has decided that I need boundaries and discipline. I need to sort out my territory, make sure all my stuff is safe, make sure the bed is made properly.

But when I hear them in the hallway, Meg barking excitedly, the door banging behind them, I feel empty and sad and left out and even a bit jealous. I'm just not sure exactly why.

CHAPTER 8
Grumpy

Archie has a laptop. Archie has a Nintendo DS and about fifty games for it. Archie spends 100 per cent of his time playing cool-looking stuff and he never offers me a go. I carry on cleaning and ironing, but the attraction's wearing off fast. In fact, I can't really remember why I started doing it in the first place.

Unfortunately, I'm only halfway through a huge job. There's a room full of books on the first floor and I stupidly decided to take them all out one by one and wipe away the dust that clings to them. It's really bad to have so much dust in your house. I'm almost certain it can give you lung cancer.

So I'm wiping books and probably catching cancer and Archie's sitting in the middle of the room hunched over his DS, chasing monsters and making shooting noises like he's about six.

I put up with it for at least ten minutes and then I say, 'Go away, Archie, you're too noisy.'

Archie laughs and says, 'But I want to stay here. I've never seen a boy do cleaning before. Isn't it a job for girls? Pretty, blonde, Polish ones?'

'Shut up, you moron.'

'What sort of boy does cleaning?' he says, 'I'm trying to work it out. Are you special needs? Or gay?'

I'm holding a large hardback book – *A History of Medieval Canon Law* – and I watch it arc across the room and crash onto Archie's DS. Annoyingly, Archie dived sideways a split second before impact. I hope he got a lungful of deadly dust.

'Temper, temper,' says Archie, wagging his finger at me. 'Better watch out, because if you hurt me, Grandpa will make you apologise again.'

I grind my teeth and start on the next shelf.

Archie switches off his DS. 'I can't believe you're my cousin,' he says, 'You're such a chav.'

'No I'm not,' I say. I'm not even that insulted because it's clear to me that Archie has no idea of the dress and behaviour code associated with chavs. He thinks it's just a general term for anyone poorer than he is, which is about ninety per cent of the British population. There were a lot of boys like him at St Saviour's.

He crows with laughter, 'You so are. And my mum says your mum—' but he doesn't get a chance to finish because I'm across the room in a flash slamming *Great Military Failures of the Nineteenth Century* splat onto his head, like I'm swatting a fly.

'Ow!' he yelps, and then he clatters off down the stairs, shouting, 'Grandpa, Grandma . . . he's hurt me again.'

Oh well. Here we go again. Meg's barking her head off, Helen's clucking over him as she examines his head – I'm hoping I've fractured his skull – and Patrick emerges from his study, and says in a bored voice, 'What was it this time?'

Archie squawks, 'He slammed a book on my head . . . it really hurt. . .' Patrick just says, 'He certainly reminds me of his father. Think yourself lucky you've still got a nose.'

Then he yells for me and I come downstairs and I have to apologise to Archie again. I couldn't care less and I can see that Patrick knows it. 'Archie, I am so sorry to have hit you with a hardback book,' I say. 'I will use a paperback next time.'

To be completely honest, fighting with Archie is about the only thing keeping me sane. I'm going crazy, cooped up in the house. I feel hot and cold and headachy most of the time and my body is sore and stiff with lack of exercise. Meg sometimes starts whining when she wants Patrick to take her for a walk. She paces around and scratches the front door. That's how I feel.

Patrick yawns and says, 'Tyler, come and talk to me.' He stomps off into his study again. I think about ignoring him and going upstairs – I mean, what would he actually do? But it's not worth the hassle. Louise would kill me.

'Sit,' he says, and I obey. I might as well be wearing a collar and lead. At least I'd get to go out.

'Tyler,' he says, 'you're going to have to try and control yourself. Stop lashing out at Archie just because you're fed up of being in hiding.'

Why should I? 'He's really annoying me,' I say. 'He's got no respect. You should be talking to him.'

'I will. But you should know that if you respond with violence, you are always in the wrong. Always. Automatically. It doesn't matter who started it or what happened.'

I think back to the mud and blood of that park in London. The knife that Arron waved as he set out to mug the boy Rio. The knife that Rio pulled out of his back pocket. The two of them struggling in the mud. And the way I slashed my own knife at Arron when he wouldn't do what I wanted and run away from Rio's dead-meat body.

I can't bear to think about it. 'Leave me alone, old

74

man,' I mutter, in Portuguese.

He says, 'Eh? What?' as I meant him to, and then, 'Who taught you Portuguese?' which wasn't the idea at all.

'Umm . . . it wasn't Portuguese. . .' I say, but he says, 'I may be an old man, but I haven't lost all my marbles yet.'

'I'm sorry,' I say, 'I didn't know you'd understand.'

He says, 'Of course I understood. Languages are my hobby. Excellent accent. Clear as a bell.'

'I don't really know much. I just had a few lessons before we had to leave London.'

'They're teaching Portuguese at St Saviour's? The place has changed a lot since Danny was there.'

'Not at St Saviour's. I got a Saturday cleaning job at the tattoo parlour and Maria the receptionist was teaching me. What I said to you – Maria used to say it all the time to Leon, the tattoo artist.'

'Indeed?' he says. 'Intriguing. Cleaning at a tattoo parlour, eh? Did you get a discount?'

'No. Leon said I was too young.' I had one of a massive python all planned out for my eighteenth birthday and I bet I would've got a discount.

'And was the appeal mostly Portuguese or Maria?'

That's actually quite clever of him because no one ever knew I had a crush on Maria.

'Both . . . but mostly Portuguese. It's a really important language for what I want to do.'

'And what's that . . . no, let me guess . . . something to do with the Brazilian football team perhaps?'

He's actually really clever. 'No, but nearly. I want to learn lots of languages and be an interpreter for a Premiership team.'

'Really? Excellent. Excellent. So Portuguese with Maria was your starting point, eh?'

'No, I learnt Urdu in the shop downstairs and Turkish in the kebab shop and French at school.'

'French, eh?' he says leaning forward. 'How do you like French?' He's speaking in French now and he's got an amazing accent.

'Very much, but the teachers at school are not very good. I would like to learn by talking to someone French,' I reply, slowly and carefully, trying my best to say it properly in French, and he's beaming all over his gruff face and asks, 'Have you spent much time in France?'

'I've never even been abroad,' I say gloomily – I was always nagging mum to take me to Paris on Eurostar, but she never thought we had the money.

'You must go to France,' he says, like I can just go and buy myself a ticket any time I want. And then he switches back to English and adds, 'I'm sure you won't remember, but this is not the first time we've spoken in French.

When you lived with us I had just retired, so I was around a lot. You were only just talking, so I put a lot of effort into trying to make you bilingual.'

When I lived with them? What does he mean? I'm about to ask, but then I remember something I haven't thought of for a long time. When I was really little I used to like a story – I'm not sure if it was a book or a video – about a giant called Grumpy who could talk in a special language that only I could understand.

I asked my gran once to tell me the story and she said sorry, she didn't know that one. Grumpy the giant was what first made me think that I could go out and learn lots of languages, that just by talking to people you could open a whole new world of words and ideas.

Now I'm wondering if Grumpy the giant wasn't a story or a video after all. Maybe he was actually. . . '*Grandpère?*' I say uncertainly, and my big, tall grandad says, 'It's a long time since I heard you say that.'

I don't get a chance to ask any more, because Helen comes into the room.

'I've had enough of you and Archie bickering and fighting,' she says. 'You're not getting any education, and it's not good enough. Come and sit down at the kitchen table and we're going to start GCSE Maths.'

What? Could my life get any worse? I'm a constant prisoner, I have to share a room with my vile cousin,

I don't have a mobile or a computer or any friends and now she wants me to do *Maths*? Unbelievable. I come and sit down at the kitchen table, but I'm skulking under my hoodie, and my arms are crossed in a way that Mum and Gran – my *real* family – would recognise as signalling that I'm not happy at all.

She's bought some books which set out the GCSE syllabus, and she has exercise books and pens for us, which all looks a bit worryingly serious, and she starts explaining how to solve equations. My mind usually goes into a bit of a panic when teachers start talking about $a + b$ – I mean what is the *point?* – but she explains it brilliantly. It's crystal clear all the way. Archie's yawning and saying, 'But I know all this, Grandma,' but I'm with her every step. And I manage to solve the first problem she sets us before he does.

She's smiling at me. 'Do you like Maths?'

'Umm . . . no, not usually.'

'That's a shame. I generally manage to turn people around so they can tolerate it though.'

'What do you mean?' I'm incredibly shy around Helen. This is as much as we've managed to talk. When I'm with her I start feeling all anxious, and I can't speak properly, the words get all knotted up. She seems to feel the same, and although I can see she wants to get to know me, I can't imagine it happening somehow.

Archie's laughing, 'Didn't you know? She was a Maths teacher.'

'Oh, OK.' And she sets us both a page of equations to complete. It's something to do, I suppose, although swapping an actual life for Maths is a bit tragic.

I'm just finishing the last one – and hoping passionately that I've beaten Archie – when Patrick comes into the room. 'I've just had a call from Penelope in Chicago,' he says, 'Archie, you and I have to go and see a school, Allingham Priory, this afternoon. They have a place in Year Eight, apparently, and the head teacher, Father Roderick, wants to meet you.'

Archie looks really upset and I kind of smirk. We're obviously both thinking the same thing: Allingham Priory sounds like it's going to turn out to be a strict Catholic nightmare of a school.

He goes upstairs to get changed. I follow. This is my chance to wind him up, and I'm certainly going to take it.

He's buttoning a clean white shirt and I clamber up on to the bunk bed. 'So. Allingham Priory, eh?' I say. 'Sounds Catholic to me. Ever been to a Catholic school?'

He shakes his head gloomily. All his normal obnoxious bounce seems to have left him.

'The monks hit you every day,' I say. 'For the smallest thing. Beat you until blood pours down your legs.

And you'll be getting up at 6 am to pray . . . for hours. . .'

'I don't believe you,' says Archie. 'I'm sure that's against the law. My parents wouldn't send me to a school like that, anyway. My dad's not even a Catholic.' He doesn't sound very certain. I pounce.

'Won't make any difference to them. You'll probably have to pray even more to make up for that. They're after your soul . . . not to mention your body. . .'

Anyone normal would realise I was teasing. But Archie looks like he's going to burst into tears.

'Wh . . . what do you mean?'

'Well those monks, they're not allowed sex, are they? And then they see some pretty young boy like you and . . . let's just say you won't be getting much sleep. . . You'll have to be on the alert twenty-four hours a day. Some of those monks are really big and strong.'

Archie blinks. He sits down on the end of the bed and does up his shoes. He keeps his head down longer than he needs to, I notice. I'm chuckling to myself. This is an excellent wind-up.

And then he lifts his head and he says, 'Ty . . . what you're saying, it's not true, is it?' and I can see that he's really scared and the tears aren't just in his eyes.

So I say, 'Nah . . . it'll probably be fine. I'm just winding you up.'

'Oh. It's just . . . I don't really want to go to boarding

school again.' He sighs. 'I thought I'd fixed it by getting expelled from the last one.'

'Can't you tell your parents?'

'I did. But they're both away a lot. They said it wouldn't be fair to leave me at home with an au pair.'

'Oh. Can't you talk to them again?'

'They're away such a lot.'

'Talk to Patrick in the car.' Patrick seems to me to be the sort of person who it'd be good to have on your side in an argument.

'I'm not sure. Grandpa doesn't like me much.'

Well, who can blame him? I bite my tongue. 'Have a go. Or swear at the head teacher. Make sure they won't take you. Good luck.'

Left alone, I think about going back to the book-cleaning job. But maybe I should limit my exposure to the dust. Helen's calling me from downstairs. Reluctantly I go and find her in the kitchen.

'They've gone,' she says, 'and I thought it might be a chance for us to have a chat. Just about how things are going . . . we don't seem to have talked much. . . You did very well with the Maths, by the way. Well done. We'll do some more tomorrow.'

She's always nice to me. She really tries to see my side when I argue with Archie. It's just the way she looks at me sometimes – like she's looking at someone else. Someone she's really worried about. It gives me the creeps.

Meg rubs against my legs. I lean down and pat her. 'It's . . . ummmm . . . it's going OK,' I say cautiously.

She laughs. 'You were such a quiet baby. I thought you might have changed. In some ways it's good to see you fighting with Archie. We worried that you'd always be a shy, nervous little scrap.'

Huh. She's talking nonsense again. It's obvious to me that she and Patrick have got really confused and they must have had Archie to stay a lot and are getting him muddled up with me. Not that I can imagine him ever being particularly shy.

It's because they're old, I suppose, and maybe they feel a bit guilty that they never had anything to do with me, so they've kind of told themselves stories which they now believe are true. I can relate to that. Maybe it runs in the family.

I was not quiet at all when I was little. When I was a toddler, I had legendary tantrums. Great long noisy storms, where I would shout and cry and thrash around and only my gran could calm me down. My auntie Emma teases me about the time I screamed for an hour solid because there weren't any red Smarties in the packet, or the day I bit the greengrocer when he offered me an apple. Anything could set me off.

I was sacked by three child minders and my gran had to give up her job so she could look after me more or less full-time.

Once I started big school, I think I did it once, and then Arron told me that I was being a baby and I stopped. End of. No more tantrums. *That's* when I turned into a quiet person. I can't actually remember these furies myself – although I've heard the gory details a lot – but I do have a dim memory of Gran holding me and rocking me and telling me that everything was going to be all right.

I wish she was here now. Helen is cooking onions in a big iron pot – just like Gran used to – and she's chopped up carrots and turnips into another bowl, also just like Gran. In fact, I'd say she was making exactly the same stew that was my favourite thing that Gran ever cooked. My mouth ought to be watering. But instead, tears are pricking my eyes. It must be the onions.

'Can you pass me that bowl, darling?'

I nudge the carrots in her direction.

'Do you remember when we used to cook together?' she asks. 'The doctor told us it was a good idea to get you involved as much as possible. Patrick told Julie when she took you – I hope she carried on – anyway it obviously worked out because you've grown up so tall and strong.'

What *is* she talking about? What doctor? I never go and see doctors. She's really confused. She's the one who needs to see a doctor. I wonder if I should suggest it tactfully – but it's hard to tell a kind old lady that she's probably losing her marbles.

I sniff the onions and then I get a weird glimmer of memory. Balancing on a high stool and smelling food cooking and putting my hand into a bowl of red sticky cubes and throwing them one by one into the pot. And I like the squidgy feeling of the meat and the sizzle of the pan, but I'm hungry and worried at the same time. So much worry that there's not much room for anything else.

I must be remembering cooking with my gran. But why did I feel so scared? It's all a bit much.

'I'm just going to the loo,' I say, and I stumble from the room. In the hallway I sit down on the floor and bring my knees up to my chest. I have no idea what the matter is. This place – locked up, a prisoner, cell-sharing with Archie – is doing my head in. It's so hot and stuffy. I need fresh air. I need exercise. Five minutes fresh air won't hurt, surely. And I go to the front door and push it open as quietly as possible.

I'm outside. For the first time for more than a week. And once I'm outside I know exactly what I need to do to chase away the scary feelings. I need a run. Surely

I could have just a short run?

At the end of their driveway is the road, and there's no pavement or anything – it's not really built for people who aren't in a car. One way goes uphill, one way down. I start running down the hill. If I meet a car on the way I'll probably get run over, but that doesn't really bother me right now.

It feels so good to be running again, even though I'm not really dressed for it. I've got my running shoes on, but I wouldn't normally run in jeans. After about fifteen minutes I begin feeling a bit hot and uncomfortable, and I'm still feeling achy. Never mind. I run on.

A dark grey cloud covers the sky, and it seems to get lower and lower until it's almost pressing on my head. Thunder growls like a pit bull, and then a raindrop spits onto my head. I pull up my hood, but it's hopeless, the rain starts and it's like running in a car wash. There's water flooding down my face, my shoes are filling up, I'm wet through to my boxers. I don't care. I keep running.

There's a path leading off the road through some fields. It'll be safer, I think, and run on past cows and tractors, squelching through mud and cow shit and all kinds of horrendous smells. I must have been bitten by some sort of insect, because my face feels incredibly itchy. My jeans are heavy with water, clinging to my legs.

And the rain is still pouring down. But it's great to be running. I just don't know where I'm running to.

My jeans are so heavy that I lose the rhythm of the run, stumble over a ridge of mud and fall, splat! into a huge puddle. I'm so wet that it doesn't make much difference – except that now I'm filthy too and I stink of God knows what. Some people come to the countryside on purpose, I don't know why.

I pull myself up and I carry on running. I'm out of the field now and into some woodland. It's getting dark already, and the path is petering out. I don't care. I run through brambles, pushing past branches, getting scratched by holly and all the time getting wetter and wetter as the rain pours down.

And then I hit a big hard lump of wood, my ankle turns under me and I come crashing down into green plants that prick and tear at my skin. I roll away and the pain in my ankle jabs like a knife.

'Aaah,' I groan with pain as I try to stand up, but my ankle can't take my weight and I collapse into the mud again.

I'm lying in a stinking muddy puddle, it's almost dark and I'm surrounded by trees. I'm in the middle of nowhere. My skin is on fire – I'm clawing at it, trying to stop the itch, but it just makes it worse – and my ankle is probably broken. I'm not sure how anyone's ever going to find me. I'm probably never going to be able to run again. I might even die here in this wood.

I'm dizzy with exhaustion and someone's got inside my head and is hammering their way out. The cold and wet and pain keep me awake – which is good , I realise, hazily, because it wouldn't be a great idea to go to sleep. Not when it's so cold and getting dark.

I'm just thinking of having a try at crawling when I look up and my heart gives a big thump.

Two silent figures are standing over me. And one of them has a knife.

CHAPTER 9
Rio

You wouldn't think that anyone could be pleased to see a ghost, but when I realise that one of the people standing there is Alistair, I let out a little sigh of relief. The other guy is shorter, his face hidden under the shadow of his hood. All I can see is the blade of his knife, shining against his dark clothes. Who is it? Is he real or a ghost? And then blood drips into the mud beside me and it all comes rushing back.

Rio. The boy who was stabbed in the park. The boy my friend Arron was trying to mug all those months ago, who pulled out his own knife rather than hand over his iPod and ended up dead as a dinosaur.

Rio, whose poor sad parents wept on TV pleading for witnesses. Especially the boy who called the ambulance. That boy was me.

It's because of Rio that I had to go into witness protection. I'm telling the truth about his death. It's just the next bit that I'm lying about. The bit where I stabbed Arron.

'You must be Ty,' he says, 'I've heard about you.'

My mouth moves, but no words come out. And then I remember the photos the police showed me of Rio's body after it'd been sliced by Arron's knife. I vomit, hot and sour, into the mud.

'Try and control yourself,' says Alistair, quietly cold. I'm gulping, trying to stop another wave of nausea.

Rio bends and puts his knife to my throat. I can feel the edge scraping my skin and I kind of whimper, 'No . . . please . . . I tried to help you . . . please, Rio, don't. . .'

He laughs. 'Go on . . . beg. . .' and then says to Alistair, 'He's wet himself, the little baby. . .'

He's right, and my stomach clenches with utter shame, but I'm so wet all over anyway that I can't see how he knew. The blade stays under my chin. Rio moves it over my skin, a prickling tickle, a tiny scratch, and says, 'How long you gonna lie about me? Make out I was the one shanked your frien' Arron?'

'I . . . errr. . .'

'Cos I never. An' my folks don't need your lies. You hurt dat boy.'

'I . . . I never said it was all you. Arron said that. I said . . . you were fighting . . . that was how he got injured.'

'And that was a lie,' says Alistair, and I sob and gulp and say, 'Yes . . . I'm sorry. . .' even though it wasn't totally a lie. Rio did hurt Arron. It's just that I did too.

'You gonna take back that lie or you gonna take my punishment?' says Rio. I have no idea what to say. Am I going to die at the hands of a ghost? Is that even possible? Or can I go on lying to save myself, to save Arron, to make sure the real bad guys go to prison?

And then something flies out of the darkness right at my chest. Something warm and loud and soft and furry, something that knocks me flat on my back and nuzzles up beside me and licks my face with its rough, wet tongue.

'Meg!' I gasp, hugging her tight, then she barks and jumps and runs away and then straight back to me again, and her face is as smiley as a dog's can be and I can't believe I was ever scared of her.

But Rio and Alistair are still there, and Alistair says, 'Get the dog,' and as Meg jumps around, tail wagging, I see a flash of silver. 'Meg . . . no. . .' I scream, and I'm holding onto her, frantically searching for the bleeding wound.

Patrick looms out of the darkness. Behind him comes Archie, clutching a torch. 'Ty . . . thank God!' says Patrick.

And then more harshly, 'What the hell did you think you were doing, running off like that? Scaring us to death? We were lucky to find you. Leave Meg alone and get up now.'

I'm desperately looking behind him, behind me, looking to see if Rio and Alistair are still there. I can't see them, but the darkness is full of rustling movement. And Meg is whining – is she in pain?

'She's hurt . . . Meg is hurt. . .' I say, and then I think I see Rio crouching in the shadows and I try and shield Meg's squirming body from the blow that's going to finish her off.

'She's fine,' says Patrick. 'Come on, get up.' And he grabs my arm and tries to pull me up, but I collapse back into the mud.

'He's gone bonkers,' hisses Archie, in what's meant to be a whisper. 'Maybe he's been taking drugs.'

'Maybe,' says Patrick, grimly, and I sense that when we get home I'm going to get the hairdryer worse than if I was Berbatov and I'd just missed five open goals against Chelsea. Which could happen, let's face it.

'Get up, for Christ's sake, boy.'

'I can't . . . my ankle. . .' I say. 'I think it's broken.'

Patrick and Archie haul me upright and I try and hold onto both of them, but it's harder than it should be because Patrick's too tall. I'm looking around all the time for Alistair and Rio, although Patrick keeps telling me to concentrate on walking and stop twisting and turning.

'What the hell's the matter?' he barks impatiently.

'They . . . they were trying to hurt Meg. . .' I say, 'They had a knife. . .'

'Who?'

'They . . . they were there, they'll come back, they were there. . .' I hardly know what I'm saying now.

'Ty,' roars Patrick. 'Calm down. Concentrate. No one's going to get hurt. I want to get to the car before it gets completely dark.' There's a silence, and all I can hear is my own gasping breath. And then he adds, 'Everything's all right, you know. You're completely safe.'

That's the point when my ankle gives out completely and my legs shoot out in front of me, and I slide back down to the ground. Archie almost falls down with me.

'Christ,' says Patrick again. 'I don't think we can carry him. Come on boy, you were doing OK there. What's the problem?'

'It's my ankle . . . I think it's broken.'

'You're going to have to try. Come on now. Up again.' And they manage it so I've got my arms round their shoulders and they haul me along. Patrick's bent almost double, which can't be great for a really old guy.

It seems to take years to get back to the car. It's parked at the edge of the wood and Patrick says,

'Thank God for that,' as he opens the door and they carefully sit me down on the back seat. But I yell and throw myself backwards on to the stony ground. Meg barks and jumps up and down, and Patrick shouts, 'Bloody hell . . . what's going on now?'

I can't get in the car. Alistair and Rio are sitting there waiting for me.

I point. I grab hold of Meg so they can't hurt her. And Archie crouches down next to me and says, 'What is it? What is it, Ty? What's going on? Why won't you get in the car?'

'Can't you see them?' I ask.

'There's no one there. Come on Ty . . . it's freezing. . .'

'Get in this car and you're dead,' says Alistair.

'I can't . . . I can't . . . he'll kill me. . .' I whisper.

Patrick's crouched down too. 'Ty, you're going to listen to me and only to me, understand? There is no one in the car. You need to let us get you into the car. You are hallucinating. That means that the things you are seeing and hearing are not real. Trust me. Now, let us get you up.'

'He means you're going bonkers,' adds Archie helpfully, 'but you'll probably be OK when the drugs wear off. I'll sit in the back if you want and you can sit in the front.'

So they pull me into the front of the car and Archie

and Meg climb into the back and when I dare to glimpse behind me, they are all that I see. No Alistair, no Rio. It's just us.

We drive in silence all the way back to the house, which only takes about ten minutes. When we get there Patrick says, 'Archie, you take Meg inside and tell Helen that all is well. I just want to have a few words with Ty, we'll be there in a minute.'

Once we're alone I look away from him, hoping that Alistair and Rio won't make a sudden reappearance now that the back seat is empty. I'm not sure that Patrick is up to fighting them off. He looked pretty tired once we got back to the car. He looks even more tired now.

'Tyler,' he says, 'Tell me what you've been taking. What drugs . . . maybe you've been drinking?'

'I never . . . I never took anything.' My voice sounds like I'm back at primary school.

'Do you really expect me to believe that? You were hallucinating . . . completely out of control. . .' He sighs. 'If you tell me, I can get help for you. Don't be scared to tell the truth.'

'I didn't, I really didn't. There were ghosts, really ghosts. I've seen one of them before.' My ankle is throbbing and my head is killing me. I wish he'd get on with it.

'You see and hear things regularly? Have you ever

talked to anyone about this?'

He thinks I'm mad. He thinks I'm like Gran's friend's neighbour who heard voices in his head telling him to throw his telly out of the window, which was a particularly bad idea because he lived above the dry-cleaner's.

'Not regularly. Just since I was here. I don't do drugs. Honest.'

'I wish I could believe you,' he says, and he doesn't sound angry, just sad. And I feel sad too, because it really matters that Patrick believes me.

'You can. . . It's true, really it's true.'

'Well,' he says, 'Let's see what they say at the hospital.' And he slams his door shut and comes around the car to get me out.

'Lean on me . . . yes, that's it,' he says as he pulls me out. It's harder to walk with only one person supporting me, and I have to put both arms around him. We stagger along, but we have to stop for a rest before we get to the front door, which just shows how massive their driveway is.

We stand there in the dark, and I say, 'Thank you for finding me,' and he says, 'Meg did the hard work. We gave her one of your T-shirts and she tracked you down. It helped that Mrs Baverstock who lives down the road called to warn members of Neighbourhood Watch that she'd seen a feral youth running past.'

'I'm not feral. . .' I say, and his arms hold me tight and he says, 'I know. It's OK. I'm just grateful that we found you.'

It's an amazing thing being hugged by my grandad like that. I can't remember ever being hugged by a man before. It's like I've been saved by Superman or Spiderman or Batman. Grumpy the giant has saved me.

The front door opens and Archie runs out, and grabs my other arm. He says, 'Come on . . . come as fast as you can. . . You've got to explain to him that I'm not you.'

'You what?' I ask, and Patrick says, 'Damn and blast. Typical.'

And then we reach the front door and I realise what they are talking about. This scruffy guy hovering behind Helen, with holey jeans and long messy hair, can only be one person. He's tall like Patrick, he's got a pointy chin like me.

My dad has turned up at last.

CHAPTER 10
Exposure

No one ever told me much about my dad. That didn't stop me thinking what he might be like.

I knew he studied law at university, and I knew he supported Manchester United so I thought maybe he was the sort of lawyer that works in football, arranging contracts and transfers and stuff like that. That was how I got the idea of being an interpreter working for a Premiership team. I thought we might be in the same world.

When people asked me about my dad I'd say, 'He's a sports lawyer.' Sometimes I threw in a bit more detail, like: 'He's very busy at the moment, working on the January transfers.'

It sounded better than, 'I've never met my dad and I have no idea what he's doing.' No one had to know it wasn't necessarily true.

Sometimes I got a bit carried away and I'd imagine meeting him in the future. Perhaps I'd get taken along to some high-powered meeting so I could translate everything for the latest Brazilian signing and then the lawyer would come into the room and I'd realise it was my dad.

And he'd realise too, but we wouldn't say anything right away, and we'd have the meeting and he'd be really impressed with how I was simultaneously interpreting from Portuguese into English. Even really technical legal and footballing language. And we'd both look really smart in suits and ties, and after the meeting we'd shake hands and say hello and maybe we'd get to know each other a bit.

Instead I am soaking wet, covered with mud, stinking of vomit and fertiliser, unable to walk and feeling incredibly ill. At least I have an excuse. He looks like some sort of tramp, and I can't think of any reason for that at all, except that he pretty obviously isn't a top lawyer.

It's like someone's died, someone I was pretty fond of. How stupid is that, believing my own lies? I just wish I was looking better, that's all. And that he was.

'What on earth has happened to him?' he says, and he sounds a bit upset too. He probably wasn't imagining a son dipped in cow shit.

Patrick says, 'Hello Danny,' and manoeuvres me straight past him into the kitchen where Helen sits me down in a chair and starts bathing my face with a flannel. My dad – Danny? Dad? – follows us, and flops down at the kitchen table next to me. His hair and clothes don't look any better close up. Patrick says, 'I'll let you get on with it,' and goes out of the room.

Helen props my leg up on a chair and wedges a giant packet of frozen peas around the ankle, which just adds another layer of pain to the massive load that's already there. 'He's running a temperature,' she says, feeling my forehead. 'Archie, run upstairs to the bathroom and find the thermometer.'

My dad is trying to catch my eye, but he's not succeeding because I'm looking everywhere else I possibly can. 'Tyler, I'm your dad, I'm Danny,' he says. His voice is soft and it's hard to know what he's thinking. 'Aren't you even going to say hello to me?'

Helen is pulling my wet shirt off over my head so he has to wait for me to come out. I'd rather not be talking to him while I'm half naked . . . it's a bit embarrassing. He might count my chest hairs. 'Oh. Umm. Hello.' I say, keeping my eyes on the table.

It's not that I never want to meet him, just not right now. Not like this. Not with Archie and Helen watching.

Helen wraps me in a big fluffy towel, sticks the

thermometer in my mouth and sends Archie upstairs to get new clothes for me – 'Something easy to put on, a tracksuit maybe. Underwear too.'

She's investigating my ankle, and I'm trying not to scream out loud. 'It's very swollen,' she says. 'I think we're going to have to cut your trousers off.'

I can't say anything, because I have the stupid thermometer in my mouth, but I make a noise of protest because these are my best jeans, the ones that Mum and I bought with police money.

'What's the matter, darling?' asks Helen, removing the thermometer and giving me a sip of lemon squash.

'It's just . . . my jeans . . . these are really good ones. Abercrombie and Fitch.'

'We can always buy you some new ones,' she says soothingly. 'Don't worry about it.'

My dad makes a loud snorting noise and says, 'I'm going to talk to Pa. Find out what's been going on.' He hardly looks at me as he walks out. I don't know what his problem is but I feel like I've screwed up before we even know each other. Maybe he's a kind of hippy who hates designer clothes. He thinks I'm a brand-obsessed airhead. Do I care?

Helen says, 'Your temperature's high. You must be feeling dreadful. I'll get you some paracetemol.'

She's being so gentle and kind. I shouldn't have run

away from her. She gives me the tablets and some more to drink, and I grab her hand and say, 'I'm sorry I got lost, I didn't mean to, I just needed to get outside all of a sudden . . . I felt a bit strange.'

She puts her arm around my shoulder. 'Ty, all that matters is that you are safe and sound. You don't know how special you are to me . . . to us . . . and how much it means that you're here. I know we're strangers to you. But you're not a stranger to us.'

Then Archie comes in with my trackies and a black hoodie – one of the new ones from Gap – and she picks up her scissors. 'Right. Let's see how we can get you into dry clothes.' And then she pauses. 'Are you all right with me helping you? Or would you prefer one of the men . . . or even Archie?'

I shake my head. Absolutely not. Is she forgetting that I've been completely brought up by women? – and she tells Archie to go away, and gets on with destroying my best jeans. Eventually she decides to cut through my boxers as well, then slings a towel over me and unpeels the sopping clothes. I don't care that she has to help me get the dry stuff on. I'm so out of it that you could strip me naked and post it on YouTube and I wouldn't be that bothered.

She takes my temperature again, then shakes her head and says, 'It's come down a little, but it's still high.

I think we need to take you to hospital, get that ankle looked at and find out why you're running a fever. Let me talk to Patrick . . . and Danny. . .'

'No . . . I can't. . .' I say, and she looks at me, puzzled. I try and explain, but the words are getting all tangled up. 'I can't talk to him, to Danny. I'm not ready for him . . . I can't cope right now, with him, with any of this. . .'

I'm rambling, I know, but she gets the message because she says, 'Don't worry, darling. I'll tell Danny you're not in a fit state to cope with a big reunion.'

She leaves me alone in the kitchen and I spy her mobile sitting next to me on the table and I think about calling Claire. Just for a quick chat. Just to tell her what's going on. But then I remember the fuss that my last call caused and I decide against it. It's hard though. It's actually physically hard to let go of the phone once I've got my hand on it.

So when Patrick comes into the kitchen he jumps to the wrong conclusion.

'Christ, boy, can't you be trusted for two minutes? What have you done with that phone?'

'Nothing . . . I . . . nothing. . .'

'Don't you understand how important it is that no one knows where you are? Are you stupid?'

I'm shaking. I thought he was beginning to like me.

I thought I could rely on him. Why is he angry with me?

'I didn't . . . I never. . .'

He grabs the phone, looks at the call list. 'I seem to have caught you just in time. Don't do it again.'

'No . . . but. . .' It's all too much to explain and I shut up. He's looking all cross and not all that well himself.

'Right. Now. Helen and Danny are going to take you to the hospital. But you have to remember not to use your own name. I think we'd better use Archie's.'

'Can't you come? Not him?'

He sighs. 'To be honest that was all a bit much for me. I'm not as young as I was. Helen thinks I need a rest. And Danny insists it should be him.'

'But you know . . . about the ghosts . . . you can tell better. . .'

'I'm sorry.' His face is grim and he doesn't look sorry at all. 'Just be honest with them at the hospital. That's all I ask you.'

Then my dad comes in and they haul me up and we stagger to the front door. Once there, they hesitate – I've got no shoes, and it's pretty obvious that my trainers aren't going to go on easily. Helen shoves some slippers on my feet and somehow they manage to get me into the car. I look carefully for Alistair and Rio but they're not there. So I sprawl over the back seat while they sit in the front.

Helen drives, and my dad's looking over his shoulder at me.

'So, Ty, what was it?' he asks, really casually. 'Skunk? Or maybe shrooms?'

'Danny, just leave him be,' says Helen. I try and ignore him.

'Pa says you were hallucinating.'

'He's running a very high temperature, Danny,' says Helen. Her voice is a bit shaky and I wonder if she's scared of her own son. Her son who beats up women. Possibly. 'It might not be drugs. He's probably delirious. He might even have . . . meningitis.'

'Oh,' says my dad. He sounds – I don't know – disappointed maybe. Maybe he thinks we can do some father and son bonding over a spliff or two. He certainly looks the part. He's just a grungy old stoner. Huh. No wonder my mum thought he was a waste of space. I hope I have got meningitis, whatever that is. That'll teach him not to make assumptions about me.

We get to the hospital and they agree that Danny will help me into A & E while Helen parks the car. We're alone together for the first time. I'm so tense that when he puts his arm around me to help me walk I'm pulling in the opposite direction. As soon as possible he finds a chair and spills me into it. We avoid looking at each other.

'I'll go and get you on the list,' he says. He stands

up and I realise that he can't give my real name to the hospital.

'Joe Andrews,' I say. Luckily there's no one sitting near us.

'What?'

'That's the name to give them.'

'Why? Nicki hasn't . . . she didn't change your name, did she?'

He doesn't seem to know what's been going on in my life. He doesn't seem to understand that I'm living with a gun to my head all day, every day.

'Whatever. Just tell them Joe Andrews. And my birthday's September 5th and I've just turned fourteen.'

He's looking at me, completely puzzled.

'What are you talking about? I know when you were born. Jesus, I'm not likely to forget that day.'

He doesn't sound like it was an especially happy memory. I wave my hand at him. 'Just do it. Joe Andrews. My leg is killing me.'

He frowns and mutters something about using Archie, but he goes off anyway. I have no idea what he was on about. Idiot.

By the time he's come back – he takes ages – Helen has found me. I'm leaning against her whilst she strokes my head like I'm a puppy or a baby and it is quite comforting actually, and it really seems to annoy my dad who starts pacing around the waiting room.

It takes about half an hour before we get taken into a cubicle to be seen by a nurse. Helen tells her the whole story, including the hallucinating bit, and I have to pee into a cup – not the easiest thing to do with a busted ankle. The nurse takes my temperature again, tutting a bit when she looks at the thermometer. Then she says she's going to arrange an X-ray and find a doctor.

Helen goes to find a coffee machine. My dad slumps down in a chair next to my bed. 'Look . . . Ty. . .' he says, 'This isn't exactly easy for me, you know.'

Like I care.

'Please don't think that I didn't want to be involved in your life,' he says. 'Nicki froze me out completely, wouldn't let me near you. I don't know what stories she's told you about me, but I always wanted to be a real dad to you.'

Fuck off is what I want to say. *Fuck off. Leave me alone. Go away. Not interested. Shut up. I don't need you and I never have and I never will and I don't want to hear it. You're too late. You weren't there for me and I'm not interested in knowing why.*

'Oh, yeah, right,' is what I actually say. My head's hurting too much to start getting angry.

He's crying. He's actually crying. For Christ's sake. I might be lying here dying of meningitis or whatever and all he can do is cry. What sort of a wimp have I got for a father?

'I have thought about you every day . . . every day. . .' he says, wiping his eyes on the back of his hand.

Where's Helen? She's meant to be protecting me from this kind of crap. I turn my head away, blinking in the bright hospital lights and then I see Alistair. Sitting at the end of the bed. Laughing at us.

'Well,' he says, 'Found your daddy, have you? Touching.'

'Go away. . .' I say, faintly.

'You should make the most of it,' he sneers, 'Enjoy it. My kid's not going to have a dad, is he? My parents don't get to see me. Rio's dad's never going to see him again, is he?'

'Go away . . . leave me alone . . . go away. . .'

My dad stands up. 'What's going on, Ty?' he asks. But I'm only thinking about Alistair. I don't know what's real and what's not.

'What's your daddy going to think when he finds out what you've done?' he sneers. 'When he finds out that you stabbed your friend?'

I gather all my strength and lunge at him, screaming as loud as I can, 'Go away . . . leave me alone, I don't want to hear it any more . . . leave me alone. . . Shut up. Shut up about me stabbing Arron. . .'

I'm spitting and swearing, using the kind of words they don't even use on TV.

I grab his neck as I lunge forward. I'm throttling the wavering phantom, squeezing tight, trying to choke the sound of laughter out of him – but my hands hit cold air and my legs can't keep me on the bed and I'm falling, falling, crashing on to the ground, slamming my head on the hospital trolley.

And then the lights go out.

CHAPTER 11
Disorder

'Apparently,' says Archie, handing me a box of chocolates, 'you thought you could fly. And you were trying to fly across the room, shouting and screaming, and when Grandma came in the room you yelled out—'

'I know what I yelled out,' I say, stuffing a strawberry cream into my mouth. I'm not so sure about this flying business, but I'm happy to go along with whatever they think.

'I don't think she'd ever heard that word before,' says Archie. 'It's the one I tried on the headmaster at Allingham Priory. But I'm not sure it worked.'

We're sitting together on the iron bed in the attic, Meg curled at our feet, and we're watching a DVD on the TV which has appeared in our bedroom.

I've been home from the hospital for three days and my ankle is feeling much better. It was sprained, not broken and the high temperature was flu, not meningitis and when I crashed off the end of the hospital bed I just got a big lump on my head and mild concussion.

They reckoned the hallucinations, the ghosts, were caused by the high temperature. 'It's not unheard of,' said the doctor, 'especially when someone's been under a lot of stress.' Since I've been feeling a bit better, they seem to have disappeared.

Now I've just got a hacking cough and an aching ankle. There's no real reason for me to be lying in bed eating chocolates really, except I'm keeping a low profile and avoiding my dad. It's pretty easy. Whenever he comes into the room I either pretend to be asleep, or so intent on whatever film I'm watching that I can't really hear whatever he says to me.

Today he's tried once to talk to me, but I just kept my eyes on Cameron Diaz – she's pretty gorgeous, shame she's so old – and kind of flicked my hand dismissively and he stopped in mid-sentence and went back downstairs. Obviously he's not all that bothered or he wouldn't let me get away with it.

If it was anything really important I think he'd try a bit harder.

Once I'd got rid of him, he had a long conversation with Helen and Patrick about my chat with the hospital's duty psychiatrist. None of them realised that Archie was hanging over the banisters, listening to every word.

'They're all pretending to get on and be very concerned about you,' he says, 'but you can tell that Grandpa and your dad hate each other's guts, and Grandma doesn't know what to do about that.'

'Yes, but why? Don't you know? Didn't your mum ever tell you anything?'

'I've never met him before,' he says, 'All I know about him is that he fell out with his parents ages ago and he hates children. So he meets up with my mum and her sisters sometimes, but he never has anything to do with me or my cousins.'

He's tapping four words into his laptop.

'Post . . . traumatic . . . stress . . . disorder. There you go. That's what they think you have. It's a reaction to having a bad experience, like being in a war or something. It says here that it used to be called shell shock in the First World War.'

'Oh yeah?'

'Were you in a war?' he asks hopefully.

'Yeah, Archie, I've just got back from Afghanistan.'

'*Really*?'

'No, you muppet, obviously not.'

I stop gazing at Harry Potter taking on a guy with a melting face. Patrick chose the DVDs and some of them are a bit random, but loads are in French, which is really cool. Lots of the others are a bit young for us, but Archie and I decided we didn't mind watching some of the Harry Potters again because it's a waste to watch new films when you're ill and can't concentrate properly, and they're quite good actually.

I've vetoed all thrillers. I don't feel great about watching people get shot. I can't watch anything that's almost nearly true to life. I'm sure Archie thinks I'm a big girly wuss.

I squint at the computer. There's about a million entries on Google.

'OK,' says Archie, 'Brace yourself. Here are the symptoms. Flashbacks. Nightmares. Frightening thoughts and memories. Shaking. Sweating. Not talking about the event. Numbness. Feeling distant from other people. Loss of memory. Fear of dying. Lack of interest in life. Problems with sleeping. Outbursts of anger – yes, I'd say you've got that one covered. Hyper-alertness to possible danger. And something called "fight or flight response".'

Most of it sounds familiar. 'What's fight or flight response?' I ask. Maybe it means that I'll start hitting people if I get on an aeroplane.

'Hang on, I haven't finished yet. Long-term

behavioural problems. Alcohol abuse. Drug dependency.'
He looks at me meaningfully. Archie still thinks I sneaked
out to smoke some weed, and refuses to believe that the
hospital tests proved I was totally drug-free.

'Is that it?' It sounds like some doctor has made
a random list of bad stuff and lumped it all together to
frighten me.

'Failed relationships, divorce, severe depression,
anxiety disorders or phobias, headaches, stomach
upsets, dizziness, chest pains and general aches and
pains. A weakened immune system, and employment
problems.'

'Oh. Well, I haven't had any employment problems.'

'You're not exactly employed are you?' he says.
He's typing some more into the search engine. I think
uneasily about how Joe Andrews was suspended from
school not once, but twice.

'Fight or flight response. Oh, this is quite interesting.
It's the way our body is programmed to respond to things
like sabretooth tigers.'

'You what?'

'It's about getting ready to fight or run away.
Your body makes loads of chemicals and stuff. But if
you don't get to fight or run away then you become
aggressive, hypervigilant and overreactive.' He flicks
through a few pages. 'This article here says, "Fear is

exaggerated and thinking is distorted. Everything is viewed through the filter of possible danger." You bottle up stress and it buggers your hormones. It can cause—' he starts sniggering 'erectile dysfunction, constipation and difficulty urinating.'

I give him a light slap on the head, 'Yeah, well, luckily I do a lot of fighting and running away.'

'Seems to me the whole thing is basically that scary events make you go bonkers,' says Archie cheerfully.

'Yeah, that's about right,' I say.

We've been getting on OK in the last few days. He's incredibly impressed because he thinks I'm a raving druggie nutcase and he voluntarily swapped beds just in case I try to throw myself off the top bunk. Obviously having a TV, a stack of DVDs, lucozade, two boxes of chocolates and a fruit bowl has also helped our relationship.

Last night, Patrick watched one of the French films with us – a comedy – and then he and I discussed it almost totally in French, which was not only really cool but also massively outclassed Archie, who has been going to France on holiday twice a year all his life but isn't nearly as fluent as I am. Patrick ruffled my hair and said he was proud of me. 'My mother was French,' he said – which explains how he speaks it so well. 'She'd have been delighted to hear how you speak

her language.' I'm beginning to think he do͜ ͟
after all. It's a bit confusing.

Meanwhile, my dad was downstairs talking to ͟
Archie heard them when he went down to make us ͟ot
chocolate. He didn't pick up much though, he told me
later, just my dad saying, 'Look Ma, believe me, that's all
behind me now.'

I help myself to an After Eight and think about
whether I'd rather be me or Harry Potter. Harry Potter,
I think, because you kind of know it'll all work out OK
in the end and at least he gets to go to school and do
fun stuff like quidditch. Also I'd like to be able to talk
snake language.

Harry Potter gets a lot of praise from people
like Dumbledore, while I mostly get told off all the
time. But that's probably because he's effortlessly brave
and makes good decisions, whereas I'm scared all the
time and I try and do the right thing but I always seem
to screw it up.

'Do you want to know the cure?' asks Archie,
scrolling through a few more pages of the millions of
websites about post-traumatic stress disorder.

'There's a cure?'

'If you're a grown-up they might give you happy
pills. But not for under-eighteens. So it says physical
exercise helps, and talking things through with a

counsellor. But you haven't got a counsellor. So you'll have to make do with me.'

Claire, I think, mournfully. *Claire, Claire. Where are you Claire? Why can't I talk to you?*

'Can I borrow your laptop?' I ask.

'Yes, if you tell me what's been going on. It's not fair. They all know and obviously you know and no one will tell me. If it's not war then what is it?'

I might as well tell him. 'I saw someone get killed, and since then people have been trying to kill me and they've almost shot me twice and the last time my mum's boyfriend got killed. Shot in the head. Blood everywhere.'

Archie's mouth is wide open as he tries to work out if I'm winding him up or not. I take the opportunity to seize the laptop. He clings on.

'You can't just tell me that. You've got to tell the whole story. Or it won't help you . . . you won't be cured. . .'

I start laughing because it's so ludicrous to think that talking to Archie is going to be in the slightest bit helpful. 'OK. I'll tell you more. But first I want to check my emails and then I might want to borrow your mobile, OK?'

'OK.'

'And no telling them downstairs, OK?'

'OK.'

'Right.' I log onto my email account. Three messages.

Three messages from Claire. Three messages telling me she loves me? Or three saying I've let her down, she's found me out, she's dumping me?

I click on the first one. Then I realise that Archie's gawping over my shoulder.

'Go away . . . this is private. . .'

'Have you got a girlfriend?' he asks. His eyes are wide. I know immediately that Archie hasn't got off the starting blocks with girls.

I shrug. 'Yeah. She's called Claire.'

'Cool . . . what's she like? Is she fit? Have you . . . you know. . .'

'She is completely stunning, blonde hair, blue eyes, great figure, really gorgeous . . . could be a model.' I'm exaggerating wildly, but Archie is never going to meet Claire and she *has* got shining blue eyes and if I was allowed to take her shopping and give her a makeover the rest might be true too. I think about the last time I saw her – all pale and sweet, looking about ten years old, wrapped in her dressing gown, silky mouse-coloured hair falling over her delicate face. I sigh. I miss her so much.

'And have you . . . you know. . .?'

'Well, of course, in the past, you know. . .' I pause, making sure he gets the impression that I've shagged hundreds of girls. 'Too many to mention, really. But this one is different. We're taking things slowly. Savouring every step of the way.' I lick my lips in quite a crude way. He looks suitably awed.

'How about you, Archie?' I ask. 'Any ladies in your life?'

'If I can just interrupt this fascinating discussion,' says a voice from the doorway. Damn. It's Patrick. How much did he hear? 'Ty, can you make it down the stairs? There's someone here to see you.'

'Eh?'

'Louise—' he says, but I don't wait to hear more. I move as fast as I can on my sore ankle, clattering down the stairs with Archie close behind me. Meg bounces behind us, barking happily, and I burst into the living room. And then stop.

Louise is sitting with my dad on the sofa, both of them looking uncomfortable and cross.

But I'm not looking at them. Standing by the piano, studying the silver-framed photographs, fogged by a cloud of cigarette smoke, is someone else. Someone who glances up as I come through the door and shoots me a look packed with rage and hate.

'Hello darling,' says my mum.

CHAPTER 12
War Film

'Don't I get a hug?' she asks, but I know she's just saying it because we have an audience. I have no choice but to go over and give her an awkward cuddle. She's still holding her glowing ciggie and ash goes flying all over Helen's cream rug. I'm trying to assess her skinny body for any sign of a little brother or sister. She's got a bit more up top I think, but nothing too horrific.

Then she asks where we can go to talk in private. I'm about to suggest the kitchen when my dad says, 'Look, Nicki, we all need to sit down together to discuss Ty's future, short and long-term.'

It's pretty brave of him because she looks at him like they're in a war film and she's in the Gestapo and he's a resistance fighter that she's just sentenced to be shot at dawn.

'I wasn't speaking to you,' she says.

'Umm . . . Nic, let's go in the kitchen,' I say nervously, tugging at her arm. But Lou says, 'It's OK Ty, we'll all go into the kitchen and you can talk to Nicki here.' And she gets up, and after a minute so does my dad. I feel like begging them to stay with me, but I manage to keep my mouth shut. Archie follows them, after giving my mum a long stare, and shuts the door, but Meg is curled in front of the fireplace, one eye closed and the other fixed on my mum.

Mum sits on the sofa and I collapse on the floor next to Meg. I somehow need to feel there's someone on my side.

'So,' she says. She's still in total Gestapo mode. 'You look quite at home.' Her eyes flicker over my Gap hoodie and brand new Abercrombie and Fitch jeans which Helen went out and got for me yesterday. 'I can see they've bought you.'

I wait for her to finish the sentence with 'lots of cool stuff,' or 'nice clothes to wear,' but then realise that's it. They've bought me. I'm that easily bought. According to my own mother. Ouch. Well. She's not the only one who can be mean.

'Should you be smoking?' I ask, 'In your . . . ummm . . . condition.'

'None of your business,' she says, stubbing her

cigarette out in Helen's favourite potted orchid. She lights up again. I'm wondering if she even *is* pregnant any more. Maybe she's been to the baby-killing clinic. I'm sure she wishes she'd paid it a visit just over fifteen years ago.

'You don't look *very* fat,' I say – which, as far as my mum's concerned, is a much worse word than anything I shouted in the hospital – and she shudders and says, 'I should bloody well hope not.'

I want to ask her why she's angry with me. What am I meant to have done? I open my mouth. But what comes out is a furious flood of questions: 'Why didn't you tell me that you were pregnant? Why was Alistair there anyway? What are you doing here?'

In a sci-fi film, lasers would flash from her eyes and zap me in the chest. In a horror movie she'd morph into a zombie with giant maggots spewing from her mouth. If I were Harry Potter, I'd huddle under my invisibility cloak or turn myself into a spider. 'I didn't have to tell you anything,' she hisses. 'I hadn't even told Alistair. That's why he was there. That's why he died.'

I'm a lot braver than I thought I was. 'Gran knew. Louise knew. But you never told me. And how come you invited Alistair over when you told me I could never see Claire again?'

'I didn't know if I was going to keep it or not until I'd talked to Alistair. Your gran guessed because she heard me being sick one day when you were at school. She must've told Louise. She always tells her everything.'

'And are you going to keep it?'

'I'm sixteen weeks, what do you think?' she says, cryptically. I have absolutely no idea what that means. I give up.

'Why are you angry with me?'

She huffs and puffs and shrugs her shoulders and says, 'Don't play the innocent with me.'

'I'm not! They had to buy me clothes, Nic . . . I didn't have anything. Doug didn't pack properly. . .'

Her hand is shaking as she helps herself to another cigarette. 'Tell me the truth, Ty. How often have you met them before? How long have you been lying to me?'

'I never . . . I never met them before. What are you talking about?'

'Louise' – she spits out the name – 'she's brought you to see them before, hasn't she? And him. You've been lying to me for years. You're all cosy here in this lovely big house, with your lovely rich grandparents, and I bet you're really looking forward to going off to France with your dad.'

France? What is she talking about?

'What do you mean?' I say, but she yells, 'Come off

it, Ty! You'll have to do a bit better than that!' And she reaches into her bag and pulls out an envelope and throws it at me. Meg growls and barks, but I shush her, pull her next to me.

'Tell me you know nothing about that,' says my mum.

'I don't even know what it is,' I say, opening the envelope. A little book falls out, a purple book. Oh my God. It's a passport. I sneak a glance at the back page. My face. My real name. The photo from Snappy Snaps.

'For weeks now I've not known where you were. *She* wouldn't tell me . . . said it wasn't safe. . . My own son. . . I've been imagining all sorts . . . so scared. And then I find out that *she's* been in touch with them . . . for years, telling them stuff about me . . . and you . . . and you . . . and he . . . and you'd betray me . . . greedy . . . disloyal . . . and. . .' She lifts her head. 'I'm not having it. You're my son. You belong to me.'

'I'm not a *possession* . . . I don't *belong* to anyone.' She's wrong, but in my heart I wish it was true. Louise should have brought me to see my grandparents. Even if it meant lying to my mum. No matter what my dad did, why did I have to lose out? It's not fair. I actually like Patrick and Helen – and even Meg – quite a lot.

I can't tell her any of that because she'd kill me.

So I ask, 'Where do you live now anyway?' hoping to head her off to neutral ground.

'They've put us in a flat. Just for now.'

'What sort of flat? Where?'

'On an estate. Birmingham. High-rise.' Her voice is getting louder again, 'You don't have to make a face like that, Ty. We can't all live in big houses. We won't be there forever. And let's not forget why we're there in the first place.'

Oh no, let's not forget that.

'But you said you'd never live on an estate,'

'Didn't have the choice, did I?' she says. 'There's three bedrooms. Lou's sharing with Emma and I'm sharing with mum and you'll have to share with Darren.'

'Who's Darren?'

'Police.'

I'm stroking Meg's fur. She licks my hand. I'm not going to live in some high-rise in Birmingham. I'm not going to share a room with a cop called Darren. I'm not going anywhere with Nicki right now, she's gone completely mad.

'Go and pack up,' she says. 'We're getting out of here as soon as possible.'

'But what about Patrick and Helen? They've been really good to me, Nic . . . really good, they didn't have to. . .' My voice stumbles to a halt.

'I'll tell them. We don't owe them anything. Get your stuff.'

I can't think what else to say. I trail upstairs and pull out my bag. It doesn't take long to stuff my clothes inside. Then I start coughing. I cough and cough, and it's exhausting. When Archie bounds up the stairs, he finds me red-faced and wheezing, sitting doubled up on the bed.

Of course he jumps to the wrong conclusion, the plonker.

'Hey . . . are you *crying*?' he breathes, sitting on the bed next to me and putting a hand on my shoulder.

'No . . . of course not.' My breathing's shot to pieces. I take a few gasps of air. 'Just coughing . . . you know. . .'

'Christ, there's a big fight going on down there,' he says, looking away while I mop my face with a hankie.

'Is there?'

'Your mum came marching in, saying she was taking you home, and now your dad's threatening to get lawyers in. Is she always like that?'

'She's a bit unpredictable,' I say.

'Your aunt said she'd been ranting all the way in the car. Two hours, non-stop. She said, "When Nicki's angry there's no reasoning with her." Is that right?'

I nod. I know my mum's scared of losing me.

Sometimes she shows her love in a strange way. But that means I feel bad about feeling bad, which makes me feel even worse.

'Your dad's really determined though that you're going to stay with him. What do you want to do? Do you want to go with her?'

I shake my head. 'She's gone a bit bonkers, she's really angry with me. And they're living in a high-rise and I'd have to share a room with a cop.' I don't even get started on the whole baby thing.

'What about your dad?'

'I dunno. . . Archie, this is all doing my head in. I don't know what to do. . . I don't want to be with either of them. . .' I'm panicking. My cough starts up again. Archie slaps me on the back.

'Look,' he says, 'Here's the laptop. Check your emails. You never got to read them before.'

I log on and open up the first email from Claire. Archie is buzzing around the room, but I'm intent on the screen in front of me.

The first email says: *It was so strange to talk to you. Sometimes I can hardly believe that we ever really met. You're like someone from a story or a film, a hero who saved me. I wish we could be together.*

The second is all about how she's going off on some Geography field trip – fossils – and how she wishes I was going, and how it's going to be fun, but it'd be better if I was there. I check the date. She'll be there now.

The last one says: *It's horrible how sometimes you're in touch but mostly you're not. It makes me feel like you've forgotten me. I'm beginning to think you've got a new girlfriend. I'm not even sure you ever thought of me in that way at all. Maybe you're more interested in girls like Ashley.*

I stare and stare at the screen. Claire has no idea. She doesn't understand how I feel about her. She'll probably go off with someone else on this field trip, someone like Brian . . . or Jordan . . . or even Max. . .

I snap the laptop shut. My head feels clearer. My body's stronger. I know what I'm going to do.

'Archie,' I say, 'Have you got any money? Can you lend me some?'

'You what?' he says, grabbing the computer. 'You didn't close it down properly, did you? I won't let you use it again.'

'Money, Archie, I need to borrow some. And you'll need to cover for me for a bit.'

'Oh my God,' he says. He's almost bouncing with joy. 'You're going to run away? Oh my God.'

Christ. Can I trust him? Is he going to go and snitch to Patrick?

'You mustn't tell them,' I growl. 'You mustn't say anything to them.'

He's looking at me. I can't tell if he thinks it's a great idea to let me run myself into trouble, or whether he'd rather go for the easy win of telling on me right away. I clench my fists. 'I mean it, Archie.'

'Chillax, man,' he says, waving his hand at me. 'It's a sick idea. But you can't do it on your own. I'm coming with you.'

CHAPTER 13
Lost

Sneaking out of the house – Archie shows me a back gate that leads straight to the village – waiting at the bus stop, buying tickets at the station . . . I'm sure the whole time that it's only a matter of minutes before we're nicked. Before Patrick tracks us down, or my mum bursts out of a taxi. . . But now we're sitting on a train, heading for London and no one has found us. I begin to feel confident. I begin to relax.

Then I remember that we're heading for a city which is packed with people who want me dead.

'So. . .' whispers Archie. 'Where are we going, exactly?'

I frown at him. I know exactly where we're going and how we're getting there, but I'm not exactly going to broadcast our plans to the entire carriage.

'That information is on a need-to-know basis,' I tell him.

'I do need to know,' he says. 'After all, I'm paying.'

I glance at the woman sitting opposite us. She's plugged into her iPod. I don't think she's listening.

'Claire,' I hiss. 'We're going to find her. I know where she is. I'll tell you where we have to go when we get there.'

'Great,' he says. 'Brilliant. You're on a mission to shag your girlfriend and I'm going to be doing what exactly?'

'I never asked you to come,' I point out. 'Why did you, anyway?'

'They've got a place for me at Allingham Priory,' he says. 'I was just working out my own exit strategy. Now, if they catch us, I can blame it all on you . . . say you made me come, threatened me . . . nicked my cash.' He smirks at me. I can't work out if he's joking or not.

'Look, just come with me as far as you want,' I say. 'If you lend me money then I'll pay you back one day – I promise. . .'

He rolls his eyes. 'Ty,' he says, 'You've got to learn when I'm joking. You take life way too seriously.'

For a moment I'm reminded of Arron. Arron who was as witty as Jonathan Ross or Johnny Vaughan. Arron, who'd make jokes – and some were about me – and I was never sure if I was meant to laugh or not. I wonder if he's still as funny now he's in a Young Offender Institution.

We've got to recognisable bits of London now – Ally Pally on the hill – and I'm feeling the sweet, sharp, familiar, choking taste of panic. And when the train stops at Finsbury Park – Finsbury Park, for Christ's sake, where I have been about a million times; where, if I were to get out and walk past the bowling alley and down the Blackstock Road, someone, anyone could recognise me in seconds – I think I am going to faint. But I don't. I concentrate on Claire. I'm doing this for her. I'm going to find her.

We take a bus to Victoria. Once we're up top, right at the front, I surprise myself by actually enjoying it all a tiny bit. Oxford Street, Marble Arch, Hyde Park Corner. I'd forgotten how much I love to watch all the different people, trying to work out where they come from, listening to the babble of languages mixing in the air. I'd never realised before that other places in England aren't necessarily like that.

At Victoria, I lead Archie into the ticket office. He'd withdrawn money from a cashpoint at Kings Cross – it's useful that he's got his own cash card – and he peels off the money we need. I'm buzzing with excitement, imagining Claire's face when she sees me. Maybe she'll actually run away with me. If Archie would lend me some cash we could go to Ireland maybe . . .

I could work as a cleaner.

'I'm starving,' says Archie. 'Stay here. I'll get food.' He sits me down on a bench, dumps both bags with me and says, 'I won't be long.'

I wait and wait and there's no sign of him. I begin to get nervous. I hardly know Archie, and I don't like him much. What if he's just abandoned me? What if he never comes back? What if he thinks it's a great joke to leave me here while he goes back to his home in London?

Shit. I'm sure that's what's happened. The dickhead. I don't have a mobile, I don't know anyone's number, I don't know anyone's address. I've got no money. There are people who want to kill me. Archie has the coach tickets. Why did I trust that tosser? Why?

I'm a little bit shaky. My chest is wheezing and my ankle's started aching again. I'm trying to focus on Claire, but all I can think of is Patrick's face when he found that we've gone. He must be furious. He must be so disappointed.

What the hell am I going to do? When I was very little Gran told me about finding a policeman and saying, 'I'm lost.' Once I've caught that memory all I can hear in my head is my voice when I was five, practising for this moment . . . I'm lost . . . I'm lost . . . except she never realised that I might reach a point in my life where I wouldn't be very keen on approaching the police.

I'm just about to get up and start searching, when Archie comes back. *Jesus.* I'm so relieved I could kiss him. Almost.

'There was a massive queue,' he says, 'Come on, we've only got five minutes.' And we sprint across to the stop, and swing onto the coach.

Once we're sitting at the back, I begin thinking about how much time we've got. I assume Archie's mummy and daddy will want to plaster the entire country with photos of their darling little lost boy. Hopefully my mum at least will realise how dangerous that would be for me. Maybe she'll just let me go. Maybe . . . but if my mum thinks one course of action is the right one, then my dad will think the opposite just on principle. I can't see them ever agreeing on anything.

I nudge Archie, who's producing crisps and sandwiches from a plastic bag.

'Archie, d'you think we should call them? Just to tell them we're OK?'

'Cheese or tuna?' he asks, 'No I do not. Are you mad? No, don't answer that. Have the tuna. Salt and vinegar OK for you?'

I nod, and eat the sandwich and watch as London melts into grey suburbs and blurs altogether. Archie's shaking me awake as the coach stops. 'Come on, Ty,' he says, 'We're here . . . we need to get off. . .'

It's strange being by the seaside again. The fresh, sharp smell, the shrieking seagulls. For a minute all I can think of is Alistair's shrouded body, the blood on Gran's slippers. But it's OK. This is the south coast. We're miles away from everything that happened that day.

Archie's rubbing his hands together. 'Starbucks,' he says, 'Come on. I could do with a hot drink and we can ring your girlfriend, tell her we're here.'

Uh-oh. Shit. I haven't actually got Claire's number, and I don't expect she'll be checking her emails if she's out fossil-hunting all day. We'll never find her. How am I going to tell Archie that I've completely cocked up?

I wait until he's bought me a latte with extra cream before I confess. But he's amazingly cool about it. 'Youth hostel,' he says. 'That's where school trips always stay.' And he pulls out his laptop and finds a list of hostels, then starts ringing around asking which one has a party from Parkview School. And amazingly, he hits the right one, and books us a double room.

The sweet coffee is warming me, and I can't keep the smile off my face, thinking about Claire, how pleased she'll be. How much I want to see her . . . touch her. . . Archie stops muttering into his phone and says, 'Result!' and we high five. He's beaming. I'm actually beginning to like him.

We drink our coffee. He says, 'It was true, wasn't it, what you told me? I thought you were joking, but it was true. The look on your face on that train. I thought you were going to have a heart attack.'

Bugger. I thought I was being calm, confident and brave. 'It's all true,' I say.

'Jesus,' he says, 'It's like a film. You're like the star of a movie.'

'Not really,' I say, taking a huge gulp of latte. 'Where we were living before, it was all just normal.'

'Is that where you met Claire?' he asks.

'Umm . . . yeah. . .'

'She's pretty special, huh?'

'Yeah.' I say. And then it hits me. My mum knows just how I feel about Claire. As soon as they discovered we'd run away she'll have got onto the phone to Claire's mum. She must know about the field trip. There is no way we can go to the youth hostel.

I leap to my feet, spilling latte all over the table. 'Shit!' yells Archie, 'Watch out for the laptop.'

I'm panicking. 'Archie . . . Christ . . . I'm so stupid. . .'

'You've only just realised,' he sniggers. 'Mop it up, you clumsy git.'

The door opens, letting in a blast of cold air. I glance over my shoulder, looking for my mum, for Patrick. But it's OK, I think, just two fit girls, one short and blonde, one tall and dark, scanning the café, looking for their mates.

And then they walk over to us. And the blonde one says, 'Oh my God . . . it is really you . . . I couldn't believe it when I got your message. . .'

Holy Mary, mother of God.

It's Claire.

CHAPTER 14
Strictly

When I first knew Claire, she was having a really hard time. Ashley, my first, very bad choice of girlfriend, was being really mean to her. Claire felt and looked like a complete loser. Hair all over her face. Huge baggy clothes. A constant scared-rabbit expression on her face.

It was a complete miracle that I realised she was actually very pretty, and her mousey hair was shiny and soft. And even I felt a bit weird sometimes about fancying her, because generally she looks about ten.

But this Claire is different. This Claire has short spiky blonde hair, smudged grey eye liner and dark mascara. She's wearing skinny jeans and silver hoops in her ears. Her lips shine with gloss. She looks at least fourteen and just like the kind of girl that might be going out with someone as cool as Joe. If I was still Joe. . .

I stand up and manage to find some words.

'Hey. Umm. Claire.'

She just stands there looking at me. What's she thinking? She looks gorgeous and obviously I like it, obviously it's great, but she doesn't look like *my* Claire, the Claire I've missed so much. What if she's changed as much inside as she has on the outside? What if she thinks I've totally changed too – and not for the better?

'Hello Joe,' says Claire's friend. I just about recognise her as Zoe, used to be in 8P, definitely fancied me. 'You never told us there was another one like you at home.'

Archie gives her what he thinks is a winning smile. 'I'm Joe's cousin,' he says, smoothly accepting my name change without a blink. 'Who are you?'

'Never mind that,' I snap. 'Archie, what's going on?'

'Well, as you didn't have Claire's number I left a message for her at the youth hostel reception,' he said. 'You must have come straight over,' he adds to the girls.

'Look,' says Claire, 'we only have one hour and then we have to get back to the youth hostel. And I really need to talk to you.' She's really brisk and almost bossy and again . . . I don't know . . . she's just not very Claire.

'It's OK,' says Archie, 'We'll meet you at the hostel. Let me give you some pocket money, young man.'

So I have to suffer the total humiliation of having Archie hand me £20 in front of Claire and Zoe – who's finding this all very funny. As we head out of the door, I hear him offering to buy her a drink.

I forget all about them once we're out of Starbucks. I'm standing there with Claire, and staring at her face, and I don't know whether to laugh or cry. I can't believe it. And there's nothing stopping us hugging, but somehow we don't, we just stand there and it's so confusing . . . so strange . . . and she's looking a bit worried, which makes her look more like herself and I want to tell her that's it's OK, there's nothing to worry about, everything will be fine, I'm here to look after her.

But my head is full of worry as well, and that's what comes out.

'Claire . . . I shouldn't really be here,' I say. 'My mum'll be on the phone to your parents right now, they'll probably have caught up with us by tonight . . . can you tell them not to say anything?'

'Have you run away?' she asks. 'I don't think it's a good idea even to mention your name to my parents, really, else they'll probably turn up too.'

Great. Nothing's changed. The last time I saw them, Claire's mum was calling me 'streetwise' – meaning 'scum' – and her dad was pretty keen to hit me. I'd kind of hoped she might have talked them round by now.

'I have tried to talk to them,' she says, 'but a lot of evil gossips have been stirring things up.'

I'm not really surprised. When people don't have the facts they start making stuff up. The less they know, the bigger the lies grow.

'Everyone thinks they know all about us. And all about you. And they don't think very good things.' Her voice is even, but she's looking into the distance and slightly frowning, and I can see that she's had a pretty horrible time.

'Claire, I'm really, really sorry. . .'

'It's OK. It's a bit annoying sometimes, but it's certainly changed the way people think of me at school. Nothing I can't cope with. And there are some people, like your friend Brian, who don't believe everything they're told. Anyway, I thought I might as well change my image as well. I seem to have failed at being invisible.'

'You look great,' I tell her, 'You always did.' It's good to see the lines on her forehead disappear.

'So you like it?' she asks.

'What you look like doesn't matter to me,' I say, and she looks away and I'm so stupid, I'm so *stupid*, I said totally the wrong thing. But I can't think how to put it right without sounding really false.

I don't fancy another Starbucks-type place; I want this time to be special. I want to get it right. And then I see a sign that looks interesting.

'Look. . .' I nudge her, 'Let's go in there.'

'What?' she says, 'Why?'

'It'll be warm, and we can get a drink, and no one that we know will be there . . . and it could be fun . . . please, Claire. . .'

She looks at me like I'm a lunatic, but she follows me in and starts giggling as I buy two tickets. The woman on the desk looks a bit uncertain, but takes my money.

'This has got to be the weirdest date ever,' says Claire, but I say, 'No, wait and see, it'll be good.'

And then we walk in and every person in the room is staring at us. We're the youngest people there by about a hundred years. Fair enough really, because you don't get many teenagers buying tickets to a tea dance.

A bloke comes over to us. 'Oy,' he says, 'Clear off. We don't want any trouble from your sort.'

'We're not here to cause trouble,' I say and Claire smiles at him and pulls off her jacket and asks politely if there's a coat rack, which is clever because he starts showing her some hooks on the wall and forgets that we're undesirables.

When I knew her before Claire was always hiding, swamped by huge shirts and jumpers, hair messed up over her face. But now her clothes have changed as much as her face. Her pale grey top has long sleeves, but clings to her body. And her body – well, either she's grown a lot in the chest area, or there's some padding going on, or she's had some of those implant things.

It's like she's in disguise, she's pretending, she's trying to be someone else . . . just like I have to do all the time. Or is this the real Claire, the Claire that was hidden? I don't know. How can I tell?

It's too weird to start falling for this completely new Claire when I still love the old one. I wanted to help her change. And she's done it all by herself. She didn't need me after all.

'So,' she says, smiling up at me. 'Are we going to dance?' And I take hold of her hand and slip my arm round her waist and say, 'Let's have a go.'

I would prefer better music – although Frank Sinatra is a favourite of my gran's, so at least I know these songs – and we do stumble over each other's feet a bit, until she gets the idea that I know what I'm doing and relaxes and lets me lead her. But the twirling and the movement and the looking into her eyes – it's just what I hoped for.

Never mind that we're in a church hall, and there're no sequins or glitter balls, no band, no Bruce Forsyth. Actually it's good that there's no Bruce, he's my least favourite bit of *Strictly Come Dancing*. All I want is to give her something to cancel out the gossips with their dirty minds and lazy mouths. Glamour and romance, that's what I'm aiming for.

And she does get it, because she's smiling and she whispers in my ear, 'What do you think the judges are going to say?' and I say, 'Oh, even Craig'll love us,' and I lift her up – she's so light, her hair smells of strawberries – and try a spin, American-Smooth-style, which makes both of us a bit giddy and reminds me that I've got a dodgy ankle and I'm quite glad when the song ends and I can put her down.

It's then that I realise that all the old folk have stopped dancing to watch us, and some of them are clapping. One old lady has her hanky out. 'Well done,' she calls, 'It's so lovely to see young people aren't all muggers and vandals.'

We go and get cups of tea and biscuits and sit down at one of the little tables scattered around the dance floor. Claire is laughing at me. 'I wouldn't have put you down for a *Strictly* fan,' she says.

'My gran is the biggest *Strictly* fan in the world,' I say. 'And she does salsa classes, and line dancing, and she did ballroom before she had kids.'

I pause. And then I tell her one of my darkest, deepest secrets. 'She sent me to ballroom classes when I was six, and I went for two years. But you're not to tell anyone. Especially Carl and Brian.' It doesn't matter if I'm not at their school any more. I'm not having them taking the mick.

'Maybe you'll be on *Strictly* one day,' she says. 'They have athletes, don't they? When you've finished winning medals.'

'Yeah right. First I have to have a life again.' And I bring her up to date on what's happened since I last saw her.

She doesn't want to talk about Alistair. 'Ellie was so upset,' she says, and she changes the subject quickly. She's most interested in my dad. She's got loads of questions about him, and I can't answer any. I don't know what job he does, or where he lives, or whether he's married or what music he likes.

'It's like you've decided not to be interested in him,' she says, disappointed, and I say, 'I have been ill, actually, I was in hospital overnight.'

'Yes but even so, Joe, it's your dad and you've never met him before.'

'Hmm.' I say, 'Did I tell you that my grandad speaks French like he comes from France?' But she's not interested in Patrick, and she says, 'You need to get to know your dad. Maybe he's good at languages too.'

And then she says, 'Joe, I have a lot of things to ask you about. That email you sent me . . . you can't do that. You can't dump something like that on me when I don't know when I'm going to see you again.'

'I'm here now, aren't I?' I say, sulkily. I grasp her hand.

'Please Claire, can't you just forget about it? It was just a stupid email. It didn't mean anything.'

'Of course not,' she says indignantly, 'It means a lot. I need to know what you meant – who have you hurt? Why are you lying?'

'It's a bit complicated,' I start, and then she looks at her watch. She gasps. 'Oh God – I should have been at the hostel an hour ago. I'm going to be in such trouble.' She slides her hand in her pocket and takes out her phone. 'Oh no . . . look . . . seven missed calls. Mr Hunt will be furious. Come on we'd better go.'

'Mr Hunt?' She can't mean it. She's here on a school trip with Mr Hunt, my old form tutor, the one who hates me, the one who will remember every detail of my two suspensions and hasty exit from her school. He thinks I'm a bully . . . someone who bullies girls for sex. He'll call the police if he sees me within twenty miles of Claire.

'Can we can talk later? Claire – please—'

She's putting on her jacket, and buttoning it up. She takes her time over it, fingers fumbling and I realise her eyes are full of tears.

'What . . . what's the matter?' I ask uncertainly. I want to pick her up again, kiss her tears away. But she's rubbing her face and looking away from me.

'We'll have to talk later,' she says. 'You need to explain . . . what you meant. And I can't really see what's going to happen after that, because either you were lying to the police or you were lying to me. Which is it?'

I open my mouth. I want to tell her the whole story, everything I've done, right and wrong.

But she says. 'Don't even bother trying to answer that.'

CHAPTER 15
Reunion

It's like she's hit me with a meat cleaver, and exposed my heart for everyone to see, and I'm bleeding to death in the middle of a bunch of jiving pensioners.

And all she does is pull a map out of her pocket and goes and asks an old lady how to get to the hostel. I stumble after her – can't she see what she's done to me? – but her eyes are firmly on the directions she's getting.

Then she's out of the door, almost running while I try and keep up with her, which ought to be easy – I'm usually faster than anyone I know – but, with a screwed up ankle and a wheezy chest, it is infuriatingly difficult.

'Claire . . . wait . . . please,' I gasp.

'I can't . . . I've got to get back,' she says, turning a corner.

I catch up with her, and grab her shoulder, 'Claire . . . this is more important – you can't just say that and rush off. What if we don't get to talk later?'

She pulls away from me. 'We'll have to . . . I'm sorry. . .'

'Claire. . .' My whole body is aching with the effort of keeping up with her and my brain is bursting trying to find a solution. But it's like a riddle – how do you convince someone you're honest when you're truthfully telling her you've been lying? And how do you promise her that you're safe to be with, when you're confessing that you've hurt someone? And how do you build trust when you're not even allowed to speak?

And what do I do with the knowledge that Claire can be a bit screwed up . . . that she might not make good decisions? That she even *liked* it when I hurt her that time?

'Claire . . . Claire. . .' I catch up with her again, and this time I manage to get myself in front of her. And I grab her and wrap my arms around her and hold her tight. Just for a second we're still, and I touch the soft skin of her face and stare into her eyes and plead. 'You've got to *listen*, you've got to talk *now* . . . you can't just *say* that. Please let me explain.'

She ought to like me holding her . . . shouldn't she? She ought to listen to me . . . but she's pushing and struggling and trying to break free, and she shouts, 'No . . . not now. . .' and I scream back, 'Yes, now. . .'

And then she kicks me hard on the shin – ouch – and I feel hands digging into my shoulders, dragging me backwards and a loud familiar male voice saying, 'Let go of her! Call the police!'

Oh shit. Mr Hunt. Great timing.

He shoves me sideways and I stagger and fall onto the pavement – I probably could've got away if it hadn't been for the ankle and the cough – and a large lumpy guy jumps onto my back, knocking the breath out of me and pressing my face against the cold wet pavement. My jaw slams against the hard surface and my teeth crunch down on my tongue and I'm gagging on the salty-sweet taste of blood. The pavement stinks of piss and worse. I struggle and cough and retch and he just pushes my head against the stone and grunts, 'Stay where you are.'

I know that voice. Jesus. It's Carl. The last time we had a fight I ended up breaking his nose. Now he's getting his revenge without even knowing it. I can't get a glimpse of Claire – all I can see is my hair and my hood and a dog turd, inches from my nose. Christ, I hope Carl doesn't see it.

'Claire . . . are you all right? What did he do to you?' Mr Hunt's trying to sound concerned and caring, but

I can also hear that he's pretty delighted with himself for bravely saving his student from the clutches of an evil hoodie mugger. 'Emily, Anna, come and look after her.'

Claire's voice is all squeaks and gasps, escaping in little breathy spurts. 'Mr Hunt . . . it's OK . . . I'm OK. . .' Gasp. Sob. 'Let him go . . . it's OK . . . it wasn't . . . it wasn't . . . don't call the police. . . It was my fault. . .'

'What are you talking about, Claire?'

And then a different voice. Zoe's voice. 'Mr Hunt. I think it's Joe. We . . . ummm . . . we met him earlier in Starbucks.'

I knew Mr Hunt as a weedy, sandy-haired Geography teacher who used to find me intensely irritating, mainly because I called him 'sir', and he thought I was winding him up. He specialised in quiet sarcasm and multiple detentions. But apparently he can also shout so loud that it hurts my ears, '*Bloody* hell! Bloody Joe *Andrews*?' he roars. 'Have a look, Carl.'

Carl grabs my hood, twists and pulls, almost choking me, and then shifts his weight slightly so he can flip me over onto my back to get a good look at my face. I'm limp as a rag doll about to be disembowelled by a Rottweiler. Luckily, the Rottweiler is well-trained and friendly. 'Whoa . . . it *is* Joe. Hello mate,' he says, cheerfully. 'Never thought we'd see you again.'

He releases me unexpectedly, and my head crashes

back onto the pavement – splat! – into the huge pile of dog shit. The smell is excruciating. I'm praying that none has gone on my hair. The only tiny comfort is that a bit flew as far as Mr Hunt's shoe. Girly cries of '*Eee . . . uw. . .*' ring out.

'Hey Carl, watch what you're doing, bro,' I say faintly. 'Hey Emily, Jamie . . . Max. . . Umm . . . hello, sir.'

'Joe Andrews. Bloody hell,' says Mr Hunt, like Satan himself has materialised in a puff of smoke. 'Claire, what's been going on? Did you arrange to meet Joe?'

'No . . . yes . . . I got a message saying he was in Starbucks,' Claire sniffs. 'Mr Hunt, he didn't do anything. He just wanted to talk to me. Please, please don't call the police. . .'

'It may be too late,' says Mr Hunt, 'Did anyone call?' There's a general shuffling, and I gather that no one has been fast enough to summon the cops. Hah. They are all pathetically slow. Good thing I wasn't really an evil mugger.

Then I realise that actually everyone here is – was – more or less friendly with me when I was Joe. They must have been tipped off by Zoe that I was in town. Even Carl was probably just playing a role – rather too convincingly, in my opinion.

'Right,' says Mr Hunt. 'Claire, I will have to ring your

parents to inform them about this. Joe . . . I don't know what you're doing here, but I suggest that you get lost as soon as possible. I never want to see you again, and you are not to bother Claire, is that clear? Now we'd better go and meet the others at Pizza Hut. They'll be wondering where we are.'

'But, Mr Hunt,' says Max, 'we haven't seen Joe for ages. Can't he come with? I mean, there's loads of people at the pizza place who'd like to see him . . . Brian, for example, and Mr Henderson. . .'

Typical Max – a completely pointless intervention. I remember his attempt to petition the head teacher after I was suspended for smashing Carl's nose, and I flash him a grin. I would really like to see Brian, and Mr Henderson, my former PE teacher, was always a decent guy. But only a total idiot would think that Mr Hunt's going to let me share a deep-pan-four-cheese-special with Claire.

'Shut *up*, Max,' says Mr Hunt, and Max shuts up. Zoe nudges him and shoots me a meaningful glance. But I'm too shattered to understand it.

Claire's dried her tears and she's looking at me with such a sad face that I have to turn away. I know what her expression means. She can't see any way forward for us.

It means she's decided I'm a lying, violent thug.

It means she'll never be able to trust me, to love me, to forgive me.

It means. . .

'Come on, now,' says Mr Hunt, and they're walking away from me. Claire's looking back, but being pulled along by her friends. Carl releases me and says, 'Sorry, mate. Had to be 100 per cent sure it was you. What were you doing to her, anyway? It looked a bit heavy.'

'Carl, tell her that I need to talk to her . . . tell her . . . tell her I love her. . .'

He gawps at me, and I know I've chosen the most useless messenger possible. But this may be my last chance to speak to Claire and, like my gran would say, beggars can't be choosers. Lying here on the ground, wet and filthy, with 50p in my pocket, no phone, no idea where this hostel is or what it's called, begging seems to be the only option.

I can't seem to get up. My body's ceased to function. I lie on the pavement and wonder what would happen if I just stayed here. Who would find me? What would happen to me? I might as well just find out. I'm not sure I really care. A pathetic tear escapes from one eye. I blink hard to stop any more. I'm not worth crying over.

Then I hear someone running towards me. Light steps. A girl? Claire? I prop myself up on my elbows. *Claire?* No . . . it's Zoe. She sees the disappointment on my face and hisses, 'It's that door there, you wally, number twenty-three. Archie's waiting for you. Room twelve. I'll talk to Claire. See you later.' And she sprints back to the rapidly disappearing group of my former classmates. Mr Hunt is interrogating Claire. He doesn't seem to notice that Zoe's gone back to talk to me.

I lie there a bit longer. What I'd really like is for someone to come and help me up, take me inside, look after me. I close my eyes and wonder if it's possible to sleep like this. Then something nudges my skull. I look up.

A policeman. His shiny boot, right by my head. It smells of leather and polish. I stink of sweat and shit.

He's not looking very caring. 'Too much to drink?' he demands.

I struggle up onto my elbows again and shake my head. *I'm lost. . .* I think, *I'm lost. . .* But there's no point saying it. He can't help me. My life is way too complicated.

'Move on, then,' he says. 'I don't need louts littering the street.'

'OK,' I say, and make a superhuman effort to scramble to my feet. I look around and see the door marked twenty-three. The hostel. I move towards it, and he walks away. And there's a rush of hot air as I push open the door.

Room twelve, Zoe said. . . There's a woman sitting at a desk in the hall and as I walk past I see her nose wrinkle. 'Where're you going?' she asks, and I say, 'I'm with the group from Parkview,' and she says, 'Oh, OK, you know where you're going,' and gestures up a steep flight of stairs. It takes me ages to trudge all the way up – I have to stop for a coughing fit halfway – and by the time I get to the dimly-lit corridor I'm dizzy and clammy, my ankle throbbing. No one would ever believe that I'm supposed to be a promising athlete. I'm kind of grateful that I didn't get to meet Mr Henderson. I really hope I can avoid him in the morning.

I bash on the door marked twelve and Archie opens it slowly. 'About bloody time!' he says, 'Where were you?' and then, 'What is that *smell*?'

The room is tiny and cell-like; two metal-framed single beds, dark grey carpet, hospital-white sheets, glaring bright overhead light. The only things that don't look like they belong in a prison or a hospital are the cream linen curtains that frame the window, and the wooden seat that's been built against it, painted light grey. There's a sink in the corner and a strip of mirror, but nothing else – no shower or toilet, no television, no kettle. I've stayed in a few hotels in the last year, none exactly five star, but they were palaces compared to this.

It's warm though, and clean – or at least it was until

I arrived.

The window is wide open and there's a cigarette burning on the sill which Archie picks up, leaning back and inhaling deeply. Most of the smoke blows out of the window, but a whiff remains and it reminds me of my mum.

I take a long, juddering breath and remember life at home, before any of this happened. I'd be stressing over some Maths homework and she'd come dancing in, plant a kiss on my forehead and demonstrate the song she was planning to sing at karaoke that night. She'd put her arm around me, and show me where I was going wrong with the Maths and give me money to get my supper from the kebab shop.

Just for a minute I miss her so much that I think about getting Archie to call Patrick and ask him to send me back to her. I could live in a Birmingham high-rise. What's the problem? Then I imagine her response to my disappearing act – *'You selfish little bastard. Do you know how much pain you've caused me? You could've killed Alistair's baby. . .'* – and I know there's no going back.

I peel off my hoodie before I flop onto the bed. Archie's looking at it in horror. 'Urgh . . . don't even bring that in here . . . what happened to it?'

'I fell in some dog shit,' I say slowly. I'm completely revolted at the thought of the germs that are smeared over my clothes. I'm wondering if any of it got into my hair . . . on my skin. . . I start stripping, dragging my clothes off frantically until I'm down to my boxers. Then I fill the sink with steaming hot water and pick up the tiny tablet of white soap and scrub and scrub at my arms and face until I glance at myself in the mirror and see they are glowing red and pink.

I refill the sink with clean water and plunge my head underwater, shaking it back and forth and rubbing soap into my hair to try and rid myself of the dirt, the crawling germs.

The hand towel is rough and small, but I rub myself dry with it until my skin burns and tingles. Archie yawns and says, 'I'm starving . . . I've been waiting for you for ages. I'm going to go and buy us some chips.'

'OK,' I say, and when he's gone I search in my bag and find a brand new hoodie, a spotless white T-shirt and some jeans. I'm clean. I'm dressed. I go and sit on the window seat so I can smell the last of his cigarette smoke and pretend I'm back home in London.

There's a cold breeze coming in, and I put my hand up to pull the window shut. Down on the pavement below I can see two men talking. And – if I push the window open wider – I can hear snatches of what they're saying.

' . . . can't believe you just left him lying here. . .' says one, ' . . . totally irresponsible. . .'

'Come off it, Geoff,' says the other, 'What was I meant to do? You were all at Pizza Hut and my responsibility was to our current pupils.'

Mr Hunt. Blimey. It's Mr Hunt and Mr Henderson and they've come back from the pizza place. To look for me?

'I don't feel at all easy about this,' says Mr Henderson, 'What on earth was he doing here? What state was he in?'

'I told you,' replies Mr Hunt, who sounds like he'd be much happier getting stuck into a pepperoni feast with a stuffed crust. 'Typically aggressive and cheeky with it. I thought he was a mugger. Twice the size of that poor girl, God knows what he was doing to her. . .'

'She says he just wanted to talk to her, it was a misunderstanding,' says Mr Henderson.

Mr Hunt snorts. 'Look Geoff, we've wasted enough time here. A former pupil with an appalling reputation was harassing one of our most vulnerable girls. If anything happens to him, that's all we have to say. Our backs are covered.'

There's a silence. I assume they've gone away. But then Mr Henderson sighs and says, 'Well, Colin, I hope you're right. But I wouldn't say that Claire was necessarily the most vulnerable child involved. Did you know that Ellie Langley's trainer who got shot was Joe's mother's boyfriend? I dread to think what's going on in that boy's life.'

And then I hear their footsteps walking away.

I slump down onto the floor, hug my knees to my chest and think about what I've just heard. Mr Henderson . . . he knows . . . he sort of knows. He thinks I'm vulnerable. He's worried about me. It's really strange – I'm embarrassed, angry and pleased, all at once.

The smell of dog shit is even stronger than before. I start thinking about the germs buzzing and breeding and I feel a sick and shuddery. I have to destroy them. It's too bad about the clothes.

I use the towel to pick up everything that might have been tainted with Alsatian turd. I stick it all in the metal waste paper bin in the corner of the room. Then I reach over to Archie's bed and pick up his lighter. I lean down and flick it at the hoodie. It takes a little time but soon it's ablaze and spreading to the T-shirt.

Staring at the flames, I'm remembering the fire in Mr Patel's shop, the explosion that was meant to exterminate us, the roaring and crackling as fire melted the chocolates and gobbled newspapers and magazines. I smell the chemical smoke that crept out of the sofa that time my mum had too much to drink and fell asleep with a ciggie in her hand.

I'm back by the fireplace in Patrick's study, when

I wanted to stick my hand into the flames. I watch, fascinated as the jeans start to catch and the orange and blue glow jumps towards the top of the metal basket.

Gran used to go on about hellfire sometimes, about the way that damned souls would burn forever, suffering eternal torments. My mum and aunties would laugh at her and tell her she was talking superstitious nonsense. Mum used to pretend to cover my ears and say, 'Ty, don't listen. I don't want you hauling around a load of Catholic guilt.' Even the teachers at school said that hell didn't really mean pitchforks and brimstone and flames. 'Hell is complete separation from God,' Father Matthew told us, 'the loneliest feeling imaginable.' But I always found it easier to imagine Gran's fiery damnation.

There's a little bit of my mind which knows this is a really stupid idea. But I feel calmer now, knowing all the germs are being cremated. And my fingers are getting closer and closer to the fire.

CHAPTER 16
Together

Something's splashing over my hand. The flames hiss and die as Archie chucks a full litre bottle of coke into the bin. I snatch my hand away. My skin is just a bit pink. The bucket sizzles and steams, crackling with foam.

'What are you doing, you dickhead?' he demands. 'This place stinks even more than it did before. How're we going to entertain in here?'

'Umm . . . what d'you mean?' I'm talking about the entertaining, but he misunderstands me. Typical.

'I mean you. Trying to burn the place down. Bloody hell. They never talked about arson on those post-traumatic stress websites.'

'Long-term behavioural problems?' I suggest.

Archie grabs the bin of smouldering kit. 'I'm going to go and get rid of this outside. Let's get some air in here.'

He opens the window wider and says, 'Can I trust you not to chuck yourself out before I come back, you nutter?'

I try and think of something to say that will get me the respect that I deserve from this kid, this boy, but I can only manage a weak, 'Yes, Archie. Sorry.'

'Good. Get a grip. Pull yourself together.'

He's right, I know, I am falling apart. But pulling yourself together is hard when you never felt very together in the first place. I was always worrying about what other people wanted me to be – my mum, my gran, my friend Arron. Thinking about what they wanted took all my time. And they all wanted me to be different things. So I was.

I've only truly felt completely together when I was running and when I was with Claire. When I could care for her. And now I can't run because of my ankle and my cough, and the new Claire doesn't need me and she doesn't trust me and she *kicked* me – I touch the bruise, tender on my shin – and maybe I'm never going to be able to pull myself together at all.

Then I remember Ellie and how she coped when her back was broken and she was stuck in a wheelchair forever. I am such a baby. Christ.

There's a knock at the door. It must be Archie, back again. I get up, and open it and immediately I feel a million times better. It's not Archie. It's my friend Brian.

And I *can* pull myself together – it's just that I pull myself together as Joe.

'Whoa . . . hello mate. Good to see you.' We're both speaking at once.

He bounds into the room and we high five, and he sits on the window seat and I sprawl on the bed. I open up one of the packets of lukewarm vinegary chips that Archie's left there and offer him some. I'm starving.

Brian says, 'I couldn't believe it when I heard you were here. Zoe told me which room you were in.'

'I thought you were all having a pizza.'

'I sneaked out. They're all fussing over Claire and no one's paying attention to the rest of us. Some of them have gone to the arcade, no one's going to notice that I'm not there. Emily said she'd cover for me.'

He kind of glows when he says her name.

'You done well, my son,' I tell him.

Brian's grown about four inches since I last saw him, and lost some of his little-boy chubbiness, and he's discovered hair gel and some sort of magic zit cream, not totally unsuccessfully. I'd still have thought Emily was out of his league.

'It was thanks to you, really,' he says, 'Everyone wanted to talk about you and Ashley and Claire and everything when you disappeared, and Emily was quite close to Ashley then, and of course, me and the boys, we were standing up for you.'

'Ummm . . . thanks. . .'

'Yeah. Well. We got quite a lot of cred for doing it. Girls noticed us a lot more. And one day Emily cornered me and said she'd had a lot of doubts about Ashley because she knew she'd been being a bitch to Claire and generally, and she – Emily – was feeling bad about it, and we had a long talk about the whole thing and next . . . well . . . we've been going out ever since. We went to the end of year party together.'

'Oh. Cool.' We've finished the chips and because there's no bin I toss the paper out of the window. I know Brian's hoping I'll ask how far he's got but I'm way too jealous to follow through.

Not jealous about Emily, obviously. Jealous, because he has a life.

'Max was hoping it'd work out for him and Becca too, but he's too short.'

'Poor old Max, the virgin midget,' I say, and we laugh cruelly.

'Anyway . . . how are you? What happened? Did you really go back to London?'

He's looking at me strangely, his eyes flicking from my face to my hair which is still a bit wet. I don't know what to say. I'm completely fed up with lying all the time, especially to someone like Brian who – I now realise –

is not only one of the best mates I've ever had, but also someone I've really missed. Without even thinking about him.

I feel a bit choked up and very grateful that I've had enough experience with girls to know that this is definitely not a gay moment.

'Brian. . .' I start, but before I can finish the sentence he says, 'There's something really strange about your eyes . . . have you got contacts or something? And what's going on with your hair?'

As I try and think of an answer to that one – bugger, my roots must be showing – the door opens and Archie's back. He's carrying a large plastic bag which clinks with alcohol.

'Hey,' he says, 'I see the party's started.' He locks the door behind him, and gets a spray out of his bag. Air freshener. He sprays it all around the tiny room until it smells like a hairdresser's. One that does pensioners' specials. Brian and I are falling about laughing.

'Urgh . . . Archie . . . what're you doing, man?'

'I didn't know you'd got a *maid*. . .'

'Yeah, this is Archie, my personal val*et*. . .'

Archie looks slightly annoyed, but he says, 'I wouldn't have to do this if it wasn't for you—' and I quickly interrupt, 'No, seriously Brian, this is my cousin Archie, a brilliant addition to my family.'

Actually, right at the moment, Archie has moved right up my personal chart of family favourites and is sitting second only to Gran. This is mainly because everyone else is on our trail and if there's one thing that can bring them all together, it'll be that they all want to kill me.

Archie pulls some bottles out of his bag and lines them up on the window seat. Another two litres of coke. A big bottle of vodka. A smaller one of Bacardi. Two six-packs of Stella. Some paper cups. Crisps. Peanuts.

'Jesus, Archie, where d'you get all that?'

'I paid a guy to go into the off-licence and get it for me. Do you want a drink?'

I can't decide. Brian takes a can of beer and Archie mixes himself a vodka and coke, which is really a girls' drink but they must have different rules at private schools. Then he mixes one for me and I take a gulp, and there's something about the sweet fiery taste that I like. It warms me.

'Umm . . . so who's coming to this party?' I ask and Brian says, '*Everyone.* Joe, you're hosting *the* party of the season.'

'Oh my God, Archie, what have you done?'

'It's OK,' says Archie, 'Zoe said she'd make sure the teachers didn't know about it. They'll all be off down the pub anyway.'

That might have been true when he and Zoe were talking in Starbucks. I doubt it'll be the case now.

'Archie, are you trying to get us found or what?' I ask.

'Look,' he says, 'You were a completely miserable git less than twelve hours ago and now I'm throwing a party for you and all your mates. I think a bit of thanks would be appropriate.'

'Oh.' I'm a bit nervous he's going to accuse me of crying again when I was actually only coughing. I pour myself another drink. 'Umm. Thanks, Archie. I do appreciate it. I'm just wondering how we're going to get away with it?'

But then there's a knock at the door and Jamie and Max are piling in, closely followed by Emily . . . and Zoe . . . and Carl, who whops me on the back and says, 'Thanks for running out halfway through the lost property gig.'

'Oh, sorry. I couldn't help it. We had to leave in a hurry.'

'You left me the real stinkers.'

'I know. I'm sorry.' I am truly sorry, but it also strikes me that this is quite funny and I start laughing. He looks at me a bit strangely and grabs a Stella.

'So . . . what happened?'

I make a kind of all-purpose apologetic noise and

say, 'My mum . . . y'know. . .' and I get away with it. And then they're all around me, slapping me on the back, helping themselves to drinks and telling me all the gossip from school – the teachers that have left, who's going out with who, how Carl's football team's doing. It's great. I feel almost normal. Everyone's so funny and so nice and Jamie's telling me jokes and I'm cracking up.

But then Carl squints at me. 'You look a bit rough. What's going on with your hair? Did you get highlights, you poofter?'

Obviously it'd be the easiest thing in the world to laugh and run my hand through my hair and say, 'Yeah . . . trying to change my image, bit of an abortion eh?' I can handle this. I can dodge the question. Carl's so thick he won't be able to come back.

I just can't be arsed any more with lying all the time. It's making me lose my grip on what's actually true.

So I say, 'Nah. It's dyed black and it needs to be redone. Roots.'

Carl splutters into his Stella and Brian stops nuzzling Emily's neck and gives me a startled look. I take the opportunity to grab the bottle of vodka and have a chug. The coke is giving me gas.

'And . . . er . . . what about your eyes?' asks Brian nervously. 'Have they changed colour? Weren't they brown?'

I think fleetingly of teasing him, 'I never realised you spent so much time gazing into my eyes, Bri boy. . .' That'd shut him up. That'd stop the personal questions.

But I can't get it together to tease him, poor old Bri. 'I'm not wearing my contacts any more. They made my eyes look brown.'

Silence falls in the tiny room. Everyone's looking at me. It's quite funny how they look, like they really want to know what's what but no one wants to ask. I start laughing. 'C'mon . . . lighten up,' I say. 'Whassup with the music, Arch?' And Archie fiddles with his iPod speakers and Girls Aloud are singing and no one's looking at me any more.

Except Zoe. She sits down next to me. 'You all right?' she asks.

What's she on about?

'Where's Claire? I ask her. I put her arm round her – nothing funny, just mates. 'Where's Claire, Zo? Where's Claire? I need . . . I need to talk to her about something.' I'm going all fuzzy round the edges and I'm not sure what it is I need to talk about. But I'm sure I'll remember when I see Claire.

Zoe sniffs, 'There's no way on earth they'll let her see you,' she says. 'And you're not in a great state for talking, let's face it, Joe.'

Zoe's a nice girl. It's good to be sitting with her,

warm and close like this. I put my head on her shoulder. 'I really need to talk to her,' I say. 'Please Zo . . . help me.'

She sighs and pushes me away. 'You're a mess, Joe,' she says. 'Look, try and get yourself to that café across the road and I'll see what I can do, OK. And don't drink any more of that vodka.' She removes my arm from around her and gets out her mobile.

Someone's standing in front of me. I narrow my eyes, try and focus. It's Brian. And Emily. I raise my hand. 'Yo, Brian.'

Brian's looking all serious, the tosser. 'Joe, what the fuck is going on? Why did you disappear? What do you mean, you dye your hair? What's going on with Claire?'

I'm a bit confused. Each question – every word of every question – seems to have such a huge story behind it . . . so much to explain. . . I keep on trying to say something and my teeth snap shut onto my tongue. I open and close my mouth like a goldfish. Eventually I say lamely, 'Thass *loadsa* questions, mate.'

Brian leans forward. 'We put our necks on the line for you. Me and Jamie and Max . . . and Carl . . . we stood up for you, we told everyone you were OK. Zoe here, she ran around telling everyone they were lying when all the stories were spreading round that Claire was pregnant etc, etc.'

I hate to think what 'etc, etc' could mean.

'So I think we're due some answers,' he finishes.

'Yeah it's jus' . . . it's jus' a bit complicated. An' dangerous.'

'OK,' says Brian. 'Try us, Joe'

'Umm . . . my name's not really Joe.' I say, and then I start laughing at the startled look on his face. He just looks so funny. My stomach hurts I'm laughing so much.

'Don't mess around,' growls Carl, right by Brian's side.

I'm astounded. 'I'm not . . . I'm not, it's *true*. I'm . . . someone wants to kill me. They tried to shoot me. They did kill someone. My life's a big mess and I really miss all of you and being at Parkview.'

I'm not laughing any more. My voice is small and shaky and no one's talking. In the background Cheryl Cole's being a Love Machine. It's my mum's favourite karaoke song. I can't remember when I last heard her singing it.

Brian says, 'Come off it. D'you expect us to believe that?'

'Um. Yes?' They think I'm raving. And then Archie says, 'It's true, actually,' and I can't really stand their faces any more. I only want Claire.

Then there's a knock at the door and a flood of kids from Parkview squeeze in. Some of them I remember well, others I never even spoke to. They're drinking vodka, opening cans of beer, smoking. I wish I was one of them. But I'm not.

In the crush of people it's impossible for Brian to go on with his cross-examination. 'Joe – we'll . . . we'll talk later, OK?' he says uncertainly, and then he and Emily and Carl drift off. Archie's arm circles Zoe's waist. His face is flushed, he's on his third vodka and coke and he's moving in on Zoe's ear, presumably because he thinks that it'll lead him to her lips. I nudge him. 'Archie . . . I need some money. . .'

He glances away from Zoe for a split second and mutters, 'Look in my bag. Under the bed.'

I fish out his rucksack and crouch over it, so no one else can see inside. There's a huge roll of cash knocking around. I peel off fifty quid in tenners, and there's still a lot left. After a moment's thought, I take another fifty. I can always give it back later.

Archie's phone is there too. My hand closes around it, and I shove it in my back pocket. I'm only going to be gone for an hour or so. It might be crucially important, you never know.

It's not technically stealing because I scoot back over to him and mutter, 'Archie, I've taken some cash and borrowed your mobile, OK?' It's not my fault if he's too busy nibbling Zoe's earlobe to clock what I'm saying.

He looks dazed and happy. He looks like I used to

look once upon a time, when I was Joe, when I was cool and confident and didn't really understand that if people want to kill you they might actually succeed.

If they'd shot the right person, then I'd be stuck in a coffin, dead and buried. Like a contestant on *I'm a Celebrity* – except you can't just shout to Ant and Dec to get out, you're there forever in the dark with rats and spiders and worms. How soon do bodies start rotting? What does Alistair look like now?

I can't cope with this. I can't cope with any of it. I need help. Someone sensible, who'll tell me how to cope with my mum and dad, someone who'll give me some direction . . . some guidance. Patrick. I need Patrick. How can I call him?

I lift myself off the bed, and push through to the door. No one really notices. I reach the corridor, and lean against the wall. I'm hot and dizzy and everything's gone a bit swimmy.

Then I hear Mr Henderson's voice booming as he comes down the corridor. 'They're all together somewhere,' he's saying. 'It's just a question of finding which room.'

I take a deep breath. Patrick's not here. But Mr Henderson is a really sensible guy. He's with Mr Hunt – damn – but maybe he'll talk to me on his own. I just need a quick chat. Maybe . . . I just have to find the words. I just have to ask.

I let go of the wall. 'Mr Henderson—' I say. My voice comes out softer than I expected and I try and clear my throat.

He comes right up to me. Puts his hand on my arm. 'Joe. . . ' he says. 'Are you OK?'

'I . . . I—' I can't go on. A sharp, sweet taste hits the back of my throat. I try and catch it, but it's too late. Out of my mouth flies a flood of yellow vomit . . . chips and coffee and vodka and coke . . . urgh . . . all over his shoes and splashing onto his jeans.

'Christ!' he yells and I cough and splutter, 'Sorry—' and then I run. I run down the stairs and out of the door and into the biting cold night.

CHAPTER 17
Twilight

Claire's sitting on her own at the back of the empty café. She's borrowed a top from someone twice her size, and her little face is almost invisible under the droop of the hood. She looks more like the old Claire, scared and sad and small.

I'm just about sure when I sit down opposite her that I've got rid of any sign of vomit – almost all of it went on Mr Henderson, with just a little dollop for Mr Hunt – but I've got a hideous taste in my mouth and I'm not at all confident about my smell. Especially my breath. Vodka and vomit. But what can I do?

'Do you actually want anything to eat or drink?' says the woman behind the counter, and Claire picks a hot chocolate and I ask for a glass of tap water. The woman glares at me and when it arrives, it's lukewarm. I take a sip and try and slosh the water round my mouth without Claire noticing.

'Joe . . . ummm . . . Ty. . .' says Claire, and her eyes fill with tears. I can read her mind. She's going to chuck me.

'Don't say it,' I beg. 'Look, it's OK. I'll just go. We don't have to do this. Forget about me, and everything will be fine.'

'No. . .' She takes out a tissue and blows her nose. My head is throbbing. I stare at her in the bright fluorescent light. 'I was so wrong,' she says. 'Can you . . . will you forgive me?'

Eh?

'Ummm. . .' I have no idea what to say. Then she tilts her head up, and her eyes are closed and her lips kind of pursed and I get the idea really quickly that she wants me to kiss her. But I can't because I don't want to totally repel her. I quickly puff air into my hand while her eyes are shut and the smell is toxic.

So I say, 'I don't know what you mean,' and Claire looks a bit annoyed and glances at the café woman and says, 'Let's go somewhere more private.'

We wander round the corner, to the road with the bus station. I look at Starbucks – warm and cosy – but she stalks past and finds a lonely bench, which would be very romantic if it wasn't sleeting and I wasn't suffering from terminal barf-breath.

So we sit there, kind of awkward, and she's looking up at me hopefully and I'm looking around, pretending that it would never occur to me to kiss her. After a while she whispers, 'Did I hurt you when I kicked you?'

'Nah,' I lie.

'Good,' she says, 'I shouldn't have done that. I was just panicking about being late.'

'What about now? Won't they be looking for you?'

She shrugs. 'I don't care. You and me . . . it's more important than anything else. They can say what they want. No one's going to stop us being together.'

I don't want to break the mood. I don't want to remind her of the bad things. But I can't quite stop myself.

'But what about the other stuff, Claire? My email?'

'I don't care. I know you are a good person. I'm sure there was a reason for everything you did.'

That's just it. There was no good reason really for stabbing Arron – how could there be? I'm not completely certain if there was a good reason for carrying a knife in the first place. And the main reason for lying to the police is to save myself from going to a Young Offender Institution, however much I try and tell myself that I'm doing it so Arron doesn't get all the blame.

'Erm. . .' I start, but she puts her finger on my lips.

'It's OK . . . when I thought about, you know,

Bella and Edward – well, nothing could stop their love, and it's the most beautiful love story, and she just totally believes in him and that's how I feel about you.'

What *is* she going on about? Do I know these people?

'Umm. . .?'

'You know . . . *Twilight*. . . Even though he's killed, like, fifty people and he really wants to kill her, she just loves him so much . . . and he loves her . . . and that's what matters.'

These can't possibly be real people. It must be some film or book or TV series about a serial killer. A girly film about a serial killer. Weird. A year ago, when I lived on Planet Girl and I read almost every magazine in Mr Patel's shop, I might have known what she meant. Anyway, it sounds like Claire's got a bit mixed up.

'Ummm . . . he wants to kill her? That can't be right.'

'Oh,' she says, dreamily. 'He's a vampire. His skin sparkles like diamonds. He's beautiful, just like you.'

Huh. 'Beautiful' is way too like 'pretty boy', if you ask me.

'Oh . . . and in the end? He kills her, right?' I know how these vampire movies go.

'No . . . but they can't touch too much . . . but that's OK, because it's just because he's a vampire. . .'

She's blushing. She's so sweet.

'Oh, right, good,' I say.

'You should read it,' she says, 'and you'll see what I mean. But you mustn't read the other books because Bella isn't really *worthy* of him. I would never mess around with a werewolf like she does.'

Good.

'And the fourth book is just really bad. I personally don't even believe the same person wrote it.'

She's mad, but so lovely, and I'm going crazy because I'm desperate to kiss her. I can smell her shampoo and it's really turning me on. Mmmm. It's either strawberry or fruits of the forest. My whole body is aching to touch her . . . hold her . . . but I can't. If she sniffs vomit on my breath, she'll go off me forever. I have to exercise complete self control. It's killing me.

Archie's phone vibrates in my back pocket. I pull it out. He's sent me a text. It says, 'WTF? U barfed? Fckwt. Wr r u? Yr mum here. on rampage. r u on run? kl. A.'

'Oh shit. Shit. Claire, she's here. My mum. Shit.'

I'm shaking. I'm not ready to be dragged off to Birmingham. I need some time to think. That's what I never do. Stuff happens and I react and I screw things up. I need to work out what I'm going to do. I wanted Mr Henderson's advice but I'll just have to rely on myself.

'We'll tell her,' says Claire, 'we'll tell her and my parents that we have to be allowed to go on seeing each other. They can't stop us. We just have to show them how strongly we feel.'

'It's not that simple, Claire. My life is really complicated. I have to work things out.' My heart is beating fast and loud, and I'm sure she must be able to hear it.

'Well, what will happen?' she asks, 'What are you going to do?'

'I think . . . I need to think,' I say slowly. 'I'll come back later. Tell them I'll be there soon.'

She squeezes my hand. 'I'll stay with you.' Her eyes are shining, and she reaches out and strokes my face. My skin tingles, and a shiver runs through me. I lean towards her . . . but I can't . . . I can't. I seize her hand and squeeze it, but turn my head away.

'No, Claire, I need to think things through by myself. I'm sorry.'

I walk with her back to the corner of the road where the hostel is. 'I wont be long,' I say. She looks upset . . . confused. . . I'm lying, but she knows it, I'm sure, so it's not really a lie. It's true in my heart.

Like most things in my life, it's almost true.

CHAPTER 18
Night Bus

I need somewhere where no one's going to find me. Somewhere I can think. Somewhere warm and dry.

I start walking aimlessly along the seafront, and I find myself back at the bus station. I glance longingly at Starbucks – dark and closed – and then I have an idea. If I get a coach to London then I can connect on to anywhere in the country. I'll lose myself somewhere random and get hours of warm, dry thinking time. The last bus to London goes in half an hour. I buy a ticket with a note peeled off Archie's stash – where did he get his money? – and climb aboard.

It's all going round and round in my head – Claire, the police, my mum – like clothes in a tumble dryer, and I'm trying really hard to concentrate and make a plan, sort it all out, but then everything's dark and someone's shaking me and saying, 'Time to get out, son.' I jolt awake to find we've arrived in London and it's freezing cold and I'm starving and my head is aching. My mouth tastes like it's stuffed with rotting cabbage. It's 1 am and there are no coaches anywhere for at least six hours. Why didn't I realise? Now I'm stranded.

London's strange at night. There's none of the usual noise and rush, so every little noise seems louder, every movement blurry and shocking. It's like a horror film before the killing starts. You know something bad's going to happen; it's just a matter of detail. It's too quiet, too empty – I need to go somewhere.

Then a name comes into my head and I know . . . I know what I must do. I know who to talk to. I don't want to, but I must.

First I pull out Archie's phone. The battery is running down and I probably haven't got much time to use it. I run down his contacts list until I find Patrick and Helen's number. I push the button.

It rings four, five times, and I'm just about to give up. Then Patrick's voice barks in my ear, 'Who's that? Archie, is that you? Ty?'

I try and speak – I really do – but my mouth is too dry. So I sit at a bus shelter, phone pressed to my ear, rocking myself slowly while I listen to him asking where I am, what's going on, can he come and get me?

He says something in French, something soothing and kind, and I like how it sounds, but I'm too tired to understand. Then he switches back to English. It's OK, he says, no one is angry. No one's going to make me do anything I don't want to do. I just need to come home.

What does he mean, *home*?

'Tyler,' he says, 'I think that's you. We're all very worried about you. Can you tell me where you are?'

No. I can't.

'You're not in trouble,' he says. 'Nicki and Danny, they know they made a mess of it earlier. Everyone's calmed down now. We've found Archie. We just need to find you and everything will be all right.'

I find a voice, although it doesn't sound much like mine. 'No, it won't.'

'As all right as we can make it, I promise. Now, where are you?'

I'm distracted by a noise – a drunk, staggering in circles, gobbing on the pavement and shouting, 'I told them, I told them.'

'Where are you?' Patrick asks again. I reply, 'I don't know,' which is a lie geographically, but true in other ways.

'Ty, listen,' he says, 'Find somewhere to go – a café or something – and call me from there. I will come and get you. Wherever it is. Just find somewhere and stay put.'

If only it could be that easy. 'Patrick, were you a soldier?' I ask.

'A what?'

'A soldier. In the war.'

He sounds a bit surprised. 'I'd have to be about fifteen years older than I am to have fought in the Second World War, Tyler.'

'Oh, sorry.'

'But my father did,' he says. 'Why do you ask?'

'Oh. I dunno.' I was kind of hoping he might know a bit about this shell shock business is the truth, but obviously he doesn't. I'll just have to get to the point.

'Patrick, did I really live with you? Why?'

'You mean when you were small?'

'Yup.'

'Danny asked us to look after you for a while. He was finding it impossible to care for you because he was studying. It was a difficult time.'

'But what about my mum?'

Patrick doesn't say anything. I think the phone's gone dead and I check the battery – it's really low – but then I hear his voice. He sounds all croaky, and not like him at all.

'He put her in hospital, Ty. Has she never told you what happened? You really need to talk to your parents about this.'

So I was right. He did hit her. If Patrick says so, it must be true. I don't need to ask any more. It's freezing cold and I've got other things to do.

'Ummm . . . look, I'd better go. Thanks.'

'Ty . . . don't just hang up, for God's sake. Tell me where you are. We'll sort it—'

But then there's nothing. The battery is flat.

I sit there for a bit with the cold, dead phone pressed to my ear. What I should've done is written down some of the numbers in the contacts list while it was still working. Then I could've used a phone box. I didn't think of that. I am stupid. But I don't even know why I was phoning in the first place. Probably just to delay what I have to do now. And now I have to do it.

I walk slowly away from the deserted coach station to look for a bus stop. I know which bus I want. This is one end of the line. I'm going right to the other end.

And here is the bus stop and there are night buses every thirty minutes and by the time one turns up my teeth are chattering with the cold. And then I realise I don't have an Oyster card, so I have to pay with a ten pound note, which annoys the bus driver. I don't belong in London any more. I'm a stranger. I'm homeless. I climb up to the top deck where there won't be so many people.

And we're driving through empty, dark streets,

and the bus fills up and empties again and I'm pleased with the way I'm coping, not jittering like I did before, quite calm . . . even sleepy . . . when a guy comes and sits next to me. He's taller than me and he's in a hoodie as well and he smells all sweaty.

I inch towards the window, and then I realise that he's got two mates with him. They're sitting in behind us, no one else is anywhere near, and they're all looking at me. I don't like the way they're looking.

Sweaty nudges me. 'Where're you going, man?'

I ignore him. I stare at the dark window. All I can see is my reflection. My dark hood. My big eyes. I don't know what I look like to him, but to me I look scared.

His mate leans over the seat and sticks his face right up next to mine. His breath smells of beer and curry. I flinch away. 'Answer the question, pretty boy,' he growls.

'Umm . . . dunno. . .' I say.

'Wanna get there safe and sound?' says Sweaty.

'Umm . . . yeah.'

Something jabs my side. I look down. There's a flick knife in his hand and it's pressing against my ribs. Right now it's unflicked, but in a second he could slice through my clothes and skin. We both stare at the knife like it's nothing to do with either of us. I can feel myself getting all hot – I must be blushing – it's like he's touched me wrong.

'What've you got for me?' he says. Just like Arron did to Rio in the park. That's what you say when you want to take someone's phone or iPod off them. It's not because you want whatever it is. It's to show who's got the power. And right now, I have none.

'Umm. . .' I feel around in my pocket and pull out Archie's phone. He pockets it and his mate laughs and says, 'What else?'

The only other thing is the money. I scrunch forward and pull the roll of notes out of my back pocket and hand it over. He takes it from me – our hands touch – his skin brushes mine and I pull away fast. Maybe the movement scares him, because the knife clatters onto the ground and out of nowhere he smashes his fist right into my face.

I fall back against the window and bash my head against the glass and the pain's crushing my head from back to front. I can hear them laughing, then thudding down the stairs, and the bus stops and starts again.

I'm lying on the seat, tasting blood and clutching my eye and wondering if he's knocked it clean out of its socket. And gradually the bright lights of the bus seep through and I can see again. I sit up and retch a bit. I'm shivering, but this time I don't think it's to do with the cold because it's steaming hot on the bus. An old lady climbs up to the top deck, takes one look at me and goes straight into reverse gear back down the steps.

The bus turns sharp left and the knife spins under my seat. I reach down and stuff it into my back pocket. Because if anyone else says 'What've you got for me?' I've got nothing to give them at all.

And then we reach the end of the line and I get off. And I know where I am and I even know why. I've come home.

CHAPTER 19
Running

My face is throbbing and blood is stiffening on my chin. My head is aching and I'm dying to pee. I'm jumpy as hell – I know that if I get spotted by the wrong people then that's it. I'll be dead on arrival. But there's still something really good about walking down the street where we used to live.

I get to our old front door and flatten my nose against the shop window. I'm like a ghost of myself.

Last time I was here, the air was thick with the smells of smoke and petrol, the crackle of burning magazines, the sizzle of melting confectionary. The glass was smashed to diamonds and the street was lit with a flickering, yellowy glow.

Now it's dark and still, and you wouldn't know it had ever happened. Mr Patel has even made a kind of window display showing his wide selection of pot noodles. And if I try very hard I can pretend that I'm about to climb the steps to our flat. Back to when I had a home. Back to when I had a life.

And then there's a sharp tap on my shoulder. *Christ.* I spin around, my hand flying to my back pocket – but I freeze when a voice says, 'What're you doing out at this time, lad?'

My hand stops in mid-air. Police. You never used to see a policeman walking on our road at night – way too dangerous – but maybe things have changed.

There are two of them. One old, one young. They look me up and down, and the younger one says, 'Don't I know you?'

'No . . . sir. . .' I think maybe he was at the police station when I gave my first statement.

'What's happened to you, son?' says the older guy. 'You look like you've taken a bit of a beating.'

'I'm OK.'

'Want me to call an ambulance? Call your folks?'

'No, thanks. I'm just going home.'

'Where's home?'

Good question. I wish I could just say 'here' and disappear. I wonder if anyone new lives in our flat now. The thought makes me feel sick. I wave my hand vaguely and say, 'Stamford Hill way.'

'OK,' says the younger one. 'That's quite a way away. So what're you doing here right now?'

I shrug. 'On my way home.'

'What were you doing, looking into this shop?' he asks.

'Umm. Nothing.'

'This shop has had a bit of trouble lately,' he says, 'There was a fire here a few months ago. Know anything about that?'

'Umm. No.' I don't sound very convincing, even to myself.

'We're going to have to search you, you're acting suspiciously,' he says, and starts gabbling a load of stuff about the powers given to him by some act of Parliament, and what his name is and what police station he comes from – like I *care* – and all the time I can feel the heavy knife tugging at my jeans.

'OK, son,' says the older guy, 'It won't take long.' And he comes towards me, arms out, but I dodge past him – 'Oi – stop!' he yells – and I'm sprinting along the high street, past the kebab shop, past the tattoo parlour, with both of them chasing me, but I can run faster, I can run faster than anyone and I'm down an alleyway and over a wall and into the park and they're not there any more.

And my ankle is killing me, and I'm coughing

my guts up, but they've gone and they never found the knife and once the coughing stops everything will be OK again.

I've been in this park about a million times, so I know it really well, but the last time I was here was the time that Rio got killed. And I never thought I'd come back ever, especially at 3 am when it's so dark and cold and if there are ghosts anywhere, they'll be here.

Gradually my eyes adjust to the moonlight. I'm right back at the place where it happened. Where Rio died and everything changed. There's a few bunches of dead flowers tied to a tree. 'Our beloved son and brother' reads one note. 'RIP fallen souljah' says another. This is where I've been running from and this is where I've been running to. But it's not a good place to be.

Then I hear it. An eerie howl, a weeping sound, like someone's crying for Rio and Arron and all of us – and it's not me, because my hand's right by my mouth, I can taste the salt of my skin – and I'm shivering all over and I fall to my knees. There's no going back – the police will be looking for me. I'm terrified of the next place I'm heading. But this is unbearable.

The knife sits heavy in my pocket, weighing me down, pulling me backwards. I can't bear knowing it's there. I'm too scared to go on without it – but then I think of blood splashing out of Arron's arm, and I know that

I have to get rid of it.

I want to throw it in the bushes, but I stop myself just in time. This is a children's playground – what if some little kid finds it and works out how to undo the catch? In the end, I put it in the bin that's meant for dog shit. Surely that ought to be safe.

And then, as I turn away, I see something staring straight at me. Two dark eyes, shining from a shadow, a long furry nose. . . I gasp, and my heart kind of jumps – *Meg!* How's she found me here? Patrick?

Words bang in my head . . . *hallucination . . . you nutter . . . you fuckwit . . .* but then the staring eyes blink and I know what it is. A fox, a beautiful wild fox, one of my favourite London things. When you see them it's like magic, straight out of a story book.

Just for a moment we gaze at each other – he must have howled, wailing to the moon – and I hold out my hand. It'd be great to have a fox as – no, not as a pet – a friend. Something to run with. Something a bit more reliable than most people. I stand up very slowly and step towards him, my hand outstretched.

And then he runs and I run and I find the bit of wall I need and I clamber over the fence and I'm running to the stairway and climbing the steps and bashing at the door. Arron's door. Even though I know Arron can't be there.

CHAPTER 20
Nathan

I'm praying for Arron's mum, but Nathan's eyes are glaring into the dark and he's trying to slam the door shut. But I've got my shoulder in and after a few silent seconds he recognises me, and in that moment of surprise I push into the hallway and collapse onto the floor.

Nathan's cussing his head off in a furious whisper. 'Christ . . . fu'ing Jesus Christ man, what the fu' you doin' here? Tryin' to get yoursel' killed? Are you mental or what?'

He's shaking and sweating and he's got a weird look on his face – if I didn't know better, I'd say he was scared. He's crouched over me, and little bits of spit shower my face.

I force out the words, 'I need your help. Nathan. Please.'

'Shut up,' he says, 'Keep quiet. In here.' And he pulls me up and drags me into their lounge, where I trip over a naked Barbie and step onto her pink car, crash into the coffee table and sprawl on to the sofa.

Nathan kicks the Barbie across the room. It's usually as clean and tidy in here as the hospital where their mum works, and I must have looked a bit surprised because he growls, 'Mum's away. She's taken Jasmine to visit Arron at the Young Offender Institution. It's best if they stay overnight.'

Jasmine is their littlest sister. She's only five. I get a sudden picture of her sucking her thumb, hair tied up with a pink bobble, smiling, all confused in a room full of sobbing mums and silent boys.

'Oh,' I say. I'd hoped Arron's mum would be there, to sort out my face and stop Nathan killing me. Now anything could happen.

The sofa feels really lumpy, and I reach underneath the cushions and pull out Mermaid Barbie. Once upon a time, Arron's little sisters were always nagging me to play with them and when I was feeling kind, I would . . . if the football we were watching was boring or something. No wonder Arron used to laugh and call me a girl.

I turn the doll over and over in my hands, hating her silly smile and false boobs. That's the problem with people who've known you a long time. They remember how soft you were before you learned to be cool. That's why I liked being Joe. He was never stupid. He was never young. He certainly never played with Barbies.

Nathan's staring at me. 'Come here,' he says. I shrink away and he grabs me by the shoulder and drags me over to the sink – their kitchen and lounge are all one room. He's taller than me – only just, though – and he's got huge muscles. There's no point even trying to fight.

He turns on the cold tap. Shit. He's going to fill up the sink and drown me . . . or torture me . . . and then there's the cooker, he could burn me . . . or just chuck me over the edge of the balcony. . .

But then he wrings out a tea towel in the water and says, 'Clean yourself up, man, you look like crap.' He starts rooting around in a cupboard until he finds a first aid box, and he fishes out some antiseptic cream and a plaster.

I dab at my face, but it stings too much, and I stumble back to the sofa, holding the wet cloth carefully over my eye. Nathan gets a can of coke out of the fridge and hands it to me. He sits down in the armchair. All we need is Arron, and the telly on for Football Focus, and it'd be just like old times. I take a little sip of the coke, and it's good to wash away the taste of death in my mouth.

And then he says, 'So, li'l Ty, you done some growing up, boy.'

'Yeah.'

'You've got yoursel' a kinda interesting look there.'

'Umm. Yeah.'

'How's your mum?' He scratches his head and looks at the ceiling when he says this, but I'm used to everyone's big brothers and dads . . . anyone male really, teachers, shopkeepers, whatever . . . fancying my mum.

'She's OK. Pregnant.'

'Pregnant? Jesus. Who's the lucky guy?'

'Her boyfriend. He's dead.'

'Shit. Bummer. That's bad.' He's staring at the ceiling again.

'How's Arron?' I ask nervously.

'He's OK,' he says. 'He's OK. Considering. Hoping the trial will be soon. They tell you anything, the cops?'

'No.'

He's looking at me straight on now, eyes narrowed to slits. 'I told you to keep your mouth shut. You shoulda listened, eh?'

I take a gulp of coke.

'Yes . . . no . . . but the police would've found me anyway. They knew I was Arron's friend, and loads of people saw me when I stopped the bus.'

'You never realised you needed to keep your mouth shut about Jukes? You never knew who his old man is? Arron never told you?'

'No.' I look back at stupid, innocent, ignorant Ty and I'm not surprised at the sneer I see on Nathan's face. He's shaking his head. 'My gran said I should just tell the truth. For the family of that boy.'

'Oh yeah. Dat boy. Dat innocent boy.'

'Yeah.' We don't seem to be getting very far. 'Nathan . . . you gotta help me, man. These people who want to kill me, you know them, don't you? You could ask them . . . ask them not to. . . I can't live like this, Nathan, you gotta help me, man, I can't do it no more . . . I'll do anything.'

It's like he hasn't heard me. He's staring at the ceiling again. I hear myself babbling like a scared little baby and then he says, 'How's your gran, Ty? Is she OK?'

'Umm . . . she's . . . she's . . . what do you know about my gran?'

He's chewing his thumbnail now and I swear I've never seen Nathan look so . . . so . . . nervous? Christ. I get it. So *guilty*. That's how he looks.

'What do you know about my gran?' I ask again, but this time it comes out slow and angry, and when he shrugs and looks at me, I know. He was involved in beating up my gran. Nearly killing her. Putting her in intensive care. Turning her into someone who's scared all the time.

I lunge at him, punch my arm across his neck to knock the air out, then slice the mermaid's sharp tail hard at his eyes.

He swipes me away, yelling out loud – with pain, I hope – and I crash to the ground and next he's got me spreadeagled on the floor and I'm biting his hand and reaching for his throat and we crash into the telly and it totters over, smashing onto the floor with a bang like a bomb going off.

We're locked together, panting fury into each other's faces, sweat and spit, blood and tears. He rolls me over and wrenches my arm up at an impossible angle, pinning my hand to my shoulder blade so I have to bite my tongue to stop myself screaming.

'Is this what you did to her?' I gasp. 'Is this what you did?'

And then there's something soft, something pink blocking out the light. Cold little hands touch my face and a voice squeaks, 'Stop! Nathan! Stop. It's OK! It's Ty!'

CHAPTER 21
Duke of York

'Shanice!' shouts Nathan. 'Get back to bed, girl.'

Shanice wraps her arms around me.

'It's Ty . . . Nathan, let him go! Let him go!' And she aims a kick in his direction.

Shanice is only seven so she's not a great fighter. But Nathan lets go of my arm. I lie still on the carpet, crunchy with glass from the busted telly.

'Stay where you are,' Nathan growls. 'If you hurt my sister, you're dead.'

'Ty wouldn't hurt no one,' says Shanice, her eyes big and teary. 'Ty . . . are you all right? Nathan didn't mean it . . . he must've thought you were a burglar, but it's not, it's Ty.'

'Get up,' says Nathan. I pull myself up and stagger over to the sofa. My arm feels like it's hanging by a thread.

Blood dribbles from a cut on Nathan's forehead where Mermaid Barbie did her work.

Shanice leaps on me, hugging me tight, kissing my sore face. I wish she'd stop. I am so full of hate that I don't want to think or feel anything else. And I especially don't want to start crying, which is a distinct possibility right now.

'Shanice, you go back to bed,' says Nathan, 'You gotta be in school in three hours, you need to sleep.'

But Shanice sticks her thumb in her mouth, shakes her head and cuddles up next to me. 'I'm staying here with Ty so you can't fight him no more,' she says. 'Ty, when is Arron coming home?'

'I don't know,' I answer, 'I'm sorry, Shanice. I don't know.'

'Not for a long time,' says Nathan, and he goes into the girls' bedroom and brings out Shanice's Disney Princess duvet. He tucks it around her. She's asleep in two minutes.

Nathan gets a wodge of kitchen roll and mops his face. He unlocks the door to the balcony and drags out the busted television. He hoovers up the glass and he tidies Shanice's toys, shaking each one carefully to make sure there's no glass tangled into a Barbie's hair or sticking to a piece of Play Doh.

He doesn't say one word to me until he sits down

again. Then he whispers, 'You're wrong. I never hurt your gran. I wouldn't do something like that. Whoever told you that was lying.'

'No one told me,' I say slowly. 'I just . . . I just knew.'

He shakes his head. 'You can't just go off on one because you think you know something. You have to make sure. Check things out. You can't jump to conclusions, man, you gotta sit tight and see what's what.'

'You know 'em . . . you know Jukes and his family, the ones that want to kill me. You could've been working for them.'

'I could've,' he says, 'but I wasn't. I never was. I stayed clear of all of that. Not like my little brother. He couldn't wait to get involved.'

'Arron? He wasn't . . . I don't think. . .'

'He never told you the half of it,' says Nathan, 'In fact he never told you any of it, did he? Your mate Arron.' He's still whispering because of Shanice, but his voice drips with contempt.

My head is buzzing and I'm struggling not to yawn. It's hot in the flat, and Shanice's warm body pins me to the sofa.

'He said . . . he said we needed protection.' I say. 'He'd been mugged. He told me to carry a knife, and he took me to meet Jukes and Mikey and he said we needed protection. And they said we could have it if we did some jobs for them and I said no, but then . . . then later Arron wanted me to help him do a mugging. So we could be in the gang. So we'd get protection. I said no, but maybe . . . maybe if I'd done what he wanted then it would've been different. Maybe Rio wouldn't have got killed.'

'Yeah, yeah, I hear you,' says Nathan. 'Arron's lawyer showed me your witness statement. Load of old bollocks.'

I'm confused. I think about what I've just said. That was all true, I'm sure of it. It's only later on, the bit where I slashed Arron's arm, that I started lying.

'Think about it,' says Nathan. 'Arron had been doing little jobs for dem boys for months. Selling drugs for dem at your posh school. And the rest. Nicking phones. Nicking iPods. He'd done 'em all the favours he needed to get protection. Why suddenly go to them begging for help?'

'He got mugged. He got beaten up. He was scared.'

'He was beaten up by the others. The rivals. The other soldiers on the street. Because he crossed into their territory.'

'Oh.'

'He saw an opportunity, my li'l brother Arron. He thought this is my chance. My chance to give Jukes what he wants.'

'Oh. . .?' He's losing me.

'You still don't get it, do you?' he says, shaking his head.

'Umm. No. Not really.'

'Still think your best friend Arron was looking out for you? Trying to get you protection on the streets?'

'Umm . . . yeah. . .'

'Huh. Arron knew Jukes wanted you in his gang. Under his wing. So he made out he was mugged by strangers. Scared you . . . wound you up. Thought he could deliver you to Jukes, like Jukes wanted.'

'But why?' I'm whispering too. But underneath, I'm screaming, *No . . . Arron wouldn't lie to me . . . he wouldn't trick me . . . he's my friend. . .*

'Jukes had his eye on you for a long time.' says Nathan. He shakes his head. 'I blame myself. I shoulda warned you somehow.'

'What do you mean?'

'Jukes's old man,' he says. 'Drinks at the Duke of York.' And he spreads his hands out in front of him like everything should be clear now.

The Duke of York was a pub ten shops along from our old flat. 'It's so near, it's like drinking in my own front room,' my mum used to say, 'except I'd keep it a lot cleaner.' It was a big, dark, dusty old boozer with velvet seats and black wood furniture and a new manager who was trying to turn around the effects of the smoking ban by bringing in stuff like cocktails and happy hours, quizzes and karaoke nights. My mum loved karaoke night at the Duke of York. My mum . . . my mum . . . *Jesus.*

I look at Nathan and I think he's telling the truth.

'My *mum*? This is about her?'

'Jukes's old man was a big fan of karaoke,' says Nathan. Then he sighs. 'So was every guy who drinks at the Duke of York. Your mother is a legend, Ty.'

I'm not sure if he's disrespecting her. I frown, and he says, 'It's a well-known fact dat she's very picky. Dat's why Jukes's old man never made a move. Dat's why he thought he'd get you involved; get her in a situation where she's beggin' for his help. To keep you outta trouble.'

'Did Arron. . . Did Arron *know* this?'

'Nah. Arron, he just thought Jukes wanted you as a soldier. To be honest, I'm not sure how much Jukes even knew. After all, there's his mum to think about . . . but his old man, he's got a few girls on the side, in flats, you know. . . And I think somewhere in Arron's thick head he thought you should toughen up a bit. Be a man. Like he thought he was.'

'So it was all a set-up? I was meant to mug Rio?'

'Rio. . .' says Nathan. 'You do realise, dontcha, dat Rio was in the other gang? Dat weren't no random victim walking though dat park? The idea was to get

Rio roughed up a bit, give dem boys a message. Revenge, like. Dat's why Jukes and Mikey showed up. Make sure you picked on the right man. The two of you walked straight into a set up.'

I swallow. This is all a bit much. I think back to the day when Arron and I met Jukes and Mikey. We'd just got off the tube. My head was full of French homework. Arron had hardly spoken on the train and I'd pulled out my exercise book so that I wouldn't look like I was being ignored.

Then he'd said, 'We're meeting some friends of mine . . . Jukes . . . Mikey . . . you know?' And I'd replied, '*Je ne sais pas,*' because I wasn't thinking, and he'd snapped, 'Can you *try* not to be too gay.'

And then later, he asked me, told me, begged me to do this little job for Jukes and Mikey. 'You'll be doing yourself a favour,' he said. 'You'll be part of something, have people to look out for you. Go on, man. I'll back you up. Don't be scared.'

But I was scared, and I ran away and I spied on him and Rio pulled out his knife and got killed.

And if I'd been the dead one, then they'd probably have had a wake at the Duke of York, and Jukes's old man could've comforted my mum and offered help and support through her terrible loss. And a flat. Christ.

'How d'you know all this?' I ask, suddenly suspicious.

'How do I know you haven't made it all up?'

Nathan shrugs. 'Arron told me some. Some I heard. Some's not difficult to guess.'

Shanice stirs in her sleep and Nathan leans forward and picks her up. 'C'mon, Shani, time for bed,' he says, and nods at me to bring her duvet. He carries her into her room and puts her in the bottom bunk. I cover her up and we stand and look at her sweet, sleeping face.

Then he says, 'You must be tired. You want Arron's bed?' I don't really, but I am shattered, so I go into the room that he and Arron share and I take off my shoes and I lie down on the bed and I stare at the Arsenal posters up on the wall. Arsène Wenger is looking straight at me, and his gloomy French face seems to sneer at the idiot who wanted to protect the friend who was lying and lying and lying. . .

Nathan sticks his head round the door. 'I'll have to take Shanice to school a bit later, but you just sleep and I'll wake you up lunchtime,' he says.

'OK,' I say, and Nathan pauses and says, 'Look, Ty, I'm not making no excuses for Arron. He's done a lot of bad things and he's gonna pay for it now.'

I turn my head away. I don't trust myself to say anything.

'You feel bad, right, because your friend weren't straight with you,' says Nathan. 'Fair enough.

But just remember one thing. He thought he was doing you a favour.'

CHAPTER 22
Edge

The sun is shining in my eyes, and although I groan and roll over and try and block it out, it's no good. I'm awake. I look at my watch. It's midday.

I stare at Arron's ceiling and I think about all the lies he told. And all the lies I told. A world where everyone tells lies all the time is like a world where everyone carries a knife. You think it's going to help you, but it only makes things worse.

And I wonder how my life would change – how I would be – if I only tell the truth from now on. No matter what happens.

But if I tell the truth about how I hurt Arron – and right now, this minute, I'm pleased I hurt him, I want to hurt him again, I *hate* him – then I will end up in court and in prison and I won't have a future any more.

But do I have much of a future anyway?

I can hear Nathan moving around, and the door creaks open. I quickly shut my eyes and pretend to be asleep. The door creaks shut again, but it doesn't completely close and I can hear him talking. Either there's someone there with him or he's on the phone.

'He's here. . .' he mutters, 'Sleeping. Came last night. Yes. Yes. Come right now. . . Not going anywhere.'

Jesus. He's telling someone about me. He must've been lying to me. He must be on the phone to Jukes's gang . . . maybe Jukes's dad himself. . . *Christ.* They're coming here. They're going to get me.

I'm breathing in little jittery gasps and my heart is thumping. Sweat prickles my armpits. There's a sharp taste of sick in my mouth. I rush to the window, but it's tiny . . . I'd never get out . . . and there's a two-floor drop underneath, straight onto concrete.

I creep to the door. No sound. Maybe I can get out. I sit down, tie my shoes and open the door, slow and silent. No one. Nothing. I move slowly towards the front door, reach the handle, push it down. Damn. It's locked. I scurry back to the bedroom.

I hear a burst of Dizzee Rascal. Nathan's phone. 'Yeah.' I hear him say. 'Still sleeping. Tell you what, I'll come down and show you where to put it. See you in a minute.' And I hear a door open and close, and he's walking to the front door . . . and it slams shut. And I run and try it again, but no, it's still locked. I'm a rat in a trap.

There's nowhere to hide. I go into Shanice and Jasmine's room, and think about crawling under the bunk bed. And then I imagine being dragged out feet first, and the mess if they shoot me there and then. The blood in their pink and cream palace.

I'm back in the living room. I'm sitting on the sofa. I'm sweating and moaning . . . I can hear myself almost crying. This is it. I'm going to die.

And then I remember Nathan unlocking the balcony door when he dragged out the busted TV – and he didn't lock it again. I leap to the door, pushing the curtain aside, fumbling to get it open. It works! I was right! I pull the curtain behind me and step out into the winter sunshine.

There's a dryer hung with wet washing, and the telly, and loads of plants and a ladder – but not a ladder that's long enough to get me anywhere. I'll just have to climb down to the balcony below. From there, maybe I can jump . . . maybe it'll be OK. . .

The barrier is half-wall, half-railings. The railings will be better for climbing – maybe I can grip them as I climb. I swing my left leg over. And then I look down.

Christ. It's a long way. I close my eyes, then open them again. It doesn't look any better. It doesn't look any more possible. I swing my right leg experimentally. And I'm hit by a fit of shaking and all-over sweating that leaves me wet through like I've been thrown in a swimming pool.

My hands are sliding off the railing. My teeth are chattering. I can't get a grip . . . I can't do this. But I can't get off the railings either. I'm stuck. If I sway backwards I'll fall. If I swing forwards I'm trapped. And I can hear voices on the other side of the curtain.

Jesus. I'll have to go for it. I sneak another look down, towards the balcony I'm aiming for. It's about fifty miles away. What was I thinking? But maybe if I slide down the railings . . . and then swing. . . I must be crazy . . . but I'm pulling my right leg up to pull it over the railings too.

A clutch of girls with prams are watching me. 'Don't do it!' one of them yells. She's pulling out a mobile. They're all shouting now. 'Stop! Help! You'll kill yourself!'

I try and speed up, but my body is against me. It won't obey my orders. My foot sticks at the top of the railings. I'm balanced, shaking, about to fall . . . eyes screwed tight shut . . . waiting for a shot . . . waiting to feel myself drop.

And then I hear a noise and I open my eyes. And I see the curtains push back, and the balcony door open.

CHAPTER 23
Rollercoaster

I'm struggling to release my foot. I lurch backwards. My hands scrabble on the railings. There's a gasp from the watching girls, a scream. . . Nathan bursts onto the balcony, yelling, 'No!'

I'm falling. . .

And somehow, someone grabs my shoulders, pulling me forwards.

I'm gripped tight. I smell leather and smoke. Someone in a biker jacket is pulling me towards him. I'm wriggling to get free, thrashing and twisting. . . 'Got him,' says a man's voice, 'Grab him . . . pull him. . .'

Someone's holding me round the waist and I'm shaking, to scared to open my eyes. Waiting for the blow. Waiting to die.

But then my legs slither back onto the balcony side

of the railings and I topple forward, pushing against the biker jacket, and we tumble together onto the balcony floor. We're sprawled among the pot plants, covered with damp underpants, and this time I recognise the voice. 'It's OK. Stay calm. It's OK.'

It's my dad.

I'm taking huge gulps of air, trying hard to do what he says, stay calm, calm down, it's OK, stay calm, stay calm. I don't feel very calm. His arms wrap around me. 'It's OK,' he says into my hair. 'Everything's going to be fine.' His voice is soft and steady. His jacket is smooth and cold against my cheek. Gradually I stop shaking. My breath steadies.

Slowly, carefully, we separate. We stand up. He moves between me and the railings. He holds on to my arm as we walk back into the flat.

'Jesus, man,' says Nathan, 'I thought you were gonna throw yourself off. What the hell were you doing?'

I shake my head. I'm not sure I'm up to speaking right now.

'This is your dad, innit?' says Nathan, 'The sports lawyer. . . I went downstairs to check him out, check he was who he said he was. He looks just like you. Ty's told us a lot about you,' he adds. My dad looks a bit startled.

'It is . . . it is him,' I say. 'I thought . . . I thought it was them. Jukes's dad. I was trying to climb down.'

'Ty, man, you gotta stop thinkin',' says Nathan. 'You get it wrong every time.'

I duck my head down, chin to chest. My dad thanks Nathan for all his help, asks if I've got any stuff with me and agrees, yes, things do get very busy for him in the transfer season.

Then he hands me a motorcycle helmet, says, 'Put it on,' and we're out in the open, out in the daylight. Anyone could see us . . . but the helmets are protection and disguise. A great idea.

We walk down the stairs and my dad goes around a corner and there's a huge silver bike. He gestures to me to get on behind him. And then we're weaving in and out of traffic, driving past our old flat, climbing up and out of Hackney, racing faster and faster . . . up past the Emirates Stadium . . . up past Finsbury Park station.

I'm clinging on to him as tight as I can and I don't know if I'm scared or excited, happy or sad. The speed is all that matters. Air whacks my body, my nose is running, my eyes streaming. My hands are blue with cold, and I'm sure that any minute they'll go numb and I'll lose my grip and fall off. It's brilliant . . . like the best rollercoaster ever. . . I wonder if my dad would ever let me borrow it. I'm kind of disappointed when he pulls in to a street of red-brick houses, slows and stops.

'Here we are,' he says, taking off his helmet and

wheeling the bike into the front garden of a massive house. My head is spinning. Does he live here? What's a loser like him doing in a house like this? You have to be a total millionaire to own a house this size in London. Maybe my dad is really rich . . . maybe he's . . . oh my God, who has bikes like these in London? He's a drug dealer . . . my dad's a drug dealer.

And then I decide that I'm going to stop jumping to conclusions and I'd better keep quiet and wait and see.

'Keep the helmet on,' he says, 'Just until we get inside.' And he opens up the front door, which leads to a hallway and two more doors, and the one my dad opens is obviously to a flat, because there's a staircase. So he's not necessarily a total millionaire after all. Phew. Unless he's only a small-time drug dealer.

It's a really nice flat. I can tell as soon as we get up the stairs. The floors are polished boards, and the walls are unusual colours – blues and greys and kind of sludgey brown. . . It looks better than you'd think. . . And there are some really cool black and white photos framed on the wall – singers, musicians mostly, some faces I know, lots I don't.

He chucks his jacket and helmet on the floor, and I can't help noticing that there's a bright pink coat hanging on a coat hook. And a purple one next to it. And there's a vase of yellow flowers on a little table. So either my dad's married, or he lives with a girlfriend or he's some combination of gay and transvestite. I can't think of any other possibilities.

'You can take it off now, ' he says, and I realise that I must look like an astronaut exploring an alien planet. I kind of wish I could keep the helmet on.

He opens the door to a large, bright kitchen. The cupboards are shiny maroon. The counter top is stainless steel. There's a big pale wood table and another vase of flowers – huge fluffy purple ones mixed with massive white things with orange middles. These are serious flowers, not the sort you pick up from Tesco. Of course I'm not impressed by girly stuff like flowers and top quality iPod docks and shiny coffee machines.

My dad has lit a cigarette, although, like Archie, he smokes it with his hand sticking out of an open window.

'I'm trying to give up,' he says. 'Do you smoke? Help yourself.'

I give him one of my gran's looks. 'Oh, sorry,' he says. 'I suppose I'm meant to be giving you a lecture on the dangers of smoking, aren't I? You'll have to bear with me for a bit . . . let me get used to saying the right sort of thing. . .' His voice trails off, and he stubs out the cigarette, half-smoked, and throws it out of the window, which is not a very good example to set, but I don't say anything.

I don't know what to do. I shuffle my feet a bit and he says, 'Why don't you sit down? I'll put the kettle on. Do you drink coffee?'

'Tea,' I say, and I sit down at the table and look at the flowers and wonder who put them there. I'm almost certain it wasn't my dad. He's such a mess himself – under the biker jacket are ripped jeans and a baggy black jumper – that I can't imagine him poncing around arranging flowers. He sees where I'm looking. 'Grateful client,' he says, and fills the kettle at the sink. It doesn't sound like drugs to me. But I can't quite think what sort of client thanks a scruffy guy with a bunch of posh flowers. Weird.

In fact, the only sort of people I can think of who talked about clients were the tattoo artists at the parlour where I had my cleaning job and the massage girls next door. He can't be a nail technician. Can he? Hmmm. . . OK. I'm going to wait and see. My judgement isn't always very good.

He puts a cup of tea in front of me – I have to ask for sugar – and he says, 'You look terrible. Have you been in a fight?' I almost start laughing – I've not really done much else recently – but I hold it back and put my head down and mumble, 'Yeah . . . a bit. . . .'

'A bit? You've got a black eye, and your face is cut. What happened?'

I sneak a glimpse at him. He looks really worried, really concerned. But this is the guy who put my mum in hospital. This is someone who hits women. There must be a whole other side to him, a scary violent side. Like when I was Joe. Like when I stabbed Arron, punched Carl, bullied Claire.

I remember Claire's face when I gripped her wrists that day. Sometimes I just hate myself so much.

He's still waiting for an answer. His hand reaches out towards my face. I pull away. 'It's OK. I just got hit by someone.'

'By that boy? Nathan?'

'Umm . . . no, not really. . .'

'He said . . . he said you've changed a lot.'

'Yeah. Well. A lot's happened.'

'You'll have to tell me . . . I want to ask you. . .' he says. He's looking a bit nervous. I'm not giving him any encouragement. I drink my tea – it's nice to have a hot drink – and ignore him.

He gets up and opens the fridge. It's one of those giant American ones. There's all sorts of interesting stuff in there. Black olives and blue cheese and purple salad.

'You must be starving,' he says. 'Why don't I make you something to eat? Then we can talk.'

Eating sounds good. Talking not.

He starts pulling stuff out of the fridge. Crusty

white bread. Organic unsalted butter. Eggs. Tomatoes. 'I'm just going to check something,' he says. 'I'll be back in a minute.'

He goes out of the room. I drink my tea. An egg rolls across the table towards me. I put out my hand to stop it. It's cold from the fridge.

Then I jump backwards, my hand crunching the egg flat. My chair crashes to the ground.

On the egg was writing.

It said, *You're dead.*

CHAPTER 24
Eggs

I want to run. I'm looking from side to side, panic rising inside me, looking for a way out.

But what if I run and then someone kills my dad?

I crawl under the table, roll up into a ball and think as quickly as I can. My fingers are slimy with egg. It reminds me of . . . OK, let's not go there right now. . .

I make a list of possibilities:

a) I have gone mad. I am hallucinating again. Any minute now Alistair will appear, juggling eggs and laughing his head off.

b) Someone has broken into the flat and left a death threat for my dad (potential drug dealer) or me. On an egg. In the fridge. Where are they now? What sort of a nutter writes on an egg? How would they even know where to find me?

c) My dad is a sicko headcase and this is his idea of a wind-up. For some reason, this is the scariest thought so far and I pass swiftly on to

d) I am dead. I did actually fall off the balcony and the whole motorcycle thing was me going to heaven . . . except I'm pretty certain I won't get in there . . . but maybe going to a Catholic school gets you extra points. . . The Death Egg was God's way of breaking the news. It's symbolic, like an Easter egg, except not chocolate.

For a moment I'm convinced this must be it, but surely you'd feel something if you died. You'd realise. Wouldn't you? What did Alistair feel? And Rio? What if they didn't even know?

Anyway, I think once in church they said something about eggs meaning life, not death. Life. I'm almost certain.

My dad comes back into the kitchen. 'Ty?' he says. And then he spots me. He ducks down and I can see his upside-down face pretending that I'm not doing anything weird. 'Oh. What are you . . . are you all right?'

I look away and he says, 'Umm . . . shall I just give you a minute?'

His legs walk from the table to the sink and back again. I hear a swoosh as he cleans the eggy mess off the table. He makes himself a coffee. He cuts some bread.

Then he puts a plate with bread and cheese and tomatoes under the table, next to me. He doesn't say anything. I grab some bread and stuff it in my mouth. I'm starving – but it's rough against the roof of my mouth and I feel vomit rise in my throat.

My dad sits at the table. His legs are right by me. I could reach out and grab them. Obviously I don't want to.

'Ty,' he says, in his soft calm voice. 'Did something scare you?'

I have a stabbing pain in my throat. I lean my head on my knees.

'Was it something to do with the smashed egg?'

I can hear a little yelping sound. Maybe he has a puppy. I look around and then I realise that it was me. Shit. How embarrassing. I stick my arm over my face.

'Was there writing on it?'

My whole body is shuddering. It must be something to do with eating after being hungry for so long. I rock from side to side.

He slides off his chair and squeezes under the table next to me. His arm is around my shoulders. I can smell the coffee on his breath. My mum smells like that when she's drunk coffee. I try to inch away, but I'm not in total control of my movements right now.

'Ty,' he says. 'Was that it? It's OK. It was just a joke.

It doesn't mean anything.'

Christ. Option c) – he is a warped headcase. I *hate* him. If I wasn't feeling so crap, I'd kill him. I'd tear him apart. But all I can do is jerk away from him, kicking out with my legs and crashing my head against the table top. *Jesus!* My skull shatters like a smashed china bowl and I let out a howl of agony.

'Oh God. . .' he says, 'Look, come out, let me see what you've done.' He basically drags me out from under the table. I'm holding my broken head and I can feel big, fat baby tears on my face, but that's the least of my worries, given that I'm probably going to need brain surgery.

He's looking in the fridge again. 'Jesus . . . we don't have frozen peas or anything useful . . . ice, maybe.' He sticks a lumpy tea towel on my head and I yowl with pain again. An ice cube slides down my nose. 'Bugger,' says my dad. 'I'm sorry. I'm not very good at this.'

He can say that again. I'm trying very hard to stop snivelling, but it's not so easy. His fingers lightly touch my head. 'You've got a lump like an egg there,' he says, and I'm shaking again. I was sure the bone was broken . . . sure . . . certain . . . but I was wrong. I can't even trust the messages I get from my own body.

'Look,' he says, 'Look. It's OK.' And he's sticking the whole egg box in front of my nose. I stare at it.

Every egg has writing on it. Someone's used a black

felt tip. One says *if you*. Another says *Danny*. The third egg says *take my*. The last one has an exclamation mark. My dad reaches over to the table and picks up the remaining egg. He puts it in the box. The writing on it says *stuff*.

'What did yours say?' he asks.

'Umm. . .' I'm still trying to sort out what's going on.

'*I'll kill you*? Something like that?'

'*You're dead.*'

'Oh Ty. I'm so sorry.' There's the hint of a smile on his smug stupid face.

'You wrote it?'

'No, look, it's to me. *Danny, if you take my stuff you're dead!* It's a joke. I'm away a lot and when I'm back I don't buy much food and the girls I live with get pissed off when I eat theirs. Look.' He opens up the fridge and pulls out some grapes. There's a post-it note stuck on them. *Mess with my grapes and I'll cut off your balls.* My dad pulls a grape off the bunch and sticks it in his mouth. He grins at me, holding it between his white teeth, then swallows it. 'See how brave I am.'

I can't help it. I smile. The tears are drying up, thank God. It's such a frigging relief to have eliminated options a) to d) that it doesn't really matter if he lives with total psychopaths.

'Who are they? These girls?'

'One's called Tess and one's called Lucy,' he says, munching away at the grapes. He offers them to me. I take one, and then another one. They're really sweet and they don't have pips.

I'm kind of reeling from the news that my dad lives with two girls. There's a phrase for that. I'm trying to remember it. 'Threesome' is what the *News of the World* would say, but I'm thinking of something French . . . something I read in a magazine once. *Playboy* magazine actually. You don't grow up over a newsagent without learning a bit about the world. 'You have a *ménage a trois*?'

He laughs. 'Christ. Where'd you get that from . . . no, don't tell me. . . No, we're just flatmates. Or actually, because this is my flat, I am the landlord and they are my lodgers.'

'So you don't actually sleep with them?' I might as well get things straight.

He starts nibbling his thumbnail. 'Umm. Well. Tess and I have a sort of . . . you know . . . on and off. Off mostly. Off at the moment.'

'Oh, right. And Lucy?'

He's looking really shifty. 'Oh. Well. Once. Or twice. But . . . ummm . . . you don't want to be mentioning that to anyone. I mean . . . errr . . . Tess doesn't really know about Lucy at all and Lucy isn't fully aware . . . ummmm . . .

of the extent of . . . all the times with Tess.'

'I get it,' I say. He does have a *ménage a trois*. It's just that the other two don't realise. And they pay him. I'm not sure if I'm impressed or not. He must be a good liar, that's for sure.

He stands up, and hands me a bit of kitchen towel to clean the egg off my hand. 'Come on. Let's go upstairs.'

My head feels a bit better. I follow him, as he shows me the living room – big leather sofas and a huge flat screen telly, totally cool – then upstairs to the sleek silver and white bathroom. It's like something out of the interiors magazines that mum used to borrow sometimes from Mr Patel's shop. They'd give her stupid ideas like painting the bathroom pink, or putting up a bead curtain to separate the kitchen bit of the living room.

He waves his hand at two closed doors. 'That's Tess's room and that's Lucy's. They're both at work. Tess is in television and Lucy's a trainee chef. That's where I went. I was just checking they weren't here. They both work long hours, funny rotas, so probably they won't be back for ages. My bedroom's over there.' Another closed door.

Then we go up another flight of stairs – this flat goes on forever – and into a massive room, with a window either side and a wall of photos in between. From one side you can see Alexandra Palace, and all the streets snaking up the hill. From the other . . . *wow* . . . the whole City of London. The Gherkin. Canary Wharf, blinking like a Christmas tree with a star on top. Skyscrapers shining in a brown-ish haze. I could look out of this window for hours.

'Like it?' he asks.

'Umm . . . yeah . . . cool. . .' I say. I look at the photo wall. It's like a patchwork of people, not framed this time, but pinned up, jostling each other for space. I pick out a few famous faces . . . Lily Allen, Cheryl Cole, Kylie. . . Claire had some pictures like these up on her wall, I remember, which looked like they'd been pulled out of magazines. But these are glossy prints. Why would a man have a wall like this?

'Do you like it?' he asks again. 'This is what I do. I don't know why you thought I was a lawyer like my dad.'

What he does is stick pictures of Cheryl Cole on the wall? I'm completely confused. But then he pulls a big camera out of a black bag and I get it. He *takes* these pictures. He's a photographer. A photographer who takes pictures of celebrities. And I don't mean one of those paparazzi guys either. These are arty pictures taken in a studio. Lily, Duffy and the rest of them are smiling, pouting, posing for my dad.

Forget sports lawyers. I have the coolest dad ever.

It's so unfair. If I'd known about this when I was at St Saviour's I could've been king of that school. Imagine being able to name-drop Kylie, Alesha Dixon, Leona Lewis. OK, I am a bit impressed, I have to admit.

He picks up his camera and points it at me. 'Hmm. . .' he says. 'I think you might photograph quite well. Interesting features – even with a black eye. You might want to think about modelling. It's a good way of making money. Can you dance? I think Lily's looking for boys for her next video.'

'I'm trying to keep a low profile,' I point out, and he scratches his head and says, 'Oh yes . . . sorry. I wasn't thinking. I'm a bit dazed just having you here, to be honest. I've imagined this so often, showing you my home . . . my work. . .'

I remember the mean way my mum said, 'They've bought you.' She must've worried for years that I'd meet my dad and his family and I'd want things that she couldn't give me. She's been struggling to pay the rent while he's living in a palace on the hill.

'This flat must've cost you a fortune,' I say.

'Well . . . I saw it as an investment. . .' He's got that shifty look again.

'My mum never had any money, but every penny she had she spent on me,' I say. It's nearly true. He doesn't need to know that she treated herself to hair extensions and nights out at the pub and her clothes came from Top Shop while mine came from down the market. It's the general principle that counts.

'You know Nicki wouldn't let me near you,' he says. 'She wouldn't take anything from me. I've put money away in an account for you. I thought you could have it on your eighteenth birthday, but it's there for you now, if you want.'

'I'm not for sale,' I snap, and he says, 'I didn't mean that.'

I haven't thought about my mum for ages. Christ. She must be really worried. Serves her right, I think, but at the same time I don't like imagining how she'll be going bonkers . . . crying. . . And there's my gran, she'll be worrying too . . . and Patrick and Helen. And then there's Claire.

'Does she even know you've found me?' I ask, and he says, 'I should call her, shouldn't I? She gave me Nathan's number and address, that's how I found you. We agreed she'd call your girlfriend's family and I'd do London. I've been to see your old landlord, Mr Patel, and I talked to quite a lot of people in the local shops . . . there was a pretty girl in the tattoo parlour, very concerned about you . . . and I went to your boxing club and asked there.'

Jesus. She's been trying to get him killed. She sent

him straight to the people who want me dead, to the boxing club which is full of Jukes's men. My mother is a ruthless woman. God, she hates him. What on earth did he do to her?

He pulls out a mobile. She answers right away. I can hear her squawking at the other end. He can hardly get a word in.

'I've found him,' he says eventually. 'He's safe. A bit battered, but fine. He just needs some peace and quiet.'

Quack, quack, quack. My dad mouths, *Do you want to talk to her?* And I shake my head quickly.

'Look, Nicki. . .' Quack, snap, crackle, crackle.

'Nicki, shut up for one minute. I'm keeping him with me for a bit. I don't care what you want. Just let him recover. I need to talk to him. I'll call you tomorrow. Tell you what we've decided.'

Blimey! I've never heard anyone dare to talk to my mum like that. There's a noise at the other end of the line like a volcano erupting. And then he switches his phone off.

He looks a bit sad. 'What a woman. . .' he says. 'She really hates me, doesn't she? Mind you, it means . . . she's not indifferent, is she? She still cares. There's a thin line between love and hate. Pretenders. Before your time. Almost before mine, but one of my sisters liked them.'

'What, Archie's mum?'

'Yes, my oldest sister Pen. It was her who rang me, told me that you were with my parents. Of course, they hadn't bothered.'

He's kidding himself if he thinks my mum could ever forgive him. It's all very well, his massive flat and his cool job and his *ménage a trois* and his celebrity mates. Ultimately he's a guy who beats women.

'My mum does not love you,' I say, 'She really, really hates you and she always will. It's your own fault. You hurt her.'

'I had to,' he says.

'What?' I can hardly believe my ears. 'You . . . you hit her! You hurt her! You put her in hospital! Jesus . . . what *are* you?'

I'd like to hit him, but I've done enough fighting for today. It's enough to shout and cuss at him.

His mouth drops open. His eyes are wide. He puts his hand on his forehead.

'Is that what she told you?'

'Not just my mum. Patrick too.'

'My father? My *father* told you I hit Nicki? Jesus. I'd believe a lot of him, but not that. Lying bastard.'

I have a moment of doubt. After all, Mum never actually told me what happened. And Patrick didn't quite give me all the facts.

'Ummm. . .' I say, but he's opened a cupboard and is pulling out a leather bag.

'I'm going out,' he says, 'You stay here. No running away – understand me?'

His voice is cold and harsh. It gives me a jolt to hear it. I kind of prefer the way he usually speaks.

'Understand me?' he asks again, face grim, eyes furious, and I nod. He shoves the leather bag into my arms.

'Take a look at that while I'm gone,' he says. 'When I get back, we can talk about what you've found.'

And he walks out of the room and I hear the door click behind him. My dad has locked me in.

CHAPTER 25
Birthday

I drop his stupid bag and slam my body hard against the door, again and again. It rattles and shakes, but I can't bust the lock. All I'm doing is killing my shoulder. After the fourth try I give up. I fall back onto the floor and get my breath back.

How could he do this to me? Is he going to keep me prisoner? It's inhumane . . . probably not even legal. When my mum hears about this she'll get the police onto him. *Jesus.*

There's a computer on a desk in the corner and I switch it on, but . . . bugger . . . it's completely password-protected. I think about smashing the monitor. I resist the temptation.

There's a packet of cigarettes on the desk – so much for giving up – and a lighter. I start flicking the lighter, passing my finger through the flame. I could burn all his photos on his stupid wall. I could make a frigging bonfire with his bloody bag. I could burn this whole poncey flat down to the ground . . . and why stop there? Burn the whole city. The Great Fire of London Part Two.

I stare out of the window. The Gherkin is like a massive blade ripping into the sky. Canary Wharf is a rocket about to explode. I flick the lighter against my skin, on off, on off, just letting it hurt a little. I wonder if flesh smells like meat when it burns. I wonder what hair smells like. . .

The leather bag is right by my feet. I pick it up and empty it. The start of my bonfire. Photos, envelopes stuffed with letters and even some baby clothes and toys. Who'd keep such a load of rubbish? They deserve to be burned.

I crouch over the pile, lighter in hand. And then stop. What am I doing? Who starts a fire in a locked room? A suicidal nutter, that's who. I have to stop this right now.

I throw the lighter hard to the other end of the room.

And then I sit, exhausted and sweaty, picking up stuff from the pile and putting it down again.

The photos are in neat little folders. I pull them out and mix them up. I glance at one or two at random. There's my mum, with a huge smile on her face, showing off some trophy she's won. She's in running kit, so it must have been for a race. She does look kind of fit, I suppose, although it's totally wrong to think that about your own mum. Long brown legs. Women shouldn't be allowed to have babies until they're about forty. I drop the photo pretty fast.

There's one of my dad. I laugh when I look at it, because he's so different. He's got the St Saviour's school uniform on – they must've made the sixth form wear it in those days. He's got the St Saviour's army haircut.

And he's got a baby in his arms, which stops me laughing right away.

The baby is all wrapped up in a blanket, so all you can see is its nose. But there's a massive grin on my dad's face. He looks happy. He looks proud. He doesn't look like I'd expect a Year Thirteen dad to look, which is pissed off and frightened and worried that the baby was going to throw up or shit all over you.

There are more photos. My mum holding me. I'm wearing denim dungarees – never a good look – and I'm as bald and ugly as that guy on *Little Britain*. She looks different – more curvy, busting out of her too-tight T-shirt. I do not approve.

The next photo is more recent. A big glossy print. Bizarrely, it's me and Arron. We're in our St Saviour's blazers. It looks like we're walking out of the school gates, on our way to the tube. Arron's walking ahead,

I'm following. We're laughing, we look like real true friends. Who the hell took this picture? How did my dad get it?

I pull a letter out of one of the stuffed envelopes. Thick cream writing paper. Spiky writing. Black ink – not a biro. My eyes are swimming in and out of focus. I read a few sentences – *'He's been so quiet and withdrawn, so emotionless. It's much healthier for him to get upset when he hears your voice. . . He should be absolutely fine.'* But I can't concentrate. Worry nibbles the back of my mind, fear. . . I need to think for a minute.

My dad went all over the place asking people about me. He went to the boxing club, where I know that Jukes's guys go. What did he tell them? What did he ask?

I'm trying to remember if he called Nathan or Nathan called him. I'm thinking about why that matters. And then I hear a click and the door opens.

'You locked me in!' I yell at him. 'You locked me in! You can't do that!'

'I didn't go far,' he says.

He's balancing a tray with two mugs of tea and a plate with two slices of cake. I want to smash it out of his hands, crush the cake into his face, smear it on the glossy photos.

I don't because my mouth is watering.

'Your one has the teaspoon – it was two sugars, wasn't

237

it?' he says, like nothing's happened. I grab a slice of cake
– chocolate, mmm – and stuff it into my mouth. 'Happy
birthday,' he says. 'I haven't been able to say that to you
since you were one.'

It's my birthday? I'm fifteen? 'You can't lock me
in. . . I'm not your prisoner,' I mumble through the cake.
I reach out for the second piece. He nods, 'Go ahead.
Enjoy.'

He must've gone out to buy me a birthday cake.
That's kind of nice of him. I wish Claire was here so we
could have our birthdays together. I wish I could've kissed
her . . . stayed with her. Maybe I'll never see her again.

My dad sits down on the floor next to me.

'I had to lock you in,' he says. 'The one thing I know
about you is that you run away. You've done it twice
in the last week.'

Oh. Huh. I still think it's frigging inhumane. What
if I'd needed to pee?

'I spoke to my dad and again to Nicki,' he says,
'two people I never speak to in normal circumstances.
They both deny telling you that I hit her. They were both
surprised . . . wondered why you would think that.'

'Patrick *said* you put her in hospital,' I say, mouth full
of cake.

'He also says he told you it was something you
needed to talk to Nicki and me about. One of the few

times I've completely agreed with him.'

'Oh yeah, well, I get a lot of chances to do that, don't I?' I'm going for a bitter and dignified tone, but the effect is slightly dented by the chocolate icing all over my hands. I lick it off.

'So listen to me. Believe me. I never hit Nicki.'

He could be lying. But somehow I don't think he is. I want this to be true. The cake is good. I'm feeling much better.

'Anyway,' he says, 'Did you look at the pictures and letters and things? Did it give you more of an idea?'

'Yeah. . .' I'm a bit puzzled by how he's managed to defuse my fury with a smile and some cake. And I don't know what to call him, which is kind of annoying when there's something urgent I need to say. What was it?

He picks up a photo. It's another one from when I was really tiny, a little bundle in a blue blanket. He's holding me and his arm's round my mum and again he's got a goofy grin on his face. It's like the opposite of all those sex education ads when they tell you how your life will be ruined forever if you don't use a condom. They look really happy.

'I'm not sure where to begin,' he says. 'I never ever talk about this time of my life. It's too painful. Only my sisters know about it really, and Louise of course.'

'You've been in touch with Louise?'

'Not very often,' he says, 'But she did let me know now and again how you were getting on.'

My auntie Louise has obviously been a triple agent dealing in secret facts about me. I don't think my mum will ever speak to her again. They never got on that brilliantly in the first place.

'Look, Da . . . Danny. . .' I say, nervously.

'Have you ever been in love?' he asks. 'This girl . . . Katie, is it? Do you really love her?'

Katie? He can't even get Claire's name right. Anyway. None of his business. 'I need to talk to you,' I say. 'Can we do the rest of this stuff later?'

'It's important that you know the truth,' he says.

'Yes I know, but. . .'

'I knew Nicki for ages, just as Louise's little sister,' he says. 'She was an annoying kid – noisy, pushy. Then their dad died and we went to the funeral. She'd really grown up since I'd last seen her. She was amazing . . . beautiful. We started seeing each other after that. We didn't tell anyone, because she didn't want people to know we'd met at her dad's funeral.'

They got off together at my grandad's funeral? Unbelievable. I am beginning to see why my gran's forehead goes noughts and crosses whenever my dad is mentioned. Which isn't often.

'I just fell completely and absolutely in love,' he says. 'I've never felt anything like it since. She was wonderful – so determined. She was going to be a champion athlete, going to do brilliantly at school, be a top lawyer, maybe even prime minister. Nicki could do anything. She was so special. . . I was drifting along, no idea what I was doing with my life. I was going to study law like my dad and my sister because I couldn't think of anything else. . . I couldn't bear the idea of losing her. I wanted to make sure I would never lose her. So I suggested that we have a baby.'

He did *what*? Jesus. But I mustn't let myself get distracted. 'Look, this is all great, but I need to ask you something.'

'Of course, anything,' he says.

'It's just, when you came and found me . . . did you ring Nathan? Or did he ring you?'

He looks surprised. 'I left a note for him yesterday. Right after you went missing, I headed straight for London. Then he rang me when you turned up, and I got down there as quickly as I could.'

'So you gave him your mobile number?'

'Well, yes. . .'

'And the others? The other people you went to see? The boxing club? Did you give them your number as well?'

'Yes, but don't worry about that. I've found you now.'

'No, it's just that' – I grab his arm – 'Dad, we're in danger, we need to get out of here. They'll realise you've found me and they'll come looking for me, and they've got your number and they can get your address . . . this address. . .'

He gently puts his other arm around me. 'Ty, I was talking to Nathan before we realised you were out on the balcony. He said you were overreacting . . . paranoid. . . It's totally understandable, given everything that has happened to you.'

'No, really . . . really it's true. The police told us that mobiles are completely insecure. They can trace your details, I know they can.' I'm shaking his arm, trying to make him listen. 'We need to leave here. You need to warn your girlfriends. I don't think it's safe. . .'

'Ty, no one was following us. I'm sure of it. Nathan seemed trustworthy. It's fine. Relax. You're safe.'

I sigh. I want to believe him. I know that I get it wrong again and again. I want to sit here and eat more cake and get to know him a bit better.

But I can't.

'They wouldn't need to follow. They'll just turn up. That boxing club, it's full of Jukes's men. When Alistair was shot. . .' My voice trails off.

I'm shaking. 'My mum phoned him. And the next day he was dead.'

'OK,' says my dad slowly. 'I don't want you to be scared. We'll go to a friend's house. I just need to call Tess and Lucy, explain to them. Maybe they can stay with friends for a few days.'

I nod gratefully. 'Thanks . . . ummm . . . Dad.'

We start scooping up the photos and letters and putting them back in the bag. He pulls out his mobile, ready to call the *ménage a trois*.

And then we both freeze.

We can hear the creaking noise of someone walking around the flat downstairs. And then the crash of breaking glass.

CHAPTER 26
Bomb Disposal

We creep down the stairs slowly. We reach the bathroom door. Then my dad points back up the stairs again. He mimes locking the door. I shake my head. I'm not sitting behind a locked door while he gets shot. What if they've brought a petrol bomb?

A door creaks downstairs. We can hear steps . . . someone moving around. I'm holding my breath . . . shaking. . .

He pats my hand and whispers, 'Don't worry . . . I've got a black belt in tae kwan do.' He doesn't realise . . . he has no idea. . .

And then we hear a voice – a female voice – saying loud and clear, 'Oh bloody hell, Danny, you thief!'

My dad laughs. 'Tess!' he calls out, 'Jesus, you scared us to death.'

I am a complete idiot. I always get everything wrong. I'm looking very hard at the black and white framed photos on the wall as Tess – I think she was the on-off, off at the moment, works in television one – comes up the stairs.

'I didn't know you were here, you thieving bastard,' she shouts – but she doesn't sound really angry. 'Who's "us"? You haven't got that tart Angie here, have you? – Oh!'

She's caught sight of me. 'Well! This is something different!' she says.

'We always talk to each other like this,' my dad says to me, adding, 'She's just joking about Angie. Angie is my assistant, as you know very well, Tess.'

'That's not what it looked like to me that time,' says Tess, who has the sort of blonde hair that looks nearly white, pulled back in a ponytail. She's dressed in a tight black blouse and a short grey skirt and she's wearing really trendy glasses, bright red lipstick and incredible high heels. Even my mum never wears heels like that. She's a bit scary. I can't imagine why she would look twice at my dad.

'Yes, well, never mind about that, it was her birthday,' he says, giving her the sort of look which means *shut up*. 'I want to introduce you to someone. This is my . . . my son. Tyler, meet Tess.'

245

I put on a smile, but Tess doesn't even try to be polite.

'Oh. My. *God*,' she says. 'You are kidding, aren't you? You did just say *son*?' She looks me up and down and laughs. 'You had a son when you were twelve? Sodding typical. Christ, Danny. This is hilarious. Why is he called Tyler Tyler?'

It seems pretty rude to talk about someone in front of them, particularly when you've never met them before. 'I'm not,' I say, and I push past her and stomp down to the kitchen. The chocolate cake is on the table, and there's a smashed wine glass on the floor in a puddle of red wine. I ignore it and I help myself to some more cake. My birthday cake. I feel a bit sick.

I can hear my dad and Tess talking at the top of the stairs. There's a lot of muttering going on. 'Well, what did you expect me to say when you drop that sort of news on me?' she says. 'How come you never mentioned him before? Never even hinted? Has he just turned up on the doorstep? Are you certain he's yours?'

Mumble, mumble. Then she says, 'And Lucy's going to kill you. You do know she made that cake for her mum's birthday?'

I look at the cake. Half of it is gone. I put my hand on the other half and slowly squish it down. Icing oozes through my fingers, and bits of cake fly off the plate.

I give the remains a few gentle karate chops. Then I wipe my hand on my shirt.

My dad comes charging into the room, Tess following him. 'Oh good. . .' he says, 'You're OK.' He obviously thought I'd run away again. I ignore him.

Tess spots the remains of the cake.

'Oh my God!' she says. 'What has he done?'

I scoop a stray bit of icing onto my finger, stick it in my mouth and suck it. I'm gazing at her. Staring, actually. Looking her up and down. Like Arron would sometimes look at girls we met on the tube.

She meets my eyes for a bit, and then she says, 'Danny. A word.'

'Look, I'll give Lucy the money for a new cake,' says my dad. He's watching me too, and chewing his thumbnail. 'We're going to have to leave here for a while, Tess, and maybe you and Lucy should find somewhere else to stay temporarily. There's a bit of a situation. . .' He trails off. He scratches his head. He looks at me.

I don't want Tess thinking I'm some scared little boy who needs protecting from imaginary attackers. Anyway, Danny probably just gave his number to Sylvia, the boxing club admin lady, who'd have lost it within five minutes.

'It's OK,' I say, 'I musta got it wrong. We don't gotta leave. There ain't no problem.' My mum would go

beserk if she heard me talk in gangsta like that. My dad
and Tess don't even blink.

So I add, 'If yo' bitch is cool wid dat.'

Tess flounces out of the kitchen. My dad gives me
a look . . . a bit of a confused look . . . and follows her.
I'm laughing inside. He has no idea. He'll let me get
away with anything.

She doesn't bother to whisper. 'Are you planning
to move him in here?' she says, 'Your long-lost little
hoodie? Because I'm not happy about sharing my home
with a foul-mouthed thug.'

'C'mon, Tess, he's my son. I'm spending time with
him for the first time since he was two.'

'Well he's *certainly* not a baby any more,' she says, and
then her voice goes a bit squeaky. 'Why didn't you tell
me about him? I didn't think you had secrets from me . . .
oh . . . Danny . . .'

I squint through the almost-closed door. My dad has
his arms around her and they're having a very long and
complicated kiss. He's undone her tight ponytail and
is stroking her blonde hair. She's hugging him close
to her.

My dad is like a bomb disposal specialist for humans.
Amazing skill! It also appears that he's a talented
kisser. Tess has her eyes closed behind her specs,
and she's pressing up against him, sighing, 'Danny,

oh Danny . . . you should've told me . . . you must have been hurting so much. . .'

It goes on and on for a bit like this, and then I think I'd better interrupt before she drags him to her lair.

I cough a fake cough. And then it turns into a real coughing fit and I hack and wheeze at full volume for about ten minutes. When I recover they've come back into the kitchen again.

'Do you think he's got TB?' says Tess. She gets me a drink of water. 'Apparently these Victorian diseases have come back among the homeless.'

'He's not exactly homeless,' says my dad. 'He has several people fighting for the joy of having him live with them.'

'Oh,' says Tess. 'I suppose you're one of them.'

'Of course,' he says. 'Look, maybe we should stay here tonight. We can get a takeaway, have a chat, you can get a good sleep, and then we'll take off in the morning.'

I'm not sure. It would be safer to leave. But then I imagine his phone number scrumpled up in Sylvia's waste paper bin. I really want to stay. I'm exhausted, and this is my time with my dad. It's so unfair if it gets taken away from me.

And I really don't want him to think I'm paranoid – and I really don't want to actually be paranoid.

'What about her?' I ask, giving Tess one last

glowering stare. She says, 'You know, actually he does look a bit like you, Danny.'

'I'm sure Tess won't mind . . . you'll give us some space, won't you?' he says. She doesn't look too happy, but says, 'Of course. Whatever you need. I was going to the gym anyway.'

My dad pulls out a bunch of menus and we order curry. Tess disappears and my dad cleans up the cake. 'You shouldn't really call women bitches,' he says, and I shrug and say, 'I didn't like how she talked to me,' and he says, 'Yes, you made that perfectly clear.' He sweeps cake crumbs into a dustpan and says, 'I didn't know Lucy had made it especially for someone. But I'm sure she'll understand. She's a great cook, she can whip one up in no time.'

Then the food arrives and we take it upstairs to his amazing room, and we eat it looking out of the window. It's dark now, and fireworks are bursting out all over London. The display at Alexandra Palace is fantastic. I remember going there with my mum once, standing in the crowds, wet and cold, looking up at the sky. This is better.

The curry is really good and my dad opens a can of beer and gives it to me. I've never really liked the taste and my mum wouldn't be too happy, so I just take some little sips and love that I'm fifteen and drinking beer and watching fireworks with my dad. With my *dad*. Oh my God.

Maybe it's the beer, and maybe it's because I feel just about safe, and maybe it's because I've always loved fireworks, but suddenly I'm flying rocket-high. The dancing stars give me hope. Fire makes beauty as well as danger. Maybe I can tame the fire inside, even make it into something special, something amazing.

As long as it doesn't get snuffed out altogether.

For a while we just eat in silence, and then he says, 'That stuff with Tess . . . you must think I'm a . . . I'm a. . .' He trails off.

'You're a player,' I say, quickly.

He scratches his head, 'No . . . that's not what I mean. . .'

What *does* he mean?

'I don't want you to think it's a good thing, to do . . . what I do. . .' he says.

I can sort of see what he's getting at. But it's kind of interesting that there's no male equivalent of the word 'tart'.

He laughs and says, 'I know I'll be sorry later. I never think these things through.'

'Oh. Umm. I'm a bit like that.' Oh God. Why did I say that? Now he's going to think I'm like him, shagging every girl in sight.

251

'Yes,' he says, mopping up some chutney with the last of the peshwari nan. 'We need to talk about that.'

What does he mean?

'When you looked in the bag, how much did you read?' he asks. 'Did you get to the medical file?'

Medical file? 'No . . . there was a letter, but I didn't read much. I looked at some pictures of you . . . and my mum.'

'You looked happy,' I want to say, 'so happy that I can't imagine why you would have left me for so long.' But I can't say the words. What if there was something I did? What could I have done when I was so little?

He takes a big gulp of his beer. 'Look. The details don't matter. I went to university. Nicki brought you to Manchester so we could all live together. It was great at first, but we were all jammed together in a tiny little flat and I had a lot of studying to do. Money was tight. It wasn't easy. Then your mum had to go into hospital. I couldn't manage to look after you, so I asked my parents to have you for a while. That was basically it.'

He rattles through this so fast that I don't have time to ask any questions.

'But then . . . what happened? Why is she so angry with you?'

'You'll have to ask her,' he says. He's got that cold, distant voice back again. 'But I certainly didn't hit her.'

'But—'

'She came out of hospital and decided she didn't want to be with me any more and that's the end of the story.'

It's not even the beginning of the story. I don't know what to do. He obviously has decided he doesn't want to talk to me. My good mood fizzles, dies, comes crashing back down to earth. I stare out of the window and watch green stars and golden sparkles and try not to care too much.

Maybe I'll never know what happened in the past. Maybe it's the price I have to pay for getting to know him now. Perhaps it's something so dreadful that it would destroy me to find out. That's why he's kept away for so long. To protect me – but from what?

Then he says, 'That's history. What matters is now. I want to hear about your life now. I've missed so much.' And he asks me all about what films I like and what music, and we talk about football and running, and my favourite and worst school subjects, and why we both hated St Saviour's.

I tell him a bit about going into witness protection, and about going out with Ashley and finding Claire. And he asks really good questions and the scared, sad, sick feeling goes away.

And then he says, 'Tell me about Arron. He was your

best friend in London, wasn't he?'

I hunch my shoulders. 'What d'you know about Arron?'

'Well, Nicki gave me his number and address and told me Arron's family might have heard from you. She said he was your best friend. And I know he was mixed up with the crime that you witnessed, and I know he's on remand right now. But I don't know what he's like. I don't know why you were friends.'

'He . . . he looked out for me. He was bigger, he knew more stuff because he had an older brother. He had lots of friends and that meant so did I. I kind of needed Arron, I didn't feel great doing stuff by myself,' I say. My voice is a bit shaky.

'Did you have a lot in common?'

'Sort of. He could be a laugh. But just recently . . . we didn't get on so well.'

I'm not going to tell him how Arron teased me . . . said I was gay, a girl . . . tried to get me to fight. I'm not going to tell him how Arron lied to me, how he was plotting to get me mugging people, dealing drugs. It makes me look weak and stupid – tricked – and that's not what I want my dad to see.

'I see,' he says. He puts down his beer can. 'You weren't getting on so well. So tell me. Was that why you stabbed him?'

CHAPTER 27
Truth

My mouth drops open and a bit of chicken jalfrezi falls out. His voice was so calm that I can't quite believe he said what he said. Maybe he didn't really say it. Maybe I was just imagining it . . . the voice of conscience, kind of thing. . .

'Why did you stab Arron?' he asks again.

'I . . . I . . . who said that? Nathan?'

'No, Ty, not Nathan,' he says. He's leaning forward, looking at me. I make myself busy scraping the last dregs of dhal out of the pot.

'You told me,' he says.

'*What*?' My mind is racing, here and there, trying to work out what he's going on about . . . it makes no sense. . . We hardly even spoke at Helen and Patrick's house.

'In the hospital. You started saying, "Go away, go away". I thought you meant me – you wanted me to go away. Then you were raving . . . talking to someone who wasn't there. "Shut up," you said, "Shut up about me stabbing Arron." I've been trying to talk to you about it ever since, but you kept avoiding me. I assumed that was why you wouldn't talk to me, but maybe I was wrong. Maybe you were just avoiding me anyway.'

'It was all wrong at their house. I was ill and I didn't want to meet you like that.'

'Ty. Don't try and change the subject.'

I can't look at him. My mind is whirling around. It all comes down to this: truth or lie?

'I can't . . . I can't talk about it.'

'Talk about it,' he says. How does he keep his voice so steady? My mum would be screaming at me by now if she thought I'd stabbed someone. Maybe it's because he doesn't really care.

Slowly I nod. I'm staring out of the window. He clears the leftover food, the empty pots and the dirty plates out of the way and comes and sits down on the window seat behind me. I can't see him, but he's so close, I can feel his breath on my neck. He's not touching me, but if I wanted to I could lean on him.

I don't want to.

I say it as fast as I can, 'It was after . . . after Rio was

killed. They were fighting and I ran off to call for help.
I was watching . . . I wasn't fighting . . . they didn't even
know I was there.'

'Why didn't you use your mobile to call for help?'
he asks, 'Why did you run off?'

'It wouldn't work. It needed topping up.'

'Who's "they"?'

'Arron – he was there with Jukes and Mikey.
They were telling him what to do. And they were
pushing Rio, pushed him on the knife . . . then they were
fighting in the mud.'

I hate thinking about this. I hate my dad for making
me talk about this. I'm trying to move away from him,
leaning forward.

'And you went to get help?'

'I could see blood. I thought Arron was hurt, I stopped
a bus, got them to call an ambulance.'

'And then what?'

'I ran back. I was worried about Arron. He shouldn't
have been doing it . . . doing the mugging. He asked me
to do it. But I said no. So I thought maybe it was kind
of my fault if he was hurt.'

'Why did he ask you to do it? Did you mug people
a lot?'

I shake my head. 'No, I didn't. I never did . . . I think
I know why he asked me. But I'm not sure.'

He waits, and then he realises that I'm not going to tell him any more about that.

'OK. And then what happened?'

'I got back, and Arron was there with Rio. The others had run away. And Rio was dead and I knew I had to get away but if I left Arron then he might . . . he would . . . get arrested. And I didn't want that. And it was kind of my fault because I'd called the ambulance. So I shouted at him to run with me, to run away. But he wouldn't.'

'Why not?'

I'm almost crying now, my voice is jerky; my nose running with slimy snot. 'I don't know why not. I was shouting at him. . . It was like he wanted to get caught, like he didn't care.'

Arron was going to get taken away by the police, disappear out of my life forever. I would have to cope without him. Alone at school. Alone on the streets.

'I had to save him. But he wouldn't save himself. And I was so angry about that, so I hit my knife at him. I didn't know . . . didn't realise. . .' I have to choose between holding back the tears or controlling my breathing. I go for the voice, and I can feel water dripping down my nose.

'How bad was it?' he asks. Christ. He's still so calm. It's like he's asking how much sugar I want in my tea.

I can't believe I've been alone with my dad for less than a day and I've cried in front of him twice. Jesus. I hope this isn't going to become a habit.

'I don't know. . .' I say, 'I saw blood, but he was bleeding anyway. Sometimes I remember it and I think the knife hardly scratched him, and sometimes I see it slice into his arm. I just don't know.'

He doesn't say anything. There's a moment where all I can hear is my jagged breath. Then I feel his hand on my shoulder.

'Ty, why didn't you tell the police about this? Do you think Arron told them? Have they questioned you about it?'

I try and shake his hand off, but he keeps it there. I think about fighting him, making him leave me alone. I can't. There's no fight left in me.

'What about the police, Ty?'

'I just didn't tell them about that bit,' I say, 'I told them about the fight, about Rio . . . that's what they wanted to know about. What happened with me and Arron, that was private.'

'And Arron?'

'He told me he'd never say anything. And I think he hasn't. But I don't think that's for my sake. I think it's because he is telling them he had to defend himself against Rio. So it's not really murder. And he did . . . Danny . . .

Dad . . . he did have to defend himself. That's all true.'

'What a mess,' he says, 'What a mess.'

'I know. . .' I say, and add, stupidly, 'I'm sorry.'

He's moved his hand now, so it hangs over my shoulder, and he hugs me close to him, and I'm not strong enough to pull away. 'I'm sorry,' he says, 'I'm so sorry. If I'd been around for you, then maybe things might have been different.'

'This is not about you! It's not my mum's fault!' I'm furious. 'I never even carried a knife until about a week before this! You couldn't have brought me up better than her! You're useless . . . you don't know nothing. . .'

'The fault is mine,' he says, 'Not hers. I was scared to fight her. I should've pushed more for access.'

Scared of what?

We sit there for a bit, and then he says, 'You need to find out what damage you did. You need to face up to this Ty. How can you live with this sort of secret?'

'But I'd go to prison.'

'Maybe. But there are worse things.'

'I can't . . . I can't.'

'I'm not going to tell you what to do,' he says, 'It's good that you've told me. If you feel strong enough to tell the police, then I will stand by you, no matter what happens. And I will make sure you get good legal advice, and I will be there for you. And

I'm sure that Nicki would say the same.'

Not true. I know what my mum thinks. She's always said that I'd better never get in trouble. 'You go wrong, and you're on your own,' she'd tell me. 'I won't be coming to see you in prison.'

'Come on now,' he says, 'You need to get to sleep. You can have my bed tonight, and tomorrow we'll leave here. If you want me to take you to your mum, then I will. If you want to go to my parents, then that's fine. We'll work it out. There's always a solution, Ty, nothing's ever as bad as it seems.'

I think I'd believe him if he and my mum had found a way that I could've grown up knowing both of them.

We go down the stairs and he opens the door to his bedroom.

'I've got something for you,' he says, and as I look around the room – unmade bed, clothes on the floor, musty smell – he opens a drawer and pulls out a small black bag. Inside are a new toothbrush, toothpaste, a comb, a flannel, a little pot of moisturiser and some aromatherapy oil. What the hell?

'They give you that bag free when you travel business class with British Airways,' he explains, 'I've got loads of them.'

Then he finds me an electric shaver, which is really nice of him, even if it's not strictly an urgent necessity.

He searches for some pyjamas – I don't get the impression he wears them much – and in the end gives me some boxers (Calvin Klein) and a T-shirt.

Then we go into the bathroom, and he pulls out a towel and shows me how the shower works. He leaves me alone to clean myself up. It feels so good to step under the steaming water, and I search around among the girly soaps and find some Dove for men, which must be his. I'm kind of chuffed we use the same shower gel.

After I've got dressed, I have a go at shaving, watching myself in the mirror. I look really convincing – it's a shame Archie isn't here. Then I have a little look in the cupboard and find some aftershave – Dolce and Gabbana. I spray on quite a bit – why not? – and I scrub my teeth for at least five minutes. I even floss.

When I go back into the bedroom he's made the bed – nice clean sheets – and picked up the clothes and opened a window.

I curl up gratefully. The bed's really comfortable. Perhaps I could come and live with him.

'Where will you sleep?' I ask, and he grins, and says, 'Well, there's a futon upstairs or, you never know, I might just get lucky.' And I feel like an idiot, because obviously he's just waiting for me to go to sleep before he dives into bed with snooty Tess. But I'm too tired to worry.

I drift into darkness, but soon I'm dreaming of blood

and mud and monsters. And then I'm running from a wild forest fire, and everywhere I turn is blocked with crashing trees and falling ash and thick dark smoke. And the flames hiss and crackle louder and louder.

And I'm scared and alone and completely desperate. And then I hear someone scream, and I don't know if it's me or Arron, and I know that I'm dreaming, so I'm trying, trying to wake up.

And I do, and I lie panting and sweating, tangled in my dad's duvet.

But the screaming hasn't stopped.

CHAPTER 28
Twister

Everything is dark as I stumble down the stairs. I should look for my dad, I suppose . . . but he's with that Tess . . . and I can't leave this person to scream all alone. It sounds like a woman. It sounds like she's in terrible pain.

There's light coming from under the kitchen door. The screams have stopped now, but I can hear someone crying and a man's voice shouting, 'Where is he? He's been here . . . tell us . . . where is he?'

I can see through the slight crack where the door's open. Two men are holding a woman's arms, and one's holding a knife to her throat. I've never seen her before, but she's about twenty-four and really pretty with huge eyes and curly hair. She must be Lucy, part three of the *ménage a trois*. Her eyes shine white and scared against her black skin and her face is wet with tears.

I ought to creep up the stairs again and find my dad. I ought to find a way of calling the police. But they're shaking her and she's screaming again and I can't bear the noise.

I burst into the room. 'Oh God,' she cries, 'Who are you?'

'Let her go,' I yell, 'It's me you want . . . don't hurt her . . . let her go. . .'

They turn to me. They're both dressed all in black and their faces are covered by balaclavas. They look a bit like the Islamic ladies that used to come into Mr Patel's shop. But the ladies had nice smiley eyes and these guys . . . these guys don't.

They let go of Lucy and she falls to the floor, sobbing and crying. They grab me, pinching and wrenching my arms. 'Is it him?' barks one to the other, and his mate sticks his head right by my face. I can't see his mouth but I can smell his stinking breath. I'm struggling and kicking, trying to get free.

'It's him,' he says. 'It's him all right.' And I nearly die of fright and shock because I know that voice.

It's Jukes. It's the guy whose family have been chasing us since the day that I gave my statement to the police. What the hell is he doing here? Shouldn't he be in prison?

'You had to snitch,' he says. 'You couldn't just shut up, forget you was there, could'ya?'

I'm trembling, and I open my mouth to beg him to leave me alone. I'll tell the police I was lying; I'll tell them I stabbed Rio . . . anything . . . anything to stay alive. But those words don't come out. Instead I hear myself shouting, 'Get off me . . . you murderer. . .' and I bring my knee up fast and hard to his balls, just like my mum practised when she went to Women's Self Defence.

He yells – the kind of noise a gorilla makes in the zoo at feeding time – and thumps me in the stomach. Then someone kicks his arm, so the knife flies across the room, and he's falling backwards. And my dad kicks him in the face really hard, and twists to kick the other guy too. Bang! Right in his teeth. He wasn't kidding about the black belt in tae kwan do.

Jukes lies there groaning on the floor and I know I should pin him down, but somehow I can't move. I don't know why. I'm all weak and hot and my legs are trembling. Tess jumps on Jukes's back, while my dad kicks the other guy again. She's armed with a Jimmy Choo, and when Jukes tries to move, she whacks him on the forehead.

My legs don't work any more. I'm kneeling down, shaking. I'll be OK in a minute. It's just the shock.

There's a banging sound, a bell ringing, shouting

coming from outside. 'Lucy. . .' gasps my dad, 'It's the police. Get them . . . tell them. . .' He's lying across Jukes's mate, who's clutching his own jaw and trying to throttle my dad at the same time.

Lucy stumbles to the door. I'm in her way. I try and move, but I can't. She looks at me and starts screaming again. I don't know why. My dad shouts at her, 'Luce . . . for Christ's sake . . . do it now. . .' and she gulps and squeezes past me. The door bangs behind her.

Jukes is twisting and turning, Tess struggles to stay on top of him. She grabs his balaclava and pulls it off. He's cussing her, spitting, calling her a bitch. She hits her sharp heel straight at his eye, and he falls backwards, hands clapped to his face, screeching. It's the best sound ever.

And then there's banging and pounding up the stairs, and the room is full of policemen. One nearly falls over me and I try and get up, but my legs have lost the plot altogether. I can't even scrunch myself up smaller. I'm just lying on the floor.

Two cops grab Jukes and haul him out of the room. Two more grab his pal. My dad is shouting and yelling now. He's shaking one of the policeman's arms, pointing at me. I can't hear what he's saying. The noise makes no sense. It's all just swirling around my head.

And then a guy kneels down next to me, touching

my body. What the hell's going on? I try and push him away, but my arms aren't working either. 'It's OK, son,' he says. 'We're going to get you out of here very soon.'

My dad's at my side shouting at the man. I can hear him now. 'You've got to help him . . . got to do something . . . please Ty, don't go to sleep, stay with us now. . .'

My dad's T-shirt is sticking to me. It feels wet, and so does one side of the Calvin Kleins. That's strange. I'm trying to focus, but the room is speeding, whirling . . . it's like being at the fair, like being on the Twister. My dad's holding my hand and all I can feel are his cold fingers gripping tight while everything else spins around.

I look down and see red. A thin red line, running down my leg. A scarlet pool on the floor. But if I was bleeding it would hurt, wouldn't it? I'm hallucinating. I must be seeing the blood . . . so much blood . . . when Rio was killed, when I hurt Arron. I'm shaking again. I'm choking. I'm giddy and dizzy and everything is glitter and dust.

'Hold on, Ty,' says my dad, 'Hold on, help is here, they're here. . .'

I make a super-human effort to get my mouth working. I turn my head to look at him. I can see his big brown eyes through the sparkling speckles dancing around my head.

'I want my mum,' I say, and I squeeze his hand. 'Please get my mum.'

CHAPTER 29
The Gate

I'm standing with my mum on a dusty road. It's so hot that the air is shimmering. I'm sweating, wishing we could go inside. It's too hot. I need water. A burning wind whips red dust around us. I can hardly see.

There's a rough stone wall and a big black iron gate. My mum rattles it. A man with a clipboard comes out, shutting the gate behind him with a clang that hurts my ears.

'This is my son,' she says, 'Tyler Michael Lewis. Is he on your list?'

'No,' he says. 'No. He's not on the list. There's no place for him here.'

My mum looks like she's going to go ballistic. *'What?'* she spits, 'Did I send him to Catholic school for *nothing*? What about all that time we spent in church? I thought you were 100 per cent guaranteed a place . . . he's been christened, you know. And taken First Communion.'

The man checks his paperwork again. Ruffles his beard. Looks to see if I'm on his list as Lewis Tyler. And then shakes his head. 'I'm terribly sorry,' he says. 'There's lots of competition, you know. Limited places. We've gone interdenominational. He must have failed one of our tests . . . you'd be surprised what these teenagers get up to.'

What is this place? Is it a new school? How did we get here, anyway? The last thing I remember is my dad's frightened face.

'Unbelievable,' says my mum. 'I need to see your boss. I'll go right to the top if necessary. D'you think I'm going to accept the other place? You've got to be joking. . .'

'I'm sorry,' he says, 'There's nothing I can do.'

Then she swallows and says, 'Do you mind me asking . . . is Alistair Webster here?' And I'm staring at her, suddenly cold and shivery and thinking she's gone completely mad and the man says, 'Yes, he got here just over a month ago. No problem with *his* admission.'

And a tornado of dust swirls around me, and a voice says, 'We're going to wheel him down to theatre now.'

When I wake up, I think I must still be at that gate with my mum, because I'm hot and my throat aches and I can hear her voice going on and on. But I'm lying down.

Maybe I'm on the dusty road – it feels lumpy – but I can't move. I can't even open my eyes.

'He's a good boy,' she's saying, 'a really good boy, no trouble to anyone, so sweet. He always does his homework. All this trouble, all this . . . it just came out of the blue. I don't understand it.'

She's obviously bypassed the man with the clipboard and is talking to his boss. But why am I lying down? I can hear a low mumble, a male voice.

'You mustn't get the wrong idea about him,' she says, 'He's not as grown up as he looks. Honestly, Danny . . . he's just a baby . . . he only stopped sucking his thumb a few years ago.'

Jesus. I force my eyes open and say, 'Nic . . . shut up!' But it comes out as a low moaning noise.

She's right by my side, holding my hand and saying, 'Oh, thank God you're all right . . . you are all right, aren't you? How do you feel, darling?'

I'm blinking. We're not on the road at all. The gate has disappeared. We're in a completely white room with incredibly bright lights. Machines bleep and flash. There's a sink, some chairs, a strong smell of bleach. I'm trying to put all the bits together. Then I catch sight of my hand, which has a tube coming out of it. Christ. I'm in hospital. Was this where the gate led? What's going on?

Then I spot my dad on the other side of the bed,

and I give up trying to work out what's going on because I feel so hot and strange and I'm not sure why I'm in hospital because nothing actually hurts.

I close my eyes and I'm drifting in space and sometimes I can hear voices and sometimes I'm just blank.

And then, fantastically clear and loud, right by my ear: 'If you all stopped messing around and just got hold of Claire and brought her here, I'm sure he'd be fine.'

I open my eyes. Archie! I knew it. He's slouching in the chair next to me. My dad's next to him and he has his arms crossed and he's looking at Archie like he's a piece of spat-out gum. My mum's really pale and she's got no make-up on and her hair is all frizzy and she's looking unusually fat.

'Yo, Arch. . .' I say, and the words come out OK, although my voice sounds kind of weird. My mum lunges forward to clutch my right hand and my dad elbows Archie out of the way to grab the left.

'Yo,' says Archie, looking really chuffed, 'Thought you were going to snuff it.'

'Yeah. . .' I say, but my voice seems to be on the blink. It doesn't hurt, though. In fact I feel great, kind of floaty and really relaxed.

Archie says, 'Did you know there's a massive bag of something that looks like piss hooked onto your bed?'

'No . . . urgh. . .'

'Why don't you leave us in peace and go and get yourself a drink, Archie?' growls my dad, sounding amazingly like Patrick. Archie gets up to go but I try and shake my head and croak, 'No . . . Archie . . . stay. . .'

And then my dad says, 'God, Nicki, are you OK?' He rushes round the bed to her side, and she grabs his shirt and says, 'I just feel a bit . . . a bit woozy,' and he puts his arm around her and says, 'You need some fresh air. Ty, she's been at your side for the last forty-eight hours, non-stop. She needs some food . . . a rest. . . Archie, you stay with Ty while I just . . . I'll be back as soon as I can.' And then he virtually carries her out of the room.

She can't have been drinking in a hospital, can she?

I'm dying to sit up and talk to Archie properly, but there's no way. There seem to be tubes everywhere – I might be seeing double – and just thinking about what Archie said about the bag hooked to my bed has made me realise that something very odd is going on in a bit of my body that ought to be completely private. I'd be a lot more worried about this if I wasn't so spaced.

I'm best off just lying very still and listening to Archie, who's making a big deal of handing over my Manchester United scarf, which I'm glad to see again.

'Bloody hell, mate,' he says, 'Trust you. Stabbed in

the sodding liver. They thought you were going to die. They were rummaging inside you in the operating theatre for hours.'

'Nah,' I say, 'Nothing hurts. You got it wrong, Arch.'

'Nothing hurts because they are pumping Class A drugs into you,' he says. 'Top grade morphine. Street value hundreds of pounds. You better enjoy it while you can.'

'Oh,' I say. 'Wow.' And then I vaguely remember that he must know a load of stuff that I missed out on. 'Claire. . .?' I ask.

'OK. So. Your mum turned up at the hostel, along with Claire's parents. Bloody hell. They were all going completely mental when they realised neither of you were there. Everyone thought you'd run off together. Claire's mum was crying and your mum was shouting and then it turned out you'd spewed your guts out over the PE guy – and then Claire shows up, and she was crying too, because you'd given her the slip.'

I try and shake my head, but I don't seem to have great control. I think I do it in slow motion.

'And then my mum turned up – straight off the plane from Chicago, jet-lagged and dangerous.'

'Claire?'

'Claire's parents were going on at her, and then the police arrived and started asking loads of questions.'

'Police?'

'Plain clothes cops. Talking to Claire and your mum
. . . and me a bit. Then my ma realised I'd liberated
some cash from her account, using the bank card
I'd borrowed in case of emergencies.'

Oh. . . Archie's stash. . .

'And she's *totally* unreasonable about it, and says
I'm definitely going to Allingham bloody Priory. As soon
as we've got the sodding uniform. So running away
didn't really work, although it was definitely worth
it because Zoe is completely amazing. Incredibly hot.
We're definitely keeping in touch. And then my mum
took me and your mum back to our house. I tell you, your
ma goes on a bit.'

I want to hear more. I want to ask him loads of
questions. But my eyes are sticky and I've got that fuzzy,
blurred feeling that means sleep.

'Archie . . . tell them . . . get Claire . . . here,' I say.

'I'll tell them,' he says, 'but I don't think they'll listen
to me. You should tell them yourself.'

'No, you . . . you tell. . .' I'm too tired to talk.
Also I may be dribbling.

'Oh OK. I tell you something, your mum is really fit.
It's amazing to think she gave birth to someone as ugly
as you.'

I open one eye and give him a look.

'He . . . your dad . . . he's always staring at her.'

'Oh yeah?' But I can't keep going any more. My eyes are shut and I'm crumbling into sleep.

Archie comes and sees me every day. He's a pain, but to be honest his stupid comments make a change from watching my dad watch my mum and my mum watch me.

Today he's bouncing around on his chair like frigging Tigger. 'Did you know there's a cop outside your room with a machine gun?' he asks, 'Do you think he'd let me hold it, if I asked him?'

'Yeah, Archie, great idea . . . why don't you go up to him and say, "Please, Mr Policeman, can I touch your great big weapon?" I'm sure he'd be only too happy to let you.'

'You're a lot better,' he says, 'You'd have totally missed that two days ago, when you were still drooling and babbling.'

I glare at him. He waves a piece of paper at me. 'Look, it's a printout of my email from Zoe. She talks about Claire. I thought you'd like to see it.'

He shoves it under my nose, but I'm still having problems focussing and I push it away and say, 'Read it to me.'

He puts on a high girly voice. *'Archie . . . I can't stop thinking about you and how fit you are. . .'*

'Not interested. Tell me about Claire.'

'Killjoy. OK, here we are. *Claire is still really sad about Joe and I've had to work hard to stop her getting all mopey again. You wouldn't believe it but she used to be a real emo, only not in a cool way, self-harming and everything, and she looked a total mess. I haven't told her about Joe being in hospital, because that might just push her over the edge, know what I mean.'*

He lowers the paper, 'Zoe's so caring and sensitive, isn't she? I'd never have thought of that.'

'Keep reading, muppet.' I croak.

'I'm going to try and cheer her up tonight by taking her to Emily's party. Don't worry though, I'll only be thinking about you.'

'Is that it? Jesus.'

'Umm . . . no. . . Claire seems to be feeling really guilty about something. I'm going to have a heart-to-heart, find out what's going on. It's amazing – no one could believe it when someone as hot as Joe turned out to be shagging her. But now all the boys are desperate to go out with her. It'd probably be best for her if she got off with someone like Jordan or Max . . . errr . . . that's it. She goes on a bit about some athletics competition. . .'

Jordan? *Max?* 'I *wasn't* shagging her,' I say bitterly. I can't begin to explain to Archie what I feel about Claire, how much I care about her, how great it is to find someone you can totally trust and who needs you, how Claire is my friend, my best friend not just someone I may or may not be shagging – and that's no one's business anyway . . . anyway.

Archie says, 'That's OK, mate, it's me you're talking to, not her granny.'

So I'm stuck in hospital full of tubes, under police guard, and Claire is going to parties to be chased by every guy there. And OK, it's not very likely she's going to go for pizza-face Jordan or mini Max, but there'll be a load of year tens and elevens after her too. Anyway, even if I lived next door, her parents would never ever let her see me again.

'Archie, did you ask if they'd bring her here?' I need someone to persuade Claire's parents that I'm so ill that she needs to dash to my side. After all, I did virtually save her life that time, so they might feel in my debt – at least, they *should* – but nothing's happened, and annoyingly I seem to be getting better, so it's not really so obvious why she'd need to be here.

I make out I'm in loads of pain and feeling really ill, but I don't think I'm managing to fool anyone except my mum and dad, who spend ages discussing whether I'm getting properly cared for. I'm pinning my hopes on them, even if it's the weirdest thing in the world to think of them as 'them'.

'I did ask your mum –' says Archie, 'I've told you this about three times already – and she said she'd think about it. But in the car, when we drove back to Fulham from the hostel, she was saying that Claire's mum was a small-minded old cow and you were too good for Claire, so I wouldn't hold your breath.'

'OK. You'll have to do it. Give me a piece of paper.'

I carefully write Claire's email address for him. My hand's a bit shaky, and the writing looks like a six-year-old's.

'Write to her. Tell her I need to see her. Please, Archie, tell her where I am and how important it is.'

'OK, but they won't let her come and visit you. No one can come and see you. Not your gran, or Grandma and Grandpa, no one.'

'You can.'

'Yes, but that's only because I come with your mum and dad. It's meant to be just them. My mum lends them her car and then they bring me.'

'They're both staying with you?'

'Yeah. Separate bedrooms. They seem to be getting on all right. They've been talking a lot. My mum is going mental trying to work out what's going on with them. She's really nosy. That's why she lends them the car . . . so I can spy on them for her.'

'Oh. And?'

'They talk a lot about you. About when you were little and what you were like at school. It's really boring. He's always fussing over her – makes her food, checks she's OK all the time. The other day he was actually spooning soup into her mouth. It was really weird.'

That is truly weird. We spend a few seconds in silence thinking about how weird that is.

'My mum's sure he's still in love with her,' he goes on. 'She said, "My little brother isn't the brightest banana in the bunch at the best of times, and he loses the few brain cells he has when Nicki's around."'

'She said that to *you*?'

'No, she was on the phone to my dad and I was listening on the other line.'

'Oh. Well. Tell me if you . . . if you see . . . or hear anything. . . Anyway, if Claire came here, they'd have to let her in. They'd have to. Or I'd have to get out of here somehow. . .'

This is about as much talking as I've done in all the time I've been in here, and I can feel my breathing getting shorter and puffier and the words dragging out slower. My eyes feel sore, and I have to close them because they're really hurting.

'You look bad, man,' he says, sounding slightly worried. 'I'd better go and find them. See you around.'

'Yeah. . .' But my voice is just a whisper and I lie back

and rest my eyes. I don't let them flicker when I hear my mum and dad come into the room. There's definitely something going on, and pretending to be asleep is the best way to find out what it is.

I can hear their voices murmuring by my side. 'He looks so peaceful,' says my mum, 'He's really on the mend, isn't he?'

My dad says something which I can't really hear. . . 'Mumble, mumble *asleep* . . .' and then she says, 'Did I ever tell you about when he was five? He took a fancy to Emma's old doll's house and he used to play with it for hours. He had two Sylvanian families – one with badgers and one with little bunnies.'

My eyes snap open – what is she *saying*? – and they both laugh and he says, 'I was right then,' and she says, 'I knew I could wake him up.' I try and look confused and sleepy – I've been stabbed in the *liver*, they don't care at *all* – and she strokes my hair and says, 'How are you, darling? Nice deep sleep?'

'Yes, until your big mouth woke me up. Telling *lies*.'

Her eyes go wide, but she's laughing again. 'Ooooh . . . lies? I don't think so . . . oh, hang on, they were sweet little squirrels, weren't they? Not bunnies.'

'Shut *up*.' She's looking very pleased with herself, I must say. I can't think why. She's not looking very good at all – none of her clothes seem to fit her. She must've completely forgotten her diet while she's been staying at Archie's house. She's even got a bit of a belly. She could do with a trip to Slimming World.

Then I remember that she's pregnant. Great. Well at least that means there's no way they could even be thinking about starting anything together, because that would be just too disgusting and wrong and possibly illegal.

'Ty,' says my dad, 'We need to talk to you about something.'

We? They've never spoken to each other for thirteen years, and now suddenly it's 'we' and 'us'. It's like the whole of my life never even happened.

'Maybe I don't want to talk to you,' I say, 'or *her*.'

He looks a bit shocked. She narrows her eyes at me. 'I'd have thought you'd be pleased that we're getting on. Don't get into one of your sulks, for goodness' sake.'

One of my sulks? Unbelievable. The lies she tells. I lie back on my pillow and close my eyes.

'Listen,' she says. 'We've been thinking about the future. Thinking about what happens when you come out of hospital.'

I've been wondering about this myself. I open one eye.

'One thing you should know is that the boy who attacked you, he's in custody again,' says my dad.

I open the other eye. 'Why was he out in the first place?'

'He got parole,' said my dad. 'The main policeman . . . DI Morris, is it? He's going to come and see you soon. Bring you up to date. Have a chat.'

I don't like DI Morris and his little chats.

'How come you two are getting on now?' I ask. 'How come you don't hate each other any more?'

My mum leans forward, 'Ty, we thought you were going to die. You were in that operating theatre for hours. Something like that . . . it makes you realise what's really important. Danny saved your life. I can't deny that. We've decided to put the past behind us. We'll do what's best for you.'

'We've both grown up a lot in the last few weeks,' says my dad. 'There's no point trying to change what's happened. We need to find a way to go forward.'

They look annoyingly pleased with themselves. I close my eyes again.

'Listen, Ty,' says my dad, 'How would you like to go to live in France for a bit? My parents have a cottage there, in a little village in Provence. They're happy to let you and Nicki and your gran stay there for as long as you need to. You like languages, don't you? Everyone seems to think you would pick up French quickly enough to manage at school. It might be the best bet while things settle down, and I could come and visit you there.'

Wow! Amazing! I'm trying to stay cross with them, but I can feel a huge smile taking over my face. They're smiling too. Then I think of a snag. 'But Nic, you don't speak French . . . and nor does Gran. . .' I can't see them learning, either. This will never work.

'It won't be easy. But we can learn. I'm sure most people will be able to speak English.' I'm not at all sure she's right and I can see my dad's looking a bit dubious as well. She squeezes my hand. 'You'll have to teach us. The main thing is to be safe.'

'Will Helen and Patrick come and visit too? And Meg?'

'I'm sure they will,' says my dad, 'My parents are very worried about you and they'll do everything they can to help.' He says all this while nibbling his thumb, so I'm guessing he still doesn't get on that well with his mum and dad.

'Wow,' I say, 'Wow. . .' Everything's falling into place. I'll go to school in France, learn to speak French really well, have French friends. . . I'll have friends and a school and a life again. I can go running on French roads. It's like I've suddenly got my future back. I'm going to have a home. I'm going to reinvent myself as a brand new French person.

Maybe my mum and gran will really get into learning

French and living in a village. They could keep hens or something. I could get a motorbike like my dad's. I could have a new French name – not Didier, not Thierry. . . Patrice is a bit close to Patrick. . . Eric. After Eric Cantona, Manchester United legend. That'd be cool.

There's only one problem, and that's Claire, but I'm sure we can write and maybe talk on the phone and perhaps she could visit too.

My mum looks at my dad and she's smiling, 'I told you he'd be really happy,' she says, and he grins back at her. Just for a minute I feel sick. I know he fancies her. I can see it in his eyes. Her smile seems really warm and friendly. Too friendly? I can't tell.

But then I'm not very good at guessing what's going on. Maybe the thing that's pulling them together is just me.

CHAPTER 30
Jan e jigar

A new doctor is looking at the scar that's usually covered up with bandages. His hands move over my body and I try and stare out of the window. I don't like being a patient. I don't like lying here almost naked while someone's touching me. My mum doesn't like it either. She's sitting next to me, and she's looking away too.

'How's he doing?' she asks.

'Very good,' says the doctor. 'First class recovery. We'll have you home in no time now.'

I haven't met this doctor before. I'm guessing he's from Pakistan. His accent sounds like Mr Patel's. 'You have been very lucky,' he says, looking at my notes. 'If help had taken longer you could have bled to death.'

My mum gets to her feet. 'I'm just going to the Ladies',' she says. She seems to be running off to the loo all the time now. I don't know if it's because she's pregnant or because she's finding the hospital a bit stressful. I don't like to ask.

The doctor watches her go. 'Tyler, I am hoping you will look after your liver from now on,' he says, 'It has suffered a very big trauma. Look after it, and it will serve you well in the future. Do you know what your liver does for you?'

'Umm. . .' The only thing I can think of is that if you drink too much, you get liver disease. So that means. . . 'Does it store the alcohol in your body?'

'Not exactly. It rids the body of toxins, such as alcohol for example. It is very efficient, a marvellous organ. It has many other roles as well. It is essential to good health.'

I get it. It's like a laundry room for the body. It can't have been good sticking a dirty knife into it.

'OK,' I say. Then I remember something.

'Do you speak Urdu?' I ask him – I say it in Urdu, and he nearly drops his clipboard.

'Well!' he says, 'This is a surprise. Such an English-looking boy, speaking the language of my grandmother.'

My hair's gone back to its normal dark blonde again. My mum brought some scissors in yesterday and chopped the ends off. Brown hair and green eyes.

English-looking. That was one thing I liked about being Joe. Black hair and brown eyes were much more international.

'The person who taught me Urdu, he used to say *"jan e jigar"*. He told me once that *jigar* was liver. But I can't remember properly what it meant, just that it was good, a nice thing to say.'

'Ah, yes,' he says, 'He was wishing you the strength of the liver. In our culture the liver signifies your soul, your strength, your courage. Not so much in Western culture, that is all about the heart.'

We chat a bit in Urdu, and it's all coming back to me, which is brilliant, but then my mum comes back into the room, and the doctor says he'd better go and see some other patients and he'll send the nurse to redo my dressings. 'You should be going home any day now,' he says.

I lie back and think about being hurt in your soul, your strength, your courage. And my mum shivers and says, 'I hate to see you like that. Ripped to pieces,' which is not the most helpful comment she's ever come out with.

She picks up the book she's reading. It's the vampire thing that Claire was going on about, *Twilight*.

'What's that book like?' I ask, dead casual, and she says, 'It's not your sort of thing at all.'

'Yeah, but what's it like?'

She looks a bit surprised – I've never shown the slightest interest in her girly books – and says, 'It's reminded me how stupid teenage girls are when they think they're in love.'

Then the nurse arrives, and I'm disappointed because it's not my favourite nurse who is called Bee, and she's from the Philippines and she's got gorgeous black, shiny hair and quick, gentle hands. She's been teaching me Tagalog, which is one of the most interesting languages I've ever come across, because most of it is totally different from anything else I've ever learned, and then you get a word or two of English or Spanish mixed in, like meeting an old friend in a room full of strangers. I hope I get a chance to tell Patrick about it.

This nurse is called Sue, and she's as old as my mum and doesn't even bother with lipstick. She was the one who pulled out the worst tube, so I think she ought to have the decency to leave me alone. She's got scratchy nails and she smells of liquorice, so I can't even close my eyes and pretend I'm somewhere else.

Sue covers up my scar and says, 'It's healing nicely, you're doing brilliantly, well done,' as if I had something to do with it.

Then she asks, 'Your husband not here today?' and Mum says, 'No, he's working. Photographing Cheryl Cole, actually,' and Sue oohs and aahs – 'You'd never think she's had troubles at home'. And my mum explains how my dad played bass in a band – *really?* – which did quite well, in fact, Sue has one of their CDs and saw them perform at Glastonbury – *wow*! And then he drifted into photography and he has lots of friends in the music business, so that's what he mostly takes pictures of, but he also travels to places like India and Cambodia to do ad campaigns for Oxfam and UNESCO.

In less than fifteen minutes, she's told Sue more about him than she's told me in fifteen sodding years. And she never actually says, 'By the way, he's not my husband, until recently I hated his guts and for years he hasn't come near us.'

Sue goes away and I wait for an explanation. But she just starts reading *Twilight* again.

I ask, 'Why did you pretend he's your husband?'

'It's easier,' she says. 'None of her business, what he is to me.'

'It's my business, though.'

'Well, you know he isn't my husband.'

'Yeah, but I don't know what's going on now.'

'Yes, you do. We're getting on, talking, because it's the best thing for you.'

'He still really loves you. I know he does.'

She sighs. 'Maybe. That's one reason why I never

wanted to see him. Selfish of me, I know, but Danny is very good at getting what he wants. He's difficult to resist.'

'Oh. And do you want to resist him?'

I'm being very clever here, just keeping her chatting casually. But she puts down *Twilight* and smiles at me and says, 'It's nice having time together, just you and me, isn't it? I've been missing that.'

'Don't change the subject,' I snap. 'I was asking you something.'

'Yes, well. . .' she says. 'Sometimes there aren't easy answers.'

'What's that supposed to mean?'

'Sometimes I sit here with you and Danny, and I think yes, this is good. We can turn back the years, to when we had this sweet little baby and everything in front of us.

'And sometimes I think of all the hurt and pain and the . . . the problems . . . and if we get too deep, it'll all start again, and how much damage that would do. I have to do all the thinking because Danny's head doesn't work like that. He never bothers about the past or the future.

'God knows, I needed someone to share the worry of the last few days with, but it's hard too. It's bringing back all sorts of memories, things that I haven't thought about for a long time. And I have to find out . . . I have to find out if he can be relied on. Pen – Archie's mum –

she says he's changed, but I have to be sure. So I can't really answer your question.'

I can't even remember what my question was.

'Don't you like him?' I ask.

'It's not really about whether I like him or not,' she says. 'It's not that simple. You like him, don't you? Is that what you want? Me and Danny back together again?'

'No!' I say, outraged.

'No?' She's watching me. I don't know if she wants my approval or my permission or what.

'No!' I say. Then, 'I don't really know. Maybe.'

She takes my hand. She doesn't say anything. She opens her mouth a few times and closes it again, like a goldfish. Then she says, 'I'm sorry, my darling, but it's never going to be that easy.'

Christ. She's twisted it round so I look like a stupid kid who's spinning fairy tales about Mummy and Daddy getting back together again. I'm not going to mess around being careful of her feelings any more.

'Are you sleeping with him?'

'No,' she says, but her mouth makes a funny sort of twisting movement.

'You want to, though, you both want to.'

'That,' she says firmly, 'is really none of your business.'

There's a pause. Then she says, 'Ty, why did you think he'd hit me?'

I'm cringing. Why does she have to bring this up? I don't want to remind her of the time she found out I'd slightly bullied Claire. What she said.

'Because of what you said . . . to Claire . . . you said it's never acceptable . . . you said. . .'

'Yes, but I never said your dad, did I?'

'No but. . .' I trailed off. What does she mean? Someone else?

'There was a guy,' she says. 'Remember him? Chris the plumber? Nice looking? You were about four.'

'Ye . . . esss. . .'

'It was him,' she says, 'But it wasn't me he hit – not at first, anyway. It was you.'

CHAPTER 31
Chris the Plumber

It makes no sense. It makes no sense what she's saying. I just about remember Chris the plumber. I'm sure I'd remember if he'd . . . if he'd . . .

'Discipline,' she says. 'That's what he called it. He said you were spoilt, a naughty boy, needing a firm hand. I didn't even realise what was going on. Then there was one day . . . in the car. . .'

I remember that day in the car. I remember. But he didn't hit me. She sorted everything out. She hid the wet patch, she took me to Gran, she saved me. Nothing bad happened.

She's looking at me. 'Do you remember?'

I'm not sure what I do remember. But I'm not going to discuss it . . . much too embarrassing.

Nothing stops her, though. 'You were making a mess

in his car – he was a neat freak, Ty, spent hours every week cleaning that frigging Ford Mondeo. He went ballistic. Shouted at you, stopped the car. Scared you so much you wet yourself. Poor little mite. I should've done something, should've stopped him. I'm so sorry, Ty. I was young and stupid and I kind of believed him when he said you needed a father figure. Anyway, he saw what you'd done and he stopped the car and he belted you. Wham, across the face. Horrific. You were so scared, you didn't even cry.'

What can you trust if you can't believe your own memories? How do you know what's true or not?

'You don't remember, do you?' she says. 'Thank God for that. I felt so guilty. After that you stayed at your gran's whenever I saw him—'

Unbelievable. 'You went *on* seeing him?'

She blushes, 'I said I was young and stupid, OK. I thought I was in love.'

I don't say anything. What can I say? But I feel like Jukes's knife carved out everything that was ever inside me.

'And then he started getting jealous. Thought I was looking at other guys. And one day he lashed out at me, gave me a black eye. And that was it. Over. You were affected. You were very quiet for a while. But then you started school, and made friends with Arron, and well . . . we moved on.'

'Why didn't you tell me before?'

She shrugs, 'When's the right moment to talk about something like that?'

I turn my head away from her. 'You never told me anything.'

'Ty,' she says. Her voice is soft and pleading. 'Ty, darling, we all make mistakes. I just wanted to make a good life for you. Make things right. I tried my best.'

I blink hard. I don't want to have this conversation any more. 'I know. It's OK,' I say.

'There's other stuff I ought to talk to you about,' she says. Her voice is hesitant, unsure. I don't look at her.

The bell goes for the end of visiting time. She gets up to go. 'You need to rest,' she says.

'I don't want to rest. I do nothing but rest. It's so boring here. There's nothing to do.' I sound like a baby, I know, but I can't help it.

She kisses me on the forehead. 'What about that iPod Archie gave you? What about the books he's lent you? What about the telly in this posh private room? And Pen's sent you a book of Sudoku.'

I yawn. Archie's iPod was full of girl bands and I've given it back to him with a list of decent stuff to add. Proper men's music. His books are thrillers and manga and I'm not in the mood for either. And as for

Sudoku. . . God knows why Archie's mum would think I'd spend one moment trying to work out where stupid numbers go in some stupid grid.

'Boring. Tell Archie to come tomorrow.'

'He's off to school next week,' she says. 'This is his last weekend. He's acting like he's being sent off to prison. He's a brat. Boarding school will be good for him.'

'He wants to stay at home,' I say, and she says, 'His mum's a top City lawyer, you know. I'd love to have a career like that. Danny's sisters were always incredibly impressive. And she's done it all with a child. Talk about inspiring.'

There are times when I just don't get how her mind works.

'This school, Allingham Priory,' she adds, 'Danny's dad suggested seeing if they had a place for you. He offered to pay. Said it seemed like a really good school.'

Oh my God. I can just imagine Patrick's idea of a good school. 'No! I'm going to France! You said!'

'No, it's probably not the best thing,' she says, 'although, mind you, Ty, private education.'

'France.'

'Oh, well, I suppose it'll be safer. Now I really am going.'

She kisses me again and then she's gone. And I'm

all on my own and I've got another boring, boring, lonely evening in the hospital to look forward to, and I really don't fancy my own company right now.

She's left *Twilight* behind, and I pick it up, but a quick skim of the first page or two confirms that she was right – it's not my sort of thing at all.

I spend ten minutes frowning at a Sudoku puzzle, and then realise I've got two eights next to each other. I chuck the book at the door. It crashes onto the floor and Dennis, my personal armed guard, sticks his head round the door.

'What's this then, throwing books?' he says, picking it up. 'You must be feeling better. Last week you wouldn't have had the strength.'

'I'm bored.'

Dennis is the nicest one of the cops that come and guard me. The others look at me like I'm scum and never talk. Dennis is as bored as I am and flits in and out chatting about football.

He sits down on the bed.

'Dennis, what's going to happen when I get out of here? They're not going to have someone like you watching me all the time, are they?' I've been wondering where I'll go before I'm well enough for France. Or maybe I'll go straight from hospital to the Eurostar.

'Doubt it,' he says, 'It'll be witness protection for

you again, I should think. Quite a lot of people involved, though, this time – your dad, those girls he lives with. Not sure how they'll deal with all of them. But hopefully, now they've arrested old man White, the threat's not so great.'

'They've arrested him? Jukes's dad?'

'Big day today at the station. The guy who was nicked with your mate Jukes, turns out his sister's been temping in the witness protection admin office. They reckon that's how they got your name and address. It's the link they've been waiting for. They've found deposits in her bank account that match one of White's accounts. They did a dawn raid this morning. We've been trying to put this guy away for years.'

'Is that good?' I don't know if that means I'll be safer or whether Jukes's dad will now hate me even more than he did before, and somehow find a way to eliminate me from inside his prison cell.

Dennis chuckles. 'It'd better be. Biggest crook in north London. Hopefully we can move on and nick a few of his mates as well.'

Then he says, 'I'm dying for a slash, and Jim's not coming to take over for another hour. I'm just going to use your facilities.'

He disappears into the loo that's attached to my room. My mum is really impressed that I've got my own shower and toilet. She says it's because they've put me in the private patients' wing, and not being in an NHS ward is the one and only advantage she can think of that's come from this whole mess.

Dennis is being ages. He's not meant to leave the door unguarded. What if someone's lurking outside? What if a gunman bursts in? I'm concentrating hard on not worrying, not being paranoid, not jumping when I hear rattles and footsteps in the corridor outside.

And then there's a knock at the door.

CHAPTER 32
Visitor

No one ever knocks at my door. I don't stop to think whether a gunman would either. I dive for the floor, ready to roll under the bed. But my arm is still attached to a tube – *oww!* – and it rips out of my hand and I crash onto the floor by the bed, bleeding all over my pyjamas.

And then the door opens and Claire comes in.

I can't believe it. I'm stunned, mouth wide open and my arm is killing me, and she's running to me, 'Why are you on the floor? Oh my God, you're bleeding! There's a gun! What happened?'

And then we hear the loo flush and the hiss of air freshener – thank you, Dennis, for *totally* ruining the moment – and he comes into the room and says, 'I leave you for two minutes and you smuggle a girl in. Well, good luck to you, mate.'

And he picks up his gun and goes and stands outside the door. I don't think he really takes this job very seriously.

'What . . . how . . . why are you here?' I ask, faintly. Claire has found some tissues, and is mopping the blood on my arm, and asking anxiously if she should call a nurse. But I have no intention of alerting anyone who might point out that visiting time is over. I climb back up onto the bed, holding a tissue against the blood, and it seems to be stopping. Claire curls up next to me and I'm so unbelievably happy. My face is one big stretched-out smile.

'You asked me to come. So I came,' she says. She's wearing black jeans and a soft pink top. Her eyes are lined with smoky kohl. She's got shiny lip gloss and turquoise fingernails and her hair is blonde feathers.

She's nothing like the Claire I fell in love with.

But when I close my eyes, I smell her clean soapy smell and we're back in her dark bedroom again. Except that this time she's the cool, attractive one and I'm the complete mess. And last time she was cut and bleeding, and this time . . . this time it's me.

'How did you get here? Did your parents bring you?'

She shakes her head. 'They've gone to watch Ellie race in Prague, and me and the boys were meant to stay at home with my granny, but I asked her if I could stay with Zoe and she said yes, because the boys are enough work for her and she's getting on a bit.

'Zoe was desperate to see Archie again, so she decided to come and stay with her aunt in London. Her mum said it was fine. I'm not going to tell my parents, they'll only worry. We'll go back tomorrow, they'll never know.'

'Oh, wow,' I say. Her mum and dad are going to totally kill her if they ever find out, but she doesn't seem too bothered.

'Zoe and Archie are going to pick me up me later,' she says.

I'm desperate to hold her, but my body's like a sweaty lump of cheese. A sweaty, painful lump. Everything feels wrong. Then Claire scrambles off the bed and switches off the light. It's not quite dark because there's a street lamp right outside the window, but in the orange glow the room feels like it's ours.

She climbs back next to me and says, 'Are you all right? You're covered in bruises.'

'I'm OK.' The black eye is fading now, but I'm not exactly looking at my best.

'Archie said you were nearly killed.' She strokes my hair. 'I've never seen you look like this. You're so thin. Is this your natural hair colour? You're so blond.'

My hair is the colour of Special K, and about as

attractive. Claire only thinks I look blond because she's used to me with black hair. Now I'm washed out, colourless, boring. . . No one would blame her if she didn't fancy me any more.

'It is natural,' I say. 'I'll probably have to dye it again when I come out of here.'

'It's nice,' she says, 'It's weird, though. Is this how you look when you're not Joe?'

'I'm still Joe,' I say. I don't care if it's true. 'Claire, last time I saw you . . . last time, you know I really wanted to kiss you. I just couldn't.'

'I worked it out,' she says, and she's shaking with laughter, but then she puts her hand on my cheek and she lifts her mouth to mine and I can taste cherry lip gloss and mint toothpaste. Her lips are so soft and so strong, and that emptiness carved inside me is filling up with joy.

Suddenly I feel alive again. Suddenly I've got energy and can sit up properly and kiss her back, and it's so great that I'm wondering if it's actually a dream . . . and whether it's one of those really fantastic dreams. . .

It's strange. When I used to kiss Ashley, it was a bit like doing beginner's Sudoku. It was all about what comes next . . . if this bit goes here, then this bit must go there . . . and nothing mattered except the final result. I never got that far – just like Suduko – although for different reasons, obviously.

But kissing Claire, it's like a diabolical Sudoku where you feel happy to have got even one number. I'm totally focussed, not planning ahead at all, and it's getting better and better . . . although I wonder why I'm thinking about Sudoku right now. . . She's so sweet and soft. . .

And then Sue comes in with my supper on a tray.

'Well!' she says, snapping the light back on. 'I'm not sure this is what the doctor ordered!' And she laughs a lot at her own lame joke and plonks a plate of fish pie and some fruit salad on the table. 'You're going to have to move,' she says to Claire, who goes and sits on a chair. 'It's important that he builds up his strength.'

And she pulls the wheelie table so it's right under my nose, and wags her finger at Claire and says, 'Visiting time finished half an hour ago. I'll turn a blind eye right now, because you've certainly cheered him up, but I want you gone within the hour, OK?' And we can hear her laughing with Dennis as she leaves.

I try and push the table away, but Claire says, 'No, she's right, you do have to eat. You have to get better.'

'I'm not going to get better eating this muck. Honestly, Claire, they treat you like dirt in here.' There is absolutely no chance that I am going to kiss Claire tasting of manky hospital haddock.

'I remember Ellie got really fed up when she was

in hospital,' says Claire, 'But it sounds like you'll be out soon.'

Is she saying I'm a whinger? Ellie was in hospital for months. 'Yeah, that's what they say.' And I tell her about France and going to a French school and possibly being called Eric, and then I notice that she's not looking very happy.

She's forcing herself to smile, and I lean towards her. 'It's just . . . France is such a long way away,' she says.

'Oh. Well. I know. But we can email . . . oh, God . . . what have I said now?'

Before, Claire was just looking a bit sad. But now big tears are welling up in her eyes, her nose is running and she's put her hand over her mouth.

'It's not . . . it's not you,' she says, 'It's nothing you've said. It's me. It's what I've done.'

'What do you mean?' I shove the table hard enough to send it spinning to the bottom of the bed. The fish pie flies into the air and lands with a splat on the floor.

Claire's really crying now. I try and reach out to her, but she shakes her head and huddles in her seat. I feel like an idiot.

'You're going to be angry with me,' she says.

'No, Claire, I'm not. I could never be angry with you.'

I've gone all cold and shaky inside. What's happened?

Who has she got off with?

And then she says, 'It was at the hostel. After you went off.'

'What. . . Who. . .?' Oh my God. That was quick.

'The police came and they talked to me, and Joe . . . Ty. . .'

'What? Tell me. . .'

'I showed them your email.'

CHAPTER 33
Hunger

Maybe she's totally overreacting. Maybe those police were just local plods, seaside cops, know-nothings, couldn't care less. . .

But any cop would be interested in something that said, 'I'm lying to the police,' wouldn't they?

'It was a Detective Inspector Morris,' she says, scrubbing her eyes and sniffing hard. 'Your mum called him when I came back without you. He drove down from London. He seemed really nice, really concerned about you. He said I had to give them all the help I could, to keep you safe. . .'

Uh-oh. DI Morris. Head of the investigation into Rio's murder. Relying on me as star witness. This is not good.

'So I told him we'd been emailing. And I showed him that one . . . I'd printed it out. I couldn't stop thinking about it, trying to work out what you meant . . . what you'd done. . .'

I swallow. 'It's OK, Claire, it's OK. I shouldn't have sent it in the first place. It wasn't fair on you.'

'DI Morris looked really angry,' she says, in a small voice. 'He showed it to the other policeman and he said, "You were right all along." And then the other one said, "Wait till the defence lawyers get their hands on it," and they asked me to make a statement.'

'Did you?'

'Yes. Just saying how we'd met and how I knew what your name really was and that you'd sent me the email. And my mum and dad read it too. . .' Her voice is all trembly, 'and they weren't very happy. . .'

I ought to be panicking, but I'm quite calm. I'm actually less jittery than I've been for ages.

It's just that Claire's tears, and the blood drying on my arm remind me of that first time. The time I saw her cut herself. The way I felt when I saw the blood creeping down her arm. The excitement. The guilt. I'm beginning to feel it again. I hate myself for it, but at the same time . . . it's there.

And I'm hungry. Really hungry. But not for fish pie.

'Come here,' I say, 'Please, Claire, come here.' She doesn't look at me, but she sits back on the bed next to me. She's not on the side with the scar, which means

I can lean right into her, hold her tight, brush her tears with my hand while my greedy mouth finds hers. . . And it's not a soft, gentle kiss this time but a hungry, thirsty, biting one and it's only the start . . . it's nowhere near enough . . . and I want . . . I want . . . every inch of my skin wants to be next to hers and even my bones are aching to . . . to. . .

And she's shy and shaky at first, but then she's kneeling on the bed and pressing against me and holding my face in her hands . . . oh God. . .

And I don't know whose tears are whose, and I don't know whose skin is whose, and my frantic hands are searching, stroking her face, her neck, pushing under her T-shirt, kissing her beautiful throat, touching her arms. . .

Shit.

My fingers stop their journey. I've found . . . what have I found? An interruption. A roughness. It's . . . it's a plaster. Shit.

I pull away. I'm gasping for air. 'Claire – Jesus, Claire – you're cutting again?'

'No,' she says. She pulls me back.

'You are. . .' I say, telling myself it doesn't matter. It's her business. There's nothing I can do. All I care about is this hunger, this need, how close she is, how beautiful, the smooth, slippery sweetness of her skin. . .

And then I stop. I can't do this. *Jesus*. What's wrong with me?

'You promised,' I say. 'You said you'd stop.'

'I did stop,' she says. 'I did. But then you . . . you . . . I didn't know what was going on. I didn't know who you were. That email.'

Oh. I see. It's my fault.

'I should never have sent it to you.'

'It's not just the email. Archie said that you started a fire in the hostel. You could've burned the place down. I don't know. . .' Her voice has gone all shaky. Thanks, Archie.

'I didn't start a fire. Not a real fire. But my clothes were all covered in dog shit, Claire, they were disgusting. I just wanted to get rid of them.'

She's looking at me with her big eyes, and I can see she's really struggling. And I'm struggling too, because I care about her so much, but I'm not really sure any more that I'm any good for her.

'I've not coped very well with everything, Claire. . . I think I've gone a bit . . . a bit. . .'

I'm trying to talk and breathe at the same time. I wish I could just shut up. I can still feel her skin, electrifying my fingers.

' . . . a bit . . . err . . . stressed. I've got this thing. Post-traumatic stress something. Google it.

It's really complicated.'

'Oh,' she says. 'But what about the email? I've made it worse for you.'

I have to stop her worrying about me. I have to stop the cutting. Even if it means lying to her.

'It's OK, Claire . . . it's fine. They talked to me. It's no problem. They were really cool about it.'

She looks at me, disbelieving, her eyes all puffy and her face red.

'I've been killing myself with worry about this, and now you say it's no problem?'

I hope she'll never find out that I was lying to her. I keep my voice steady.

'Nah. Just a stupid email. You shouldn't have worried.'

'But what did you mean?' she asks. Her tears have stopped. Her eyes are round. 'Who did you hurt? What lies did you tell?'

'Oh, nothing really. I just had a small . . . argument . . . with my friend Arron. I accidentally hurt him. But not very much. Really nothing. A tiny scratch. I don't think the police are very worried about it. He didn't even tell them about it. That's all I was lying about. Just that. Nothing else.'

'So why didn't you say that in the first place?'

'I . . . errr . . . I suppose I wanted to feel that we were

really close again. Maybe I overdid it a bit.'

I never knew Claire could look this angry.

'You. . . I thought I could trust you! I thought we were going to be honest with each other!'

'Yes . . . I know. . .'

'But you just wrote me a load of crap . . . why? What's going on?'

'I . . . ummm . . . errr. . . I don't know really.' Christ, I sound lame.

'God. Joe . . . Ty. . .'

I put my arm around her. 'Claire, you're going to have to go soon. Can we just . . . just talk about something else? Just be together?' The hunger is still there, and my skin tingles at her closeness, but I know it's no use.

She sniffs. She looks like she'd like to pull away. But she doesn't. She holds my hand. And then she spots my mum's copy of *Twilight* and picks it up. 'Wow . . . you're actually reading it . . . isn't it amazing?' she says. She sounds hopeful. Happy. Even loving.

More lies. I have no choice. 'Yes,' I say, gazing into her eyes. 'It's brilliant. It makes me feel closer to you.'

And she sighs and snuggles next to me, with her head on my shoulder. I can feel my body getting heavy and my eyes trying to shut and I'm yawning. Her voice is a soft murmur and I'm only getting odd words here and there. She's talking about the book, I think. . .

Bella this, Edward that, some bloke named Jacob. I'm trying to stay awake, trying to make sense of it all. But I can't do it. I fall asleep, head on her shoulder, cuddled up next to her.

And sometime in the night she must have sneaked away without waking me, because when Sue bustles in with my breakfast, there's no Claire by my side.

CHAPTER 34
News of the World

My hospital room is kind of crowded. There's my mum. There's Mr Armstrong, a lawyer. There's DI Morris and his sidekick DC Bettany and a woman DC called Pam who's set up a tape recorder – a really old-fashioned one. You'd think the police would have better equipment.

They've all dragged chairs in and they're jammed close together. I'm sitting on the bed, but luckily I'm in jeans and a T-shirt, not pyjamas, although I have to wear tops that hang loose over the dressings, so I don't look at my best.

How I look doesn't really matter a lot right now.

Mr Armstrong has advised me to think carefully before I answer any questions and to stay silent if I want to, but to remember that if I don't answer, then a jury might draw conclusions from that. I don't know what he wants me to do. I don't know that he really cares.

I've heard it all a million times from the police, anyway.

Mr Armstrong told us that I could only have one adult to stay in the room with me, to protect my interests. My mum and dad both wanted to do it, but she just gave him a really hard stare and he kind of mumbled, 'Oh, OK then, you stay.' He gave me an encouraging smile when he left the room. My mum examined her fingernails and ignored him.

I might have known that their new, mature, we're-getting-on-for-your-sake relationship wouldn't last.

The bust-up came yesterday while my dad was explaining how Mr Armstrong was going to be there when DI Morris came to talk to me. 'It's your chance, Ty,' he said, looking hard into my eyes. 'Your chance to get things straight.'

My mum looked puzzled. 'What do you mean?' she asked.

'Ty's not told the police everything, Nicki. I think it's bad for him. It's weighing on his mind.'

My mum looked from me to him and back again. She got right away that he knew about the knife I'd been carrying in the park. She doesn't know what happened next with Arron. But just the knife was enough to set her off.

'Are you *joking*? Are you *crazy*? What do you know about Ty? You should mind your own business.'

'Come on, Nicki, anyone can tell things aren't right at the moment.'

'That's because of what he's been going through. No need for him to tell the police stuff that's going to get him into trouble. Jesus, Danny, don't tell him what to do. Don't ruin his life.'

'Do you want him to live a lie? It's up to him. Isn't it, Ty?'

I was reading one of Archie's manga books. It was about this guy who has a notebook which kills anyone whose name he writes in it. That'd be a really scary thing to own – so easy to kill, so easy to lose. The guy used it for good, but it was doing his head in.

I didn't look up.

'It's an interview with the police, for Christ's sake,' said my mum, her voice trembling. 'Not one of your sessions at the Priory.'

She must mean Allingham Priory, where Archie is now completely miserable, according to his letters. I didn't know my dad had been there too. And I have not a clue why he glared furiously at my mum, said, 'I thought we agreed to leave the past behind us, and anyway it wasn't the Priory,' and slammed out of the room.

And they don't seem to have made it up now.

'Don't tell anyone anything,' my mum said to me after he'd gone, and I just shrugged and looked at the book and kept my mind completely empty of police and emails and parks and knives.

And here we are, with DI Morris and DC Bettany and Pam, and they're explaining that anything I say may be taken down and used in evidence against me, blah, blah, blahdy, blah.

DI Morris asks about my health. He says he's glad to hear that I'm getting better. 'I hear you were very brave,' he says. I shrug. I gave them their statement about the stabbing a few days ago – another lot of police, another story to sign. Now I'm trying to forget it. Not so easy.

DI Morris is asking my mum how she is, how the pregnancy's going, how she's managing. So far, so boring. I fill my head with good stuff, like Meg's soft fur and *The Simpsons* and the feeling you get when you pass the only other runner ahead of you in the race and you know you've got the power to beat him.

He's explaining about Jukes's dad being arrested. He's saying that lots of his associates are also in custody. They've done a clean sweep, he says. They think that I can feel much safer now, and so can my dad and his flatmates, because they'll be witnesses when Jukes goes on trial for stabbing me.

It's a shame I've stopped believing anything the police say. And now, presumably, they've stopped believing anything I say. Which makes us kind of even.

'Now then,' says DI Morris. 'I have something to read to you, Ty, and then some questions to ask. And he pulls a piece of paper out of his briefcase.

'Hey Claire, my Claire,' he reads.

I imagine I'm at my gran's flat in London, eating shepherd's pie and watching *EastEnders*.

'I've been thinking a lot about why we got so close so quickly, and it's still a mystery. One minute I was being mean to you – and I am so sorry, you know, don't you – and we were fighting, and the next I just felt this incredible closeness and trust.'

DC Bettany coughs. My mum says, 'What the *hell*?' Mr Armstrong mutters to her, and I think he's telling her to shut up.

I think about watching DVDs with Patrick and talking to him about it afterwards. In French. With an excellent accent.

DI Morris says, 'Just let me finish, please, Miss Lewis. I think you'll see the relevance. Where was I? Ah, yes, *I always will, even if you never want to speak to me again when I've told you this. I have to be honest with you. It's what we're about.'*

My mum reaches over and tries to take my hand.

I brush her away, hunching my shoulders. There's a thick, fleshy bit inside my cheek and I bite on it hard. No one can see.

'*I'm a liar, Claire,*' says DI Morris, and my mum gasps. '*I'm lying to the police and if I get into court as a witness I'm going to lie there too. I'm not just a liar, I'm someone who did something terrible. I hurt someone. I've never admitted it to anyone before.*'

I'm trying very hard to remember what colour we painted the walls of my room in our old flat in Hackney. I know they were blue, but what blue? I can see all the tester pot patches up on the wall, but I can't quite get which one we chose. I feel sick. How could I have forgotten?

'*It's up to you what you want to do,*' says DI Morris. '*You could ask me lots of questions, and I will answer them all. I'll tell you anything. Maybe you will understand why I did it and forgive me.*'

I think about my mum saying, 'One of your sessions at the Priory.' I remember one early morning in Mr Patel's newsagent's shop, looking at the *News of the World* before it went into my paper round bag. A story about a model with a drug problem. She'd gone for treatment at a place called The Priory.

Oh my God.

DI Morris is still reading. '*You could never contact me again, and I will understand. Or you could pretend you never got this email. It's your choice. Whatever you do, take care of yourself. I'm trusting in your strength.'*

He pauses. Looks at me. I stare back. I yawn. I'm not going to give him the satisfaction of thinking that I'm upset.

'*I love you,*' he says, looking straight at me, and there's something hard and cruel in his voice.

Mr Armstrong says, 'I need to ask you about the provenance of this document.'

DI Morris says, 'I'm nearly finished. *I love you. I always will. You are my best friend. I know you think of me as Joe, but it was Tyler who did this and that's who I want you to love or hate or forget.*'

There's complete silence. I sneak a glance at my mum and look away as fast as I can. Two black stripes of mascara are running down her face.

'So, Tyler,' says DI Morris. 'Let's make a start. Can you confirm that you wrote this email?'

CHAPTER 35
Almost True

It's like he's playing darts in the pub, except words are his arrows and I'm the bullseye. The only way I can make his questions bounce away is silence. So I say nothing as he asks me: did I write it? What did I mean? How am I lying? Who did I hurt?

Mr Armstrong asks him lots of questions about where the email came from and how he got it. When it comes out that Claire handed it over to the police I think my mum's going to scream. She nearly jumps out of her chair and her mouth is wide open.

And then the questions start again: what, where, how, why?

And eventually my mum says to Mr Armstrong in a loud whisper, 'Can't you get them to stop? He's crying. He's been through a very hard time.'

I hate her and I hate the police and I hate Arron most of all. I'm absolutely not crying. She's stupid.

DI Morris says, 'Ty's facing very serious charges here. Perverting the course of justice, just for starters. I don't need to tell you he's rendered himself worthless as a witness.'

That word – *worthless* – buzzes in my ear like a wasp drunk on Dr Pepper.

'I may not know right now what he did to Rio, but I certainly intend to find out. This email is pretty damn near a confession.'

'It wasn't *Rio*,' I say. I'm not crying. I'm really not.

'So who did you hurt?' asks DI Morris, and his voice is suddenly a million times kinder.

I don't care any more. So what if I go to prison? I've hardly had a lot of freedom since Alistair was shot, anyway. This hospital room feels like a cell. Maybe prison is the right place for someone like me. Maybe that's where I belong. I'm worthless. He just said so. No one disagreed.

So I tell how I pulled my knife out of my pocket and waved it at Arron, with Rio's dead body lying at our feet. I tell them I wanted to help him, save him. I say I was scared, panicking, out of control. I describe the downwards swoop of the blade and the way it cut into his arm – and I can see it now, the blood that ran along his arm and dripped onto the ground.

It wasn't just a scratch.

I don't tell them that Arron promised to keep quiet. I don't tell them how great it felt when I saw respect in his eyes. I don't tell them how scared I was after Arron's mum took him to the hospital, or how I threw up in their loo, again and again, crying like a little girl.

I just tell them enough. I don't want to lie any more. But I don't really believe that anything can ever be the whole truth. There's always another bit of the story, something deeper. I keep on finding out things that were part of the whole story.

Who knows what else there is?

'That's it.' I say. 'That's what happened. That's all.'

They're looking through their files and they pull out a photograph of Arron stripped to his boxers, showing the scars on his legs and his chest and his arms. And they make me point out the one that I did, and I'm still not absolutely sure.

I look at his angry dark eyes and his curly hair, the face I know better than my own. I know why I needed him to be my friend, but what did he get from me?

And I wonder if he thought he was looking after me, like I wanted to look after Claire – although not like *that*, obviously. . . Just . . . just . . . it makes you feel good if there's someone around who's weaker than you. That's all.

They take the photograph away. They say they'll have a statement ready for me by tomorrow. And DI Morris says they will have to conduct other interviews and look at the forensic evidence and I think it's all over when he says there's just one more thing he wants to ask me about.

My mind is blank. I can't think what it can be.

And he pulls a plastic bag out of his briefcase and puts it down in front of me. And I let out a little 'Oh!' of surprise, because it's something I'd forgotten all about. It's the flick knife. The one from the bus. The one I threw away in the park.

And we're off again: do I recognise this? Where did I get it? Did I use it? Why did I run away from the police? Did I know my fingerprints were all over the knife and the bin?

And Mr Armstrong does his bit, but I'm not too bothered because it wasn't even mine, that knife, and it wasn't really anything to do with me, and I'm actually quite proud of how responsibly I disposed of it.

So I answer all their questions.

And DI Morris says that's two counts of possessing an offensive weapon that I'm looking at, a possible charge of GBH or even attempted murder relating to Arron, and perverting the course of justice as well. Mr Armstrong is scribbling in his notebook and he doesn't look too happy.

Then DI Morris says he's arresting me. There's complete silence in the room. Then my mum's wobbly voice asks, 'Are you going to take him away?' and they say no, I'll be on police bail and I'll have to report every month to a police station until the Crown Prosecution Service can consider the case, and they will be in touch and let us know what comes next.

And they chat for a bit and I work out all by myself that I won't be going to France.

The cops leave. There's no sound in the room except my mum's choking sobs. I'm reaching for my manga book, but she's in the way and I don't think I can ask her to pass it.

My dad comes back. Mr Armstrong tells him what they said and what I said and what might happen to me, which turns out to be quite a long time in a Young Offender Institution if the worst comes to the worst. 'But of course they might not charge him with anything. A lot will depend on what Arron has to say – it's notable that he has made no accusations against Tyler up until now.'

'I can't believe this,' says my mum. 'We've put our lives on hold for months. My baby's father . . . a totally innocent man . . . he's, he's dead – a young man, an innocent man. My boy, my son . . . he nearly died.

And they're talking about charging him? Sending him to prison? They ought to be ashamed.'

'The problem is that once a piece of evidence like this comes along, they can't exactly ignore it,' says Mr Armstrong. 'I should warn you, Tyler, that when you come to give evidence at Arron's forthcoming murder trial, the defence lawyers will tear you apart.'

Wow. That'll be fun. I'm really looking forward to it.

Mum says, 'I want to sue the police. They didn't look after us properly. We're lucky it was just one person that got killed. There could've been a massacre.'

And then she's crying, and my dad virtually jumps over the bed to hug her and she's weeping into his chest and he's kissing her hair and her eyebrows and Mr Armstrong and I are trying not to stare. I guess they're over their argument. It's totally embarrassing.

Mr Armstrong leaves and my dad says, 'Nicki, you look shattered. Why don't you get a taxi back to Pen's house?'

And my mum says that yes, she will, and she's not even really looking at me when she kisses me goodbye and as she goes off I can see she's crying again.

It's just my dad and me. He looks at me, and he opens his mouth, and I think about prison and then I remember The Priory and I wonder how I'm going to ask him about it. I'm waiting for him to start going on about the knife and the email and the rest of it.

But he asks, 'Where's the remote?' and he switches on the telly and we watch *Top Gear* and *The Simpsons* and *Who Wants to be a Millionaire*. And when the nurse comes to say that visiting time is over and it's time to go, he goes out into the corridor with her, and then he comes back and sits down again and we watch *EastEnders*. We only switch off when *Holby City* comes on, but then he shows me some games on his BlackBerry and we see who can get the best score and I beat him every time.

And when I'm eating my supper – macaroni cheese, revolting – he tells me a bit about being in a band, and how he never thought it would be more than just messing around with some friends, but suddenly they had a manager and a recording contract and they were on the festival circuit.

I don't think I'd like his band very much. He asks me if I like indie rock and when I say no, commercial hip hop, he looks pretty snooty and says, 'I'll have to educate you.' Yeah, right, I think not. He describes their sound as being highly influenced by The Pixies and Nirvana – 'some guy at *The Guardian* called us the British Pearl Jam.'

'Why did you stop?' I ask politely, wondering how anything which sounds so rubbish ever got off the ground. He says, really offhand, 'Oh you know . . . the lifestyle. It didn't really suit me.'

'Oh, right,' I say, feeling like an idiot, and he says, 'I thought I could handle it, but I was wrong. I've learned my lesson. Nicki was right to keep you away from me. I didn't really accept it at the time, but I wouldn't have been good for you. I'm so sorry. I'm going to try and make it up to you now.'

'Oh, right, OK,' I say.

The nurse comes in to take the plate away and says I need to get ready for bed. 'Big day tomorrow,' she says. 'You're going home.'

'Yeah, right,' I say, and I think I'm OK, but when she's gone I begin thinking what it would be like to be really going home, back to our little flat and seeing Mr Patel and none of this had happened at all.

But then I'd never have met Claire or been Joe. I still wouldn't know that I could run. And I'd never have met Patrick and Helen, and Archie and Meg.

And I still wouldn't know my indie rocker dad. He's watching me, and asks, 'Are you all right?' and I'm taking off my T-shirt so I can say, 'Yup,' without him seeing my face.

But when I've spent five minutes frozen inside the shirt, not moving, hoping he won't notice, I feel him sit down next to me.

'Hey,' he says, 'It's OK. It's good news. You're getting out of here.'

He pulls the T-shirt gently over my head, and he drapes my pyjama jacket over my shoulders and helps me stick my arms in one by one and carefully does up the buttons. As though I'm a baby.

He puts his arm on my back, and I want to push him away but I don't seem to have the strength. Then his arms go around me and he pulls me towards him and I'm so tired, so exhausted that I just lie there. I can hear his heart thumping like a drum. He holds me close and there's a moment when it feels, I don't know, normal. Familiar.

And after a bit he says, 'What was the worst thing, Ty?' and I hear the buzzing of that word – *worthless* – but I can't say it, and I shake my head, and he says, 'It will work out. I promise.'

He shouldn't really make promises as big as that. But I'm glad he did.

CHAPTER 36
Cold Turkey

I don't know why people say that playing games on the PlayStation or the computer can make you violent. I saw it when I was on my paper round: 'Killer video games fuel teen violence' in the *Daily Mail*. I don't know why they call them video games, either. Who has a video any more?

Anyway, they're wrong, because gaming is the opposite of violent. When you play, you're completely safe, because no one can hurt you. You're busy and using your brain, so you're not bored. You can't hurt anyone else. So how does that fuel teen violence?

There's a huge difference between these games and real life. When real people get killed, there's no music booming in the background. Killers aren't always pig-ugly and dressed in black. Life would be better if it was more like games. You'd always get another chance.

In fact, if everyone played a lot more of these games I bet crime levels would fall. Newspapers like the *Daily Mail* ought to promote them.

I know all this because when I came out of hospital, Archie's mum gave me his old PlayStation and loads of games and an old telly to plug it into. And since I moved into the high-rise in Birmingham – which is just as minging as you'd expect – that's what I've done. All day, every day. For a whole month. Working up the levels and moving on. It's fantastic.

My mum moans a bit that I ought to be catching up with school work before I start at some Brummie sink school in January, but when I think about being plunged into the middle of year ten with no friends and no idea what they've learned for the last six months, I get breathless and my scar starts hurting and I have to lean forward into the screen to block her out.

My gran tried to talk to me about the whole stabbing thing – 'Why, Tyler? What did we do wrong? How could you do such a thing?' – but I'd just reached level fifteen of *Wolverine* and I muttered, 'Another time, right, Gran, OK?' She hasn't tried again. The way she looks at me – disappointed, upset, confused – just makes me want to run back to my console.

It's Christmas Day and they make me stop playing

for dinner even though I'm not really hungry, and I gobble down some turkey and potatoes as quickly as possible, then turn down Christmas pudding to get back to *Grand Theft Auto*. Man, I wish I'd played this game before Arron got involved with Jukes and them. I'd have had way more idea about how things work. They should teach this stuff in schools. It'd be a hell of a lot more useful than learning about Shakespeare or Vikings.

My dad arrives about 6 pm. It's the first time I've seen him since we moved here, because he's been working in New York. He rang a few times but it wasn't easy to talk to him on the phone. I'm not used to having him around enough to know what to say when he disappears again.

He leans up against the door frame of my room and looks around. 'It's not so bad,' he says. 'Nice and light. Perhaps a lick of paint. . .'

Not so bad? There's a yellow stain running from the draughty window to the floor. The carpet is full of holes and brown stains and it peels at the edges. It smells of damp, and there's a constant thudding bass line booming from the ceiling. There are needles in the stairwell and dried vomit and dog shit in the lift. I think about my dad's American fridge and leather sofas. I don't bother to reply.

'Why are there two beds?' he asks.

'There was a copper living here with them before,' I say. 'Gone now. Emma's going soon. And Louise.'

Emma's going back to Spain to hook up with some guy she met when the police moved her and Lou and Gran there in the summer. He's called Carlos and he has a boutique in Marbella and Em says he looks like Enrique Iglesias. Yuk. Lou's got a job as head of English at the British School of Tashkent. That's in Uzbekistan. I suspect she's trying to get as far away as possible, because things are a bit brittle between her and my mum.

I'd be pretty excited, I suppose, if there was any chance that I might be able to go and visit. But there isn't. Even though I've got a passport now, there's no way the police will let me leave the country. So I'm keeping focussed on working my way through as much of GTA as I can before I get shipped off to prison.

I'm assuming there's no PlayStation in Young Offender Institutions. The thought makes me a bit shaky, so I don't think it very often.

'I've got a copper protecting me,' says my dad, 'just until Jukes White goes on trial. Even though they think the threat's very small now because they've got most of his associates inside. Tess and Lucy have protection too. It's a pain in the arse. I'm going to be spending quite a lot of time abroad in the next few months.'

'Yeah, right,' I say, leaping, running and – wham bam! – blowing away a rival, 'Sorry 'bout that.'

'Lucy asked me to thank you for what you did for

her,' he says. 'She thinks you're very brave.'

'Yeah . . . right. . .'

'Ty, can you switch that off for a minute? Just pause it or something?'

'Umm . . . not right now. . .'

'I've got your Christmas present.'

Oh, for God's sake. Can't he see I'm busy? Why doesn't he just leave it for me to open later? This present had better be good. He's making up for fourteen years of no present at all. Reluctantly I freeze the game.

He hands it over. A phone. A mobile. Great. Brilliant present. Something I should have as a basic necessity. I mean, who gets a phone as a present when they're fifteen? That's your big exciting gift when you're about eleven. Anyway, it's completely useless to me now because I have no friends and no one to call. It's about as pointless as the running gear my mum gave me. Does she really think I'm going running in a strange city where anything could be out there waiting for me? I don't think so.

I must admit that he's chosen a particularly cool handset, with lots of features.

But my fingers are itching to start the game again.

'Ta,' I say.

'It's pay as you go,' he says, 'I've given you quite a bit of credit. And I've put some numbers in. The battery's charged up. It's ready to use. I've written your number down for you, here you are. . .'

'Ta,' I say again, and I hit play. The engine roars, I'm speeding along the mean streets. . . Jesus. He's still here. What does he want from me?

'Ty,' he says, gesturing at the pulled curtains, the clothes on the floor, the bowl of ancient, half-eaten cereal mouldering by my side. 'Do you think maybe you should cut down a bit on the gaming? Nicki says you've been spending all your time in here.'

'Yeah, right, no,' I say.

'Ty. . .' he says, but I'm off, I'm into the game, I've got no time to listen to him or think about anything other than survival and killing and building up my criminal reputation and it's fine, it's safe because it's not real. Thank God it's not real.

I don't think I ever want to do anything much that's real again.

But later, when he's gone and my mum's insisted that I switch off and go to bed, and I'm lying in the dark waiting for everyone to go to sleep so I can switch it on again, I reach for my phone. And I look at the numbers he's programmed in – his own, Patrick and Helen's, Archie. Patrick's called me a few times since I've been living here but I haven't talked to him. I've been too busy, too concentrated. And I don't know what he'll say about the police stuff, and I'm not sure I want to know.

Perhaps I should ring them. Wish them a happy Christmas. Maybe arrange to go over to see them, take Meg for a walk. . .

But maybe they don't want to know me any more. Maybe that's what Patrick was calling to say. And anyway, they don't have a PlayStation. I don't call them. Instead I call the 118 people. I get Claire's number. And I punch in the numbers.

Claire's mum answers. I can't cope with her. 'Can I speak to Ellie, please,' I say, trying to disguise my voice with a Brummie accent, although that's got to be the first language I've had no interest in learning. 'It's . . . ummm . . . tell her it's Brian.' I can hear Ellie's voice in the background. 'Brian who?' she's saying. 'Who's calling at 11 o' clock on Christmas day?'

Then she picks up the phone. Her voice is clear and breezy and strong. I get a whoosh of nostalgia for the days when Ellie was my trainer, and all I had to do was obey her orders, and everything was going really well. When I was Joe. A lifetime ago.

'Hello?' she says.

'Ellie,' I mutter, 'It's me. It's Joe.' My voice is all croaky. I don't use it much at the moment.

'Oh my God,' she says. 'What's going on? Why did you want to speak to *me*? What about—'

I interrupt before she can say Claire's name.

'I just wanted to tell you something,' I say. 'I think Claire's cutting herself again.' And I cut off the phone. Just like that. I lie there in the dark and I know Claire's never ever going to speak to me again.

And after about half an hour I get up again and start playing GTA. Level sixteen. I only stop when my head's so full of cars and guns and pimps that I think it'll be safe to try to sleep.

When I wake up I'm scrunched under my duvet. My watch says 11.30 am. That's strange – normally they wouldn't let me sleep this long.

I swing my legs out of bed and then freeze. If I was in a cartoon my eyes would bulge from my head and there'd be a crash as my jaw hit the floor.

They've gone. My telly, my console, all my frigging games. Gone. Disappeared. We've been burgled in the night.

I haven't moved so fast for ages. I run out of my room, into the living room which doubles as a kitchen. Thank God my mum's there. Thank Christ she's all right. But where's Gran? Where are my aunties?

'Mum . . . Mum, we've been burgled. . . Someone's got in. Is Gran OK? She might be . . . oh my God, she might be hurt.'

She's sitting there, drinking coffee, like nothing's wrong at all. She's even smiling. I try again, 'Mum . . . Nic

. . . they've taken my stuff. They've taken the PlayStation and the telly and the games . . . all of them. . .'

'Ty, love, you need to go and get dressed,' she says. 'It's a bit cold to be running around in your boxers.'

It's beginning to dawn on me what's happened. There's been no burglary . . . no burglary as *such* . . . it's . . . they've. . . 'It's you, isn't it?' I scream at her. 'You've taken them. Where are they? Where are they?'

'There's no need to overreact,' she says. 'Calm down.'

Calm down? How am I meant to calm down with no games?

'You've got no right. No right. They were mine. She gave them to me. It's . . . it's *stealing*.' I don't quite say it like that. I don't think my mum's ever heard me cuss like that.

'Charming,' she says. 'It's not stealing. Don't be silly. Danny and I had a chat with your gran and we all felt that you were spending too much time in your room on the PlayStation.'

Unbelievable. *Unbelievable*. The three of them plotting against me.

'*Jesus*. . .' Even I can hear that I sound shrill, hysterical and slightly deranged. I change tack, try and sound reasonable. 'OK, maybe I have been overdoing it a bit. I'll cut down . . . just a few hours a day . . . please,

Nic, please. . .'

'No,' she says. 'Cold turkey. Just right for Boxing Day.' She snorts at her own lame joke. 'Your gran's taken them to a charity shop.'

What??? 'But it's a bank holiday . . . nothing will be open. And how's she going to carry a telly?'

'She's taken a taxi. Islamic Aid is open all day. Normally she wouldn't touch a non-Catholic charity but she's making an exception, just this once. For you, Ty. And listen, I've arranged a nice surprise for you. . .'

I interrupt. 'Islamic Aid won't take it. You've got to be joking. They'll really disapprove of stuff like that. Plus I'm sure charity shops don't take electrical goods. Ring her. Tell her to come back.'

A flicker of doubt crosses her face. Then her phone pings with a text and she reads it and says, 'Actually, the taxi driver's just offered her fifty quid for the lot, so she's taking that and going to meet Emma in town for the Boxing Day sales.'

Jesus! 'But that's *stealing*. I hate you! I hate her too!' I kick out at the table leg, and a chair topples over. It hits her knee and she winces. 'Ty! There's no need to start throwing furniture about!'

'I'm not! It was an accident! You're so selfish! You never think about me at all!'

'Ty, we're doing this for you. You can't shut

340

yourself away from everything. Look, I know things are hard for you. I know you're scared about being charged by the police—'

'I'm not scared! Shut up!'

'But you have to have a life; you have to keep on with your running, with your languages, darling. You need to get ready for school. Otherwise you might as well . . . be. . .'

She stops. Her hand covers her mouth. Tears flood down her face. The scar on my stomach is blazing like it's been ripped open and someone's trying to weld it back together with a blowtorch.

'Be what? Be dead? Maybe you should never have had me in the first place.'

'Ty. . .' she gulps, but we're not alone. Louise comes into the room carrying a Londis bag full of milk and bread and eggs. 'What the hell is going on?' she asks.

'Ty . . . he's upset. . .' sobs my mum, and Lou turns on me. 'For heaven's sake. What have you done?' She clocks the chair lying on the ground. 'You threw a chair at her? For God's sake, Tyler. Are you OK, Nicki?'

'I never . . . I didn't . . . she's taken all my stuff, Lou, my games and my telly and my console.'

'I know,' says Lou, 'I helped her.'

My breath is coming in short puffs. I'm shaking. I slam my fist onto the kitchen table. 'Get them back!

Get them back! Or I'll . . . I'll. . .'

'You can go to your room right now,' says Louise in her best classroom voice. 'You're acting like a five year old. Go and calm down and then we can talk about this.'

I need to get away from them before I make a complete fool of myself. Also, I am a bit cold. I'm shivering. 'I'll go in my room because I want to,' I yell. 'Because I can't stand looking at you . . . traitors . . . liars . . . *thieves* . . . for one more minute.' And I slam my door so hard, the entire sixteen-storey block shakes.

All I can see is the emptiness where the PlayStation used to be. There's nothing else. Two beds and a table. An empty table. I punch the wall, again and again. Plaster flakes fly into the air. But it doesn't make me feel better. I fling myself onto my bed, fists to my forehead, full of rage with nowhere to go.

And then someone stirs in the other bed.

CHAPTER 37
Health Crusader

All I can see is a tuft of dark hair. Who . . . what. . .?
And then a face emerges and he stretches and yawns.
Jesus Christ. It's Alistair.

I feel my forehead – am I running a high temperature
again? That's why they said I was hallucinating before,
wasn't it? But I don't feel hot. Alistair looks over at me
and smiles, quite kindly. 'Don't worry,' he says. 'It's stress.
Understandable.'

I'm not talking to him. He's not real. He's not.
Perhaps if I turn my back on him he'll disappear.
I lie still for five minutes. But it's no good. I can hear him
humming *Silent Night*.

'They did the right thing, you know' he says.
I'm not answering. He's not real. If I talk to him,
I'm talking to myself. Like a mad person.

343

'You were getting addicted,' he says. 'Forgetting to exercise. That's not healthy.'

'Shut up,' I growl very quietly between clenched teeth.

'You should listen to me,' he says. 'I've got a degree in Sport and Exercise Science from Loughborough University.'

'Big sodding deal.'

'I know people think that trainers in gyms are dumb, but there's actually a lot of expertise involved,' he says, sounding a bit hurt.

'Yeah, right,' I snarl back.

'You should try yoga – it's very good for stress reduction. I'll give you a leaflet,' he says.

'You can't, you're dead,' I point out, brutally.

He shrugs. 'Yoga's very big here,' he says. 'Some wonderful teachers. I'm learning a lot.'

'Oh.' I don't know what to say. 'Umm, that's good.'

'Anyway . . . look, Ty, you can't yell at Nicki like that,' he says. 'She's at a difficult stage.'

Hah! That shows how much he knows. She's always difficult. 'Shut up,' I hiss. 'You know nothing about her.'

'I knew everything the minute I saw her,' he says dreamily. 'So beautiful and so fragile. I see lots of girls like her at the gym.'

I don't want to hear this. But he goes on and on.

'I felt a connection the minute we got talking. I wanted to help her . . . get her exercising . . . help her quit the smoking . . . healthy eating. . .'

For God's sake. He's making out he was some sort of Health Crusader, instead of a sleazy guy trying to get his leg over.

'You wanted to get her into bed.' I've turned round to look at him now and I'm back to my normal voice. It's hard to remember someone's not real when they're totally winding you up. 'You knocked her up. Not very healthy, was it? What about safe sex?'

He shrugs. 'We got carried away. Heat of the moment. You'll understand one day.'

Patronising git. Patronising *dead* git.

He leans forward. His hands grasp mine. They're so cold . . . so icy cold that I start shivering again. I want to pull away but I can't move. 'Look after her,' he says urgently, his grey eyes staring into mine. 'Look after her. She won't like it. It'll upset her. . .'

'Wh . . . what?'

'Ty, you know what I'm talking about. You know. Really you do. Look after her. Look after the baby.' His eyes flicker over me, unimpressed. 'You're all I've got.'

Then he's gone. Dissolved into the air. I'm left, sitting on the bed, staring at nothing, shaking and shivering, skin bumpy as an Iceland chicken. *You know*, he said. *You know.*

What did he mean?

I pull on some clothes. I'd like to have a shower but it's not my day on the rota. You try sharing a flat with four women. Your personal hygiene suffers, believe me. I'm breathing in and out, in and out, replaying his words, trying to focus, concentrate, remember.

And then there's an explosion of noise and I fall off the bed in shock . . . but it's great, it's fine, it's amazing because the noise is a dog's happy barks! And it's Meg! And she's jumping up and licking my face and I'm hugging her close and breathing her dusty smell. Her beautiful, beautiful smell.

I know she's not a hallucination. Nothing could be more real than Meg. But what's she doing here? She can't have tracked me cross-country, through the streets of Birmingham, up in the lift?

Meg snuffles at me in a way that would be a purr if she was a cat. 'What are you doing here, girl?' I ask her soft ears, her shiny brown eyes. 'How did you find me?'

My mum is standing at my bedroom door. 'Well,' she says. 'I never thought I'd see you so fond of a dog.'

I still haven't even nearly got over the outrageous

PlayStation theft. I ignore her and concentrate on scratching Meg's tummy.

'Patrick and Helen want you to go and stay there for a few days.' She says it in a totally neutral voice, like she's reading the football results on 5live.

'You *what*? When I was there before, you acted like I'd been kidnapped.'

She's gone a bit pink. 'Yes, but things are different now. I think you need a change of scene. Anyway, aren't you going to get dressed and come and say hello to Patrick?'

Oh my God. I can hear his voice rumbling in the distance. I'm still not sure how I'm even going to face him.

Five minutes later, I sidle into the living room, Meg by my side. Patrick's standing in the middle of the room examining a large patch of damp that's made a dark shadow of mould on the wall. 'It's a complete health hazard,' he's telling Louise. 'Really, they should pull these places down. No wonder some of the people who live in them behave like animals. Oh, hello, Ty.'

That's what I like about Patrick. He tells the truth. We've all been pretending that patch doesn't exist. Patrick just says what he thinks. I give him a big grin.

'Having a good Christmas?' he asks, looking me

up and down. I'm suddenly self-conscious about my unwashed hair and crumpled jeans.

'Umm . . . yeah. OK.'

'I gather there's been a touch of family disharmony,' he says, raising his eyebrows.

Blimey. Mum must've been really worried about the gaming to have told Patrick about it. Pregnancy has softened her brain cells.

'Why don't you sort out your bag, Ty?' she says, picking dog hairs off the sofa. She's looking like she's already regretting letting Patrick and Meg through the front door.

I scuttle off to stuff a few things into a bag, but I leave the door open so I can listen to what they're saying, although I don't really need to, because Patrick's voice is so loud that he can probably be heard by the people upstairs with the sound system from hell.

'This is no place for a baby, Nicki,' he says, and for one astonished moment I think he means me. Then I realise he doesn't. I can't hear her reply, but I work out it's something about money. Beggars can't be choosers, I should think. She's been saying that a lot recently.

'You've got my idle son to tap for fifteen years' worth of child support,' booms Patrick. 'He's made a small fortune, as far as I can work out, with his so-called music, and I don't think all of it disappeared up his nose. Just because you wouldn't take money from him before doesn't mean you can't take it now.'

Mumble, mumble from my mum. Louise says, 'He's got a point, you know, Nic.'

Patrick again: 'And what about the new baby? Surely you have a claim on the father's estate.'

Blimey. I'm suddenly aware, out of the corner of my eye, of Alistair, pressed against the wall, listening intently. But when I turn to look at him, he's gone.

I've missed my mum's reply if there was one. But Patrick says, 'You should try and contact them. They've lost a son, why should they lose the chance to know and support their grandchild?'

This seems as good a time as any to break it up. I haul my bag onto my back and walk into the living room just as my mum, red in the face now, says, 'Look, just because I've said Ty can come and stay with you for a few days doesn't mean you can walk in here and start telling me what to do.'

'Patrick didn't mean—' says Lou, just as I open my big, fat mouth and say, 'He's right, actually, Mum.'

'*What?*' says my mum, shooting me a filthy look.

Maybe if I make this happen, then Alistair will leave me alone. Finally. Forever.

'You should – it's the right thing – Alistair would

really want you to, I know for sure. It's not fair on the baby if you don't.'

Right next to me, I can see Alistair. I think he's giving me the thumbs up.

There's a silence. My mum's red face has faded to white. Lou's hand is over her mouth. Patrick pulls out his handkerchief and blows his nose. His eyes look a bit funny. Maybe he's allergic to mould.

'We'd better get going,' he says. 'Nicki, I'm sorry if I spoke out of turn. I didn't mean to interfere.'

'Oh,' says my mum, 'OK.' She sounds a bit sour but she's not going to explode in the next five minutes. I give her a quick hug, tell them to say goodbye to Gran – still out looting the shops with her ill-gotten gains – and check that I'll be back before Lou and Em skip the country.

'Oh, yes,' says Mum again, 'They're going on the first of January and you have to be back to report to the police here on the thirtieth.'

They arrange that Patrick will take me to the police station on the way back, and that's it. We're out. Escape from the fortress of women. We get downstairs and his car's safe, amazingly, although it turns out that's because he's paid a kid five pounds to keep an eye on it.

And we're driving away, and the city turns into green fields and country lanes and Meg's whining in the back to go and have a run. Patrick pulls in at the side of the road and we find a footpath and Meg bounces out of the car. She rushes off, every centimetre full of joy to be free and running and following her nose. I wish I could turn into a dog. I'll never get to be that happy.

It's cold, and my breath puffs out in front of me. Someone's driven a tractor down this path and ice sparkles in the frozen mud stripes and ridges of the tyre tracks. It's good to be outdoors, good to breathe in the fresh cold air. My mind's getting clearer and sharper. Everything is coming into focus. Memory bites, like the cold.

'We have a lot to talk about,' says Patrick, as we walk after Meg. 'You need to tell me what's happened with the police and your lawyer. I hope that Danny's found you a good one.'

He doesn't sound too cross with me, but at the same time I'm not stupid enough to think that Patrick's going to be super cool about what I've done. 'He's called Mr Armstrong,' I say. 'He seems OK.'

'What on earth happened?' he says. 'I thought you were a witness, not a participant. According to Penelope you're facing a long list of serious charges.'

I sigh. 'I don't know. It was just . . . one thing kind of led to another. Danny thought I should tell the police. It was sort of screwing me up, not telling.' Not, mind you, that I feel especially un-screwed up now.

'What was the first thing?' he asks. 'You say one thing led to another. What was the first step in this mess?'

I'm not sure what to say. The obvious answer is the knife. The first knife. The knife that Arron said I needed for protection. If I hadn't had that knife, then I couldn't have stabbed him. I'd have had nothing to lie about. So much would have been different.

I remember the day he told me to carry it. I gave it, oh, about a minute's thought, and just stuck it in my back pocket. My biggest worry was whether I would cut myself if I sat down.

But maybe that wasn't the first step. Maybe it went back before then. Maybe the trouble started the day I decided to ignore that Arron was almost definitely dealing drugs at school. Maybe it was the first day I let him get away with calling me names – pretty boy, gay boy – and decided I could take anything, as long as we went on being friends.

Maybe it was all those days stretching back to reception class, when I didn't want to make my own decisions, and instead asked Arron what to do. I got into a habit of letting him do my thinking. I never considered that I might do a better job for myself.

'I don't know,' I say. 'I shouldn't have listened to my friend.'

'Really?' says Patrick. 'All his fault, was it?'

Maybe, I think, it all goes back further than even being friends with Arron. Maybe it's something to do with the things that I can't quite put together. Things that are nothing to do with me. Decisions and events that happened before I was born.

'No,' I say slowly. The truth is as cold, hard and slippery as the patches of ice crunching under our feet. 'No. It was my fault. It was the knife. The day I chose to carry a knife. I thought it was for protection, but I didn't think through what I was doing.'

Patrick takes a deep breath and I think he's going to blast off at me. I brace myself for the roar. But then he says, 'Life is tough now, eh?' and there's a moment when I think I'm going to be able to just nod and say, 'Yup,' but what comes out is a weak little wobbly voice saying, 'They tried to kill me, *Grandpère*, they stabbed me. I was bleeding . . . I was bleeding. . .'

And he pats me on the back and says, 'Frightening stuff,' and then Meg bounces back to us and it's OK again. It's really OK. Just for the moment I'm fine.

Back in the car we talk about Archie's new school and Louise's new job and what GCSE subjects I'm going to pick – Patrick is weirdly prejudiced against Media Studies, although I think I've got a head start because of growing up over a newsagent's.

But my mind keeps going back to Alistair and what he said about my mum, and how that fits in to all the new stuff I've learned and all the old stuff I always knew.

I need some answers. I'm after the truth. But who can tell me the whole story? And how will I know it's true?

CHAPTER 38
Family

Driving to Patrick and Helen's house, I'm looking forward to peace and quiet. No booming bass line, no squabbling neighbours. Space. Time to think. Maybe I'll be allowed to take Meg for walks; she might even come with me for a run. Perhaps Patrick and I can watch films together . . . and there's a lot of good football on. . .

But the driveway is packed with cars – big, expensive four-wheel-drive cars. As we come through the door I hear a buzz of talk coming from the living room. Helen comes out, a huge smile on her face, and I can hear the chat die down. There's a crowd of people in there, waiting for me. I know it. Helen takes one look at me and says firmly, 'Come on, Ty, let's take your stuff straight upstairs. You can meet everyone later.'

There's no peace and quiet in the attic, though. It's been turned into a campsite, full of blow-up mattresses and multi-coloured sleeping bags. Archie is lying on my iron bed watching *Lord of the Rings* part one, full volume, and two little boys are bouncing up and down next to him. I'm kind of stunned.

'When Nicki called, I was so excited,' says Helen, 'I told everyone to stay on to meet you. They were all here for Christmas, anyway. It's my chance to introduce you to the whole family, darling. I'm hoping that Danny will come too. It'll be a real reunion.'

She's almost jumping on the spot, she's so happy. No one would think she was showing off a grandson who's about to go to prison, or welcoming back a druggie son. In fact, no one would even think she'd ever heard of knives or drugs. I like Helen a lot. But there's something about her that makes me nervous.

'Oh. Umm. Cool,' I say. 'Hey, Archie.'

'Hey,' he says, pausing the DVD.

'This is Ludo and this is Atticus,' says Helen pointing out the little boys. How on earth can she tell the difference? They both have black hair and blue eyes and exactly the same little nose and freckles. They're about six years old. They're identically hyper and loud. Some idiot has dressed them both in jeans and blue jumpers.

'Archie's in the big bed,' she says, 'but you can have

the top bunk, Ty, is that OK?'

'Yup,'

'Why don't you unpack, and then come down and meet everyone?'

'Umm . . . yeah . . . OK.'

She gives me a quick hug – she smells of mince pies and roses – and a kiss. It's totally weird, like getting a kiss from a teacher.

I sit down on the bottom bunk bed and Ludo and Atticus rush over to me. 'Hello,' I say. I've already forgotten which one is which.

'Are you Tyler?' says one.

'Umm, yeah.'

'Wow! You go round fighting people!' he says. The other boy looks solemn and says, 'Mummy said you had a knife stuck in you.'

'Umm, yeah,' I say. I'm incredibly nervous about meeting the whole family. How many people can fit in that room?

'Wow! Can we see where it went in?' says one of the boys.

'Oh. Umm. I don't know.'

'Please . . . where the knife went in,'

I don't know what to do. Archie sniggers, and says, 'Go on, show them.'

'Oh. Umm, yeah, OK.'

I pull up my hoodie and T-shirt and I show them the scar. It will fade eventually, I've been told, but right now it's still pretty raw. Both boys are completely awed, although one of them looks a bit sick.

'Sorry,' I say to him

'I'm OK,' he says, but his freckles stand out against his pale skin. Maybe I shouldn't have showed them.

His brother has gone back to bouncing up and down on the iron bed like it's a trampoline. Archie snaps, 'Stop it Atticus,' and he stops for an instant and shrieks, 'Did you fight? Did you have a knife? Do you have a gun? Are you a criminal?'

'No,' I say. 'Look, umm, Atticus. Ludo. It's not fun getting stabbed like this. It's much better not to get involved with this kind of thing in the first place.'

I'm quite proud of this piece of mature advice, but the bouncy one just laughs and says, 'I'd have stabbed them back in the eye and the gut and the bum.' Archie snorts and says, 'Ooh, listen to you, Ty, you've gone very responsible.'

'Yeah, right,' I say. 'How's it going, Arch?'

'OK,' he says, 'Good to be on holiday. I've been talking to Zoe every day on Skype. We're going to meet up for New Year, she's coming to London, staying with her aunt.'

'Oh, cool,' I say, although just the mention of

Zoe's name sends a sharp, Claire-shaped pain through my body.

'How's school?' I ask, to change the subject.

'Oh, you know. It's complete crap. Effing monks drilling us all the time.' He doesn't actually say 'effing', and I see the little boys glance at each other, eyes wide.

'It's just – you have no idea what it's like being in a boarding school. Nothing but frigging rules and regulations' – he doesn't say 'frigging' either – 'and you might as well be in prison.' Then he covers his mouth with his hand. 'Oops. Sorry.'

At first, I think he's apologising for swearing in front of the kids. Then I realise that's not it.

'I didn't mean. . . I mean, you might not go down . . . isn't that right?'

Atticus and Ludo's eyes are identically round and fixed on me, and I'm hot with embarrassment and shame. 'Yeah, right.' I say.

'Zoe's dad's a policeman, and he says lots of cases don't ever get to court.'

I think about this. I think some more. 'You *told* Zoe?'

Archie nods. 'Of course. Because she knows you . . . and I thought. . .' His voice trails away. He's looking at my face. 'Umm . . . sorry,' he says in a small, un-Archie-like voice.

Zoe knows I might go to jail. She'll tell everyone

at Parkview. That means Brian and Jamie. Carl. Max. Mr Hunt. Mr Henderson. *Claire*.

Claire and Ellie and all their family. They'll know that I might be going to prison.

Yesterday, I thought I'd given up hope that Claire would ever want to speak to me again. But I did have hope, after all. Because if I didn't, then what just died inside me?

My eyes are blurring. My mouth is full of a squeaking, wailing sound that I can only hold back by clamping my lips shut and breathing through my nose. I have to get away. I need to find a private space to hide, so that I can do what I have to do without completely shaming myself in front of hordes of new relatives.

I spin around, crash out of the room, run down the stairs. They don't seem to be following me, but just in case – I need to escape. Fast. Jesus, help me. Help me, *please*.

I get as far as the front door. I'm not going to run away . . . just find somewhere private. But then the doorbell rings and I jump away. I run through the empty kitchen and into the laundry room. The peaceful, calm, cosy laundry room. The whirring of the washing machine might just cover any other noise.

I grab a newly-washed towel and press it against my face. I breathe in its Comfort smell, but it's no use. The sobs are coming in great shuddering waves, my eyes are flooding with hot tears and it's lucky I have the towel to muffle the noise, because otherwise the whole house would hear me wailing like a baby. What the hell can I do? I'm going to have to hide here forever.

It feels like hours, but eventually my body stops shaking. The tears dry up. I wipe my face with the damp towel and hiccup a few times. I must look terrible. I can't go out there, I can't meet anyone. There's a big, scary bubble of panic at the back of my throat.

And then I spot the big pile of ironing just waiting to be done. Surely it'd only be helpful . . . no one would mind . . . just one shirt. Maybe two. To calm me down. I plug the iron in.

I can hear my dad's voice in the hallway. Helen's so happy he's here, you can tell by the way she's burbling. 'Ty's here,' she's saying. 'Poor thing, he looks exhausted. He's upstairs with the boys. Maybe you want to find him there, bring him down?'

I can't hear his reply. I spit on the iron, just like Gran taught me, and the saliva sizzles into a ball and disappears with a hiss. Just right. I start with the sleeves. The spray squirts and the iron sighs and it's fresh and smooth and just like new. I run my finger along the cotton. It's perfect. Nothing else in the world is as perfect as this.

Louder voices. Helen's in the kitchen. The tap's on, and I hear the click of the kettle. I tense, praying she won't find me, but she's talking to someone and clattering around with teacups and plates. I start on the other sleeve.

'It's so wonderful to meet you at last,' says a woman's voice. I know that voice. Who the hell is it? I miss Helen's reply.

'Oh, a long time,' says the mystery woman. 'We've been close friends for years. It's lovely to meet Danny's family at last, fill in all the gaps.'

Tess. It's that Tess. *Ménage a trois*. Ice bitch. That's who it is. What's she doing here?

'It's really a sign that Danny's put all his problems behind him,' says Tess, 'Introducing us . . . building up a relationship with Ty again. Poor kid. He's had such a rough time.'

Does she mean me? Or my dad?

'It's a joy for all of us having Ty back in the family again,' says Helen. I think she'll be pleased I've done the ironing for her. I shake out the first shirt – smooth, fresh, shiny white – and pick up another.

'How devastating for you,' purrs Tess, 'when Nicki refused to let any of you see him. How vindictive. I'd have thought she'd have understood . . . been grateful that you wanted custody.'

There's a silence. Then Helen says slowly, 'So . . . Danny's told you about that? You must be very close.'

I'm frozen. I can hear the blood rushing around my body, the rhythm of my heart, the breath rattling in my lungs.

'It must have been torture for you,' says Tess. 'Knowing that little boy was growing up in such an unstable home. You can't blame her, I suppose. She was ill. It was terrible for Danny. . .' I'm straining to hear, but there's a crashing sound which drowns her out and all I catch is the end of the sentence ' . . . hospital.'

'Grandma! Grandma! Where's the tea? I want cake!'

'Oh,' says Helen. All the happiness has drained from her voice. 'We're just coming, Atticus darling. Just waiting for the tea to brew. Where's Archie? And Ty?'

'Ty went downstairs,' says a little boy's voice. 'Archie's watching *Lord of the Rings*. Archie's very silly, Grandma.'

There's a smell . . . a weird smell . . . not a nice smell. I look down at the shirt. Oh no. No. I've been pressing too long in one place. There's a shit-brown mark on the snowy white shirt. I've scorched it . . . spoiled it . . . ruined it. Tears prick my eyes again. I clutch the edge of the ironing board. I can't – mustn't – start crying again. Not over a shirt. For God's sake.

'Run up and call him, Ludo,' says Helen. 'Danny must have found Ty and brought him downstairs. Open the door for me, Atticus. Tess, dear, would you mind taking off your shoes? I don't like high heels on the parquet.'

And they're gone. And I can breathe again. But almost instantly there are more voices. My dad. Helen.

'Where the hell is he?' he's saying, 'Has he run away again? My God . . . he's not safe for a minute. Nicki said he was angry about the PlayStation but I didn't think he'd disappear. Did you tell him I was coming? Where can he be?'

I can't move. Everything's kind of muffled and slow and I really need to pee, but I can't take one step.

'Danny,' says Helen, 'This girl . . . this woman . . . your friend. She seems to know everything. Every detail of what happened. She was talking about it so casually. Is she . . . are you. . .?'

'What did she say?' he asks.

'What didn't she say?' I never knew Helen could sound so bitter.

'I don't understand,' he says. 'I don't know how she found out. I'll talk to her. Find out. Tell her not to say anything to Ty. Nicki and I agreed it would be better if he never knew about . . . you know . . . when I had her sectioned.'

Sectioned. I've heard that word before. On *Casualty* or *Holby* or maybe *East Enders*. . .

'Oh, Danny,' says Helen, 'I think Ty . . . I think he might be. . .'

And she must have pointed to the laundry room door, because suddenly he's opening the door, looking at me like I'm a ghost.

'Oh my God,' he says. 'What did you hear?'

Sectioned. Mental Hospital. That's what it means. It means he put her in a loony bin. Jesus Christ. He put her away.

'What did you do to her?' I ask slowly.

'What?'

'To my mum. What did you do to her?' Little fragments are coming back to me now. 'The hospital. Patrick said . . . he said . . . she had to go in. . . She hates hospitals.' That's all I can think of. She hates doctors and hospitals. What happened to her? How could he?

'She was ill,' he says. 'Really ill. She needed treatment. She couldn't look after you. She was bad for you.'

What? What is he saying? I clutch the hot iron. My voice is kind of choking in my throat. 'You can't . . . you shouldn't. . .'

And I lift the iron up to my shoulder, so I can throw it bang smash into his face.

CHAPTER 39
Helen

I hurl the iron at him with all my strength. But it's still plugged into the wall. It jerks, and for a horrible moment I think it's coming straight back at me. Then it falls to the ground. The plug tears from the socket and whips over my shoulder, whopping me in the face as it goes.

'Ergh . . . oww. . .' I whimper, holding my jaw.

My dad's staring at me. Patrick looms behind him. 'What's going on?' he barks. He must've come into the kitchen just in time to see my temper take over. Treacherous tears are gathering again, tickling my throat, prickling my eyelids. I dig my nails into my arm and bite my lip.

Then Helen pushes between the two men. 'Let me talk to Ty,' she says. Her voice is calm and gentle. 'Danny . . . Patrick. . . You go into the other room for a minute. Everything's all right now. Ty just needs a few minutes.'

They leave. 'Ty—' says my dad and I raise my head and give him what I hope is a furious glare. But I don't know how well it worked because I'm just concentrating on keeping my mouth shut and not letting any embarrassing noises out. I can't read his face. He's not as obvious as my mum.

Then it's just me and Helen. I wish she'd go away. She asks, 'Do you want to come and sit in the kitchen?' and I shake my head. My legs feel all shaky and I lean against the washing machine, and slowly slide down to the floor. So I'm sitting with my back to the dryer. My ears are full of the noise of the machines. I'm holding my jaw where the plug hit it. It's throbbing with pain.

She picks up the iron, and puts it away. She takes the shirt I've ironed and says, 'You have done a good job.' She folds up the ironing board, and spots the scorch mark and says, 'Never mind. It was an old one.' She's so kind. I wish she'd just tell me off and leave me alone.

Then she sits down next to me, on the cold tiled floor. I turn my head away. 'Ty,' she says. 'You know, I've been a teacher for the best part of forty years. There's not a lot that I don't know about people your age.'

I hunch my shoulders. I'm not in the mood to chat about Maths GCSE.

'All my experience didn't help when it came to bringing up my son, though,' she adds. I have nothing to say. I'm counting the folded towels stacked up beside me.

'I remember Nicki when she was thirteen,' says Helen. 'Sitting in the back row, pretending she wasn't paying attention, then getting full marks in every test. Full of energy, and pushing at every rule she could.'

It takes me a minute, but I get there. 'D'you mean you taught my mum? She said . . . I thought . . . they were all nuns at her school.' Maybe Helen was a nun . . . but no, she couldn't *possibly* have been.

'Not all,' she says. 'For some subjects they brought in teachers from outside. Julie sent all the girls to my school, even though it was a bit out of the way for them. Actually, come to that, I taught Julie as well. I was newly qualified and she was in my O level class. I was her form teacher. That's how we knew each other. When she left school, I was looking for someone to help with my first baby, so she came to work for me. '

'Oh,' I say. 'Wow.' This is totally bizarre. How can one grandmother teach another one? Mr Lomax, who taught me Maths at St Saviour's and was completely obnoxious suddenly floats into my head. I swallow a nervous laugh.

'Nicki was top of everything. An athletics star as well. I don't think I've ever met anyone so competitive.'

'Oh, right.' She's got my attention, although I'm trying not to show it.

'The whole family had a hard time when Mick – your grandpa, Ty – was ill. He had cancer and he couldn't work. Julie was run ragged, trying to earn money and care for him and the girls at the same time.'

He was my grandad, I think, not my grandpa. And I never even knew him, so it's a bit unfair that she did.

'Nicki went a bit wild. She was always in trouble. The nuns thought she was a bad influence. First they suspended her. In the end they asked Julie to move her to a new school. I tried my best – argued for her – but to no avail. Julie was so upset. It was terrible timing. Mick died about a month later.'

My mum was excluded from school? I never ever knew that. When people talked about her getting into trouble, I always thought that I was the trouble she got into.

'We went to the funeral. It was awful . . . three young girls without a father, poor Julie in floods of tears. We went back to the house for the wake. I was so sad for Julie – widowed before she turned forty.'

'Oh.'

'Then one day, a few months later, Danny didn't come home.'

'Why?'

'We didn't know. We were terribly worried. We called

all his friends. Danny had lots of friends, girls and boys. Especially girls. The phone was always ringing for him. But no one knew where he was.'

'And he was . . . he was with my mum?'

'No. I phoned Louise. She told me she hadn't seen him since her father had died. I was surprised, and I was worried. It wasn't like Danny to go off by himself.'

'Oh.' The door creaks open and we both look up. Meg pushes into the room, tail waving, mouth smiling. She curls up on my feet with a huge doggy sigh. I wish Meg lived with me.

'Then we got a call from the Whittington. The Whittington hospital. Danny had been found in Waterlow Park, unconscious. He'd been drinking. The hospital had him lying on a mattress on the floor, sleeping it off. That's how they treat drunks. He looked like a prisoner in a cell. It was grim. They kept him in for three days with alcohol poisoning.

'We had absolutely no idea what had happened. Why he'd done it. He wouldn't talk to us about it. Patrick was furious – well, you can imagine. I suspected some girl trouble, but we hadn't realised that one girl was more important than all the rest. I mean, Danny was a normal teenage boy. He played the field. He never talked about anyone special.'

'Oh,' I say. I don't seem to be able to come up

with anything else.

'I used to call Julie quite often to see how she was getting on. And Julie was a good person to talk to – she knew my girls so well. I didn't really want to share this with my friends . . . it was difficult. . .'

I get it. She could tell my gran she had a problem with her son, but she couldn't tell her posh mates because they'd look down on her. Huh.

'Julie told me that Nicki was pregnant. She was beside herself. No idea who the father was – Nicki wasn't saying. Julie hadn't realised she even had a boyfriend. An abortion was out of the question – Julie was so devout, is she still? – and Nicki was four months gone before she told anyone. It seems so ironic now – I was worrying about Danny, she was telling me about Nicki, and we had no idea . . . no idea at all.' She smiles at me, 'You probably think we were a bit slow.

'We thought perhaps Danny was anxious about his A levels. He'd floated through school really, underperformed in his GCSEs but achieved reasonable grades. He didn't seem to know what he wanted to do in life. Patrick sat him down, talked to him about universities. Maybe that was a mistake . . . maybe we should have suggested a gap year – but we were worried that he'd just float away from education, never make anything of his life.' She shakes her head and smiles.

'We thought we could help.

'The only idea in Danny's head seemed to be to get out of London. So he opted for Manchester, and said he'd study law. I don't think he was really interested. He was doing it because his father and two of his sisters had done so before him.'

She stops. She looks at me. 'Don't do that, Ty darling. Don't let other people make choices for you. Work out what you want to do for yourself.'

She's obviously forgotten I might have my future decided for me by a judge and jury. 'Then what happened?' I ask quickly, so she won't remember.

'Danny disappeared again. One morning he wasn't there – he'd left the house during the night. I was frantic with worry. But then I got a phone call from Julie. Oh, Ty, I have never been so shocked. She told me that he'd turned up at her house. She thought he was there to see Louise, but he was begging to see Nicki. And they were reconciled, together, in love. Ty, we had no idea at all. Everything fell into place, but nothing seemed to make sense.

'We went over to Julie's house. Danny and Nicki were defiant. They sat there, holding hands, telling us how they were going to be parents, get their own place. They were so young, Ty, it was pitiful. Nicki didn't look a day older than when I used to teach her. And Danny . . . Danny was always the baby of our family. Three older sisters . . . no one ever took him seriously. It was . . . Patrick didn't react well, I'm sorry to say. And Julie was angry with Danny too. It wasn't easy.'

It all sounds like a complete and total and absolute *nightmare*. I'm imagining the whole thing and substituting Claire and her parents for Mum and Gran, with Mr Lomax floating around too. I'd rather die. My dad should've just run away as fast as he could. I actually feel quite sorry for both of them.

'When you were born, there was really no question that Danny was your father,' she says. Obviously there had been quite a lot of questions beforehand. 'You looked just like my daughter Marina when she was a baby. And a little like me, perhaps.'

Huh. I obviously looked like a total girl right from the start.

'Huge blue eyes,' she says. I widen my eyes and show her. 'No . . . Helen . . . my eyes are *green*.'

'Children's eyes turn from blue to green very late,' she says. 'Marina's eyes changed when she was seven. Anyway there was no question at all that Danny was the father. Nicki juggled school and the baby. We helped Julie out with some money so she could cut her hours and help care for you. Danny – to our surprise – got his head down and started studying hard for his A levels.

He spent a lot of time round at their house, but it wasn't easy. Julie was very hostile. Sometimes Nicki would bring you around to us, but she was always on edge – very touchy – taking offence at the slightest thing. She and Danny were fine one minute, having big rows the next. It wasn't the easiest time.'

My mum hasn't changed much.

'Danny finished school. Nicki took her GCSEs. I don't know how she did it, but she managed to get some good grades. Nothing like she should have got, though, Ty, she had such high potential. They were spending a lot of time together. You were such a sweet baby – a really good boy. Everyone adored you. We didn't know what would happen if Danny got into university. We thought perhaps he'd take a year off, transfer to a London college. Then he got his grades. He got into Manchester. And they announced that they were going off together.

'We were all horrified. Patrick tried to make Danny see sense – to persuade him that he should either go by himself or take a year off, earn some money, apply to a London university. But Danny can be so stubborn. He insisted. Nicki was desperate to escape from her mother, it turned out. Julie had been giving her a hard time. Danny was probably desperate to escape from us, who knows? They wanted to be together, they said, they wanted to be a family. He'd been in touch with the university authorities, arranged that they could have a one-bedroom flat. There was no arguing with them. They went off to Manchester with you – Patrick drove them. There wasn't room for Julie or me in the car, because of all their stuff – the baby equipment. I remember that day so well – their excitement, how Patrick was. . . I sat down and cried when you all left, Ty. I just couldn't see how they were going to cope.'

I can hear voices. People in the kitchen. People moving around. Archie's voice saying, 'Where's Ty? Where's he gone?' I don't want them to interrupt. I need to hear the next bit of Helen's story.

'They didn't cope, did they?' I say, and then someone coughs. Someone's in the room with us. We both look up.

'I'll take it from here,' says my dad.

CHAPTER 40
Danny

'Go away,' I say. Helen thinks I'm talking to her. 'I'll leave you to it,' she says, and I have to hold onto her sleeve to stop her getting up.

'No, you stay. You tell me more. I don't want him. He told me nothing. Nothing at all. You have to tell me the true story.'

My dad slides down to the floor. This room can't really take any more people, and his long legs have nowhere to go. He pushes at Meg's bum to make some more space. She shifts in her sleep, growls softly and then spreads herself a bit more comfortably, leaving him even less room.

I could move up, I suppose, but then I'd be virtually sitting on Helen's lap. I don't.

'It's OK, Ma. You stay. I don't care who hears this.'

There's this tiny part of me that wants to bury my head in a towel, hide from him and her and the truth and everything about it. I have enough fresh problems in my life right now, without adding some decaying dug-up old ones.

'Ty,' he says, 'Ty, it all worked fine at the beginning. We were having an adventure. We liked being independent, looking after you. You were great – you were doing something new and different every day. It was good. A really good idea.'

He's looking at Helen, and I immediately discount most of this. I know when someone's trying to make their mum think everything was fine. I do it all the time.

'I was trying to balance studying and making new friends at uni, and working – I got a job in a bar – and being with Nicki and you. It wasn't always easy. Nicki was lonely, and she hadn't been able to find a college with childcare, so she was a bit bored. We finished the first term and we came home for Christmas and we missed each other a lot. I went over to her mum's house on Christmas day, and she – Nicki's mum – just didn't want me there. We were really happy to go back to Manchester.'

He's looking at me now. I don't want to fall under his spell again. Get drawn into the way he sees things, start believing in him. I need to keep myself separate. So I concentrate on the tiles on the floor, which are big and red and someone's had to cut them in half to fit the corners.

'But then . . . I don't know . . . things started to go wrong. Nicki . . . she got an idea into her head that I wasn't so . . . wasn't into her any more. She got jealous. She thought it was her, that she wasn't attractive. She thought she was fat. She went on a diet.'

I get the distinct impression that he's hiding something. I suspect my mum had every reason to be jealous. Anyway, all women think they're fat. They're all on diets. I'm surprised he doesn't know that, with his vast experience and his *ménage a trois* and his celebrity mates.

Archie sticks his head round the door. His eyes boggle when he sees us all sitting on the floor. 'What's going on?' he says, 'I'm hungry, Grandma.'

'Go *away*, Archie.' My dad and I say it together. He grins at me. I look away.

Helen says, 'I'm coming in a minute, darling.' Archie retreats. She looks at me. 'Do you still want me here? Maybe you need some time together on your own.'

I never needed Helen before; I already had too many women in my life. But right now, I don't want her to go.

So I say, 'No, stay, please,' and she stays. I don't think my dad's really delighted.

'Oh God,' he says, 'Where was I?'

'You were explaining why you had my mum locked

away in a loony bin,' I say through gritted teeth.

'She just stopped eating Ty. I didn't realise at first. She sort of pretended to eat, or I'd get home and she'd say she'd eaten. She got thinner and thinner. I didn't realise . . . didn't know.'

I yawn. When will he get to the point?

'And then she got a cold. She was in bed, ill, and I took time off from lectures and work to look after you. I realised . . . from the way you were. . . I'd been blind, hadn't realised what was going on. I was stupid.' He gulps, and stops. I'm amazed to see tears running down his face.

'You were very young,' says Helen. 'Maybe I should tell Ty what happened next.'

He nods. He's biting the back of his hand.

'We got a call from Danny,' she says, 'He'd got the doctor at the student health centre to see Nicki. She'd cut down too much on her food, become ill. The doctor said she needed treatment, proper treatment in a hospital. She wasn't going to get better without it. He diagnosed anorexia. You get to a point of no return, where you end up starving yourself to death. It's a terrible thing but very common in teenage girls.'

'Oh right,' I say. I know about anorexia. I've skimmed articles about it in *Cosmo*. But I thought girls with anorexia looked like living skeletons. I can't imagine my mum ever looking like that.

'So that's why . . . that's why the hospital. . .'

'Nicki wasn't just denying herself food,' says Helen. 'She'd somehow persuaded herself that you needed to diet too. Danny took you to a paediatrician. You were failing to thrive, darling. Underweight.'

'I thought they were going to take you into care,' says my dad. His voice is flat and sad. 'I had to call them. I didn't know what to do.'

'Them' means Helen and Patrick, I think. He must've been desperate.

'Nicki didn't accept any of it,' he says, 'I don't think she really even accepts it now. We spent all that time together when you were in hospital skirting around the subject. Not talking about it. I suppose she must have got over the eating disorder now . . . but she doesn't eat much, does she? Louise calls her a functioning anorexic.'

It's like looking in those strange fairground mirrors that squash you and pull you, and everything's the same but totally different. My mum's not got an eating disorder – or has she? She eats a pot of low fat yoghurt in the morning, she makes a sandwich and has half of it for lunch and the other half for supper. If she eats a piece of cake or some chips, she cuts down the next day. My gran was always asking her what she'd eaten, what I'd eaten, filling our fridge with food. I learned at an early age that I needed to take money from Nicki's purse to meet my own needs.

But she's not ill. She looks as good as a celebrity. She's not sick and dying and in hospital and mentally ill and needing treatment.

'She had to be sectioned,' he says, 'to get help, because she wouldn't admit . . . wouldn't accept. . . I knew she'd never forgive me. I'll never forget her face . . . her face. . . Anyway, I called her mum and she came up to Manchester to be with Nicki. I called them' – he jerks his head towards Helen – 'and they came and took you. And then I just . . . I just. . .'

'He disappeared,' says Helen. 'About a month later. Walked out of his flat in Manchester, quit his course. We didn't know where he was and what had happened to him. We didn't hear from him for two years.'

'I'm sorry,' he says in the same flat, sad voice, and she says, 'We've waited an awful long time for you to say that. You might want to repeat it to your father.'

Yeah, right, *that's* going to happen, I think, and I bet my dad's thinking the same.

'It was just . . . you were looking after him better than I could. Even Pa. Nicki made it perfectly obvious she never wanted to see me again. I was . . . I couldn't cope. I didn't think anyone needed me.'

'Your sister was pregnant,' says Helen, 'The stress

of worrying about you may well have caused her miscarriage.'

I'm kind of surprised that it's not just my mum and gran who guilt-trip you about stuff that's nothing to do with you. It's obviously a general female thing. Danny rolls his eyes and says, 'Thanks for that.'

'What happened to *me*?' I ask, to remind them why we've having this conversation in the first place.

'Oh, you were sweet, you were gorgeous,' says Helen. 'We took you to the doctor and he advised us how to feed you, get you to put on weight. I had to cook with you, offer you a selection of different foods. You were very quiet at first, missing Nicki, of course, and Danny. You didn't cry, which was strange for a toddler, you were withdrawn. Sad. But then you got more used to us. Patrick had just retired and he took on the lion's share of looking after you. He would take you to Hampstead Heath for walks. He was trying to teach you to speak French. He loved you so much – it was very nice to see how much you enjoyed each other's company.'

'He had more time for you than he did for any of us,' says my dad, and Helen shakes her head at him and says, 'That's not fair, Danny. He worked very long hours.'

'Where did you go?' I ask him, and he says, 'Amsterdam, at first. Then I came back to England, stayed with friends. I used to travel around a lot, go to festivals . . . then we started the band. It's all a bit of a blur, to be honest.'

'Your mum came out of hospital,' says Helen, 'And Julie came to us. She demanded that we hand you over. We were worried – not sure what to do. We weren't sure about Nicki's health, whether she'd be able to look after you. Danny wasn't there to stand up for his rights. Patrick talked about trying for custody. But Julie said that she thought Nicki's heart would break if she didn't get you back. She promised she'd bring you back for visits. So we let you go with her.

'And then they cut us out. I kept calling Julie, asking her when we could see you, but she just said there was no arguing with Nicki, she didn't want to jeopardise her health, there was no way your mum would allow you anywhere near us. In the end Julie changed her phone number, moved house. We'd lost you. Thank goodness for Louise, who would come and see us sometimes, tell us about you, give us photographs. I don't know about Patrick, but that kept me going. She used to send you pictures as well, didn't she, Danny?'

'I took my own,' he says. 'I used to go and sit outside your school, Ty, and take pictures with a long lens. Like a paparazzo. I thought about going up to you, saying hello, but I was never brave enough.'

'You were *spying* on me?'

'It was all I could do,' he says.

I'm not wildly impressed. Even my gran seems to have behaved pretty badly. Although perhaps it's best not to judge anyone until I hear their side of the story.

Anyway, I'm starving hungry, which is kind of ironic, really, in the circumstances.

I stand up, waking up Meg, who starts barking and jumping and waving her tail right in my dad's face.

'Umm . . . thanks for telling me,' I say.

'Maybe best not to mention to Nicki,' says my dad, as he and Helen stand up too. I shrug and say, 'OK,' and then, 'Helen, can we have some food now?' And I don't know why she's crying, but my dad wraps her into a big hug, so I go out into the kitchen and find Archie's making himself an enormous turkey sandwich, with mayo, pickles and – weirdly – beetroot. I steal half of it and then we start looking in the fridge to see if there's any Christmas pudding left.

Helen and my dad are still talking in the laundry room – God knows what about – so Archie suggests we take the pudding and go and watch the next *Lord of the Rings* upstairs, but on the way up, Patrick catches us and insists that I come and meet everyone. So I get introduced to my other aunts and uncles, who are all sitting around trying not to look like they've been speculating about what the hell was going on in the laundry room.

There's Marina, who works at the BBC and doesn't look anything like me at all, thankfully, as she's a woman with dark hair and scary black-rimmed specs and a kind of sharp-edged face. She's the one who called her children Ludo and Atticus, so she's obviously a bit strange, and she has a husband – grey hair and beard, specs, unfortunate sweater – called Robin.

Then there's Elizabeth, who teaches Philosophy at London University and her husband, George, a journalist. Luckily, they've got two tiny daughters Mia and Evie who are making huge amounts of noise, so no one can ask me any questions and I can just smile and not really say anything. I completely ignore Tess, who's sitting in an armchair reading *Country Life*. She looks bored out of her skull.

Then Archie and I escape upstairs. We have to evict Ludo and Atticus from the bed, and replace *Shrek Three* with the next *Lord of the Rings* – Archie does a brilliant impersonation of Gollum hissing, 'My precioussss' – but we explain kindly that *Shrek Three* is crap. They might as well not bother with the last twenty minutes. Then they see our bowls of Christmas pudding and go rushing downstairs to get some too. We don't tell them that we've finished it off.

And it's just me and Archie, and I think I've probably forgiven him for telling Zoe, because, let's face it, I'd already messed up me and Claire all by myself. Zoe's a nice girl and maybe she won't gossip.

'What were you all talking about for so long?' he asks, mouth full of pudding, and I say, 'They were telling me stuff. About when I was little and I lived with Patrick and Helen.'

And he rolls his eyes and says, 'Oh bloody hell, not that crap again. They were yattering on about it yesterday, my mum and her sisters. So boring. All about how your mum had to go into hospital and then your dad went walkabout, yatter, yatter, blah, blah. It was like an episode of *Holby* frigging *City*. I don't know why everyone has to go on and on about *you* all the time, when it's me who's *suffering* at boarding school. . .'

He's stupid, Archie and he's a pain, but there are times when I quite like him and I even find him quite funny, and that's why I'm still laughing weakly, holding my stomach, when Patrick comes to find us.

'Everything's all right, then?' he says, standing in the doorway and frowning under his fluffy eyebrows, and that starts us laughing again. He says, 'I see it is. I'm glad. You'd better come down now, Ty, and say goodbye to Danny and umm. . .'

'Tess,' I say, and I follow him reluctantly down the stairs. Tess is balancing on one leg, putting her heels back on. Danny's shrugging on a leather jacket. I'm beginning to suspect his clothes aren't as rubbish as they look. I think they might actually be designer scruff.

'Hey,' he says, 'OK? I'll see you soon. Take care.' And before I can step aside he gives me an awkward hug, grabbing me round the shoulders and pulling my face into the cold leather. 'I'm off to New York again,' he adds. 'Work . . . and the police say it'll be safer if I'm out of the country.'

'How long for?' I ask, and he shrugs and says, 'Four weeks, maybe more.' I'm kind of shocked that I feel a little bit upset. He ruffles my hair. 'I'll miss you,' he says.

'Bye, *Dad*,' I say, to make it clear that Tess isn't included. She's too busy gushing all over Helen and Patrick to notice.

Then they're gone, and I'm just heading back upstairs to rejoin Archie when his mum appears at the kitchen door and says, 'Just a minute, Ty – come in here.'

I try and think of a polite way to refuse, but I can't, so I follow her. Helen's in there, sitting with Marina and Elizabeth. They've opened a bottle of white wine. 'Sit down,' says Archie's mum, pulling up her own chair and taking a big gulp of Chardonnay. I obey. 'Now,' says Archie's mum. 'You have to tell us. Who is this Tess girl? How serious is Danny about her?'

I open my mouth. Helen puts her arm around me. 'It's OK,' she says. 'You don't have to answer. Danny's got three nosy sisters, poor thing.'

'No, it's OK,' I say. 'She's his flatmate . . . lodger
. . . and he says they're on and off. More off than on, but
when she gets cross with him, he kind of . . . he starts it
again to stop her being cross, I think. And she works in
television.'

They're all gazing at me, completely silent.

'So they live together, then?' says the BBC
one – Marina.

'Yes, but there's another flatmate too, a girl called
Lucy,' I say, 'And he's . . . ummm . . . y'know . . . with
her too, but that Tess doesn't know. And I think there's
another girl who's his assistant and he might've . . . I don't
know . . . that's what Tess said. . .'

They're all laughing. Even Helen. I feel my face getting
hot, but then Elizabeth says, 'Oh, thank you so much,
Ty, we were worried she'd got her claws into him, but it
sounds like he's found safety in numbers,' and suddenly
I feel OK. It's just like being at home with Gran and Mum
and Louise and Emma when they're taking apart the finer
details of someone's love life. The same laughter. The
same smell of wine.

'Don't tell him I said anything,' I say, and Archie's
mum says, 'Don't worry, we won't scare him off.' And
then they're filling up their glasses again, and I escape
upstairs before they can ask anything about my mum.

Actually, I'm pretty grateful to Tess for turning up today. I'm feeling quite good for a number of reasons.

But I know that things won't stay that way. Because in just a few weeks I'm going to have to stand up in court and tell my story.

CHAPTER 41
Angel

There's an angel on the roof. *Jesus.* It's got robes and it's glowing through the misty morning. I can't see its wings, but there's a sort of halo, rays beaming from its shining head. I wonder if any one else can see it. Maybe this is it. I've finally crossed over. I've gone mad.

It's completely still – oh, it's a statue. Obviously. I knew that all the time. Duh. It's got a massive knife – a sword really – in one hand and something weird – a bag? scales? – in the other. As I step out of the car I'm meant to rush into the door that's being held open for me. Instead, I stand on the wet pavement and stare up at this strange creature. The angel of death.

Patrick nudges me. 'Come on, Ty. Get inside.'

This is the day they didn't want me to see. This is the day when I have to tell the truth. The whole truth.

Nothing but the truth. This is the day of Arron's trial, Jukes's trial, Mikey's trial. This is the day of justice for Rio and his family. I am the only witness who actually saw what happened. This is it.

I don't know if I can do it. Is it too late to change my mind?

My mum wanted to come with me, but the baby's due in a month and her midwife said that long journeys and stress would be a bad idea. Apparently her blood pressure's up a bit. I'm not sure whether blood pressure is meant to be up or down, but I'm guessing it's not good from the way Gran was fussing over her. My dad's still in New York.

So, Patrick got the job of sitting next to me in the cop car from Birmingham to London. They picked us up at 5 am, so he had to stay over in the flat – Gran gave up her room – which was a bit of a strange experience for everyone. That's probably just got into the *Guinness Book of World Records* as the biggest understatement of all time. And now he's striding through wood-panelled corridors at my side, explaining the angel on the roof.

'This is the Old Bailey,' he says, 'the Central Criminal Court. The statue represents Lady Justice. She carries the sword of punishment and the scales of equity. Traditionally she is portrayed with a blindfold, but not in this case. Don't they teach you anything at school nowadays?'

The Old Bailey. *Jesus.* How did I miss that we were coming here? That's the court they talk about on the news, on television. It's the one for really serious cases. This is a really serious case. *Jesus.* I feel like the angel statue just stuck her sword in my guts.

There's a court official showing us where to go, a woman with grey hair. She takes us to a small, brightly-lit room, and shows me a chair and a table. 'That's where you'll sit when you're giving evidence,' she says. There's a video camera set up right by the table, and a TV screen. It's nothing special, not a big plasma screen or anything. She puts a glass and a jug of water on the table. 'It shouldn't be too long,' she says. 'They'll tell you when they're ready for you.'

Patrick wishes me luck and says he'll be watching from the public gallery. 'I probably won't be able to see you, but I will be able to hear,' he says. When he leaves, I sit at the table and try and focus my mind on what I've got to say, but I can't concentrate at all. The only way I can clear my mind is by thinking about Claire.

'Tom,' says the woman, interrupting me, which is probably not a bad thing.

'I'm called Ty,' I say, 'not Tom.'

'They'll call you Tom in court. To protect your identity. And there will be screens in the courtroom, so only the jury and the lawyers can see you give evidence. And the judge and the barristers will take off their wigs so you won't be intimidated. Has this been explained to you?'

It has, and I felt more than a slight prickle of irritation at the time. Why are they treating me like a baby? It takes a hell of a lot more than some stupid fancy dress to intimidate me. Haven't I proved that? Huh.

But at the same time that DI Morris was telling me all that – he came to Birmingham to see me a few weeks ago – he was also explaining that the defence lawyers would be attacking my character, making out I was a liar, 'Someone who fantasises, has a vivid imagination, isn't reliable with the truth.' He doesn't need to tell me that I've handed them their evidence on a plate. After that, I kind of forgot the details about wigs and names.

Suddenly the screen flickers into life, and I can see all the barristers taking their wigs off and putting them into little bags, and my mouth goes dry and my stomach twists and turns. I pour myself a glass of water.

'Here we go,' says the woman. She asks me my religion and asks if I want to swear on the bible or affirm that I'm telling the truth. I'm not exactly sure what affirming means, so I say I'll swear. I do think it's a stupid, out-dated way of making people promise to tell the truth. Hardly anyone English really believes in God any more. Not 100 per cent, anyway. They should make a new system. Otherwise, they can only really trust old people, priests and Muslims. They need new technology. Something like the lie detectors they have on the Jeremy Kyle show.

As I say the words, 'the truth, the whole truth and nothing but the truth,' my voice squeaks, suddenly high and young. My hand shakes on the Bible. Great. I've just embarrassed myself in front of a whole courtroom of people that I can't even see.

'Good morning, Tom,' says the first lawyer, and we've off. We're away. There's no going back now. At least, I don't think so.

DI Morris told me that the first lawyer would be the nice one. The gentle one. The lawyer for the prosecution, the one who wants to show the court how trustworthy and truthful I am. He's OK, I suppose. But he seems to think that Arron was a much bigger villain than he was, a big man, dealing drugs at school, mugging and bullying and hanging out with gangsters. It's like reading *The Sun*. You know the facts are probably right, but there's something strange about the way they've been put together.

He leads me through all the statements I've made. Arron's little envelopes at school and what I thought about them. Meeting Jukes and Mikey outside the shop. Arron asking me to help with a mugging. Me refusing, running to the park, watching.

And what I saw. Arron and Rio fighting. Jukes and

Mikey pushing, jostling. Pushing Rio onto the knife. And how they ran away. And how I ran for an ambulance.

Then we get to the difficult bit. The bit where I made Arron run out of the park. The lawyer's in neutral mode: 'Can you tell me, Tom, what happened when you came back to the park?'

'Speak clearly, look at the camera, stay calm,' was Patrick's advice in the car. I try my best. 'I realised that the boy – Rio – was dead. I knew that when the ambulance came they'd think Arron had done it. I didn't want them to . . . to think that. I told him to run away. He wouldn't do it. So I got out my knife and I threatened him. I hit him with it. I cut him . . . I think. And then we ran to his house.'

'And did you tell the police about this when you made your initial statement?'

'No. I was too scared, and I thought they wouldn't believe me . . . about the rest of it. I told them later.'

'Can you tell me why you came clean to the police later?'

'Umm . . . there was an email I wrote. To a friend. I was feeling bad because I hadn't told the police everything. So I told her I'd been lying – but only about that, nothing else – and she told the police. So I told them.'

'Let's be clear about this, Tom. You lied to the police, but only about this one incident?'

'Yes.'

'You understand the difference between the truth and lies?'

I'm not really sure that it's as simple as that. The truth is more complicated than he's making out. But I nod my head and say, 'Yes, yes I do.' What else can I say?

I can see the jury over his shoulder. Twelve blank faces. They're not giving anything away. I can see the judge, she's blonde with massive pearl earrings. The prosecution lawyer thanks me and sits down. The judge asks me if I'm all right. I nod. She calls Arron's lawyer. I'm holding my breath. Here we go.

Arron's lawyer is a thin, gingery guy with a shiny bald patch, which I'm sure he'd prefer to cover up with his stupid wig. 'Good morning, Tom,' he says. He's trying to sound friendly. I'm not fooled.

'Would you describe Arron Mackenzie as your best friend?' he asks.

'Well . . . he was. Then he was. Not now.'

'And would your expectation be that friends tell each other the truth?'

'Well . . . yes,' I say. I don't know where this is going. Maybe it's about the way that Arron covered up the drug-dealing at school.

'What does your father do for a living, Tom?' he asks.

My head jerks up. I can't tell him that. My dad's going to be a witness against Jukes . . . they already know too many details about him. . .

'Let me re-phrase that, as it seems to be causing you some difficulties,' smarms the lawyer. 'Do you recall telling your friend Arron Mackenzie on numerous occasions that your father was a lawyer working for football teams including Manchester United, Arsenal and Tottenham Hotspur?'

Oh. Bum. 'Umm . . . yes . . . but. . .'

'And is he a lawyer working for Manchester United, Arsenal and Tottenham Hotspur?'

'Umm. No. But I didn't . . . I didn't. . .'

'Do you actually know the difference between truth and fantasy, Tom?' he asks, smirking through his tortoiseshell specs.

I can feel that my face is hot and red. 'Yes.'

'Well, now,' he says. 'Let us turn to your statement.'

Arron's story is completely different from mine. According to Arron, we met Jukes and Mikey at the bowling alley, joked around a bit, never saw them again that day. Arron's lawyer quotes back at me lots of things that were actually said, but changes them here and there, gives them another meaning, leaves out crucial bits.

I stay calm. I speak clearly. 'No, it wasn't quite like that,' I say. 'No, he didn't say it like that.'

According to Arron, he and I were due to meet at the park, in the playground. He was walking up the path to meet me when Rio jumped out at him. Rio waved the blade in his face, Arron looked for me. I didn't come and help him. He panicked, all on his own.

'You were watching all this, weren't you?' says the lawyer.

'I was watching – but it wasn't Rio who jumped out, it was Arron.'

'Your friend was fighting someone attacking him with a knife, and you didn't come to his aid? Even though you had armed yourself?'

'I – it was all really quick. I didn't think there was anything I could do. Then I saw blood and I ran for an ambulance.' It's kind of true, that is what I did. But I don't tell him how I was frozen and terrified, sweating and trying not to wet myself. And how, when I unfroze, I ran away. The ambulance came into my mind as I ran.

What would I have done if I'd known this was Arron's story? Would I have lied for him? Why is he letting Jukes and Mikey off the hook?

What's more important, truth or friendship?

'So, you abandoned your vantage point, leaving your friend fighting for his life in the dirty ground, and you ran off in a north-westerly direction – the direction of your home, in fact?' he asks.

'Yes . . . no . . . I mean, I wasn't going home, I was going to call an ambulance for them . . . for Arron.'

'Indeed?' he says.

'I stopped the bus and I told them to call the ambulance and I ran back. I'm fast – I'm a fast runner – I wasn't gone for long.'

'And when you came back, when you believed the ambulance was on the way to help save the life of your friend, your best friend, lying there bleeding in the mud – what happened?'

'I told Arron he had to run, to run away.'

'You told Arron he had to run away? Just after calling an ambulance to save his life?' He makes it sound like it's impossible that anyone could ever believe me about anything.

'I didn't want the police to catch him – I didn't want them to think it was just Arron, not Mikey or Jukes as well.'

'You thought it was more important to hide from the police than to get immediate medical aid for your friend?'

'Yes – for him, not for me, for him. It wasn't all

Arron's fault, but if they found him with the body, it'd look like it was him by himself.'

'If they found you both with the body it would look like it was the two of you acting together, wouldn't it?'

It's getting harder to stay calm. 'I didn't – I wasn't. It wasn't anything to do with me.'

'It would be quite normal for you to feel guilty, Tom. You failed your friend, didn't you? If you'd intervened earlier, perhaps the whole fight might have been avoided.'

The judge interrupts. Tells Arron's lawyer he's over-stepping the mark. Asks me if I'm OK. I take a big gulp of water. 'Yes,' I say.

'You felt bad and guilty and you begged Arron to run away so you wouldn't be found at the scene?'

'No, it wasn't like that.'

'Arron was prepared to stay with the body, wasn't he? He would have told the police and ambulance exactly what happened. How Rio attacked him. You made him run away, didn't you?'

My voice is a whisper. 'Yes . . . but. . .' I trail to a halt, because it's true I was feeling guilty and scared – and I am now – but it was Arron doing the mugging, not Rio, and I was trying to help him when I slashed him with the knife.

God, we were all so stupid. We were all guilty.

Any one of us could have been dead. Any one of us could have been in the dock.

And then he starts on about my email. The email to Claire. And he picks it apart sentence by sentence, but the one he keeps coming back to is, 'I'm a liar . . . I'm lying to the police.' And I try and explain, but he says it so many times that in the end I snap, 'Look, you've said it enough. They've got the message.'

'Yes, indeed,' he says and he sits down.

CHAPTER 42
The Weakest Link

Mikey's lawyer is next. Mikey's story is simple. He was nowhere near that park. He was at home, watching telly. *The Weakest Link,* to be precise. I'm a liar, I'm a liar, I'm a liar.

His lawyer picks up the bit in my statement where I say that maybe Mikey gave Arron some money, maybe it was to do with drugs, and he has fun with that – what an imagination I have! Did I spend a lot of time alone in my room? Watching people out of the window? Making up stories about them?

Liar, liar, pants on fire. He doesn't actually say it, but that's what he means.

Sweat is trickling down the back of my neck. I've drunk all the water they put out for me, and I need to pee. I'm shifting around in my seat, rubbing my forehead.

It's so hot in here. I feel like I've been here forever.

Mikey's lawyer sits down. Someone says something about the court . . . I can't hear it . . . 'All rise!' someone shouts, and all the lawyers stand up. Then the screen goes blank.

'Lunchtime,' says the court official. 'I'll go and organise some sandwiches. You can use the facilities if you need to – across the corridor, but you need to tell the police officer outside where you're going and come straight back. You are not allowed to discuss the case with anyone.'

I stumble towards the door, brush past the policeman guarding it and head into the Gents. And lock myself into a cubicle.

It only seems like five minutes later that there's a knock at the door. 'Ty?' says Patrick's voice. 'Ty, you've got to come now. They're going to start again soon.'

I lean my head against the cubicle wall.

'Come on, Ty. It'll be all right.'

I take a deep breath. I open the door. Patrick's standing there, looking at his watch.

'Patrick, I can't . . . I can't . . . he was saying. . .'

But Patrick wags his finger at me and says, 'You know we can't discuss anything. You need to get right back in there now before the judge comes back. I need to get to the public gallery, too. Splash your face with water . . . that's it. . . Blow your nose, and I'll see you later.'

And he's gone, and I'm back in the stuffy little room.

I sit down at the table. The screen flickers to life again. I can see the lawyers chatting, rustling papers. Then I hear them say, 'All rise' and they stand up. The judge is back. We're on again.

Jukes's lawyer. A little fat man, with a black beard. He's got a big smile on his face. He's looking at me like he's just wandered into Krispy Kreme and I'm chocolate iced with sprinkles. He's rubbing his hands together.

'Good afternoon, Tom,' he says. 'Let's talk about what you saw at the park.'

And we go through it all again. For the fourth time. He's trying to catch me out on details – who was standing where, who did what when.

And it's hard to remember exactly what I've said, and a few times he wins, 'But, forgive me Tom, didn't you say that Mr White was standing to the left of Mr MacKenzie, when you were speaking to my learned friend Mr Belweather, is that not correct?'

'Umm, yes . . . I mean no . . . I mean, well, it kind of depends which way you were looking at them.'

And so it goes on. And he makes me tell every detail again of the knife-waving and the cutting and how I wanted Arron to run away.

Then he says, 'This accusation of yours against my client, this was part of a long-standing feud between your families, was it not?'

Eh?

'Umm. No . . . I don't know what you mean.' I say.

'Since your mother took out an injunction against my client's uncle, Christopher Richardson, nine years ago.'

'I don't know anything about that,' I say, and it's totally true. I don't know anything about an injunction. But I'm thinking – *Jesus*, Chris the plumber? Jukes's uncle? – and God knows what my face looks like.

'Are you sure?' he says, 'This is the truth we want now, Tom, not one of your stories.'

'Yes,' I say, 'I'm sure. I'm absolutely certain about everything I've told you.'

'Completely certain?' he sneers. And I can't stand it any more. I push my chair back from the table, leap to my feet. I pull my shirt out of my trousers and tug it up as far as I can. 'Please sit down!' says the judge, but I'm not listening. I turn to my side, to show my scar to the camera.

'Please sit down!' says the court official, but I'm shouting, 'That's what he did, your client. That's how he tried to shut me up. And Alistair got shot, and they hurt my gran. They petrol-bombed our home. Why would they do that if I was lying? You tell me.'

I thought Jukes's lawyer would look angry, but he's smirking like I've just handed him a Christmas present. 'My Lady,' he says, 'a matter of law arises which I would like to raise in the absence of the jury.'

I sit back down on the chair. I'm trembling. I pick up the glass and drink some water, but my hand is shaking so much that I spill some on my shirt. I can see the court official shaking her head.

The jury file out. The judge says, 'Tom, remain seated while giving evidence, please.' Then the screen goes dark.

The court official is tutting at me, but she refills my glass and she says, 'Look, dearie, calm down and eat your sandwich, because it's not good to miss your lunch and it's going to be a long afternoon.' So I choke down a few mouthfuls of slimy ham and cotton wool bread, and I sip some water and I wonder what's going on in the courtroom.

They take ages. Ninety minutes later the screen comes on again. My anger's as dead as the slivers of pig in my sandwich. All I want is for it to be over. They can say what they like about me. I don't really care.

The judge tells the jury to ignore my outburst, 'which is not relevant to your deliberations.' She says to me, 'Tom, do you understand what I've said?' I nod. I don't accept it for a minute, but I'm not going to argue.

She nods to Jukes's lawyer. 'Proceed.' And he does.

When he finishes, I think that's it. I've done my bit. It's over. But then the first lawyer gets up again. The prosecution one. And he starts all over again. Perhaps I'm going to be here forever. Perhaps they all get to question me again and again and again.

He's talking about truth and lies. Asking me what I was taught at school. Asking me about going to church . . . what the Catholic religion says about lying. Making me say, 'Yes, I know the difference between truth and lies. I really do.'

'The injunction mentioned by my learned friend, you had no knowledge of it? Any idea what it relates to?'

'I can guess,' I say. 'When I was little, my mum had a boyfriend who hit me and who hit her. Maybe that was him. Jukes's uncle.'

'Do you know his name?' he asks, and I say, 'He was called Chris and he was a plumber. That's all I know.'

Then he asks me again about that moment when Arron and I ran away. What can I say? 'It's really hard to think when you're standing there and there's someone dead,' I say. 'I did the wrong thing. I'm sorry.'

That seems to be it. The camera's red light goes out, the screen goes blank. I sit at my table, staring at my hands, wondering what's going to happen now. Do we wait to see if Arron's found guilty or not? Will the screen come back on? Then the door opens and Patrick comes in, and the court official hands us over to a policeman who takes us to a door where there's a cop car waiting.

As we drive off, I look up to see the angel – Lady Justice – again, but she's up too high. I can't see her from this angle.

In the car, Patrick tells me I did well, apart from the bit when I showed them the scar. 'You almost got the whole trial aborted,' he said. 'When the jury was sent out, the defence lawyer was arguing that you'd made it impossible to try his client fairly. It was good that you stopped when you did.'

'I didn't want to,'

'I know. But there's a time and a place. Anyway, don't expect a verdict for a week or two. These things take time, and they've got a lot of evidence to hear.'

'Oh, right.'

'Ty,' he adds, 'About the injunction . . . Nicki's boyfriend. . .'

I shake my head. I'm not talking about that. But I can't stop wondering if Nathan maybe didn't have things quite right. Maybe it wasn't because of my mum that Jukes wanted me involved in the gang. Or maybe it was because of her, but for a different reason. Revenge.

Patrick's looking at me, and his face is so concerned, so worried that it's actually hurting me to look at him. I stare out of the window, but trickling raindrops get in the way of London. It's like the streets are crying.

'Arron's evidence seems to have omitted your assault

on him,' says Patrick. 'He's presenting himself as Rio's victim. Maybe it was a bit too much to expect the jury to believe he could be bullied by you as well. A big, tall youth like that. It suits him to say you had the idea of running away, but he wants to make sure they think all his injuries were inflicted by the boy who supposedly mugged him.'

'What did he look like, Arron?' I ask.

'Sullen,' says Patrick. 'He was looking down most of the time. His mother was sitting in front of me and he only glanced at her twice.'

'Were his sisters there? Two little kids?'

'No. There was a brother, I think. Anyway, he's going down for manslaughter at least, one way or another. It's just a question of whether the other two go with him. His best hope is that the jury will believe his story that Rio was the aggressor – it all depends what the jury make of you – and if there's any evidence to corroborate your account.'

My worst fear in the world used to be that Arron wouldn't be my friend. I used to fret over stupid things, like name-calling and being picked for teams at school and what I'd do if I had to admit that my best friend didn't seem to like me any more.

I never ever thought we'd be enemies. He must hate me now I've tried to demolish his story in court.

But why didn't Arron change his story? Why didn't he tell the police that I hurt him? He could've deflected some of the trouble onto me, confused the jury, made me look like a potential killer too.

I can't think of a reason. Unless, maybe, Arron's still my friend after all.

CHAPTER 43
Brother

Patrick's telling me about his house in France, and the little village which has a *pâtisserie* and a *boucherie* and an *école primaire* and an *église*. It's as soothing as doing a vocabulary test in school – always my best moments – and I can feel the hammering of my heart slowing down and the horrible retching taste die away.

And when I fall asleep, I dream of eating French bread and French cheese and walking along a French village high street and feeling free and safe and normal again.

It's quite a shock when he shakes me awake and says, 'We're here now, Ty. Time to wake up,' and I remember that home is a high-rise in Birmingham, not a cottage in Provence.

I'm shivering as we take the lift upstairs and I'm really looking forward to Gran making me supper and a cup of tea. I'm starving. But when we get to our front door it's all dark and quiet. There's no answer when we ring the doorbell.

I start thumping at the door. 'Where are they? What's going on?' I say, trying not to even think what I'm thinking. But why would someone attack when it's too late . . . when I've already given evidence?

Unless it's not this trial they're worried about any more, but the next one. Jukes's trial. *Jesus.* Where *are* they?

'Calm down,' says Patrick. 'I'm sure there's an explanation. Where's your key? Your mobile?'

But I haven't got my key. It's in my jeans pocket, on my bedroom floor. And I forgot to charge my mobile. And I keep on thumping the door, shouting their names, thinking of all the things people have told me – the Whites and their mates are all in prison now, there's no real danger of witness intimidation, there's no point because the police were on the scene so quickly and saw Jukes with the knife in his hand – and I know they're lying, they're all lying, oh God, they're lying. . .

Then the old woman from next door comes out and says, 'For God's sake, stop the noise, will you? You won't find them there, they went off in an ambulance about three hours ago.'

It's true. I was right. I think I'm going to faint.

'Were . . . were they alive?' I ask, and she looks at me pityingly and says, 'As far as I know.'

'Was there blood? Had they been attacked? Were the police here?' My words are coming out in little jumpy bursts. She looks a bit confused, and says, 'They'll have taken her to maternity, won't they?'

'Aha,' says Patrick. 'Come on, Ty,' and we run back to the lift while I try and remember which hospital my mum was due to have the baby in. My mind is completely blank. In the end, Patrick punches some keys on his sat nav and shows me a list of hospitals and I pick out one that sounds familiar. And off we go.

It's only when we're walking into the maternity unit that it hits me. *Christ*. This baby is real. This is massive. Nothing will ever be the same again. And I've hardly thought about it.

Patrick goes and talks to a woman at a desk. It doesn't help that I can't remember what name we're using in Birmingham. I stand there, jabbering, 'It might be Andrews . . . or Ferguson . . . or maybe Webster. . .' because Mum was talking about using Alistair's surname for the baby. The woman looks at me like I'm completely stupid. I'm sweating.

She points out a waiting room. There are a few people in there already, some ladies in hijabs, a big tattooed bloke pacing up and down. It's going to be difficult to have a conversation in here. I hover around the door, trying to get a word with Patrick.

'Come and sit down,' he says. 'She's going to find out what's happening. Shouldn't take long.'

'No . . . it's just . . . Patrick—'

One of the hijab ladies is looking at me. 'What is it?' asks Patrick.

'It's just . . . look, maybe I shouldn't be here. Maybe if I just came home with you? We could find out later.'

Patrick puts his hand on my shoulder. 'What are you worrying about?'

'It's just . . . I'll probably get in the way. When they've got a baby to look after.' And it'll cry all day and all night and who can blame it? Then there's the nappies and the vomit. . . How can anyone think it's a good idea to have a baby? You might as well adopt a skunk.

Patrick's looking quite sympathetic, so I add, 'Maybe I should – maybe I should come and live with you?'

'They're going to need your help,' he says, and I'm not sure if he's saying it because he doesn't want me. 'And besides, you're due to start school next week, aren't you? You've missed quite enough of your GCSE courses.'

This doesn't exactly cheer me up. My mum took me into school a few weeks ago to meet the head of year ten, and although he seemed perfectly nice, and it was kind of cool to pick my GCSEs (French, Spanish, PE and Media

Studies, which are all good; unfortunately English, Maths, Religion and Double Science are compulsory) the school was big and loud, which made me feel small and quiet. He gave me some coursework to make a start on at home, and I'm due in for the first time on Monday. I've been trying to forget all about it.

I heave a sigh. And then the woman comes back and asks Patrick to come and talk to her in the corridor. I can hear her say something about the baby . . . a baby . . . and I can't hear any more because the volume suddenly turns up on the blood rushing though my ear drums, so it sounds like the sea, and my heart is crashing and booming in my chest. The hijab ladies are looking at me, and shaking their heads and one of them pats my hand and says, 'Don't worry, it'll be fine. Your lady-friend will be fine,' which is so totally embarrassing that I rush out of the room, banging straight into Patrick as he comes back in.

He takes my arm, and we walk along the corridor together, out of the maternity unit and into the cold night air. I'm shivering again. 'Ty,' he says, 'Nicki – she's not very well. Her blood pressure went up – dangerously so – and they had to do an emergency Caesarean. She's sleeping now. It's probably a good thing we didn't know what was going on.'

I sway against him, and he grabs my arm and pulls

me over to a bench. I sit there, leaning into his tweed jacket, taking big gulps of air. And then I remember. 'The baby?' I ask.

'The baby's fine. She's in Special Care, but just as a precaution. We can go and meet her now. Julie's with her. Are you OK? Let's go.'

Patrick leads me up some stairs, and into a ward – a ward full of babies in little transparent cots. They seem really small to be all on their own, out in the world with no families. There's a nurse bustling around, but that's not the same. For some reason they make me think of Arron banged up in his cell. I don't want to think about Arron. I don't want to think about cells.

Only one baby, right at the end of the row, has a mum with it. The mum is . . . urgh . . . she's breast-feeding it. Disgusting. I hope my mum hasn't got any ideas about that. I hope my mum . . . oh God . . . I can't even think about her.

Patrick steers me round a corner to a bit where there are just four babies. 'Here she is,' he says, and there's my gran. And I rush to hug her, and then I stop.

She can't hug me. She's holding a tiny bundle wrapped up in a white blanket, and there's a little pink face and a tuft of black hair. I step back, feeling a bit stupid. Why can't she leave it in its cot like all the other babies?

'Congratulations, Julie,' says Patrick, 'This brings

back a few memories.' I remember how my gran lied and stole me away from them, and it's like there's electricity in the air, crackling and snapping and waiting to explode. But my gran just gives him a tight little smile and says, 'I'll say one thing for Nicki, she does give me beautiful grandchildren.'

Then her face creases up and she shoves the bundle into my arms and collapses into a chair, almost howling because she's crying so much. Great shivers are going through her body. I'm frozen. I don't think I've ever seen my gran cry.

Patrick pulls out a clean white handkerchief and gives it to her. He puts his arm around her. 'There, there,' he says. 'She'll be fine. Your Nicki is a real fighter, Julie, she'll be OK. Hush now, we don't want to wake them all up.'

'I thought she was going to die,' says Gran. I'm all cold inside. But then she adds, 'I had no choice,' and Patrick says, 'We realised, we didn't blame you,' and I get that they're talking about the past.

I sneak a look at the bundle in my arms. The baby's eyes are open. Alistair's eyes, staring into mine. Alistair's spiky hair. It's Alistair's face looking up at me from the white blanket, and I really don't think I'm going to be able to live with that every day.

I look desperately at Patrick. I'm silently begging him

to take the bundle from me, let me escape . . . run away
. . . never see this baby again. He catches my eye, frowns.
Then he says – and it's a command – 'Stick out your
tongue.'

'Wha . . . what?'

'Stick out your tongue. And then give her a few
minutes.'

I stick out my tongue. Alistair's eyes drill into me.
Gran's sobs are dying down; she's looking at me in
surprise.

And then the baby's mouth begins to twitch.
The tiniest wrinkle creases her forehead. And the tip of
her little pink tongue appears between her lips.

It's amazing! Unbelievable! She's so tiny, just a
little blob really, and she can't do anything, but she can
look at me and *copy* me. Wow! My sister is really clever.
And I blink, and I can see that she doesn't really look like
Alistair after all, but she's got Mum's blue-grey eyes and
Gran's dimply cheeks.

'Has she got a name?' asks Patrick, and Gran gives a
big shuddering sniff and says. 'Alyssa. A-L-Y-S-S-A. Don't
ask me. Not even a saint's name. But she's calling her
Maria as a middle name, after my mother, which is some
comfort, I suppose. Give her back to me now, Ty. How
are you, my darling boy? Have you had anything to eat?'

'Nope,' I say. I don't really want to let go of Alyssa

yet. I sniff her dark hair. She smells of smoke and iron. It's very strange and not what I expected, and I hand her back to Gran, who cuddles her close and says, 'Well, my little darling, what do you think of your big brother?' A little bit of sick dribbles out of Alyssa's mouth.

'How's Nicki?' asks Patrick, and Gran's eyes tear up again, but she says that the doctors think she'll be OK and everything is stable and she's expected to come round in a few hours.

'Maybe Ty should go back with you for a few days,' she says. 'I don't want him to be all alone in that flat, and I have to stay here. I'm going to call Emma, get her to come back for a few weeks, but until then. . .'

'We'll sort Tyler out, don't you worry,' says Patrick, 'but I don't think either of us are up to a long drive at this time of night. Maybe you could give me some keys and I'll stay over in the flat with him tonight. Then we can visit Nicki in the morning.'

Gran's going to cry again, I can tell, and I can't really take that, so I bend over her and give her a kiss and say goodbye to Alyssa. And Alyssa looks up and into my eyes again and I feel a kind of whoosh of amazement that anyone can be so small but so aware. My sister. My sister Alyssa.

'My mum's going to be OK, isn't she?' I ask Patrick as we walk out of the hospital, and he says, 'I'm sure she is. It sounds as though they acted just in time.'

My mum is going to be all right. She has to be. I'm not even going to think that she might die.

I'm just focussing on Alyssa. Her life is just starting and she's lost her dad already. She can never find him, like I've found mine. He's gone forever.

So she's going to need a really good big brother. No one's going to hurt her, nothing bad's going to happen to her, she's always going to have me to look after her.

I've not always done a great job at growing up so far. But now I'm a brother, I'm going to have to step up my game.

CHAPTER 44
Connected

Arron's eyes are full of hate. 'It's your fault this has happened to me,' they're saying. 'You betrayed me.'

I slide the *Daily Mail* back across the table to Gran. I don't want to read it. It's enough to know that Arron and Jukes and Mikey were all found guilty of murder. The judge made a special order so that Arron could be named in the press reports, because the case was so serious. His photo is on page eleven of the *Mail*.

They're all locked away in a Young Offender Institution. Arron won't come out for years and years and years. Will he come looking for me then?

Gran's rustling the pages. 'There was more evidence against them than we realised,' she says. 'There's a lot here about the gang they were in. Who'd have thought Arron would get mixed up with something like that?

Terrible. And they were caught on a CCTV camera going into the park. No wonder the jury believed you. They knew the difference between a nice honest boy and a group of thugs.'

'Yeah, right,' I say.

'Look, there's an interview with the boy's parents. Rio's parents. They say they've got a lot to thank you for.'

'I'll look later, Gran.' I say. 'I've got a lot of homework to do.'

She puts the paper back in front of me, kisses me on the forehead. 'You read it now. You should feel proud of yourself. You don't have to spend all your time doing homework, darling. You've been working since 5 am. I saw the light in your room when I did Alyssa's bottle. I'm going to make you a cup of tea.'

So she puts the kettle on and I gaze at the paper. At the picture of Rio's family. Words jump off the page. *Heart of Gold. Gang Culture. Broken Britain.*

Rio's mum said he was a good boy really. He loved his music. 'He'd just got in with a bad crowd.'

And then comes the bit that Gran's biro has starred. 'We owe everything to the boy who told the truth about what happened that day. If it wasn't for him, our poor dead son would have been branded a criminal.'

I push it away. Gran gives me my steaming tea.

I stir it, watching the bubbles form as the sugar dissolves. The tea whirls round and round in the cup. 'It's not true, Gran, what they say in the paper,' I say. 'He did have a knife, Rio. He wasn't just an innocent victim.'

And she sits opposite me and says, 'What that family is going through, I cannot imagine. I thank God every day that you are alive. We're all sinners, Ty, but that doesn't mean we can't try and do the right thing. I'm sure it's going to be all right today, Ty. I'm sure they'll realise you're a good boy.'

Then Alyssa starts to cry and Gran rushes out to grab her before my mum wakes up. So I don't have to talk to her about what's going to happen today. And I pick up my cup and go back into my bedroom, where I've made a desk for myself where the telly used to be and pinned up a big GCSE coursework timetable on the wall.

I've turned into a geek. I've discovered that you can lose yourself in schoolwork, just like you can in PlayStation or Xbox. It's not as exciting, obviously, and not fun at all, but there's that same comforting feeling of blocking yourself off from the world and – even better – the stuff that's going on in your own head. No one can criticise you for it, the teachers think I'm amazing, Mum and Gran are baffled but delighted.

It's a great way of making sure that no one's very interested in you, which suits me fine right now.

Especially today.

But right now, I'm finding it difficult to immerse myself totally in my English coursework. (We're studying a play – *An Inspector Calls*, which is ironic really, all things considered.) I'm staring into space and biting my fingernails and wondering what's going to have happened by the end of the day. Wondering if I'll feel better or worse.

Then I hear my mum's voice calling me, and I walk into the living room, and I see that my dad's arrived. He's sitting on the sofa, Alyssa in his arms, and he's blowing raspberries at her. He looks really stupid.

'Hey, Ty,' he says, 'How's it going?'

'Have you seen the paper, darling?' asks my mum. I'm glad to see she's nibbling a piece of toast. She's OK now, my mum, completely recovered, but pale and tired all the time and mostly she doesn't look attractive or like a celebrity, but just very thin. Like they say on magazine covers, too skinny. I buy her chocolate sometimes, on the way home from school, but she never seems to want it.

I worry about her a lot. It doesn't help that she's worrying about me.

'I saw it,' I say. And then, to change the subject, 'I might have to go to the library. I can't really work properly here. Of course it'd be different if I had my own laptop.' I look meaningfully at my dad, hoping he'll pick up the hint, but he's staring into Alyssa's eyes and giving her his finger to suck. It's a bit irritating.

'You probably won't have time,' says my mum. She drops the piece of toast onto her plate, half-eaten. 'How about a yoghurt, Nicki?' asks Gran. Mum shakes her head. 'Are you sure the lawyer shouldn't go with you?' she asks my dad.

'He said not,' says my dad, looking up. 'He said it'll be quite routine. Just like before, when they arrested you, Ty, except this time we'll find out what they're charging you with. Hopefully nothing at all. Come on. Let's get it over with.'

Here we go. My big date at the cop shop. They're charging me today. My mum couldn't face it, so my dad's coming with me. Gran's a bit put out. She's the one who's done all the counter-signing at the police station when I go to report in. She's not used to my dad muscling in.

'And then perhaps we can talk about the christening,' she says. Gran and Mum have had a lot of rows about Alyssa's baptism. Mum's all jumpy about it because Alistair's parents have agreed to come. And Gran's not too happy about my dad being a godfather.

'What's there to talk about?' he asks now, and I can see her forehead begin to crinkle. 'You just have to say, 'Yes, whatever,' don't you, when they ask you whether you believe in Jesus and the rest of it. I remember from Ty's christening. You have to denounce Satan.

It's no big deal.'

It's not that I'm religious or anything, but I'm going to decide exactly what I believe and what I don't well before there's any danger of anyone asking me to take part in a christening.

'Time to go,' says my mum quickly, before Gran can open her mouth, and she gives me a tight hug. I don't look at her face. I don't like it when my mum cries.

So we get into my dad's car – he's got a BMW, we have to walk miles to where he's parked it, because he doesn't seem to have Patrick's skill for finding the right person to guard it – and he takes me to the police station.

We go in, and I say hello to the man on the desk. I've seen him a few times before, he's OK. Quite friendly. Supports Aston Villa. My mouth's dry and I feel a bit dizzy. Normally I'd just sign my name and Gran would sign too, but this time he asks us to wait. So we wait. And I'm trying to think about how to bring up the subject of laptops again, but I'm distracted by wondering if it's fear that's giving me stomach cramps or if I'm going to have to sprint to the bogs.

'How's Tess?' I ask my dad after a bit, because it seems polite to ask about his life, especially if I'm going to persuade him to fork out a ton of money at PC World.

He screws up his face, taps his index finger against his thumb. 'Oh. I . . . well . . . we quarrelled. Really badly.

She admitted she'd been through all my stuff, all those papers and photos and things. She had no right.'

'Oh,' I say, 'Right. That's umm . . . a shame. . .' *Yes!* If it wasn't for the police business, then I'd be feeling almost happy.

'I used to need Tess – such a strong person – to keep me . . . to keep me going. But that's not the case any more,' he says.

'Oh,' I say. 'Umm. Right.' He looks a bit sad. Lost. Worried.

'It's good that you're going to be Alyssa's godfather,' I say, to cheer him up.

'Really?' he says.

'Yeah, you can take cool pictures of her. Introduce her to celebrities. Buy her stuff like laptops.' He doesn't seem to pick up the hint.

'I suppose so,' he says. 'I feel guilty about her. It's because she lost her father that I got back in contact with you. If Alistair hadn't died, if the boy . . . Rio . . . hadn't died, then none of this would have happened. We'd still be strangers to each other. They paid the price for us to be together.'

It's really strange having a conversation like this with someone who's meant to be older and wiser than me. He's not really like a dad at all, it's like talking to Archie or Brian except he's a bit brighter, and he's got a cool motorcycle and a BMW, and he knows Cheryl Cole.

'They didn't pay the price,' I say reassuringly. 'We can't go back in time, and we can't say how things could have been different. Maybe Alistair would've walked under a bus. Maybe Louise would've told me how to get in touch with you. No one can know.'

'It's all connected,' he says. 'Cause and effect.'

'It's not,' I say. 'We don't have to feel guilty because something good happened to us. Everything isn't really connected.' I sound quite convincing. I almost believe myself.

And then the policeman tells us we can come through now.

CHAPTER 45
Let's Get it Started

It must be really boring being a policeman. On TV it's all car chases and fights and solving murders. But actually, it's loads of paperwork and weak tea in windowless offices and saying the same old boring crap again and again about arresting you and having the right to remain silent and things being used in court against you and blah, blah, blah, blah, blah.

By the time the custody sergeant gets around to telling me what I'm charged with, I've virtually fallen asleep.

And then he starts banging on about the Offensive Weapons Act of 1953 and I gather that I'm being charged with two counts of carrying a knife. And that's it.

No perverting the course of justice. No stabbing Arron.

There's a big smile on my dad's face as he asks the

sergeant about the other pending charges, and he's told that the CPS decided not to proceed. I'm a bit confused about why that is – I mean, they've got proof of one and a confession to the other – but I'm not going to tell them how to do their job. While he signs the papers and gets the details of when I've got to go to court, I'm trying to take it in. Work out what it means. I don't get very far.

We're free to leave. We get back into the car. My dad turns to me. 'Great!' he says. He's grinning, thrilled. 'What a result! I'd better phone Mr Armstrong.'

He calls the lawyer and then my mum. Apparently this is good news. It's better than everyone expected. But how good is it really?

We get back to the flat – I suggest stopping off at PC World on the way, but he says, 'Look, if you really need a laptop, I'll sort it out on the internet,' which is encouraging but not very definite – and Gran and Mum are all smiles, and happy and no one seems to notice that I'm a bit down. Everyone is too busy telling each other how much worse it could have been and how it's incredibly unlikely that I'll get sent to prison because I'm so young and I've never done anything bad before.

They're conveniently ignoring the fact that we sat and watched the news a few weeks ago and saw the Prime Minister call on lawyers and judges to jail more young people for carrying knives. He talked about deterrents, about safer streets, about tough measures.

'Knives are unacceptable,' he said, 'and we've got to do everything in our power to deter them.' It's hard to argue with. If I'd known that a knife in my pocket meant going to jail, then I probably wouldn't have taken it. Almost definitely.

Gran's ringing Emma in Spain, and my dad's on the phone to Archie's mum, when my mum puts her hand on my arm.

'Are you all right, Ty?' she asks. 'You don't seem very pleased. It's good news, darling . . . really, better than we had hoped for.'

I slam my hand down on the table. My gran drops the phone, she's so surprised. My dad says, 'Sorry, Pen – I'll call you back.'

'It's not good news,' I say – I shout. 'How can it be? I could still go to prison – you all know that.'

'But not for so long,' says my mum soothingly. 'They've dropped the most serious charges.'

'Mr Armstrong said that they must have realised they couldn't proceed without a statement from Arron on the assault,' says my dad. 'He testified that he had no idea that you'd called an ambulance, he thought you were running off together to get help. No mention of your knife.

'And the email didn't mean as much after you'd been a key prosecution witness. All of them, Jukes, Mikey and Arron, they're all appealing against their convictions. Prosecuting you would be like opening the prison doors.'

'Yes, but . . . but . . . I still did those things, didn't I? They're still true. I still have to live with what I did. And nothing's going to take that away, no matter how much you're celebrating.'

'Ty, sweetheart—' says my mum, but then Alyssa starts crying and she rolls her eyes and says, 'There she goes again.' I spot Gran and my dad glancing at each other, which they don't do all that often.

So I shrug my shoulders and say, 'I'm going to do my homework,' and my dad says, 'I'll get onto the laptop for you, don't worry.'

I go into my bedroom, and instead of sitting at my desk I lie on my bed. I'm going to have to go to court again. Some judge is going to decide what's going to happen to me. I've given up the right to make my own decisions. I never even realised how precious that was.

And then my phone buzzes in my pocket.

It must be Archie, he's the only person who ever rings me. I can't cope with his bounce right now. So I go to turn it off. But his name isn't there. *Arron?* I think, and my heart does a big, painful thud. 'Hello?' I breathe into the mobile.

'Joe? Ty?' says a voice, and I can't believe it. I can't believe it's her. It's Claire. Claire is calling me. It's Claire.

'Claire? How did you get my number? Are you OK? Claire?' I'm trying not to sound too hopeful, but I can feel a stupid big smile cracking my face, and my hand is all sweaty, clutching the phone so hard that it's in danger of sliding out of my grip.

'From Zoe . . . from Archie. . . Joe, that was you in the paper, wasn't it? That court case . . . there's an interview in my dad's *Mail*. . .'

'It was . . . it was me.'

'I thought it was,' she says, and I can't tell from her voice whether she's forgiven me or not. I doubt it. There's too much to forgive.

'Claire, I'm sorry,' I say, 'I rang Ellie. I was worried you were cutting again, I thought she could help. It was – it seemed like the right thing to do.'

Claire's voice is soft and high, but there's a strength there which never fails to surprise me. 'I was angry,' she says, 'but I'm not any more. You did the right thing. I did need help. Ellie told my parents and they talked to me, and I had to admit what was going on. I had started again. They're making me talk to some specialist counsellor now. She's annoying, but I haven't been cutting any more. Honestly, Joe, you can believe me.'

'So it is helping? Talking to the counsellor?' Mum's been hinting that maybe I need some counselling too. Gran thinks I should talk to the priest at her church.

So far, I've resisted both.

'Maybe. It's good to talk to someone who's not involved with my family. I'd prefer to talk to you though. You . . . you're the easiest person to talk to.'

When you've been feeling crap for as long as I have, it's odd when you start feeling better. It's like getting warm after a long, cold walk. I'm all tingly. 'Thanks, Claire,' I say, soft into the phone.

'Ellie said that you wouldn't have called if you didn't care,' she adds. 'You knew I might never talk to you again, but you cared so much that you called anyway.'

Thanks, Ellie, I think, and I say 'I do care. I really do.'

'The paper says you made a big difference to the trial.'

'Claire, I sent my friend to prison. He's going to be there for a long time.'

'He killed someone. He deserves to be in prison.'

'I feel bad,' I say, 'about my friend. I feel like I should have – could have – stopped him. He shouldn't be in prison. It was my fault.'

Claire snorts, as only Claire can. 'That's just rubbish, though, isn't it?' she says, 'It's like I used to feel guilty because Ellie was in a wheelchair and I wasn't. Your friend did what he did, that was his choice. He was in a gang and he armed himself with a knife. He threatened someone with it. He had a fight, and he killed someone. And now he's in prison and you—'

'I might still go to prison,' I say. 'They've charged me with carrying a knife. Twice. They could send me away. You won't want to know me then.'

That's it. Said. Out in the open.

'You might,' she says, 'and it'd be bad, but it won't be forever, will it? They had someone come to our school the other week, telling how he got involved in crime, how he messed things up. You could do something like that one day. When you're a top athlete, you can be a role model, tell kids how to stay out of trouble.'

'Yeah . . . right . . . maybe. . .' I say. The relief that she doesn't hate me, that she understands, is fantastic.

'Not *maybe*,' she says. 'Decide to do it now and you'll be all right. We'll be all right.'

And I'm half-laughing and nearly crying, because it feels so good to be talking to her and to know that she believes in me. That she can see a future that I didn't think I had.

Then I tell Claire about Alyssa, how cute she is, and my new school and what it's like doing GCSEs, and she tells me she's joined the drama club and she's got a small part in *Romeo and Juliet* and she's slightly gone off *Twilight* but she still thinks I should see the film.

'Claire,' I say, 'My dad's getting me a laptop. We'll have an internet connection.'

'Download Skype,' she says. 'I can go to Zoe's house and use her connection. Get Archie to help. And I'm on Facebook and we can chat online . . . and you've got my number now. It'll be fine. We can be in touch all the time.'

Then she says she has to go, because her mum's calling her and she tells me she'll ring again and she says she loves me. She loves me. And I tell her I love her too, and then the phone goes dead, and I make sure I save her number before I lie down again, re-running the conversation in my head over and over again.

I lie there quite a long time, thinking. About everything she said. About the past, and how all the bits fit together. About Arron. About friendship and love, truth and betrayal. Can I live up to Claire's belief in me? Can I take control of my future?

I start looking through my stuff, and I find the new trackie my mum bought for my Christmas present and I dig out my trainers. Joe's trainers. The trainers I was wearing on the beach that day when Alistair got shot. My hands shake as I lace them up.

Then I go back into the living room. Three faces look towards me. They've all done bad things in the past, made stupid decisions and told lies. Even Gran. They're all doing just about OK now. And they all really care about me.

'Are you feeling better now, darling?' asks my mum, and then, hopefully, 'Going out for a run?'

'Yes,' I say, 'I am.'

Then I let myself out of the flat, go down in the lift and sniff the toasty Birmingham air. I fiddle with my iPod. I haven't listened to it much recently. Too many memories. But I find the Black Eyed Peas, *Let's Get it Started.* One of my top ten favourite tracks of all time. Sometimes the old songs are the best.

I start at a slow jog to warm up. I stretch. I'm stiff and unfit – I've got a lot of work to do. I'll have to find a gym . . . there's the athletics club at school . . . a guy in my tutor group is a member, maybe I could talk to him. . .

And then I lengthen my pace and my breathing kicks in and I remember how this feels.

And it feels good.

The End

Acknowledgements

Deep and heartfelt thanks to the following:

For their knowledge, wisdom and experience; Jeremy Nathan (hallucinations and stabbing wounds), Tony Metzer (courts, law and the way lawyers talk), Karen Wilson (police procedure) and Saviour Pirotta (hellfire).

For constructive and re-constructive criticism and the occasional hobnob; Amanda Swift, Anna Longman, Becky Jones, Lydia Syson, Pauline Rochford, Fenella Fairburn and Jennifer Gray. Hannah Marcus, fast and perceptive reader; Phoebe Moss, great proofreader; Jimmy Rice and Cat Clarke for much helpful advice, and Mum for spotting Alistair's little problem.

For making dreams come true; my agent, Jenny Savill and everyone at Frances Lincoln Children's Books, especially Maurice Lyon, Emily Sharratt, Nicky Potter and Jane Donald, designer of great covers.

For their love and entertainment value; Laurence, Phoebe and Judah, Mum and Dad, Deborah, Jeremy and Alun, Josh, Avital and Eliana, plus assorted relatives and cavies. And all my friends, corporeal and virtual.

Almost True is dedicated to the memory of three extraordinary, inspiring women, all terribly missed – Min Moss, Melissa Nathan and Nina Farhi. Always remembering Daniel, whose name is written on our hands.

Keren blogs about her life and books at
www.wheniwasjoe.blogspot.com

You can also follow her on Twitter
@kerensd

or find out more about *When I Was Joe* and
Almost True on Facebook on the **When I Was Joe** page

Growing up in a small town in Hertfordshire, **Keren David** had two ambitions: to write a book and to live in London. Several decades on, she has finally achieved both. She was distracted by journalism, starting out at eighteen as a messenger girl, then working as a reporter, news editor, features editor and feature writer for many and various newspapers and magazines. She has lived in Glasgow and Amsterdam, where, in eight years, she learnt enough Dutch to order coffee and buy vegetables. She is now back in London, and lives with her husband, two children and their insatiably hungry guinea pigs.

Keren's debut novel was the acclaimed *When I Was Joe*.